SHEPHERDS & BUTCHERS

Shepherds
& Butchers

Chris Marnewick

arrow books

1 3 5 7 9 10 8 6 4 2

Arrow Books
20 Vauxhall Bridge Road
London SW1V 2SA

Arrow Books is part of the Penguin Random House group of companies
whose addresses can be found at global.penguinrandomhouse.com.

Penguin
Random House
UK

First published in South Africa in 2008 by Umuzi, an imprint of
Penguin Random House South Africa
First published in Great Britain by Arrow in 2017

www.penguin.co.uk

A CIP catalogue record for this book is available from the British Library.

ISBN 9781784753436

Text design by Cherie Collins
Original design and layout by William Dicey
Set in 10.5 on 13.65pt Minion Pro

Printed and bound by Clays Ltd, St Ives Plc

Penguin Random House is committed to a sustainable future for
our business, our readers and our planet. This book is made
from Forest Stewardship Council® certified paper.

MIX
Paper from
responsible sources
FSC® C018179
FSC
www.fsc.org

To the great loves of my life, Ansie, Jacques, Michel

Il faut, dans le gouvernement, des bergers et des bouchers

– A government must have shepherds and butchers

VOLTAIRE (1694–1778)

OPENING

Preparation: May–October 1988
Execution: 10 December 1987

Palace of Justice, Pretoria

The Judge's scarlet robes signified that this was a capital case, that he had the power of life and death. I watched the serious figure in the centre of the bench as he moved his high-backed chair slightly forward and picked up his reading glasses. His two Assessors, elderly gentlemen dressed in sombre suits, leaned back in their chairs. Their first task had been completed, helping the Judge to arrive at a verdict on the question of guilt or innocence. It remained for the Judge to announce the outcome and to explain the Court's reasons.

'The defendant may be seated,' said the Judge. 'The judgment will take some time.'

Leon Labuschagne sat down and almost disappeared behind the wood panelling of the dock where Nelson Mandela had stood trial on a charge of high treason more than twenty years earlier, his life similarly at stake. Mandela had escaped with his life, and is due to become our new President in a month's time. The preparations for his inauguration brought back these memories.

It was October 1988, and it was spring in Pretoria. I was tired. The trial had run for only two weeks, but they had been hard weeks and there had been many anxious moments, long stretches of concentrated action, dark hours of nightmares and despair. I was exhausted; physically and emotionally drained by the effort. I turned slightly in my seat to look around.

Court C of the Palace of Justice was tattered, its furniture and fittings in dire need of refurbishment. Large flakes of paint hung from the high walls. Some of the bulbs in the antique light fittings lining the walls needed to be replaced. The once plush carpet was threadbare and worn through in areas of heavy traffic, its once sombre ox blood-red now faded to a dull pink. The wood-framed windows above the architraves bore the stains of many years' worth of accumulated dust and grime and the droppings of the ubiquitous pigeons.

The Judge was Mr Justice J P van Zyl. He tested his voice by coughing softly behind his hand before he opened his bench book. Spectators in the back rows of the public gallery craned forward to hear. I sat at counsel's table with my Junior on my left. The prosecutors were within whispering distance from me. A door slammed elsewhere in the building, its sound muted by the thick stone walls and the carpeting as the Judge started reading in measured tones.

'The extraordinary defence in this case has its origins in a process of which very few details have been known until this trial – the execution of a condemned criminal by the State.'

I felt my concentration begin to wane as the performance stress started to abate. I had played my part in the trial. There was nothing more I could do, in any event. They were either going to find Labuschagne guilty and sentence him to death, or they were going to acquit him. Either way, my job was done. For once I could afford to let my thoughts run free.

I thought of my childhood friend Oupa Venter. We were sitting in the shade of the camel thorn tree behind the kitchen of Welgedacht Primary School, taking a break from our sword and shield battles, Oupa playing the Roman centurion to my Spartacus. I never told him that according to the encyclopaedia we had on the farm the centurion was supposed to win and Spartacus was supposed to end up on a cross, broken and dehydrated. We were flicking seed pods, floating them in the air like pebbles on water. The only constant in our games was Oupa's smile, his white teeth flashing in the light – whether he was on the winning or losing side, always that dashing smile.

I remembered the blond hairs on Oupa's arms, bleached even whiter by exposure to the sun and contrasting with the tanned skin underneath. I felt my facial muscles tighten as I thought of his battered body, lying in his bed, with his blood spattered on the walls and the ceiling of his grandmother's house in town. His sister and his grandmother had been murdered during the same frenzied attack that took his life. By then I was in high school, and had been overcome with curiosity. I went to look at the murder scene, a house in a dirt road on the poor side of Potgietersrus.

As I sat in Court C I could still see in my mind's eye the photograph of Oupa's murderer on the execution notice. It had been posted on the public notice board at the Magistrates' Court. It was still there when I went for a job interview after I had finished school four years later. The photograph showed the murderer, a smiling man in his thirties, in a prison jacket. There was a number pinned across his chest – 1266. The notice said that Johannes Buchling had been executed for murder. I wondered if he was still smiling when they put the rope around his neck.

My father also appeared unbidden from the recesses of my memory, another smiling face in his thirties. I remembered the journey from Johannesburg to Pretoria in the car many years earlier, with my father driving and acting as tour guide at the same time. I had never been to Pretoria.

'That is the place where they are going to hang van Buuren,' he had said as we entered the city from the south. He pointed at the corner of a large building complex on the left. The words over the entrance gates were long for my not yet nine-year-old eyes, but I just managed to get them all before we passed the windowless corner of the last brown building.

PRETORIA SENTRAAL GEVANGENIS
PRETORIA CENTRAL PRISON

I remembered van Buuren, a suave, handsome young man wearing sunglasses, staring arrogantly at me from the front page of the Sunday paper. How could I have known at that time, during that miserable Johannesburg winter when I was racked with croup, that one day I would be the public prosecutor in the very same courtroom where the photograph had been taken?

I glanced up at the Judge – he was still dealing with preliminary matters – as I paged through the register on the table in front of me. I found the right year and scanned down the pages, one by one. There he was, immediately after Gideon Sibiya:

NO.	DATE	NAME	JUDGE	PLACE	OUTCOME	DATE
517	28.2.57	Clarence Gordon van Buuren	Broome, J	Durban	Executed	10.6.57

As I turned more pages of the Capital Cases Register, my eye fell on another name I recognised:

537	20.5.57	ROLAND ROBERTS (EM)	J T van Wyk	Cape Town	Executed	8.11.57

He had even made it into the *Law Reports* and I later had to study his case in Criminal Law 1 under the heading INSANITY. The letters EM next to his name intrigued me. I looked more closely at the other entries. There were other similar codes, and I deciphered them quickly. NM appeared the most frequently, Native Male. There were also lots of CMS, for Coloured Male. Occasionally there would be an EM, a European Male. I started looking into the register from a different angle. Why are there no IMS, Indian Males? I wondered. Yet I found one quickly. I also found two NFs on one page, Native Female. The search for an EF, European Female, did not take long either:

592	25.11.57	Margaret Elizabeth Rheeder (EF)	A G Jennett	Port Elizabeth	Executed	6.5.58

Rheeder was hanged for poisoning her husband. I remembered the case well. The hanging of a woman always made the headlines, and my reading skills had advanced by one year since van Buuren. Before I could find a CF or an IF, Judge van Zyl started to describe the execution process. I had to pay attention once more. The Judge turned a page and stared at the skylight above our heads briefly before he spoke. The clouds had returned for the judgment, great banks of them rushing over Pretoria in waves, their effect felt in the courtroom as alternating sheets of light and gloom as the judge read in and out of the paragraphs of the judgment. It was a judgment crafted for inclusion in the *Law Reports*. In the pages of the *Death Sentence Register* I found an escape from the tedium of words that were read and not spoken, of ideas that were emasculated by legalese and precedent.

'The execution process can only be described as a dramatic and traumatic experience for everyone involved.'

The stress of the trial lingered in my robes as a sweaty mix of fear and apprehension.

Maximum Security Prison, Pretoria: 10 December 1987

An hour is a long time on Death Row, but on the day of an execution it is an eternity. Yet for some it may pass too quickly.

The seven men in the Pot waited anxiously for the footsteps they knew would come soon to the doors of their individual cells. They had slept fitfully during the night. Even the nights of the previous week were by now a dim memory of bleak images from their childhood days, of black nightmares, their vain illusions of escape or reprieve shattered by the regular beat of the warder's boots on the catwalk above their cells. All through this last night the man on the catwalk had marched up and down slowly. Each time he approached the end of the cell-block the prisoners' hopes would light up as the warder's footsteps dimmed; then he would return and peer through the barred windows of their cells and extinguish the candle of hope again.

At exactly six o'clock the reveille bell signalled the start of the day in the cheerless complex known as Maximum Security Prison. The seven prisoners and the seven warders assigned to them shivered, mentally rehearsing what lay ahead of them in the next hour. The rest of the prison went into standby mode and no sound or movement signified life in any form within the grey walls. The nearly two hundred prisoners were usually roused from their bunks at the first sound of the bell, but they were left alone on hanging days until the gallows machine had done its work.

In the other sections of the prison the prisoners turned their worry inwards, knowing that the hour to seven o'clock would be a long one for them too. They were eager for the hour to pass so that they could return to the relative comfort of the tedium of prison routine. They did not want to think of the main business of the morning, the execution of their fellow prisoners, seven men who until a week ago had occupied cells among theirs.

The seven warders of the day shift who had reported for duty early faced the Warrant Officer in Charge of Security outside his office. By

15

title this man was in charge of security, but the prison was so secure that such a job would have been boring in the extreme. In reality he was the man in charge of executions, which, in any event, outranked security as the most important pursuit of the prison.

The warders were to be the day's gallows escorts, their duty to accompany the condemned men through every phase of the carefully planned activities of their final hour. The escorts, young men in khaki green, watched the Warrant Officer in silence and waited for the countdown to begin.

After checking their names against his duty roster, the Warrant Officer read the names of the prisoners to be executed that morning from an alphabetical list on his clipboard and allocated a warder to each prisoner.

'Gcaba!' The Warrant Officer pointed to a warder. The warder nodded.

'Gcabashe!'

'Maarman!'

'Mbambani!'

'Mjuza!'

'Mkumbeni!'

'Njele!'

One by one the warders nodded as they received their allocations.

They received their allocations patiently; there were no new warders on this watch and they knew full well what was expected of them. These seven men, some barely into their twenties, were gallows escorts, the men who would accompany the condemned men on their last journey, from the cells to the gallows, and from the gallows to the grave.

The escorts followed the Warrant Officer to the security grille at the entrance to A1 Section and paused behind him while the door was being unlocked. The door was locked behind them again, even though they were to return within minutes. The clatter of the keys and the tumblers in the lock were the only sounds to be heard.

The seven condemned men waited. They had been in these special cells for a week now, and twice they had heard the footsteps approaching at this hour, only to hear the warders stop at adjoining doors and take away other prisoners, seven on each occasion. Twice their minds had played games with them, suggesting that the footsteps were for them, that they were to be called out, and twice they had watched through the barred windows in their doors as others were taken away.

The agony of the wait was worse than anything, for some it was worse even than the prospect of death.

Exactly a week earlier a different set of footsteps had stopped at their doors while they were still in the general cells. It had been a hanging day, the third of December, and after the hangings had been completed the cell doors had been opened as usual at seven o'clock for the prisoners to clean their cells and be given breakfast. Later in the morning the whole prison had been put in lock-down mode again and a roll call was taken. The prisoners knew what that meant. Then, as now, they waited, but on that occasion there had been uncertainty. At whose door would the footsteps stop?

They had stopped at the doors of the men now waiting for their appointment with the Executioner.

'Pak!'

The single most feared word in the whole of the prison's vocabulary. The prisoners who were told to pack their belongings would not return to the general cells of Maximum Security Prison. They would be taken away to await execution or to leave Maximum for total freedom or to be taken to another prison to serve an alternative sentence. The Sheriff would tell them which, but first they would have to accompany the warders and the Sheriff to the admin office.

For the seven men now waiting the news had been that the State President had decided not to grant them mercy and that they would be hanged in a week's time.

When the prisoners elsewhere in the grey complex were not hurried from their cells immediately after the bell, their suspicion that today was a hanging day was confirmed, and they immediately started singing. At first there was only the lone voice of a tenor in A3 Section, then baritones and basses from other parts joined in.

Kumbaya, my Lord
Kumbaya
Kumbaya, my Lord
Kumbaya
Kumbaya, my Lord
Kumbaya
Oh Lord, Kumbaya

The chorus engaged the next verse, and the next, in the same melancholic and plaintive tones, verse after verse, reverently yet insistently. In the past week so many men had been called out for their appointment with the Hangman that the singing had been almost continuous. For more than ten days now the prisoners had been singing and the warders had been too exhausted to stop them.

Someone's praying, Lord
Kumbaya
Someone's praying, Lord
Kumbaya
Someone's praying, Lord
Kumbaya
Oh Lord, Kumbaya

In A1 the escorts quickly took up their positions, a man at each door, and the Warrant Officer produced a large key on a lanyard. He glanced sideways to make sure that all his men were ready. Then he brusquely opened the cell doors one after the other. As he opened each door, an escort stepped into the eight-by-six-foot cell and faced its sole inhabitant.

The waiting was over.

'Trek jou dagklere aan! Geen onderbroek of kouse en skoene nie!'

Each warder spoke with the authority of the Warrant Officer behind him.

The language of the prison was Afrikaans.

One of the prisoners was slow to rise from his bed.

'Maak soos ek sê en maak gou!'

The prisoners complied mechanically, conditioned to do exactly as they were told. Their minds were numb with fear as they undressed sluggishly. Out of habit they neatly folded their blue-and-white-striped pyjamas and placed the fear-filled rags at the head of their bunks. They stepped gingerly into the green prison trousers and pulled their shirts over their heads. When they were dressed they were almost indistinguishable from their escorts, frightened young men in faded prison green.

The armed guards on the catwalk, sweating already under the heat of the steel roof above their heads, looked down, ready for any eventuality, but there was no resistance, no complaint, nor a plea for mercy from any of the prisoners.

What little residual hope the prisoners might have entertained when they entered this prison had been abandoned, as had their faith in their Court-appointed lawyers and the appeals system. They had known since the day they were sentenced how they were to die. 'Hanged by the neck until you are dead,' their judges had told them. They had also known for a week precisely when they were to die. The Sheriff had told them: 'Thursday next week, at seven o'clock.' Their time was near. What good would resistance do?

One by one the prisoners emerged from their cells. Each escort took his man by the sleeve of the upper arm and the escorts quickly lined up the prisoners in alphabetical order, as on the Warrant Officer's list.

Gcaba, Gcabashe, Maarman, Mbambani, Mjuza, Mkumbeni, Njele.

'Dit is tyd om te gaan.'

The Warrant Officer spoke to the prisoners for the first time. He checked that the formation of escorts and prisoners was ready and then turned on his heel. He walked stiffly to the security grille. The escorts and prisoners followed in pairs and in silence.

The procession came to a halt at the grille. The Warrant Officer rapped on the door with his clipboard and the door was unlocked and opened just long enough to let them through. Two men were waiting at a table in the passage, directly opposite the Warrant Officer's office. The prisoners immediately recognised one of them: it was the man they knew as Squala, the Sheriff who a week earlier had brought the news that the State President had decided not to extend mercy to them.

The other man was a senior police officer, a lieutenant colonel, no less, in full dress uniform.

The policeman rose and with the informality born of years of experience quickly took the first prisoner's right thumb, rolled it across an inkpad and placed a sheet of paper at the edge of the table. The form had already been completed by the admin staff, who had inserted the policeman's details, the date, and the name and v-number of the prisoner.

The policeman rolled the prisoner's right thumb over the marked spot on the sheet. Next he took a small but powerful magnifying glass from his top pocket and quickly compared the print he had taken with the right thumb print on the death warrant. When he had satisfied himself that the prints were identical, the policeman signed the form. The prisoner looked on mutely, not making eye contact with anyone, as he had been taught.

```
PRISON REF. NO. V3664

I, No. W39520T Rank LIEUTENANT COLONEL Name WILLEM JACOBUS
DU PLESSIS, a fingerprint expert in the SA Police, stationed
at the South African Criminal Bureau, Pretoria, confirm that on
1987/12/10 at 06h00 at Central Prison, Pretoria, I physically
took the right thumb print of MNUXA JEROME GCABA Prison Ref.
No. V3664 and compared it with the right thumb print of MNUXA
JEROME GCABA appearing on the death warrant J 221A and found
the two to be identical.

PRETORIA W J du Plessis
DATE: 10.12.87 SIGNATURE


Right thumb print
```

One of the prisoners moaned and started sobbing. The Warrant Officer fixed him with a stern look.

'Staan stil en staan regop!'

He spoke as if to all of them. He cast his eye over the escorts, surreptitiously; he knew that they had been performing beyond the call of duty during the last week, mere boys doing the work of men.

'Ruk jou reg, man! Staan stil!'

The prisoner perked up slightly but his whole body was caught in an uncontrollable shudder that ebbed and flowed like the tide. Each time the shivering reached its highest point, the prisoner allowed a primitive groan to escape his contorted lips; it seemed to come from the very core of him. He caught the Warrant Officer's penetrating stare and wilted under it, but his fear of the Warrant Officer paled against his fear of his own imminent death.

The escorts stood next to their prisoners, in two's, stiff and ashen-faced. Each held his prisoner by the right sleeve. They were entitled to ask why they should do this job, why they could not withdraw or walk away, but they did not. They faced their duty stoically, masking their own fear under military poses, standing almost to attention, in a column, every man looking straight ahead, a well-drilled unit whose individual members were able to hide their fears and shortcomings in collective action. The shivering and fear in the column was contagious and sympathetically transferred from prisoner to escort, and apprehension passed from escort to prisoner. Each pair had become a pitiful symbiosis, shaking and breathing in unison, at the very edge of self-control as the line snaked towards the table.

Thus they stood, the seven prisoners and their escorts, each having been trained and indoctrinated by the prison culture to perform their respective tasks for the morning, to obey without question, to react immediately and without thinking to every command, to go where they were sent, to march in unison, every man in step. Like a robber and his victim, they shared the fear of the moment.

When the policeman had completed the first certificate he handed it to the Warrant Officer, who in turn slipped it into the folds of the death warrant on the clipboard. Then he motioned to the escort to take the prisoner further into the corridor and with his index finger beckoned to the second prisoner to approach. The policeman did his job with practised ease while the escorts looked on.

The process of identification, fingerprinting and certification in respect of all seven prisoners was completed in half an hour.

The policeman had no further duties to perform at the prison and left immediately through the main guardhouse as the Executioner, a nondescript, elderly man, a retired policeman, arrived. They exchanged a perfunctory greeting in passing each other, each knowing full well the purpose of the other's presence at the prison. The Warrant Officer and the Sheriff checked their records a second time. They had to be sure that they were hanging the right people.

At exactly six-thirty the prisoners were herded down the passage to the chapel. At least two further security doors had to be unlocked before they could enter. Unseen by them the Hangman joined the back of the procession and slipped through the door leading to the gallows building.

Fifteen minutes was allowed for a short service. The prisoners and escorts sat paired in the pews.

The Hangman went upstairs to wait for them. The Warrant Officer and the Sheriff had time for a cup of coffee in the Warrant Officer's office.

While the chaplain was engaged in the business of salvation, the Hangman went about his final preparations upstairs in the gallows chamber. He started by examining his equipment. Seven well-used hemp ropes had been laid out for him on the table under the window. He checked each rope for wear or defects that could interfere with his task. Some of the ropes showed signs of wear, but the steel rings and rubber washers appeared to be in good condition. He nodded in approval. The ropes were fine; he preferred the old ropes, made supple by frequent use. A stiff new rope took more time to adjust to the right tightness and position anyway.

The Hangman stood with one of the ropes in his hands, turning the noose inside out for a detailed inspection. He knew this would be the last hanging day of the year. The Department of Justice had advised him that he could take a break for a few weeks. He could not remember how many he had hanged during the year, he would have to check his records, but he had had a busy year and a hectic fortnight and, although his part of the job was easier than that of the escorts and the Warrant Officer, he still felt the tension in his back muscles before every hanging. Things could go wrong so easily, and then the blame would fall on him.

He had work to do. He started by inspecting the rope in his hands more carefully. The rope was standard hemp, an inch thick. The one end was tidied by a string, wound tight to ensure that the rope did not fray. The other end of the rope ended in a fist-sized knot where the rope had been spliced back onto itself, encasing a steel washer. The rope ran through the steel washer, forming the noose, and in the Hangman's hands the hemp moved smoothly through the steel washer. A heavy-duty black rubber grommet had been set in position to create a noose matching the thickness of the prisoner's neck. The Hangman slid the steel washer to the grommet and pushed hard against the resistance. The rubber grommet did its work and held the steel washer firmly. The Hangman nodded absently as he picked up the Warrant Officer's list of prisoners with the relevant measurements against each name. He decided to do a spot check of the first prisoner's details and calculations.

The list gave the prisoner's neck size in inches, to the quarter-inch, and his weight in pounds. The Hangman carefully measured the inner circumference of the noose with the steel washer flush against the rubber grommet. The noose was fine and its calculations correct. The Hangman next checked the prisoner's weight against the Table of Drops and nodded again when he found the calculation of the drop to be correct to the last inch.

With the calculations in order, the Hangman started attaching the ropes to the beam overhead. He used the articulated measuring stick, eight feet long, to mark the precise length of the drop. By means of a special knot he fastened the rope to a shackle attached to the beam overhead. Then he meticulously checked that the length of the drop was exactly in accordance with the calculations. When he was sure that he had everything right, he tightened the knot securely with a special wooden mallet so that the ropes could not slip under the weight of the prisoner. He repeated the process until all seven hanging ropes were securely attached to the beam.

The preparations by the Warrant Officer and his staff had been meticulous and there was little else for the Hangman to do. When he had finished fixing the ropes to the beam he lifted each noose to head height and tied it with a rubber band to the rope. He stood back and looked down the line of nooses. They were out of the way and ready to be attached to the prisoners.

In the parking lot outside Maximum, the first relatives were arriving in small groups. Only two members of each family would be allowed to attend a funeral service in the chapel. They stood around in silence looking at each other, suspecting that they were sharing a similar fate, to be witnesses, but not eyewitnesses, to the destruction of their sons. They would not be allowed to enter the prison until ten to nine but had come early. They could not hear the singing inside the walls, nor could they know that the words reflected their mood exactly.

> Someone's waiting, Lord
> Kumbaya

The Hangman waited and studied his surroundings with a knowing eye.

There were four items of furniture in the gallows chamber: a mahogany cupboard in the corner next to the door and a table with two straight-backed wooden chairs against another wall under a row of small windows. Natural light streamed through the windows onto the Warrant Officer's list of prisoners with the drop calculations on the table.

The gallows machine with its appurtenances dominated the room and, as befitted its status, occupied the centre of the room.

The machine consisted of a number of integrated pieces. A rust-brown steel I-beam was attached to the roof immediately above the trapdoors with steel bolts. It ran the length of the trapdoors with a bit to spare at either end. Suspended from the beam, at various points, were the shackles to which the hanging ropes were attached. There was also a moveable block and tackle attached to the beam. It was used for the heavy lifting, to raise the heavy trapdoors into position and to haul the dead bodies back up into the gallows chamber.

The trapdoors fit into an eight-by-two-yard opening in the floor. The opening was lined on all sides by metal framing of angular steel tubing. The steel frame was part of an elaborate mechanism designed to keep the trapdoors in place and to allow them to open when their release mechanism was sprung. Each of the doors was made of six two-inch-thick hardwood planks glued side by side with epoxy. The undersides of the trapdoors were reinforced with steel straps. At the end of each reinforcing strap was a heavy-duty hinge where the door was attached to the frame.

On either side of the trapdoors was a waist-high handrail running the length of the trapdoors. At the end of the left handrail was the lever. It stood about four feet high and had two safety devices built into it. One was a simple pin that was inserted into the lever mechanism just above the floor and prevented the lever from being pushed forward accidentally. The other was a clutch on the handle of the lever itself.

The Hangman methodically checked each item in the gallows chamber before he removed the safety pin from the lever. He was ready. He looked at his watch. It was twelve minutes to seven. Even though he had used the same equipment without mishap twice already earlier in the week, he decided to take the stairs to the pit room below in order to inspect the main mechanism in the undercarriage of the trapdoors. He descended slowly into the windowless room below the gallows.

The Hangman stood directly under the trapdoors, in a square pit in the floor of the room. The pit gave the room its name and was approximately a foot deep, with a drain in one corner.

The singing in the chapel slowly increased in intensity and could now be heard clearly throughout the complex. When the hymn reached its chorus the escorts joined in and the call for salvation rose to a crescendo.

The singing stopped abruptly as the sermon ended.

When the singing stopped the Hangman knew that it would be no more than ten minutes before the prisoners would be on the trapdoors. He looked up and with his eyes followed the metal tubing to the points where the frame was braced against the ceiling of the pit room. A set of pins on a steel rod supported elbow extensions under the trapdoors, holding them in position. The release mechanism ran the length of the left-side trapdoor and consisted of a steel rod with pins at points opposite the elbow extensions. When the lever was activated, the rod moved backwards and the pins slid out from under the elbow extensions. The trapdoors, devoid of support, then dropped down.

The Hangman took special care in his examination of this crude contraption. Satisfied with the state of the main mechanism he looked cursorily at the rest of the equipment.

More metal tubing and strips cradled six stopper bags on each side below the trapdoors. The stopper bags were suspended from the ceiling by metal cradles. Their function was to catch the trapdoors when they opened and to mute the noise of the trapdoors slamming against the sides of the frame. The stopper bags were made of heavy-duty canvas and were filled with straw.

Footsteps in the room above alerted the Hangman to the fact that the senior officers who had to attend every execution had arrived. He went back into the gallows chamber and shook hands with them. They made small talk, the Head of Central Prison, the Head of Maximum, the Medical Officer and the Hangman. Four warders on standby duty stood to one side.

It was ten to seven. In the chapel the escorts produced standard police issue handcuffs, prodded the prisoners into line and cuffed their hands behind their backs. There was an unexpected though undemonstrative gentleness in their actions. But for the brief moment when the Hangman would slip the nooses over their heads and tighten the ropes around their necks, for these prisoners this would be the last skin contact with another human being. The escorts wasted no time. They gently tugged at the sleeves of their prisoners and led them to the first door. A warder stood at the ready with a key and as the column of prisoners and escorts approached he put the key in the lock and turned it in the same motion.

The heavy door swung open and a whiff of teargas wafted down, partly masked by the smell of disinfectant. It brought back unpleasant memories, of a day when the prison had been filled with shouts and curses and teargas and everyone inside it had been gagging and wheezing, with tears streaming from their eyes. The door slammed shut behind them, locking the column into the narrow stairwell.

The prisoners had never been to this part of the prison. When they looked up, all they could see was the staircase, the grey wall on their left, the steel grille on the right, and the handrails on either side. The handrails were not for them; their hands were firmly cuffed behind their backs. Not that such a precaution could ever match the desperate ingenuity of a man about to be hanged. The stairwell was narrow and windowless at the lower reaches. At the top sunlight filtered through a solitary window.

In the crush of the stairwell the procession made steady progress to the first landing, but when the prisoners in front saw yet another landing ahead they baulked and reared back, bumping into the prisoners and escorts behind them. One man turned and started making his way down when his escort was caught in the stampede of retreating prisoners. The escorts further down the stairs stood firm, blocking the way, but it is always easier fighting one's way down the stairs than up, and for a moment it looked as if the retreating prisoner would get all the way down, but his escort caught up with him and grabbed him by the collar of his shirt and dragged him back to his place higher up in the column.

The escorts held onto their prisoners with a firm grip of the shirt collar and another hand on the handcuffs, lifting the prisoners' arms high behind their backs. This was not going to be an easy hanging, they knew from experience. With kicks and smacks they settled the column down and made their way up, grunting and cursing, with more kicks and smacks as the need arose. The prisoners put up a token resistance, their spirit broken after a year or more of unremitting conditioning and abuse and by the futility of the uneven contest. The procession came to a halt a number of times when a prisoner's legs gave in or a manacled hand would not let go of the handrail. Prisoner and escort alike had to fight gravity and fear at every step, on unwilling legs. The escorts' shouts and exhortations filled the stairwell but could not be heard outside.

The smell of teargas was stronger the higher they went. A prisoner wet his trousers. An escort gagged and struggled to hold his breakfast. The column coiled its way upwards, to the light.

When the procession arrived at the top of the stairs most of the men in the column were breathing hard, their uniforms untidy, their eyes wild in their flushed faces. The pungent smell of urine blended with the smell of unwashed men. They entered a large ante-room with some cell doors on the left.

The Sheriff stood waiting with folded arms at the far side of the room with the Warrant Officer. The escorts once again prodded the prisoners into line and turned them to face the Warrant Officer and the Sheriff. The prisoners complied mechanically and stood in a bedraggled line, heads down.

The Warrant Officer held his clipboard in his left hand, with seven white hoods draped over his arm. He studied the prisoners and escorts briefly and then raised his arm to look at his watch. It was five to seven; they were a minute ahead of schedule. He liked things to go exactly according to plan, so he took his time.

'Staan vorentoe!'

The escorts pushed their men a yard to the front and held them there.

The Warrant Officer walked slowly down the line of prisoners. They kept their eyes on his shoes.

'Ek wil niks kak van julle hê nie.'

The prisoners stood mute; the escorts peered over their shoulders.

The Sheriff came over to join the Warrant Officer in front of the first prisoner in the line. Standing face to face with the prisoner, the Warrant Officer made a show of comparing the prisoner's features with those in the first photograph on his clipboard. It was the photograph taken on the prisoner's admission more than a year earlier. The Warrant Officer did not speak; this was not his show but the Sheriff's. He took a step to the side as the Sheriff stepped up to the first prisoner.

The Sheriff addressed the prisoner by his name, exactly as it was written on the death warrant.

'Mnuxa Jerome Gcaba, do you have anything to say before the sentence of the Court is carried out?' he asked. He struggled with the pronunciation of the Zulu names.

The prisoner mumbled something incoherent. He wanted to speak but did not know what to say. Before he could change his mind, the Sheriff stepped back and made a tick on his own clipboard. The Warrant Officer reached behind the prisoner and handed one of the white hoods to the escort. The custom-made hood was an elasticised headcloth with an additional flap, also elasticised, which would in due course be hooked under the prisoner's chin and cover his face completely. The escort adjusted the hood on the prisoner's head and pushed the flap back over the prisoner's head. When he was satisfied that the hood was properly in place, the Warrant Officer handed the escort the prisoner's name tag. The escort pocketed the tag and held his prisoner in position in the line. The first prisoner was ready.

'Thank you,' said the Sheriff with exaggerated politeness as he went up to the next prisoner to repeat the formality.

'Joseph Gcabashe, do you have anything to say before the sentence of the Court is carried out?'

From here on things would happen fast. In less than five minutes these prisoners would be hanging from their ropes, destroyed by order of the law.

Yet every second would feel like an eternity for those in the gallows chamber.

Immediately after the last white hood had been put in place, the escorts pulled their prisoners by their shirtsleeves into the next room, following the Warrant Officer's unspoken command. The prisoners looked around curiously. They had heard the rumour that the condemned were not really hanged, that they were to be taken to secret dungeons below the prison to work as slaves in the Mint, to produce banknotes and coins. But there were no machines in the room and it was devoid of furniture. There was only a row of windows high up on the one side and a second door obliquely ahead.

Ahead of them the Warrant Officer stopped at the door and stood next to it. The Warrant Officer waited with his hand on the door handle.

Behind him the Sheriff stood at the front of the column, followed by the prisoners and escorts in pairs.

Here in this last stop before the gallows, the prisoners had a moment to reflect. They tried desperately not to look at the door, tried not to think of what lay behind it. But their thoughts took them to another world of horror and pain and death as an array of events slipped into focus, as in a dream, flickering without colour or sound. Disjointed incidents reared up from their past, a past that was distant yet real, a past that could not be ignored in this final act before the fall of the curtain.

Picture a slightly built, elderly man, walking with a stick, carrying his Bible in the early evening of a Cape Town autumn, being robbed of his meagre possessions, even his dentures. He cries pitifully for help, but to no avail, as he is stabbed repeatedly by his three young assailants. Some women rush to the scene, but the killers ignore their pleas to leave the old man alone. The killers run from the scene only when the police arrive unexpectedly.

Move to a farmhouse attached to a small hotel in Natal. A gang of four lies in wait for the lights to be turned off in the bedroom of the elderly couple they have been stalking. The gang is impatient; it is taking too long. One of them enters the house on a reconnaissance but creeps out again on finding the couple still awake. They decide to wait. At last the lights go out and the gang steal into the house. They grab the sickly old man from his bed and wrest his pistol from him. They stab him in the lung and ransack the house even as his distressed wife shields him from further injury. They rush off into the night. On the way to the hospital the old man drowns in his own blood, in his wife's arms, while his killers sit down to argue over the fairest way to divide the spoils.

Imagine a middle-aged man in the Transvaal, pleading pitifully for his life with his three youthful attackers. But they taunt him, 'Do you know what the date is tomorrow? It is the sixteenth of June. You know what that means!' They rob him of a few meaningless possessions. They discuss ways of killing him before they strike him repeatedly on the head with a hammer. When he does not die quickly enough they pull at opposite ends of a rope around his neck to strangle him. It takes him a long time to die. They drive around with the body in the boot of the dead man's car before they finally return to the scene to build a pyre of wood and abandoned car tyres and dispose of the body by reducing it to ashes. Even as the body burns the three killers go for another ride in the car. They stop to pick up their girlfriends and have a party during which they distribute the loot.

Then picture Cape Town, where two young men surprise a kindly seventy-three-year-old woman in poor health and living alone, in her kitchen. The one stabs her in the shoulder and takes her to the bathroom where he allows her to wash off the blood. He rapes her in her bedroom. He stops from time to time to shout instructions to his companion about which items to collect from the rest of the house. He smashes the pleading victim's skull with an ornamental stone she uses as a doorstop. The killers pack the day's takings and go drinking.

But there was little time for reflection.

The Warrant Officer looked at his watch again. It was one minute to seven.

Then he turned and opened the door without another word. The column followed the Sheriff through the door where they passed the Hangman without seeing him, their eyes fixed on the scene ahead. They were in the gallows chamber.

Immediately in front of the column was the gallows machine with its seven ropes ending in the nooses hanging at eye level, coiled and ready. The ropes so dominated the scene that the prisoners did not notice the officials waiting against the wall. In a row under the window and well clear of the gallows machine stood the Head of Pretoria Central Prison, the Head of Maximum Security Prison, the Prison Medical Officer and the four standby warders. The two officers were dressed in their most formal uniforms: prison-green trousers, shirts and ties and fully buttoned tunics. The doctor wore a businesslike white safari suit. The Hangman was in shirtsleeves, the warders in their fatigues. Like the Hangman they were not spectators, they had work to do.

The escorts did not break their stride as they walked the seven prisoners onto the trapdoors, still holding their charges by their shirtsleeves. The prisoners went onto the trapdoors between the two handrails while the escorts took a line on the outer side of the right handrail. Under the combined weight of the prisoners the trapdoors gave way ever so slightly and the prisoners instinctively looked for a handhold, but their arms were cuffed behind their backs. The escorts quickly manoeuvred them precisely into position, a prisoner on each of the seven pairs of painted feet on the trapdoors and a noose hanging from the beam exactly above each hooded head. The prisoners stood with heads down, their eyes averted from the ropes. But for the prisoner in front, who faced a blank wall, the entire view of each prisoner was filled with the spectre of the shivering prisoner in front of him.

The ropes smelled of the blood of recent hangings. The hemp in the noose was stained.

Overwhelmed, a prisoner in the middle of the line stumbled and his legs started to buckle. One of the standby warders sprang forward to the rail on the left and grabbed the prisoner by the arm as he fell away from his escort. Together the two warders raised the prisoner and held him upright in position. The prisoner swayed in their grip, oblivious to the further proceedings. The white hood had slipped to the side of his head. The standby warder held him steady as the escort quickly readjusted the hood.

The moment the last prisoner was in position, the Hangman moved up to the back of the line and, starting with the last prisoner, slipped the noose over the hood and around the prisoner's neck. Then he expertly adjusted the noose to ensure a tight fit. The steel ring on the noose sat in exactly the desired position, flush against the jaw immediately below the prisoner's left ear. The aim was for the combined effect of the rope slamming the head over to the right and the rest of the body continuing its fall to shatter the cervical vertebrae of the prisoner's neck and to crush the spinal cord. This would happen at the point where the cord exited the skull, between the two vertebrae known as the atlas and axis. As soon as the fit of the noose was exactly to the Hangman's liking, he turned the flap of the white hood down and hooked its elastic seam under the prisoner's chin so that it covered his face completely.

The Hangman took but a few seconds with each prisoner. Slip the noose over the head. Slide the steel ring over to the rubber grommet. Pull tight to ensure a good fit. Drop the flap of the white hood over the face. Next prisoner.

Slip noose. Slide ring. Pull tight. Drop flap.

Seven times the Hangman completed the sequence. Slip. Slide. Pull. Drop.

When he had completed the process with the prisoner at the front of the line, the Hangman was right next to the lever.

When the clock in the Dutch Reformed Church in front of Maximum Security Prison began to strike the hour of seven, the condemned men were on their marks on the trapdoors, the ropes around their necks and their escorts by their side.

For a second, time stood still. The moment so long awaited had arrived.

The prisoners stood still on the trapdoors for that eternal moment. They were about to pay the price for their greed, for their rapacity, for their callous, murderous hearts, for the opportunities they had missed to do good things, for the opportunities they had denied their victims, for the pain they had caused to so many others. Their hearts were beating in their ears. Their lungs were drawing quick, shallow breaths. They hyperventilated and the white hoods billowed out in front of their faces with every exhalation, only to be sucked in by the next desperate gasp for air. In this last moment before death every synapse, every sinew was alive with the most acute sense of the present, the here and the now.

Time stood still also for the escorts. They stood on their side of the rail, each next to his allotted prisoner. They were in empathic distress, their pulses racing and their chests heaving with strained breathing. For them too the here and the now was overwhelming, the stench of fear and the smell of the ropes in their nostrils. What fate ordained who should go on the right and who should go on the left of the rail? The escorts knew what was in store for them. Doesn't everyone who kills die a little with each killing?

That long second ended as the Hangman, in a smooth and practised movement, disengaged the clutch and pushed the lever forward. The escorts, acting as if on an unspoken command, simultaneously let go of their charges and took a step away from the rail. The Hangman looked backwards and down over his right shoulder as the metal cam-rod device supporting the cross-supports under the trapdoors slid forward and allowed gravity to take over. The officials and standby warders on the far side of the room stiffened.

The trapdoors opened with a mechanical thud.

Kellunck!

The prisoners' bare feet desperately sought purchase on the receding trapdoors and a rush of air escaped upwards between the doors.

Shooosh!

The prisoners fell straight into the dimly lit room below, some in silence, some with a desperate groan, one barely conscious. They experienced the instant dread of all mammals: uncontrolled free fall. Their bowels and bladders voided compulsively, the muscles controlling their internal organs responding to some primordial command to prepare for flight or battle. Their abdominal muscles involuntarily contracted and they gasped vainly for breath. As they plunged towards the end of their fall, the crimes that had brought them to this cruel end flashed through their individual minds, not as a logical sequence of events with discernible causes and consequences, but as a dark hole into which every memory was sucked with irresistible force.

A moment later the trapdoors slammed against their stopper bags with a double blow that reverberated throughout the building and could be felt by everyone in it as a faint tremor.

Whabam!

The singing in all sections of the prison below immediately rose an octave.

> Someone's dying, Lord
> Kumbaya

The ropes snapped tight as the prisoners reached the end of their pre-scribed drops. The steel rings on the nooses smashed into the muscles and blood vessels on the left side of the prisoners' necks and slammed their heads over to the right. Their bodies continued to fall for a short distance, stretching their necks to an obscene length, until the downward momentum was stopped by the neck muscles and tendons.

Simultaneously a round of loud cracks echoed in the gallows room upstairs as the prisoners' spinal cords broke. The bruised flesh and the tortured neck muscles held the bodies up and pulled them back a short distance. Signals from the tormented brains took their usual route down the spinal columns, but found their path largely terminated in torn nerve endings. The prisoners' tongues were squeezed upwards and out of their gaping mouths. Their eyes gorged on the blood and tissue being forced into their eye sockets by the constrictive force of the ropes around their necks. Blood and mucus spurted into the white hoods, mainly from their mouths and noses. In two or three cases necks were torn open on the side of the steel ring on the noose. In another an ear was partly torn off. Bodily fluids immediately stained the white hoods. Excrement, urine and blood started dripping into the pit in the floor of the room below.

The bell in the spire of the Dutch Reformed Church still resonated in the background, slowly sounding to the final strike of the gong.

But the prisoners were not dead yet. While their brains may have had no means to send signals to their vital organs or muscles, there was still sufficient oxygen to allow conscious brain activity for about five minutes. Electrochemical discharges continued to send impulses to the prison-ers' extremities through what nerve conduits remained intact, causing their limbs to twitch in a fine flutter. Their hearts lost their rhythm and in the absence of any coherent signals from their brains were soon to stop beating altogether. Their lungs collapsed and their internal organs slowed in their usual functioning.

Together the condemned men hurried towards the very gates of Hell as their own awareness of their physical existence dimmed towards absolute darkness.

But one of them was not to die quickly or quietly. He was twisting and jumping at the end of his rope, his shoulders hunched up. The prisoner kicked wildly with his feet as his companions turned slowly on their ropes, their lives ebbing away. He groaned and breathed noisily through clenched teeth. The white hood billowed in and out over his face as he struggled for air. As he spun on the rope, kicking and gagging, the third escort in the line doubled over and reeled away from the rail. The Warrant Officer, his attention riveted on the squirming prisoner at his feet, paid the warder, now heaving in the corner of the room, no attention.

'Trek hom op! Maak gou! Maak gou!' The Warrant Officer motioned with his arm to one of the standby warders who immediately rushed over to the other side of the rail.

Three warders grabbed the rope, two from the one side of the trapdoors and one from the other, and strained and heaved to haul the prisoner back up into view.

'Slow down. Don't touch him, don't touch him.' The Warrant Officer spoke with a hiss. 'A little higher, watch my hands.' He held his hands slightly apart and indicated how far the prisoner still had to be lifted, to where his feet were exactly at the original level of the trapdoors.

The three warders wrestled with the rope as they raised the struggling and kicking prisoner. They held onto the rope for dear life, with the full weight of the prisoner hanging from their extended arms. Slowly the gap between the Warrant Officer's hands reduced until his palms touched. A fourth warder stepped over quickly as the Warrant Officer nodded in his direction. The standby warder helped to steady the prisoner with his feet in line with the floor.

'On the count of three, let him go,' the Warrant Officer commanded. 'Een, twee, drie!'

The four warders simultaneously released their grip on the rope and the prisoner fell through the opening a second time. This time the neck muscles were too bruised and too tired to resist the downward pull of gravity on the body and the sideways push of the steel ring against the side of his head. There was a resounding crack as the axis vertebra was smashed and the spinal cord within was crushed.

The Hangman, the Warrant Officer, the escorts and the Medical Officer looked down into the pit for signs of life, but there were none now, only the faint fluttering of hands and feet, the sign of a successful hanging. They stepped back from the trapdoors. The warders who had hauled the last prisoner up by the rope breathed heavily from their exertions and leaned on the rail, their strained breathing the only sound in the chamber. Sweat stained their fatigues.

Elsewhere in the prison the song had reached its final stanza.

Someone's crying, Lord
Kumbaya

So the prisoners died like their victims had, pleading, screaming for help and kicking out, vainly praying for a miracle to save them, fighting for air with every grain of energy, resisting the impending darkness, groaning and bleeding. Death did not arrive quickly but with a deliberate and slow inevitability, with compelling and frightening certainty. The prisoners hung on their ropes, their bodies broken and defiled, soiled with their own body fluids, with vomit and excrement, in an obscene parody of their victims.

When there was no longer any sound or untoward movement in the pit room the men upstairs in the gallows room gradually relaxed. They stood in silence, watching the hooded heads slowly turning just below floor level.

Down in the prison the singing had stopped and the institution swung into its daily routine as cell doors were opened in preparation for the morning roll call, the emptying of night soil buckets, and breakfast. Slowly the prisoners in the condemned cells settled down as the familiar sounds of a new day reached further into the depths of the prison. For them the ordeal was to survive the nights, when they were haunted by the twin ghosts of the past and the future, of regret and fear, the two relentless hounds that bayed incessantly at their heels. The drudgery of their daytime activities allowed them a temporary escape, trapping them in the mundane present, in trips to the showers, cleaning their already spotless cells, writing letters, reading their prison-issue Bibles, eating their tasteless prison fare, the dry bread sticking to the back of their throats.

But for the gallows escorts the nightmare was continuing. They still had to take care of their wards, now hanging lifeless on their ropes.

They would be busy all day.

Supreme Court, Grahamstown

3

As the escorts were nearing the end of the day's work in Pretoria, a judge in another town reached the end of the Court's judgment on extenuating circumstances and the bureaucracy of the death sentence was about to be set in motion again.

The Judge hesitated slightly, as if to emphasise the solemnity of the occasion.

He faced Bakiri Nelson and announced the verdict.

'Our finding, and it is a unanimous finding, is that there are no extenuating circumstances present in respect of either of the offences of murder.'

Neither of the two Assessors flanking the Judge on the bench stirred, but the prosecutor and defence counsel half rose from their seats and said, almost in unison, 'As the Court pleases.'

As the interpreter translated what the Judge had said to the man in the dock, the tension in the courtroom grew. The main participants in the trial knew that the outcome was now fixed. What remained was a mere formality, the law's response to the Court's findings.

The registrar rose and addressed the interpreter. 'Mr Interpreter, please inform the accused that he has been duly convicted of murder without extenuating circumstances. Ask him if he has or knows anything to say why the sentence of death should not be passed on him according to law.'

The law moves with a slow, deadly beat. Every word had to be spoken twice, once in English for the record, and then again in the language of the accused, isiXhosa.

The Judge waited for the interpreter to repeat the Court's finding in Nelson's mother tongue.

The answer came without emotion.

'I have nothing to say, M'Lord.'

The Judge acknowledged this with a stony, 'Yes.'

The registrar held up her hand and said, 'I call for silence in Court while the sentence of death is being passed.'

Then she sat down.

The man in the dock was strangely unmoved, as if worse things had already happened in his life. Neither the regular meals nor soap and water he had enjoyed while awaiting trial had changed his essential appearance: that of a castaway, one used to deprivation, hunger and despair.

'Bakiri Nelson,' said the Judge when the spectators had settled down, 'you have been convicted on two counts of murder and one of theft. On the charge of theft the sentence that I impose upon you is two months' imprisonment.

'In respect of the murders there can never be any justification for what you did. Your actions were wicked and vicious, and you showed a callous disregard for two old ladies who, according to you, were kind to you.

'Having found that there are no extenuating circumstances, I am obliged to impose the following sentence upon you: on each of the counts of murder of which you have been convicted the sentence is that you are to be taken to the place from whence you came and at a time and a place to be determined by the Minister of Justice you are to be hanged by the neck until you are dead.

'And may the Lord have mercy on your soul,' he added.

Counsel rose to their feet again and muttered, 'As the Court pleases.'

Defence counsel remained standing. 'M'Lord, I have instructions to note an application for leave to appeal against the convictions on all three counts and also against the finding that there were no extenuating circumstances in respect of the two murder counts. May I ask when it would be convenient for M'Lord to hear my application?'

'Are you ready to argue now?' the Judge asked.

'Yes, M'Lord.'

The debate about leave to appeal was over in minutes.

'The result is that leave to appeal is refused,' the Judge announced. Then he stood up, bowed slightly in counsel's direction, and retired to his chambers.

The registrar went to her office to take care of the formalities. The Court's judgment had to be converted into an order. In her office next to the Judge's chambers, she took three copies of the standard death warrant form from the drawer together with two sheets of carbon paper.

The death warrant had to be prepared in triplicate. She started typing in the details of the case with meticulous care, taking her time, as the details had to be exactly right.

She had performed this task on a number of occasions previously and knew that there was no purpose in hurrying.

And then there were the death certificates. Only a judge or a magistrate could issue a death certificate in case of violent or unnatural death.

She quickly prepared death certificates for the victims. Inserting the cause of death she typed: *Strangulation – Homicide.*

When she had finished typing in the details in the appropriate spaces on the forms the registrar rose with a batch of documents for the Judge to sign.

It had been a busy term and there was still one more trial on the roll before the Court would close its doors for the summer recess. She reread the death warrant at the top of the pile as she walked down the passage to the Judge's chambers.

WARRANT: DEATH SENTENCE

J221E

IN THE SUPREME COURT OF SOUTH AFRICA

(EASTERN CAPE LOCAL DIVISION - GRAHAMSTOWN)

To the Sheriff of GRAHAMSTOWN

or his deputy and the Sheriff of Transvaal and his deputy.

THE STATE AGAINST BAKIRI NELSON

WHEREAS it appears of record that at a Criminal Session of the

SUPREME COURT OF SOUTH AFRICA (EASTERN CAPE **Division) held before** THE

HONOURABLE JUDGE M.P. JENNETT **(Me or the Hon. Mr Justice)**

at GRAHAMSTOWN **on the** TENTH **day of** DECEMBER

One Thousand Nine Hundred and EIGHTY-SEVEN

the above-named BAKIRI NELSON

was convicted of the crime of 2 (TWO) COUNTS of MURDER **and sentenced to**

death by the said Court:

THIS IS THEREFORE TO COMMAND YOU, <u>after receipt by you of a notice, in</u>

<u>writing, signed by the Minister of Justice, or any other Minister of State acting</u>

<u>for him in his absence, that the State President has decided not to extend</u>

<u>mercy to the person under sentence of death,</u> **to cause the said sentence to**

be executed upon the said prisoner in the Central Prison, Pretoria, as soon as

fitting arrangements can be made for the execution thereof:

AND to detain HIM **(him or her) in custody in the said prison until the said**

sentence is executed, or HE **(he or she) is discharged therefrom in accordance**

with a written notice under the hand of the Minister of Justice, or any other

Minister of State acting for him in his absence, that the State President has

decided to extend mercy to the said prisoner.

GIVEN under my hand at GRAHAMSTOWN

on this TENTH **day of** DECEMBER **One Thousand Nine Hundred and** EIGHTY

SEVEN.

....

Judge of the SUPREME COURT OF SOUTH AFRICA

(EASTERN CAPE **Division)**

Registrar

NOTE. – The Central Prison, Pretoria, is the place designated by the Minister of

Justice as the place for the execution of Capital Sentences.

Name and address of the Advocate for the Defence: MR A.D. OSLER, St

GEORGE'S

CHAMBERS, GRAHAMSTOWN

Thumb-prints taken by me this .... day of .... 19 .....

....

Detective-in-charge

Thumb-prints taken in my presence this .... day of .... 19 .....

....

Deputy Sheriff

Left thumb   **Right thumb**

Satisfied with her work, the registrar knocked politely on the door and went in. The Judge hardly glanced at the batch of documents as he signed them. Once the registrar was back in her own office, she called the usher on an internal line and asked him to fetch the warrants and to take them down to the Chief Registrar's office for his signature and the official stamp. Then she returned to other tasks. She made a mental note that the details of the case still had to be entered in a special register in the Chief Registrar's office. From this moment the case would be tracked through all possible legal procedures to ensure that when the time came there were no pending appeals or applications for clemency outstanding.

A few minutes later the elderly usher came wheezing down the steps to the cells and handed the signed documents to the investigating officer through the grille of the cell section. Only one prisoner remained in the cells: Bakiri Nelson. The policeman used an inkpad and special roller to place the condemned man's left and right thumb-prints at the bottom of the death warrant. Then he signed the warrant in the appropriate spaces and watched as the Sheriff signed there too. From this moment the prisoner's body was legally in the hands of the High Sheriff and his deputies. It was their duty to execute court orders and they would be responsible for the prisoner until his execution.

Upstairs the registrar found a quiet moment to walk down to the main admin office. There she stood over the clerk's desk and watched as the Clerk of the Criminal Court started a new entry in the Capital Cases Register. When the clerk was ready, the registrar supplied the first details to be inserted in the columns running across the two facing pages of the register:

DATE	CASE NO.	ACCUSED	DATE SENTENCED TO DEATH	PLACE AND JUDGE	DATE JUSTICE NOTIFIED	DATE TAPES SENT TO CONTRACTOR	DATE RECORD RECEIVED FROM CONTRACTOR
10/12/87	CC479/87	BAKIRI NELSON	10/12/87 (2 DEATH SENTENCES)	Grahams-town Jennett J P			

DATE OF APPLICA-TION FOR LEAVE TO APPEAL	DATE JUSTICE NOTIFIED	OUT-COME AND DATE	DATE JUSTICE NOTI-FIED	DATE ORDER SENT TO AP-PEAL COURT	DATE RECORD TO APPEAL COURT	FINAL OUTCOME
10/12/87		REFUSED ON 10/12/87				

The remaining details would be inserted from time to time as the various administrative steps were taken. 'Remember to send a telegram to Justice as soon as possible,' the registrar reminded the young clerk as she left his office.

What remained was for Nelson to be transported to Maximum Security Prison in Pretoria. The impending weekend meant that the journey would be delayed and that he would first have to be locked up in the local jail. His death warrant had to go everywhere with him. Each time he was to be handed over by one official to another, or transferred from one place of incarceration to another, his left and right thumb-prints would be taken and compared to those on the warrant. At each handover a written acknowledgement of receipt of the person of the prisoner would be signed by his new custodian and filed by the one relieved of further responsibility.

Nelson would eventually arrive in Pretoria three days after being sentenced and would be allocated number v-3912, dressed in recycled prison garb and photographed. Neither the Chief Justice nor the State President would find any reason to interfere with the sentences of the Court. And on 13 January 1989, after all the procedural safeguards had been taken to ensure that he was in fact the person who had been sentenced to death on this day, 10 December 1987, Bakiri Nelson would be hanged by the neck until he was dead, exactly as the Judge had ordered. Within a week both death warrants, now bearing the condemned man's thumb-prints, would be returned to the Chief Registrar in Grahamstown together with a return from the High Sheriff in Pretoria that the orders of the Court had been carried out.

Accompanying the return would be the photograph taken on

admission, pinned to a public notice, to be displayed in a prominent place at the Grahamstown Magistrates' Court.

The Chief Registrar would complete the formalities by inserting the details in the last column of the Capital Cases Register:

No clemency by State President. Executed on 13 January 1989.

Old Johannesburg Road

4

The young man in the grey bakkie and the seven members of the Diepsloot Karate Club in their white minibus battled on through the rain to their mutual destiny.

The clouds had at first risen stealthily in the south, arctic white against a light-blue sky. But soon the atmosphere turned nasty. The heavy smell of impending rain filled the dry, dusty Highveld air before anyone had taken notice of the ominous bank of clouds building up on the horizon in the direction of Jan Smuts International Airport. As the clouds approached, the colour of the sky directly overhead turned slowly to a darker hue of blue, then more rapidly to grey, and finally to a dull blue-black as the thunder clouds arrived directly overhead and filled the entire sky.

Long before the first raindrops fell all species of suburban wildlife had disappeared. The animals, so finely tuned to nature, quickly sensed the drop in barometric pressure ahead of the storm and took refuge. Bees returned to their hives, hornets to their nests. Birds, their proud sheen now dulled by the filter of cloud, hid under eaves or deep in the shelter of the foliage of trees and shrubs. Other birds, kept as pets in cages or in fenced backyards, were unable to obey their natural instinct to seek shelter and sat uneasily on their perches, some hiding their heads under their wings. Scrawny chickens gathered in the far corners of their coops and dogs and cats returned to their favourite hiding places, in their kennels or baskets, under beds, or on the sofa. Even the ubiquitous small reptiles of the veld, accustomed to the dangers of suburban life, burrowed deeper in their holes and crevices.

The cloudburst caught the stragglers still on the roads after the rush hour and dumped loads of water on their cars. Engines stalled. Tyres lost their grip. Windshield wipers became mere metronomes, struggling ineffectively to clear sheets of water from windscreens. Headlights failed to penetrate the walls of water and taillights alternatively signalled doubt and panic as drivers struggled to keep their cars on the road and to avoid colliding with the cars in front.

The pelting rain was accompanied by a gusting wind that drove the rain horizontally across the streets and tore branches from the trees and flung them into the roadway.

In the midst of this chaos, the young man in the grey bakkie gripped the steering wheel tighter in his white-knuckled grip and ploughed relentlessly along the Old Johannesburg Road through the screen of water in front of him, his mind trapped in the swirl of a different storm. His nerves were raw and the slashing rain on the windscreen combined with the squeaking wipers and the thundering wash against the chassis of the bakkie to compound a dull, numbing headache.

The incident started, like so many before it, with an unimportant misunderstanding, to which was added in rapid succession a sudden burst of adrenaline, copious quantities of testosterone and a touch of madness. The driver of the bakkie was lost in his own thoughts, alone, his mind in turmoil, his eyes flicking left and right in time with the windscreen wipers but unseeing. The young men in the minibus were in high spirits, on their way to a karate competition, dressed in their light-grey tunics, proud of the coloured belts which proclaimed their rankings, and sporting the white headbands that had become the fashion amongst karateka since Ralph Macchio wore one in *The Karate Kid*. They were singing merrily, clapping their hands and swaying in time with the music on the radio, township jazz, rap, whatever came up. The young man and the driver of the minibus peered into the rain but did not see each other until the last moment.

The bakkie had heaved around the gentle left-hand curve and

straightened out as the intersection came dimly into view. Then it picked up speed as the road dipped. The tall eucalyptus trees on the top of the bank surrendered seeds and leaves and even small branches to the wind. Loads of debris washed downhill and discharged a thin brown layer across the road surface towards the intersection. The minibus entered the Old Johannesburg Road from Saxby Road just as the bakkie was about to cross in front of it. A flash of lightning froze the moment in a surreal black-and-white negative, of a young white man clinging to the steering wheel of the bakkie and the young black men in the minibus, caught in the middle of a beat, their hands apart, alarm and surprise on every face.

The two drivers barely managed to avoid a collision, more through luck than driving skill, as the bakkie squeezed past the right-hand side of the minibus. Inside the two vehicles the outside world suddenly became real again, and the two drivers waved their fists at each other, angry when they should have been grateful for their narrow escape.

Then the chase started.

First the minibus came right up to the rear bumper of the bakkie, hardly a car's length behind it, and flashed its lights. The driver of the bakkie responded by pumping his brakes. He grimaced when the minibus swerved left and right to avoid running into his rear bumper. The minibus countered the move by accelerating to overtake, but the driver of the bakkie milked the last bit of power from his jaded engine to pick up speed and simultaneously veered to the right. This manoeuvre forced the minibus so far over to the wrong side of the road that its wheels left the tarmac surface momentarily. The driver had to fight hard to control its drift onto the muddy verge, and applying brakes merely exacerbated the swaying and swerving of the minibus. The vehicle careened danger-ously close to the point of capsizing, and the young men inside were flung about like puppets without the comfort or restraint of seatbelts. At last the minibus found its way back onto the tarmac and to the left side of the road, but even there the grip of its worn tyres was tenuous. The rain kept pouring down.

Soon the minibus caught up with the bakkie again where the road divided into severed lanes for north- and south-bound traffic across the Hennops River. The river was already swollen to its banks. The bakkie and the minibus jostled for position as they came alongside each other in the left-hand curve approaching the narrow century-old bridge. The bridge, designed for the gentler days of horse and carriage, was barely the width of two cars but the two young men managed to cross the river side by side, with centimetres to spare between their vehicles and the steel railings of the bridge on either side. On the bridge the two vehicles met fleetingly before they separated again. The minibus struck the right-hand verge a second time. The bakkie left the tarmac on the opposite side and spluttered on at low speed in high gear until its driver, who had slid across the front seat almost into the passenger seat, recovered sufficiently to pull it back into a lower gear.

This close shave, instead of bringing the two drivers to their senses, spurred them on to greater effort. Nothing learned, the minibus set off in pursuit of the bakkie again. Malice joined inexperience as the game turned deadlier.

The duel continued until they reached the outskirts of Pretoria. Eight kilometres after their initial encounter they entered the sweep around the Voortrekker Monument into Jan Smuts Road. The road widened into two lanes, and now they had more space to execute their swoops and passes, punctuated by threatening gestures, swerving this way and that, with feints and counterfeints and flashing lights. As they passed the De Groen Magazine on the hill to their left, the Danville and Pretoria West exit came up. Oblivious of the rain shrouding the Voortrekker Monument on the right, the driver of the minibus pretended to be stay-ing on Jan Smuts but then, at the last moment, steered sharply to the left across the zebra crossing into the glide-off. The bakkie, however, stuck to the minibus as if they were held together by an elastic band. They swept downhill at speed in a left-handed curve around Magazine Hill, neither on his intended route.

Halfway around the hill the minibus braked and escaped into a minor road to the left. It took them uphill, but neither driver knew where it was to lead them. It came as a surprise that the road ended at the walled and gated compound of the military signal station. The driver of the minibus made a desperate, sharp turn but found his way blocked by the bakkie. Then he found a rough dirt track running downhill away from the signal station and into the trees. The minibus bounced on along the uneven track. The bakkie kept up the chase.

The two vehicles splashed and bumped and ground their way down the narrow winding track until their way was suddenly obstructed by a concrete reservoir. They steered towards the left to get around it but the track ended abruptly. There was no turning around and they had to stop. For a moment no one moved. The rain continued to drum on the roofs of the minibus and the bakkie. The driver of the bakkie stared at the side of the minibus through a muddy window and the rain. The young men in the minibus looked anxiously at the bakkie. They could vaguely make out a pale face behind the steering wheel. No one moved, yet someone had to do something sensible to break the deadlock.

At first they sat there in the rain, staring at each other. Then the sliding door of the minibus opened suddenly with a clang as its locking mechanism disengaged. The sliding door grated across on its rail and slammed against the lock with another clang of metal on metal. As if they were acting on command, all but the driver swarmed out of the left-hand side of the minibus facing the bakkie. The driver came storming around the front. They were barefoot, wearing their loose-fitting light-grey karate trousers and jackets and white headbands. As one they moved towards the bakkie only a few strides away and dimly visible in the rain and fading light. Then, like a succession of thunder claps, a burst of gunshots stopped them in their tracks and felled them one by one.

The shooting stopped as abruptly as it had started. Each of the thirteen rounds in the pistol's magazine had found its target. The seven bodies lay in the mud, in disarray, the disciplined postures and formations of their sport awry, the grace of their youth lost forever as they lay where they had fallen, awkwardly, in random poses, some jerking in their death throes. Their blood poured from their punctured lungs and hearts and mingled with the rain in rivulets running down the hill towards the reservoir.

The gun fell from the young man's hand. It slowly sank deeper into the muddy slush. After a while he started working feverishly at the bodies, arranging them until they were exactly to his liking, on their backs and in line next to each other, with their hands folded solemnly across their chests. When he had finished he looked at what he had done and sank to his knees and howled into the rain. His throat raw with abrasion, he stood up, and remained fixed to the spot with his face turned into the wind, no longer conscious of the bodies at his feet, his subconscious mind already engaged in the process of erasing what it would not allow him to remember.

Later, when the wind had abated somewhat, he took a tentative step forward. He stepped away from the bodies with unseeing eyes; then walked faster and faster until he broke into a run. He ran and ran, always downhill, frequently slipping and falling in the mud, until his lungs were burning and he'd run out of energy. He fell to his knees and sat there heaving in the grass. His head sank lower and lower until it touched the ground, then he clasped his hands around his knees and rolled over on his side. He lay there while the storm continued to batter Pretoria. Darkness settled over the veld.

When he found his feet again he was somewhere among the trees below the reservoir. He started walking away from the hill and crossed a number of roads until he was in the dark open space of the approaches to the Voortrekker Monument. He leaned against a tree as his stomach retched, but there was nothing to void; he hadn't eaten anything all day.

At the reservoir muddy water ran down the track and found its way around the bodies lying there, piling twigs, leaves and earth against them. Soon the members of the Diepsloot Karate Club would be no more than debris left in the wake of a storm, their blood washing down into the waterways that would spill it into the ocean.

Less than a kilometre from the reservoir, on the city's side of Magazine Hill, the overhead security lights warmed up quickly, bathing Maximum Security Prison in an eerie light refracted in the waves of rain that swept across the city. Inside the various sections of the prison, warders and prisoners alike were oblivious of the rain as they were all locked in for the night, isolated from the world by bars of tungsten-hardened steel and thick walls of reinforced concrete, locked into a common fate for the night. The prisoners were confined to their brightly lit cells while the warders did their rounds, restricted to the passages and walkways. Every door was locked, its keys kept off the premises for security reasons.

On the south side of the cell blocks only the gallows building was in darkness. It was shut down for the year to be given a good service before being put to use again in the new year. But none of the prisoners inside knew that there was to be a brief respite from the weekly hangings. For them the nightmare would return night after night until the call came for them. It was a time to study their Bibles, to reread old letters and to write new ones, to think and to regret, to fear. And eventually to fall into fitful sleep punctuated by uncontrollable sobbing and desperate pleas. Hardened men cried unashamedly, unaware even that they were doing so, as the past and the future came together to haunt them in the harsh light they could not escape, even in their dreams.

So they waited and prayed.

> Someone's pleading, Lord
> Kumbaya

Court C, Durban

5

Judge Steyn was baiting me deliberately and was beginning to irritate me. We both knew what he was doing. We had been friends for a long time and played tennis at his house or mine every week. Owing to our personal friendship, I had to be even more deferential than I would have been with any other judge. So I had to bite my tongue throughout.

'Why should we provide a forum for the wandering litigants of the world?' he demanded.

I was upset with him but dared not show it. Not even original, you asshole, was the thought that went through my mind, but my mouth spoke the soothing language of advocacy. 'If it pleases M'Lord, there is a perfectly good reason.'

He interrupted me again before I could tell him that there was a Court of Appeal decision in my favour. I really wanted to wipe the smirk off his face by telling him that the phrase 'wandering litigants of the world' had been used before in a judgment and that the underlying line of thought had been dismissed as being contrary to the law. I also wanted to remind him that a large number of lawyers – myself not the least of them – depended for their livelihood on the legal work these same wandering litigants brought to our jurisdiction each year, even that we might need fewer judges too if it wasn't for the maritime cases the courts had to hear.

'Why should the taxpayer provide the courts, the staff and the judges to hear disputes between foreigners who can litigate to their heart's content in the courts of their own countries?'

He didn't wait for an answer. 'I am not disposed to grant this application,' he said.

I stood motionless and kept quiet for a while, a trick I had learnt from one of my mentors years ago. I kept my eyes on the robed figure on the bench.

We were in the Motion Court in Durban, a stone's throw from the busiest port in the southern hemisphere, where the ship I was trying to arrest for an American client was moored. The wood panelling of the court was still in good shape even though the paint on the ceiling and walls was stained and mottled in places. I looked up at the acoustic wires overhead, then down at the floor. The parquet floor tiles were lifting in parts and made movement about the court a tricky affair. Apartheid South Africa was beginning to look shabby, its support systems breaking down one by one.

I waited until I was sure I had his full attention before I spoke. 'Well, M'Lord,' I began, 'it is in the taxpayer's interests that the Court should grant this application. Apart from the fact that the papers before the Court make out a sound case for the relief sought,' I added somewhat tartly.

He changed his line of resistance, saying as he folded his arms, 'I have a discretion in the matter, don't I?' It was a statement and not a question. 'And I can take the taxpayer's interests into account when exercising that discretion, can't I?' He was wrong.

I had anticipated trouble from the moment his registrar had informed me that he would hear the matter in open court. I had to send for my robes in a hurry and now stood sweating in them. The usual procedure for urgent applications was to be heard in chambers and I would not have had to dress up for that.

'Hello, Johann.'

'Good afternoon, Judge.'

'So what have you got for me?'

'I have an urgent security arrest in a shipping matter, Judge. The ship is due to sail tomorrow morning.'

'Do I need to read the papers?'

'No, Judge, I don't think so. The case is rather ordinary and the order is in the usual form.'

'Yes, thank you. You can tell my registrar to make a note on the file that I have granted an order as prayed.'

'Thanks, Judge.'

'Say, Johann, what do you think of Edberg's chances to win at Wimbledon this year?'

Or so it would normally go. Not this time, though. We wrestled with the matter and we wrestled with each other, this way and that, with point and counterpoint, going round and round, the Judge wielding the power and me wielding the facts and the law. Eventually he relented as we both had known he would do.

'All right then,' he said suddenly. 'What order do you want?'

I directed him to the order I wanted. His black eyebrows obscured his eyes as he scribbled on a piece of paper. Then he tapped with his pen on the edge of the bench in front of him and his registrar stood up and turned to face him. He handed her a folded slip of paper.

'Very well,' he said, 'I grant an order as set out in the draft order attached to the notice of motion.' Then he stood up and left the court-room without waiting for the usher to escort him off the bench. His hasty retreat relieved me of the duty to bow deeply and kiss his behind with the customary 'As M'Lord pleases.' He was gone before I could say anything. The registrar came over to me as I was collecting my papers and handed me the slip the Judge had given her. I opened it: *We have to finish the tennis early tonight as I have to take my wife to the Symphony Concert at 7:30. Don't be late.*

I arrived at my reception desk with my brief under my arm and my advocate's bag containing my robes slung over my shoulder. I was still hot under the collar. In the streets outside people were already making their way home after the day's work or shopping. Traffic was picking up on the main road outside my chambers.

My secretary was on the telephone when I walked in and when she saw me shake my head she told the caller that she would make sure his call was returned as soon as I walked in the door. Then she made a note of yet another call to return and impaled it on the message spike. I put my bag on her desk and leafed through the afternoon's messages. They could all wait.

Five minutes later I was sitting in my chair with my feet up on the desk. I had a harbour view, a calming influence even on the worst of days. The port worked day and night and I watched the cranes at the container terminal as they expertly placed one container after another precisely in the right spot on the waiting ships. Spider-like straddle carriers scurried around with containers in their bellies. My secretary came in with a cup of black coffee.

'Thanks, Cora,' I muttered. I slid the security arrest brief over to her side of the desk. 'Would you do a fee note and send it out tomorrow morning, please?'

She looked down at me and smiled. 'There is someone who says she has to see you.'

I hadn't noticed anyone in reception when I came in. 'But I am off to play tennis,' I said.

'It is Roshnee Kissoon Singh and she wants to brief you in a criminal case.'

'I don't do crime, Cora. You know that.'

My secretary held firm. 'I think you can tell her that yourself, Johann. May I bring her in?'

I walked to the door with her. 'No, it's all right, I'll meet her in the front.'

Roshnee Kissoon Singh was sitting by herself with a thin file on her lap. I looked for a client but there was no one else in my reception area. I asked Cora to arrange tea for Roshnee and she and I went back to my chambers.

Roshnee is not one for levity, so I got straight to the point. 'So, Roshnee, what's this I hear about a criminal case?'

She looked down at her file before she made her case in short sentences.

'I am here on behalf of Lawyers for Human Rights. Your name is on the LHR list of volunteers for pro bono work. This man has killed seven people. He needs an advocate.'

I sat back in the chair. While I had always half-expected that LHR would call on me for something, I had hoped that they would somehow overlook me. I subscribed to LHR's ideal of advancing a culture of human rights in South Africa, but I had not had anything to do with the organisation's main activities, which appeared to be the provision of pocket money to prisoners under sentence of death and the conduct of appeals for clemency.

'Why does it have to be me?' I asked. 'I'm a maritime lawyer. I don't even know why I am a member of LHR.'

'You allowed your name to go on the roster.'

I did not respond. I looked at Roshnee more closely. A distant relative of the great Mahatma, she had a stubborn streak that went beyond the duty owed to the client or the Court. She was dressed in a sari, her only compromise to Western tastes the more subdued colours: aubergine and olive green with flecks rather than splotches of gold. Her thick raven hair was pulled tightly in a bun, lifting the corners of her eyes to give her a slightly oriental appearance. A red dot on her forehead signified that she was married.

She fidgeted with her file. 'Do you remember that case in Pretoria where seven men on their way to a karate competition were killed next to a reservoir?' She did not wait for me to answer. 'LHR has decided to provide a senior advocate from its pro bono list to lead the pro Deo Junior in the trial.'

I remembered the case only too well. It had been plastered all over the newspapers and television for a week. 'I don't need racially motivated mass murders on my slate,' I said. 'Surely they have someone in Pretoria or Johannesburg who specialises in this type of thing?'

'No one wants to touch the case.'

'Is it a political case?' I asked.

'No, I don't think so,' she said, but there was an uncertain note in her voice. 'At least, LHR told me it wasn't.'

I shook my head. 'No, that can't be right. If they are involved it has to be a political case. They only take the political ones.'

Roshnee held my gaze. When she spoke again, softly, she sounded desperate.

'Every death sentence case is a political case.'

I tried another angle. 'The case is hopeless anyway. No one gets away with killing seven people.'

'Maybe, maybe not. But you can't say no.'

'Why not?'

'Because you delivered a paper on it at an international seminar and listed cases where innocent men had been hanged. How would it look now if you refused to help?'

This was tantamount to blackmail, and she had a point. However, speaking out against the death penalty was easy as an intellectual argument but far removed from the harsh truth of real cases, which speak to the emotions rather than the intellect.

Your client is as good as dead, I thought, but kept it to myself.

The tea arrived and I watched as Roshnee poured. I thought some more about the divergence of principle and practice, intellect and emotion. Was the death penalty a subject to be decided by majority vote or was it a subject that dwelt on a higher plane, where principle checked expediency and the popular vote? Many people opposed the death penalty when you asked them for their views, but in practice even those opposed were sometimes quick to agree that a particular killer deserved to die. An opposing voice was easily drowned out by the horrors of the crime and the din of the crowd. The more I thought about the case, the more I was convinced that our feeble voices would fall on deaf ears.

I sighed heavily. I really had no choice. All I could see ahead was hardship.

Roshnee must have read resignation in my sigh. She scribbled a note on the file cover. I read upside down as she wrote my name in the space for *Advocate briefed*.

'So where do we go from here?' I asked.

'I'll set up a conference with the client in Pretoria. He is in custody. We'll have to bear the cost of our own air tickets and accommodation, by the way. I'll arrange a convenient time with Cora.'

'What have you got in there?' I pointed at the file on my desk.

Roshnee smiled for the first time during the meeting as she opened the brown manila folder to reveal a typical brief to counsel, folded over once, length-wise, and tied with the pink ribbon traditionally used for briefs to senior counsel. She turned the brief around and slid it over to my side of the desk.

I looked down at the brief again. My eye fell on the space at the foot of the brief where the fee was to be marked when the work had been completed. *Pro bono*, for the public good.

I tugged at the pink ribbon and opened the papers. I flattened the folded documents on my desk. There were only three documents, an indictment, a summary of facts, and a list of witnesses. It took less than a minute to read them.

His name was given as Leon Albert Labuschagne. I played with the French surname on my tongue. Lah-boo-shayne. I wondered whether he pronounced it like the Huguenots did when they originally came to these shores, or whether for that family, too, the name had lost its romance under the weight of the Dutch and German that accounted for the bulk of Afrikaans names. Then it would be Lah-boo-skach-knee, with a soft g and the emphasis on the third syllable.

He was twenty years old and he would likely be nicknamed Lappies, I thought.

The indictment alleged one count of murder even though there were seven deceased. It specified that the events had happened at or near Pretoria, and that Labuschagne had unlawfully and intentionally killed seven men. They were named in the indictment. I thought it unusual to have only one count of murder when you had seven people dead, but that meant that there could be only one death sentence.

I read the summary of facts aloud:

On 10 December 1987 at about 18:00 on a deserted road near the Magazine Hill reservoir the accused forced the minibus in which the deceased were travelling from the road. He then shot each of the deceased at least once with a pistol. The cause of death of each of the deceased was loss of blood caused by multiple gunshot wounds to either the neck or upper body. After the attack the accused disposed of the pistol and fled from the scene.

I looked at the list of witnesses again and then scanned the statement of facts a second time.

'There is something wrong here,' I said. 'They have chosen to charge only one count of murder. Only one count,' I said again. 'The summary is shorter than the indictment.' This was an exaggeration, but not by a large margin. 'And there is no psychiatrist or psychologist on the list of prosecution witnesses. In fact, there are only nine witnesses on the list, and that includes the pathologist, the investigating officer and a ballistics expert.' I did not count the relatives who would have had to identify the bodies.

'Last but not the least of it, they haven't given you the client's statement.'

Roshnee rose to the implied criticism. 'There isn't one. I asked them for any statement our client may have made to the police or a magistrate and they said that he has refused to speak to anyone.' She called him *our client* now, I noticed. 'In fact, he has not spoken to the police, to a magistrate or even to the pro Deo counsel. He wouldn't see his family when they came to visit him in prison. He has not applied for bail and appears to be quite content to stay in custody.'

It had been more than six months since the date of arrest. Why would anyone be content to sit in jail for six months?

'Curiouser and curiouser,' I said. 'Didn't they send him for observation under section, uhm, section seventy something, or whatever?' I added, trying to cast my mind back to the days when I still had to defend capital cases.

'Sections seventy-seven to seventy-nine,' she said. 'And no, they didn't. I think the prosecutors are afraid to initiate a psychiatric evaluation because that might open the door to an insanity defence.'

'So what did he tell our colleague from Pretoria?' I asked.

'He refused to discuss the matter with him and told him he didn't want a lawyer.'

'Didn't want or didn't need?' The thought crossed my mind that our client – *I* was beginning to think of him as our client now – was one of those religious or political zealots who actively seek their own death in pursuit of their faith or politics.

'Want,' she said, wasting no words.

I cradled the brief between my elbows on the desk. 'Are you telling me that he has not spoken to anyone at all about what happened?'

'Yes.'

'That's the best news you've given me so far.' I was pleased. 'Now this is what we are going to do. But I have to speak to my secretary first.'

I went out to my reception area and asked Cora to call my wife and to ask her to arrange for someone to take my place at tennis. His Lordship is not going to have the pleasure of my reliable serve to drag his butt out of another losing five-setter again, I thought. Not this time.

I had hardly reached my desk when my wife phoned and asked what the arrangements were for tennis. 'Who is coming and what do they drink?'

'Colin and Mark and Paul and Andrew, if you've found him,' I answered.

'Yes, I'll phone him. I can see his car in the driveway.' Andrew lived across the street from us.

'Liesl …' I forgot what I wanted to say.

'We'll need to get more beer. You know how fast Paul can down them,' Liesl suggested. 'Can you pick up some on the way home?'

I smiled. That's what I wanted to tell her. I would be late and would be unable to help.

Roshnee and I conferred for another hour.

She made notes as we spoke of evidence gathering, potential witnesses, fact analysis, a comprehensive theory of the case, and strategy.

'That's a lot of work and most of it will have to be done in Pretoria,' she said as we were waiting for the lift. The floor was deserted by now, except for the cleaning staff doing their rounds to prepare the building for the next day.

'I suspect that we are on the back foot. The prosecutors probably think they have an unanswerable case,' I said.

'They probably do,' she agreed as the lift doors opened. She was echoing what I thought, but there was a hint of a smile on her lips when she spoke.

'Damn right they do,' I said to myself when the lift doors had closed.

As I was packing my briefcase twenty minutes later I remembered something. I dialled Roshnee's office and kept dialling until she answered.

'Roshnee?'

'Yes,' she said, slightly out of breath.

'I forgot to ask you not to mention to anyone that we're going to do the case. I'll speak to the Junior tomorrow morning. I want the prosecutors to think that they are up against pro Deo counsel alone. If they find out that there are three of us they'll just work harder. Okay?'

She thought about it for a moment. 'I'm going to have to tell LHR that you have accepted the brief.'

'Well, tell them that we have agreed to take the case on the strict understanding that they will keep our involvement absolutely confidential.'

She promised to do her best.

When I got home at last the game was over and the sweaty members of my hastily rearranged tennis school were walking up from the court swinging their racquets at my geese. The geese escorted them all the way up to the steps to the veranda, hissing as they went, their heads lowered and their wings spread menacingly. I watched the noisy approach in silence. My sons ran past me in the opposite direction, eager for a bit of tennis before they had to turn to their homework.

'Hello, Dad,' I shouted after them.

'Hello, Dad,' they shouted back over their shoulders in unison. They ran along for a while as I watched their carefree bounds downhill. Then the little one slowed down, turned and came back up to the house. He arrived with the tennis quartet and gave me a hug.

'Hello, Dad,' he said shyly.

'Hello, Bozo,' I said, using his nickname, and mussed his hair.

I sat down at the table and watched as he ran back towards the tennis court.

'He knows where the pocket money comes from,' said my neighbour. Andrew was a property lawyer and often worked from home.

'Thanks for taking my place at such short notice, Andrew,' I said.

'No problem,' he said. 'I needed the exercise and the escape from the boredom of life as a conveyancer.' He patted his stomach where the middle-age spread was beginning to show.

'How did it go?' I asked, making small talk while I eyed the Judge. He was quiet.

'I arrived a little late and had to partner Colin. We won handsomely. In fact, we gave them a good hiding.'

Andrew's comment elicited a torrent of abuse from his opponents. They blamed the Judge for making bad line calls and each other for poaching and leaving half the court open.

I handed some beer and glasses around. There was a pot of tea as well and I poured some for myself. I looked over the floodlit tennis court towards the city, but the haze around the lights obscured the suburbs below and beyond. Insects darted in and out of the light; some hurt their fragile wings against the filaments of the powerful lamps and fluttered to the ground in erratic spiral dives.

The Judge had been unusually quiet and I studied him as he fiddled with a beer bottle. He had the broad hands of a builder. Colin was a member of a famous legal family, the Steyns. They had produced a number of Supreme Court judges and even Appellate judges over the years. For all that Dutch heritage, Colin Steyn was more English than Afrikaans.

'What kept you?' Colin asked when he caught me looking at him. 'Or are you sulking?'

I looked at him. He was still sweating profusely and his hair was plastered to the side of his head. 'I've been lumped with a pro bono case, Colin,' I explained.

'So you are not going to make any money, are you?' he ventured.

'Too true,' I said.

'So you *are* sulking,' said Mark from the shadows. Mark and his brother Paul were partners in a textile business that manufactured moth-proof blankets for the Prisons Department and for the Army and Navy.

'Colin did fuck me around today,' I said. I turned to Colin. 'What was that about?'

All four burst out laughing. 'Pay up,' Colin said to the other three and turned to me. 'I told them you would be in a foul mood.'

'You put me in a foul mood,' I said. 'Why did I have to robe up for it? Why couldn't I do it in chambers as usual?'

'I was bored.'

I shook my head. 'You were bored and I had to sweat for your entertainment?'

He grinned behind his beer. 'Don't worry, man. You'll be able to mark a bigger fee for having argued the matter in Court.'

If only, I thought.

The beer was disappearing rapidly down Paul's throat. He drank straight from the bottle and downed the second while reaching for a third. 'You look miserable,' he said as he twisted open the third bottle, 'and it can't be what happened this afternoon. Colin has told us everything.'

He was right. I was amongst friends so I unburdened a little. When I had finished, Colin said, 'Everyone gets a bad case now and then, a hopeless case even.'

I did not respond – he was telling me nothing I did not know – and he added, 'No one gets away with killing seven people. You know that.'

He then used my own words, 'He's as good as dead.'

I thought so too. That was the problem.

'I had a case like that once,' he said. 'My client was a witchdoctor who had killed five children and disposed of the bodies after removing body parts for muti. They were never found. So we had a murder trial without bodies or postmortem reports. He was given five death sentences.'

Paul piped up. 'I remember that. We played tennis that afternoon.' He stabbed his finger at Colin. 'You arrived in a foul mood. You smacked the cover off the ball all afternoon but never got a first serve in. And you said they were going to hang him five times.'

We chuckled because we all remembered the incident, but I also remembered the anguish in Colin's eyes when he had come to my chambers to ask for a lift home. He told me the outcome of the trial and I tried to cheer him up. 'Don't worry, you can always appeal.'

'No,' he had said, 'this one is as good as dead.'

I later read in the newspaper that his client had been hanged.

Colin was the first to leave and after I had seen off the other three I sat down to dinner and had to tell Liesl that I was going to do a murder trial in Pretoria.

'You are not going to enjoy this,' she said. 'Remember what happened the last time you did a murder case?'

I remembered only too well.

That night I dreamt I was an official at an execution.

I stood facing the prisoners on the scaffold. I turned my head slightly so that I did not have to look at them directly. In my peripheral vision I saw four vague shapes, hooded and dressed in brown overalls. The ropes around their necks disappeared into a misty haze above their heads.

A man walked down the row of prisoners, peering into their hooded faces. He had the neat parting of his curly black hair, the narrow moustache, the teasing mouth. It was the Executioner.

Without warning he pulled a lever. I felt my body stiffen as three of the men suddenly disappeared from view and the fourth body hung suspended in the air above the void where the trapdoors had been.

Still averting my gaze I saw out of the corner of my eye the remaining prisoner, in slow but deliberate motion, first remove the hood and then the noose. Leisurely almost, he began to float up into the air, looking over his shoulder defiantly. The Executioner and I stood motionless as he drifted away into the mist.

We were dressed in the same brown overalls as the floating prisoner.

When I arrived at my chambers early the next morning I asked Cora to get me the Junior's phone number. He picked up on the second ring.

'Pedrie Wierda, hello,' he said. It was a youngish voice, slightly shrill. He must be in his late twenties, I thought, maybe early thirties.

'Can you talk?' I asked after introducing myself. We addressed each other by surname, as is the custom among advocates, lending the conversation a formality it did not quite warrant and neither of us intended.

'Ja.' The answer came in the overrounded accent of a Pretoria Afrikaner.

'I've been asked to lead you in the Labuschagne case, the man who killed those men at the reservoir.'

'You mean the karate boys?'

If this was an attempt at humour I ignored it. 'Yes. I need to talk to you but I want to make sure that no one other than you and I and our attorney will know that I'm on the case.'

'You don't want to be associated with the case?'

I had been asking myself that question, and my answer to Wierda was probably not the whole truth.

'No. It's not that. I don't want the prosecutors to prepare any surprises for us, which is what they will probably do if they find out that this is not going to be a typical pro Deo case.'

There was a long pause. I could not make out whether clients were being ushered out of his chambers or whether he was weighing up the options.

Then his voice came back.

'I can live with that. What do you want me to do?' He was quite businesslike.

'I'd like to meet Labuschagne, but I don't want him to know I'll be coming up to see him. I also don't want the police to find out I've been there to see him. Do you know how we can achieve that?'

This time there was an even longer pause. I heard something tapping.

'I think I could requisition him for a bail application,' he said eventually. 'The police would have to bring him to the Magistrates' Court. Then we could see him in the cells.'

I had my doubts about his plan. 'But won't the investigating officer have to be notified that there'll be a bail application?'

'You are right,' he said, 'but I could arrange for the application to be heard late in the day. Then we could see him early, before the investigating officer arrives, and I could appear in the afternoon only to withdraw the application. They won't suspect a thing.'

'That sounds fine,' I said. 'How soon can you set this up? I am free for the rest of the week.'

He would not be rushed. 'Before we go any further, why do you think he'd speak to you? He wouldn't speak to me except to tell me he didn't want to discuss anything with me. He wouldn't apply for bail. He wouldn't even meet his family. What will you do if he refuses to co-operate with you too?'

'It seems to me that a man who is on trial for his life and refuses to say anything in his own defence is in dire need of help. If not necessarily legal counselling then some other kind of help. The purpose of the first meeting will simply be to find out what we can do to persuade him to open up, to us or to someone else. And if he refuses to talk to me, you and I are going to have to see the Judge President.'

'What does the JP have to do with the case?' Wierda was not afraid to ask questions, a good sign. He would be useful to have as a Junior.

I explained. 'We are going to ask him either to release us from the case, or to invite us to appear as amici curiae. And that, by the way, will be the end of your pro Deo fee.'

He laughed. 'Friends of the Court, eh? More like poor relatives.'

After a discussion about the best date for the bail application, we agreed to meet at his chambers in Pretoria once he had made the necessary arrangements.

The capital city glistened in the early morning light as we crossed at the corner of Pretorius and Schubart streets. Even though the sun had been up for more than two hours I found the air a little chilly when Wierda and I entered the cells below the Magistrates' Court.

The cells were not designed to make their occupants feel welcome or comfortable. Maybe it was the damp. The walls and linoleum floor were matching shades of grey, the ceiling off-white. A table and four straight-backed wooden chairs were the only items of furniture in the cell doubling as a consulting room.

Wierda knew the cell warden. 'Could we please see Leon Labuschagne?' he asked.

The warden opened the cell and we sat down facing the door. They brought Labuschagne in. He was dishevelled and had black rings under his eyes, but he was not cuffed or shackled. He made no attempt to conceal his animosity as he looked at us across the table, still standing.

'Sit down,' said the cell warden. He obeyed immediately.

After the cell warden had left, Labuschagne fixed his attention on Wierda.

'I've told you more than once that I don't want you to defend me and I don't want to talk to you.' He turned slightly to face me. 'And I don't know who you are but I don't want to see you either. Please – just – leave – me – alone.'

He was angry, I noted, but still said please.

I watched him closely. He sat with his elbows on the table facing Wierda. I wandered around the cell, feigning lack of interest and taking my time making an assessment of him. Our prospective client was about five foot ten, stocky with broad shoulders. He had thick wrists, a muscular neck and his eyes were set deep under heavy, bony ridges. Physical strength exuded from every pore. He struck me as the arch-typical Afrikaner, a Boer from farming stock, but not much more than a boy.

His gaze followed me as I paced the room but when I moved behind him he did not turn his head. When I entered his line of vision again he cast a brief look in my direction. His attitude said: who the hell are you? I ignored that. I wasn't the one who was in trouble. I stopped next to Wierda's chair.

Wierda introduced me by name. 'Leon, this is Johann Weber. He is a senior advocate from Durban. He is willing to defend you.'

It was a bit of an overstatement, but I did not correct Wierda.

I spoke for the first time. 'Mr Labuschagne, I did not come here to ask you to speak to me. I came here to tell you something.'

He did not respond. I waited patiently for eye contact before I continued.

'I have been asked to defend you. I don't particularly want to do it.'

'Well, why don't you go home?'

I met his stare. 'Good question. You haven't exactly made us feel welcome. The fact is that I have the freedom to go where I want to when I want to. You, on the other hand, have no choices. If I leave right now, my life will continue exactly as before.'

It was not true; it could not be. Walking away from a difficult and unpopular case meant breaking a cardinal rule of ethics in the advocate's profession. So I was stuck with his case, though he did not know that. I was also stuck with it in another sense: afterwards I'd never be the same again. Every client takes up permanent residence in his lawyer's mind, like a brooding ghost, to remind you of past battles, the vicissitudes of life and the mistakes you inevitably make while defending your clients.

There was just a hint of a sigh as he took his elbows off the table and crossed his arms. His gaze was defiant and distrustful, but something was missing. What was it? Where had I seen that emptiness before? I thought about it while I continued to hold his gaze.

I waited for a response but there was none. 'So why am I here?' I asked.

Answering my own question I delivered a sermon. 'I am here because I have been asked to defend you and cannot refuse. I am here because your case is so bad that nothing I do can make it worse. I am here because no one else wants to touch your case. I am trapped in this case as much as you are. Even if you tell me that you don't want to see me anywhere near the case, I am still going to have to appear as a Friend of the Court. It will be my job to help the Judge by testing the evidence against you and by arguing legal points and points of evidence in your favour. It is not easy to do a case as amicus curiae, but if you don't get your own lawyer, that is what I am going to have to do.'

When there was still no response I turned to Wierda. 'That's it,' I said. 'We've done our duty. Let's go.' I picked up my writing pad and pen. Neither had been used.

I walked to the cell door. I motioned to the warder to let us out.

At the door I turned. Labuschagne was facing the other way and I addressed his back. 'I see that you were a warder in the Prison Service. You should know then what is in store for you if you continue on this path, keeping to yourself, shutting out your family and refusing to have a lawyer defend you. Talk to the warders this afternoon when you get back to prison. Ask them what happens over at Death Row. They will tell you that it is a place from which no one has ever escaped. Hell, even suicide is a luxury available to no one.'

I turned to Wierda. 'Let's go,' I said again.

The cell warden put the key in the lock and the tumblers gnashed under his hand. I stepped out into the corridor and turned to wait for Wierda. He was still standing at the table, shoving papers into his battered briefcase.

'Listen,' he said looking down at Labuschagne. 'I have had enough of this crap. You're going to have to talk whether you like it or not. But you had better pray that it is not too late when you finally get a grip and start talking to us.'

Labuschagne lowered his head into his hands and covered his eyes.

'Come on,' I said to Wierda. 'Let's get out of here.' I could tell Lawyers for Human Rights that we had tried and that the man had rejected our offer of assistance.

'No,' he said, still looking down at Labuschagne, 'not before I have given him a piece of my mind. I have done a shitload of work on his case and I am not just going to walk away from it.' He was leaning forward with his knuckles on the table.

'Listen, Leon, you may feel sorry for yourself now, but you'll be feeling a lot sorrier when you get the death sentence, man. And that just because you are too stubborn to talk? I have done enough work on your case to know that something has gone wrong and that it will be difficult to explain that, but I also know that unless you talk there will be no explanation, and no explanation means death. Or life imprisonment, but I think it will be the death sentence because without an explanation nothing can save you, not even your youth.'

When there was still no reaction from Labuschagne, Wierda adopted a softer tone. 'I've met your parents and your sister. They told me everything they know about you. They want to help you, even though you've rejected their attempts to see you. They can't understand how things have come to this, but they miss you and they want to help.'

I thought I saw a slight shift in the angle of Labuschagne's shoulders.

'I spoke to your wife and your in-laws,' Wierda said.

This time there was an immediate reaction from Labuschagne. When his hands came away from his face I saw streaks of tears on his cheeks, but he quickly closed his hands over his eyes again.

Wierda was relentless. 'I went to see your wife and your in-laws at their house. I saw your daughter. Your wife wouldn't speak to me while her father was there, but at the door she asked me what was going to happen to you.'

Labuschagne was crying behind his hands now, no longer able to stop the flow of the tears or mask the rasping sobs. He cried from deep inside of him.

Wierda knocked on the table, emphasising every word. 'What must I tell her? You tell me, what I must tell your wife is going to happen to you?'

No response.

'When did you last see your daughter?' Wierda then demanded. 'Six months ago, huh? Well, she has started walking, and you know what? Soon she will be saying her first words. But if *you* don't start talking soon, you will never hear her speak. Even if you get away with life imprisonment you won't see her again. If you ever come out of jail alive, it will be too late and your daughter will have grown up and will probably have married, with a daughter of her own.'

Whispering now, Wierda said, 'What do you want me to tell your wife to tell your daughter when your little girl is old enough to ask, Where is my Daddy? You tell me, what shall I tell her?'

The cell warden motioned that I should get back into the cell and he locked it behind me.

I sat down at the table and watched our client cry.

Eventually Wierda asked, 'Come on, Leon, are you going to talk to us or do you want us to leave? We need an answer and we need it now.'

Wierda sat down next to me. We waited for the sobbing to subside.

I was near to giving up for good when a faint voice spoke through the last sobs.

'I don't know what to say.'

Wierda and I exchanged glances and I gave him the nod to take the lead. 'If you tell us what you know, we can try together to make sense of everything that happened,' he suggested.

'The place is called Maximum.'

I pounced immediately. 'What do you know about Maximum?'

'I worked there,' he said.

'You were working in Maximum when this happened?'

He nodded. This came as quite a surprise. I would have thought that he was too young to work there. Surely they wouldn't have mere boys working in that environment?

I took a moment to consider the importance of the new information. It could be entirely irrelevant, I thought, but we had to find out. We managed to keep him talking for an hour. Wierda and I spoke from different hearts. His was the softer and kinder, mine that of the cynic. I let Wierda do the bulk of the probing.

Finally, we spoke about bail, which Labuschagne declined. 'I am okay where I am,' he said. His handshake was firm, but he held on to my hand just a fraction too long. I was glad to hear the steel door being unlocked to let me out.

I shivered involuntarily when the cell door clanged again behind me as it was locked.

Wierda left to make arrangements for the bail application to be withdrawn, as we had planned, and I made my way to the exit. Once outside I found that the day had improved considerably while we were working. I waited on the steps of the court until Wierda rejoined me. I paused for a moment at the top. The sun had warmed the air. There was an expanse of clear blue sky above the city, which had in the meantime swung into the beat of the day. Attorneys carrying their robes passed each other on the steps of the court.

I felt like an outsider here and did not enjoy the prospect of spending weeks in Pretoria, fighting opponents I did not know before judges who did not know me.

'Shall we go for a coffee or shall we go straight to chambers?' Wierda asked as we reached the street.

'I'm sure you'll be able to find us some coffee at chambers.'

As we were crossing the street I said, 'At times you were a bit rough on him in there, weren't you?'

Wierda snorted. 'If we had stuck with your aloofness you would be in the business class lounge by now.'

It was not an unattractive proposition.

'What did his wife have to say?' I asked.

'She wouldn't talk to me.' Wierda half turned to look at me. 'Actually, she was not allowed to talk to me. Her father was hovering over her all the time. He said they didn't want to be dragged into the matter.'

Pretoria had turned its back on Labuschagne. The city was ashamed, I thought. Quite understandable, given the circumstances. The killing had made the city's inhabitants look like a bunch of redneck racists, and they took their revenge on Labuschagne by refusing to become involved in his defence.

I asked Wierda if he knew the reason for the father-in-law's hostility.

'How would you feel if your daughter was dragged into something like this?' he asked. 'First he made her pregnant when she was still at school, then he treated her badly, and now this.'

I worked out the dates. Their child was a year old. They must have got married immediately after they had finished school. I could understand the father-in-law's anger, his daughter made pregnant, and that while still a schoolgirl.

'What do you mean he treated her badly?' I asked.

It turned out that her father had obtained a restraining order against Labuschagne. There were allegations of drinking and abuse. The case that had started out badly took a turn for the worse.

'It may not be as bad as that,' said Wierda, reading my thoughts. 'I think she will talk to us if we can get her away from her father.'

'What's her name?' I asked. I was irritated.

'Magda. We can always serve a subpoena on her,' Wierda suggested.

'You want to call a witness who refuses to speak to you, do you?' I was being sarcastic.

Wierda responded in kind. 'Well, I don't see too many names of potential defence witnesses on the List of Witnesses.'

When I looked up he was smiling. He was testing me, but I was not about to silence him.

We walked the rest of the way to his chambers near the Palace of Justice. 'Look,' I said, 'there is a lot of work here and as we speak we have no witnesses and no defence to speak of.'

He nodded. 'I can see that.'

We needed witnesses. Most of all, we needed a defence. But to have a defence you need evidence. And evidence comes from witnesses. Circle complete. We needed witnesses.

As we crossed Church Square we walked past the burghers guarding President Kruger's statue. The rifles they held at the ready gave me an idea. I mulled it over as we walked on.

'Where are we going to get witnesses in this town?' I asked Wierda.

He thought for a while. 'I'll start at the prison to see if they can throw any light on his behaviour,' he said. 'And we are going to need a psychologist or a psychiatrist if we are going to advance any defence relating to his state of mind.'

I agreed and asked Wierda to make enquiries at the University of

Pretoria. We made our way through the throngs of pedestrians. We were at the lifts when Wierda spoke again. 'I think he is in a state of denial, happy to be in limbo as an awaiting trial prisoner. He doesn't have to face up to what he has done while he is in that condition.'

Wierda's chambers were a mess, a typical advocate's room: unpretentious, worn furniture, dusty, outdated paintings on one wall. A row of sagging bookcases lined another. There were briefs everywhere, on the table, on the chairs; some were even stacked on the floor in the corner. He might have been youngish but he was obviously very busy.

'How long have you been at the Bar?' I asked.

He was quick to catch on. 'Not long enough. I still have to do pro Deo's,' he said. That meant he had less than six years experience in practice.

I watched him as we sipped our coffee. While I could be described as tall and skinny, gaunt even, like Cassius, he was more of a Brutus, short and round and soft. He was also balding prematurely. I knew, though, that eventually his innocent face would be lined like mine; the job does that to you sooner or later.

'Let's get down to business,' I suggested. 'I can see that you have a good practice going here. If I am right you can't afford to run about spending days on a pro Deo case while your paying briefs are queuing up on the floor. We are going to have to get someone to help us with the investigative stuff, for which neither of us has the time.'

We discussed the matter for a while. I mooted the idea that had been forming in my mind since we had walked past the burghers on the Square.

'I'm going to speak to my brother-in-law. He lives up here in one of the eastern suburbs. His name is Pierre de Villiers and he is on extended sick leave from the Army.'

'How can a soldier help us? Why don't we get our attorney to do the dirty work?'

I explained that Roshnee was a divorce and personal injury lawyer who was not experienced in criminal cases, but he was not convinced. 'Who exactly is this brother-in-law of yours?'

I gave him the thumbnail CV. 'He was in the intelligence section of the Special Forces Brigade, the Recces. He has a BMil Honours from Stellenbosch. He can be our investigator. We won't have to pay him either. Look, we are unlikely to get any assistance from the Prisons Department, and the police are on the other side. We need our own investigator, one who has connections.'

He was still not convinced, so we agreed to have lunch and talk it over with Pierre.

Magazine Hill, Pretoria

7

I took a seat with my back to the rear wall of the restaurant, and waited. Wierda had dropped me there before fetching his children from school; his wife was writing a Unisa exam.

Pierre de Villiers arrived quietly, a tall, handsome cat of a man. The one moment I was alone watching the door, the next he was looming ominously over me.

'Can I sit there?' he said, pointing at my chair.

I stood up and moved around the table. Pierre quickly took my place and then, still standing, took a good look around the restaurant before he shook my hand. His grip was firm and in his demeanour a hint of power kept in reserve. He was taller than I; about six feet two, with a shock of thick blond hair and light-blue eyes. There was an angularity about him, heavy bones anchoring a lean and sinewy body, wide wrists and big powerful hands.

At the same time there was a delicacy to his facial features belying the sense of physical strength his wiry frame exuded. The thought crossed my mind that my brother-in-law really was a cat, a big, distrusting, eternally aloof, scheming Siamese. Or maybe not; maybe more of a tiger.

We didn't have much time before Wierda was to join us so I got right to the point. 'I need to learn about killing and I need to learn quickly.'

73

Pierre pushed himself back with his hands on the edge of the table, looking ready to leave.

'I can't talk about that,' he said, shaking his head. 'I've had enough of it and I won't talk about it. You should know that by now.'

I felt the reproach keenly; my sister had warned me not to attempt to delve into his past. He doesn't talk, Annelise had said. It is as if there is a gap of three years in his life, the three years he spent in Angola fighting Swapo and the Cubans. Don't even think of mentioning any of that.

Pierre wouldn't meet my eyes and I had to pacify him quickly. 'It's not like that,' I said. I tried to cram as much as I could into as few words as possible.

As I continued my brother-in-law slowly unclenched his fists.

'I need to learn about the men who take part in the legal execution process,' I said. 'Why do they do it? How does their work affect them? How do they feel when they kill, knowing that they have the authority of a court order to kill? What sort of people are they?'

He shook his head. 'Not all of them do the killing there. Only the Hangman does.'

It was my turn to shake my head. 'That is true only in theory, and not what we've heard.'

Wierda arrived before Pierre could respond. I introduced them. They shook hands and eyed each other with mutual distrust. We passed the time with small talk while we ate. When the coffee arrived, Pierre asked, 'What do you want me to do?'

The blue eyes did not waver or register surprise as I explained. 'In short,' I said in conclusion, 'we want as much detail as you can lay your hands on about what happens in Maximum Security Prison generally, and on execution days in particular.'

Pierre nodded again. Then he said, 'Can I go now?'

He was out of his chair before I could answer. I shook his hand, then changed my mind. 'I'll walk with you to your car.'

I turned to face Wierda. 'Back in a minute.' Then I followed Pierre out the door.

I stood blinking in the sun next to his car. He had his hand on the door handle.

'I am sorry if I am opening old wounds.' Pierre fidgeted with the key. 'But I really need help and I could think of nobody who could help as much as you can,' I said.

'It's okay,' he said, 'as long as it is not about me.'

'No, of course. That goes without saying.'

'In that case I can tell you now that you are looking for the impossible.'

'What do you mean?'

He shook his head. 'No one kills without a reason.'

'That's what I thought,' I said after a while when he didn't elaborate.

He turned his head sideways as if he was listening to a voice in his head. 'That's why we are going to have to find out exactly what they do in there,' he said, echoing my thoughts.

'But they won't talk,' he added. 'Men who kill don't talk about it. They never do.'

He faced me squarely as he bent over to insert the key into the door lock. I squinted over his shoulder and saw a battered vw kombi minus front bumper approaching, a long-haired man in his forties at the wheel. The engine revved up for a double-declutch change of gears and the van backfired, a silly grin on the driver's face. Suddenly I had my breath knocked out of me, and the next thing I saw was the tarmac under Pierre's car. It took a few seconds to gather my wits about me, and when I had, my brother-in-law was picking himself up off me. Avoiding eye-contact as I dusted myself off, Pierre cast a resentful glare at the disappearing vw.

'I'm sorry,' he said at last. 'The war is still messing with my head. I thought someone was shooting at you,' he added unnecessarily.

I used the opportunity while he was uncomfortable. 'It's alright, Pierre,' I said. 'I understand. I need some help here and you are the only one I know who knows enough to be able to help me.'

He shook his head.

'I need to know what it takes to turn an ordinary man into a killer, someone who kills for his job, for money,' I said.

'I'm not a killer,' he said, hitting the door of his car for emphasis with the side of his fist. 'And I never killed for money.'

'I know. I am not talking about you. But you know people who are like that, and you understand them.'

My brother-in-law and I stood together in the sun. He was still breathing hard.

'The ones who talk are not the real killers. The real ones don't talk.'

He got into his car and drove off without a backward glance.

'Why is he no longer in the Army?' Wierda asked as we were heading towards the airport.

'He is still on their payroll, but he's become too dangerous for them, too much of a liability. Bosbefok.' I toyed with the word for a moment.

Wierda nodded. 'Has he been in the war in Angola?'

I thought about it for a while, about the stories my sister told, about the snippets we could read in our heavily censored newspapers, about the sanitised and politically skewed images we were allowed to see on television.

I caught Wierda looking at me. 'Watch the road,' I said. 'You don't want to do this case on your own.'

I weighed my answer to Wierda's question carefully. 'He went in a nice guy. He came out mean and dangerous. And now he is on forced sick leave.'

'So why are you asking him to help us when this case has nothing to do with the military?' Wierda wanted to know.

'He knows a thing or two about killing,' I said. 'Plus, Pierre can help us with our inquiries at the Prisons Department, I think.'

'What time is your flight?' Wierda asked. We were still in the suburbs and I had not taken note of the route.

'Just before five, but I'd like to try getting on an earlier flight,' I said. We made half a turn around a traffic circle and headed west towards the Fountains.

'The reservoir is on the way,' said Wierda, pointing almost directly ahead to a koppie rising between other koppies. 'It is there, on that koppie there,' he pointed. 'Should we perhaps have a look at it while you are here and we have the time?'

Wierda had couched his question very carefully, leaving it to me to decide. It was a good idea and I started paying more attention to the route we were taking. We reached Fountains Circle with Unisa strutting over its hill on our right and the Voortrekker Monument just visible ahead to the left. I felt apprehensive as we drove slowly up Magazine Hill. Wierda's car rattled and groaned as it bounced along the steep track to the reservoir. When we stopped it stood squat in front of us, the ground sloping down towards it.

We got out of the car after the dust had settled and stood in silence in an open area above the reservoir, a grey concrete structure with no markings. I could hear cars passing along the highways and roads on three sides of the hill, but they were out of sight. I felt strangely alone and exposed.

Wierda unrolled an aerial photograph on the bonnet of his car. It showed the area in grainy black and white. I traced the route we had taken up the hill. Wierda pointed at the structures at the foot of the hill on the northern side.

'That's the prison over here, with Maximum nearest to the hill, here.' I followed his finger and turned to look, but the trees and the slope of the land isolated us at the reservoir and obscured our view. We could not see more than twenty or thirty metres in any direction.

'Where did you get this?' I asked Wierda.

He smiled. 'At the municipal offices. They asked me what I needed it for and I said for a court case. I think they thought I was doing a traffic case.'

I looked at the photograph again. 'The Prisons people are not going to be happy with the municipality handing out photographs that show the prison complex in its finest detail, are they?'

'For sure.'

I took my time; having abandoned the idea of an earlier flight there was nothing else to do until departure.

The trees around us were tall exotics, mostly saligna, with nondescript shrubs fighting in vain for sunlight and nutrition. The grass was sparse and brown, the early onset of winter having taken its toll. The air was dry and the sun beat down on us. I walked around the reservoir slowly.

The ground was uneven and strewn with rocks. There was no sign that anyone ever visited the place. I counted seventy-five paces around the reservoir back to the point where I had started.

'Where did it happen?' I asked Wierda.

He walked straight to the spot. 'This is where they found the bodies.'

I looked at the ground, expecting some sign of the violence that had brought us there, but the earth where Wierda pointed was as unmarked as the rest of the ground. Tufts of dry, brown grass. Dirt. Small stones. Shrivelled leaves and twigs. Ants in line, marching to their orders.

Wierda lined up a tree with the reservoir and paced out a distance from it. He put a rock at the place where he had stopped and repeated the exercise, measuring this time from the reservoir. Then he moved the two rocks with his foot until they were adjacent.

'This is where the front of our client's bakkie was.'

I estimated the distance from the bakkie to the bodies as no more than five paces.

'Point blank range,' said Wierda.

Wierda's self-assuredness intrigued me.

'Have you been up here before?' I asked.

'Of course,' he said. 'How can you prepare for a trial without visiting the scene?'

He was right and I didn't argue the point. 'What else is there to see?' I asked.

'We can take a walk and look at the prison from the ridge over there,' he said, pointing into the trees behind me. I was curious and followed him through the bushes, over and around rocky outcrops. The prison complex gradually came into view.

We crept closer to the edge of the ridge. My eyes were trained on the guard towers at the corners of Maximum Security Prison when a man rose like a ghost from under my feet. I don't know who got the greater fright, he or I, but I nearly fell over.

'Jammer, Baas. Ek rus net hier.'

I was shocked out of my wits, the breath knocked out of me for the second time in less than an hour. I shook my head to clear the drumming of my heart from my ears and watched as the vagrant picked up his greatcoat and a plastic bag and scampered down the hill.

Wierda stood smiling at my embarrassment. Then he clambered onto a rocky outcrop behind me and peered over some shrubs. I saw that he had a camera with him. He pointed it at the complex below and snapped off several shots in different directions, angling the camera up and down and sideways to get the best shot. I looked down at Central Prison with Maximum Security Prison in the foreground. There were rows and rows of shiny roofs beneath us, like sheds of a battery chicken farm, with high walls and guard towers along the perimeters and towering lights placed all around. Brown brick buildings clearly housed the admin sections. There was no vegetation within the complex, but immediately behind Central sprawled the warders' sports fields. Several prisoners were working in the sun, tending the grassy surface of a football field, and two were bent over a machine marking the lines in white chalk.

Maximum Security Prison lay between us and Central, separate from the greater prison complex but included in its security perimeter. It sat flush against the hill but the trees and shrubs on the side of Magazine Hill partly obscured it from view. It had similar rows of roofs – I counted three – and some brown brick buildings towards our right but I could not see much more. There was no way to get nearer. I wanted to look more closely at the three-storeyed building in the foreground. It had to be the gallows building. It stood clear of the rows of cell blocks.

I was concerned about the guards in the towers. All I could see from the hill were dark uniforms in the shadows. Could they see us up here? I turned back towards the reservoir.

'They'll lock you up one of these days,' I said to Wierda as we walked back to his car.

'It's a free country,' he said, 'and how do I know that the buildings in my viewfinder are secret prison buildings, eh?'

We completed the rest of the journey to the airport in relative silence.

As I stepped out of his car I said, 'I heard that no one in Pretoria would touch this case. Why are you doing it?'

His handshake was firm. 'It's a pro Deo. What choice do I have?'

It was not as if I hadn't ever done a capital murder case before. The consultation with our client in the cells below the Magistrates' Court had rekindled memories I had thought would have been buried under more pleasant ones since I had last been involved in a murder trial.

In my first few years in practice I must have done between forty and sixty capital murder cases. They were too many to remember and too ordinary to bother counting. That was the seventies, when the rand equalled about one dollar fifty and we were paid thirty rand per day for the trial and ten rand for the consultation with the accused. Most cases were done on Circuit, away from the provincial or local divisions of the Supreme Court, in the sticks, as we would say. It meant travelling and sleeping away from home in strange, uncomfortable beds, in local hotels with no star ratings of any kind. Once, the prosecutor and I ended up sleeping in the police cells when the only hotel was full.

We struggled in small courts without air-conditioning or heating, sweating in our robes in summer and freezing our butts off in winter. We fought by day and drank by night.

It was the custom that prosecuting counsel and defence counsel would join the Judge at the dinner table every evening. The Judge would usually bring his wife along on the month-long excursion, and we would have to entertain her and the Court's Assessors too. The Assessors were usually the Chief Magistrate and one of the town's senior attorneys. The dinners were informal but stiff and we would escape to the nearest drinking hole with the prosecutors as soon as we could. There we would swap war stories and try to settle the next day's case.

We were able to plead most cases down to culpable homicide or, when it really looked bad, to murder with extenuating circumstances, murder with ECs for short. We needed the ECs to avoid the mandatory death sentence. Often the judges intervened in the plea-bargaining process.

'What, you want to run an alibi defence? You know these people don't wear watches; they tell the time by the sun or the stars.'

These people.

'But Judge, I have an alibi for the whole day.'

'Oh, and your witness has a calendar, does he? Or is it the accused's wife or mother?'

The judges bullied the prosecutors too.

'It happened at a party, for God's sake, man. There must be ECs. Go and draw a statement of agreed facts. And put the ECs in it.'

We fought mostly over the presence or absence of extenuating circumstances. Their absence meant a death sentence, their presence a reprieve.

On the defence side we looked desperately for the slightest provocation or evidence of alcohol or cannabis, and we often presented a single beer or a puff at the pipe as an intoxicated stupor that had dispossessed our client of the understanding and control that would ordinarily have attended his actions.

Our friends the prosecutors, on the other hand, looked for premeditation, concerted action and lack of remorse. Some we won, some they did.

Yet I cut my teeth on these cases; they were the best training school for those who were newly admitted. Apart from divorce and personal injury cases, murder was all we got as newly admitted members of the Bar. We needed the money badly, even though it was only thirty rand per day, and we needed the experience even more.

When I was no longer obliged to accept capital cases on the pro Deo system, I stopped doing criminal cases altogether, and now I was going to have to explain to my wife why I had accepted this one. I had no clear answer for myself either. I had secretly hoped that Leon Labuschagne would send me packing and that the Judge President would say, 'Well, if he doesn't want counsel, that is his right.'

Palace of Justice

8

When I returned to Pretoria for the trial, I went for a run up one of the many hills as soon as we had checked into the hotel that would be our base during the trial. The overwhelming smell of the city was that of the sweet flowers of the jacaranda tree, the oily muck of millions of flowers crushed under feet and wheels. It was October and we were as prepared for the trial as we would ever be, although we could, of course, never be sure that we knew everything we needed to. Every trial is virtually guaranteed to produce surprises for the participants, but for now I was content that we had prepared as well as could be expected.

I ran up to the Union Buildings, the seat of the executive branch of government since 1910. As I bounded up the last few steps to the top plateau in front of the building, it struck me that this was where the Cabinet met twice a week to consider, amongst other matters, who should hang and who should come off the rope. 'We refer to those who are under sentence of death as being on the rope,' Labuschagne had told us. 'When they receive clemency or when their sentences are set aside on appeal, we say that they have come off the rope.'

We also learned that the language of the prison was Afrikaans. The Afrikaans has a much better resonance to it: Aan die tou. Van die tou af.

In Maximum the rope dominates everything.

The windows of the Union Buildings were dark. I turned to look back over the city, over the sprawling lawns where the late Sunday strollers and picnickers still enjoying the last of the weekend were beginning to leave. I leaned against the stone wall to stretch my calf muscles.

Pretoria is also a city of history. The defeat of the British in the first Anglo-Boer War had been organised from here. By the time of the second Anglo-Boer War the British were better prepared. This time they were able to occupy Pretoria long before the war finally ended in 1902. Then they took control and imposed the British model of government on every institution.

I couldn't say that I had ever been comfortable in Pretoria. On the one hand, it was the symbol of resistance to British imperialism, but on the other, of apartheid repression. It was equally representative of clear African skies as it was of secretive State organs working away behind the scenes. The city's overwhelming impression was that of rigidity, in thought and in structure. Even the city blocks were all of the same dimensions, and the main street, Church Street, is proudly said to be the longest straight main street in the world. Pretoria was the bastion of Afrikanerdom, yet so English in its buildings and institutions and attitudes. Thousands of its inhabitants were employed in the Civil Service, that huge monster that implemented government policy by keeping its foot on the neck of every citizen.

This was a place where others told you what to do, and how and when to do it, the seat of executive Government.

The building behind me had been designed by Sir Herbert Baker. I was standing on Sir Herbert's parapet. I could see Magazine Hill in the distance to the south, with Maximum Security Prison nestled at its foot and row upon row of the shiny roofs of Central Prison lower down. The Voortrekker Monument stood squat on its own hill behind the reservoir at the apex of Magazine Hill. When my eyes found Maximum, the hanging tables Pierre had uncovered during our preparation appeared uninvited in my mind's eye. I remembered, for no logical reason I can think of, that the drop for my weight would be exactly six feet, calculated in imperial measures in the table. It had struck me that I was the template for the formula in the table: *Thus a person weighing 140 pounds in his clothing will require a drop of 840 divided by 140 = 6 feet.*

As I jogged back to the hotel I reviewed our preparation.

We had taken an early decision to divide the work. Wierda and Pierre were to investigate the facts of the case and Roshnee and I would be responsible for their analysis. We did all of this in secret; Wierda was, to all appearances, the defence team in its entirety. He communicated with the police, the prosecution and the prison authorities. He paid visits to the prosecutors at the Attorney-General's office and liaised with the junior prosecutor, a sharp but stern woman who gave no quarter and reported to a senior who was older and more experienced, and less intense. Wierda reported them to be polite and competent but a tough team. The woman was the brains behind the prosecution, Wierda reported to me, but the senior was likely to do the talking in court.

Our arrangement worked well. Wierda elicited more information from our client and the prosecutors each week and as Roshnee and I received and analysed the new information we sent suggestions to the two in Pretoria about new lines of enquiry. In ways never disclosed to us Pierre obtained confidential, perhaps even secret, information and documents from government files. We did not need to know, he said enigmatically.

Wierda and I pulled a shroud of secrecy over our preparation. We applied as best we could the only tactics available to us: preparation and ambush.

A picture of a warder's work in Maximum Security Prison emerged during our months of preparation, though I am not sure that we ever got the full picture from anyone, not even from our client. In fact, we were most suspicious of any information emanating from him. He had, after all, the most obvious of reasons to lie: if you don't lie in the face of a death sentence, then I don't know what circumstances could ever force a lie from you.

Roshnee had found a forensic psychologist who was prepared to give evidence for the defence. I had to travel to Johannesburg to meet her at Wits University. Dr Schlebusch – 'Call me Marianne, please' – said that she did not have the expertise to deal with all aspects of the defence and that we should look abroad for cover. She referred us to an American psychiatrist, a Professor Shapiro from UCLA. While Marianne was prepared to provide her services for free, the American demanded a first-class air ticket, a five-star hotel and all expenses paid. So we had to raise the funds for a very expensive flight across America and then across the Atlantic, plus the hotel and other costs.

Roshnee somehow managed to persuade Lawyers for Human Rights to provide the funds. They, in turn, must have got the money from their secret foreign supporters. How she came by that piece of information, I couldn't say, but according to Roshnee, the money had come from Denmark.

The law books were a problem. We needed to find a legal pigeonhole for the defence we wanted to raise, but the law books painted a bleak picture. In case after case we found that the defence we were planning to present had been rejected for lack of evidence. There was resistance to it, not only from the courts but even more so perhaps from the psychiatric profession.

As we worked on the case new avenues of investigation opened up for us as a result of the directions given to us by our expert witnesses. We had to achieve two goals: find out everything we could about our client's circumstances at work and as much as possible about what had happened in the prison during the last two weeks or so immediately preceding the events at the reservoir. The experts would in due course perform their standard psychometric tests and evaluations before they would give their final reports, but they needed this information as background material.

We gave Wierda the difficult task of speaking to Labuschagne's relatives and acquaintances in order to build up a convincing picture of his past. Wierda spoke Afrikaans; he was one of them, but they were less than forthcoming, to say the least. Sometimes it felt as if the entire city had conspired to obstruct us. It was far from easy to obtain what we needed. It took time and it took effort. And all along, each of us had our own practice to run and our personal lives to live. But overall, we succeeded in keeping our preparations and plans secret. Our defence was a difficult one, one that did not succeed often, but we were going to be able to spring it as a surprise.

Eventually we felt that we were as ready for the trial as we could ever hope to be, given the circumstances. It was unlikely that the prosecution would have any surprises for us. From their names and job descriptions in the List of Witnesses we could work out what the prosecution witnesses would say.

However, the reverse, on the side of the defence, was not going to be so easy – that much we knew. If there were going to be surprises, they would be lurking in the defence case.

Wierda and I had carefully spun a spiderweb of facts and circumstances that would enable us to argue for an acquittal, with each strand of the web strong enough to support the weight it was expected to bear and the web a unit impenetrable to all but the insignificantly small and the overwhelmingly powerful. Every strand of it had to be in balance with every other strand, otherwise weaknesses would make our whole case fall apart.

A week before the trial was due to start Roshnee suggested that it might be useful to know something about the men who had been hanged in those last two weeks before the shooting at the reservoir, and about our client's relationship with them. This would add another strand to our web.

We sent Pierre off to secure the files, but we were to receive a full set only when the trial was well into its third day and the prosecution's case was already near its close.

What we found put the case in a completely different perspective, one not even hinted at during any of Wierda's meetings with our client. We found that in that year, 1987, they had hanged a hundred and sixty-four men in Pretoria, the highest tally for any year in history, and thirty-two of them in the two weeks before the events at the reservoir.

The morning of the first day of the trial Roshnee, Wierda and I met at Wierda's chambers and walked to the Palace of Justice. Pierre arrived later and kept in the background.

We had a difficult job to do and we did not have a good start.

When we arrived at the Palace of Justice we found a gaggle of media people and scores of policemen in riot gear. The police outnumbered the spectators and journalists and photographers two to one. They were crowding around a dishevelled woman chained to a tree right opposite the entrance to the court. One of the policemen wrenched a placard on a broomstick away from her. She screamed abuse at the man. He threw the placard into the back of the police van before I could read the message on it. We were living under emergency regulations at the time and it was illegal to protest within a hundred metres of a court building, which explained why the riot squad was out in heavy boots and carrying automatic weapons. I saw some policemen, unrecognisable behind the visors of their helmets, confiscating cameras and notebooks. One ripped the film from a camera and held it to the light as if to look at the images on it.

We slipped behind the crowd into the building. Labuschagne was already in the cells, we knew.

'What is all that about?' I asked Wierda.

It appeared a man had entered the third-class carriage of a passenger train and shot some people, choosing his victims carefully for their race. The woman was his wife, protesting the fact that he had been refused bail.

In the robing room Wierda introduced me to the prosecutors in our case, James Murray and Sanet Niemand.

I extended my hand. 'Hello, I am Johann Weber.'

We shook hands. There was a tiny smile on Murray's lips.

We went with the two prosecutors to be introduced to the Judge and his Assessors. It felt awkward, as it always does, just before the start of a controversial case. We engaged in the customary chit-chat, sizing each other up.

Our judge was J P van Zyl. In Pretoria the advocates called him Japie.

It was van Zyl who mentioned the woman outside. 'How many did her husband murder?' he asked.

I did not know, but Wierda did.

'He killed one and wounded several others, Judge.'

Judge van Zyl pursed his lips and shook his head. It was all we needed – for the Judge to be reminded that we had racist whites shooting black people at random.

'Are you ready to start?' he asked Murray and Niemand.

When they nodded he turned to me. 'And you?'

'We are,' I said. What else could I say?

'Let's start then,' he said. His robes lay draped over his desk, still in the dry cleaners' plastic cover. 'We'll enter at exactly ten o'clock, and I expect the proceedings to run smoothly.'

Wierda gave me a I-told-you-so look – the Judge was tough but fair, he had told me. He wouldn't take any nonsense from anyone.

Murray and I followed Wierda and Niemand down the carpeted passage. 'I expected someone like you to turn up,' Murray told me. 'Wierda is too lightweight for it, and there has been too much activity for a pro Deo.'

He walked with his hands in his pockets and spoke with the assurance of a man who knows what he is doing.

I looked up to see if Wierda, who was engaged in conversation with Niemand, had overheard, but he gave no sign that he had. They were on first name terms but were walking a good two feet apart.

Although we were fifteen minutes early, we took our seats in Court C immediately. I sat at the advocates' table, contemplating the days ahead. Wierda and I were on the left-hand side of the court with the jury box immediately to our left. The jury box was reserved for the press. Roshnee sat in the row immediately behind us. The prosecutors had claimed the seats closest to the witness box, where they could observe and control the witnesses from up close.

The jury box reminded me that a criminal trial in a South African court was conducted in a style familiar to English lawyers and to English-speaking people across the globe. While we would be speaking Afrikaans throughout the hearing, as the mother tongue of the witnesses and all the other participants was Afrikaans, we would essentially behave like Englishmen. Our rules of criminal procedure were based on English law and so was the law of evidence, but the underlying law was Roman-Dutch, a curious consequence of the history of the country, whose colonial masters had imposed overlaying systems of law on this remote part of Africa at different times. We even dressed like English lawyers, minus the wigs; our climate would have rendered a wig of horsehair on a sweating brow intolerable.

The Judge too would be dressed like an English judge, in scarlet robes, or hanging robes as we referred to them.

We called our judges My Lord and My Lady, as the occasion demanded, even though we had been a republic for more than twenty-five years, harking back to a time when our provinces were British colonies. But now we didn't have jury trials anymore. Instead of a jury of twelve ordinary folk we used two professional Assessors who sat on the bench with the Judge and decided questions of fact with him by majority vote. The Assessors were usually retired magistrates, men experienced in the conduct of criminal trials in the lower courts, almost invariably tough, unforgiving characters who had heard every lame excuse or far-fetched defence and every tearful plea for mercy.

Murder trials were a common feature of the South African legal landscape, an unfortunate fact of life for us. We had so many of them that we had become somewhat careless in our handling of them, perhaps even a little blasé. In practice the most junior members of the Bar acted as defence counsel and the prosecutors were usually equally inexperienced.

This trial was different, though. We had senior counsel on both sides, each with a junior to help carry the load of a complex case. While the prosecutors were to be assisted by the investigating police officer, we had the assistance of an attorney.

I listened to Wierda's breathing. It was even but I knew his pulse must be racing. He was drumming on the table with his pencil. Behind us, Roshnee was shuffling papers and moving the heavy lever arch files around. She had done an excellent job in the preparation. Like a general marshalling her troops she had led Wierda and me to the point where we were ready for battle. Roshnee was in charge of the logistics of the defence and, when we asked to see a potential witness, she would produce the witness along with a draft statement or a list of suggested questions. When we asked for a document she produced the original with copies. When we asked for official records she bullied and harried civil servants until she got them for us.

The only place where she could not gain access was Maximum Security Prison, but we had Pierre de Villiers with his military connections to get us that.

Pierre was already in the gallery, talking to a grey-haired man in a suit sitting next to him. His and Roshnee's work had been done during the preparation stage; the trial was my responsibility. It was about to start. There would be long periods of mind-numbing monotony punctuated with unpredictable bursts of gut-wrenching action.

I looked across at Murray and Niemand. They exuded calm and readiness as they sat there, huddled in whispered conversation. Would we be able to cope with the surprises our witnesses would inevitably produce? I looked up at the bench and the empty seats behind it. What about the Judge? He could deliver some of his own.

I felt my pulse. Ninety-six. It would return to normal only when the Judge and Assessors had taken their seats. The worst time is always just before the beginning. The nerves would dissipate once we had started, I knew.

The better prepared for a trial I am, the more nervous I always am at the start of it. Perhaps it is the knowledge that comes with preparation, that I am not completely in control, that there are risks, that there will be surprises, that a single witness or a single piece of evidence can determine the outcome, and that I may be helpless in the face of it. A trial isn't over until the last witness has answered the last question.

I prayed for the Judge to come in so that we could start.

The white noise made by the spectators who had filled the gallery behind us was interrupted by a door being unlocked, followed by heavy footsteps on stairs. I turned to see the cell sergeant coming up the stairs with Leon Labuschagne behind him. The sergeant led our client into the dock and told him to sit down. Labuschagne obeyed every order with a wordless nod and sat down in the dock with his head down. I was five or six paces away from him, but he did not acknowledge my existence.

DAY ONE

Defence: 4 October 1988
Execution: 26 November 1987

v3208 Simon Ramoatshe Moatche
v3421 Joseph George Scheepers
v3615 Johan Christiaan Wessels
v3695 Jim Kgethang Mokwena

Maximum Security Prison

9

The seven escorts followed hard on the heels of the Prison Medical Officer as they took the stairs down into the pit room below the gallows chamber. The doctor swung a stethoscope like a lasso in his hand, a cigarette dangling between his lips. He was still a young man, with the lean body of a medical school student, but his face was prematurely old, lined with the creases of too many examinations of assault and rape victims, of countless autopsies on the broken bodies of adults and children who had died unnatural deaths, and of witnessing too many executions.

Two of the escorts were still breathing heavily from their prior exertions. The others took the stairs equally gingerly. By the time they reached the bottom the doctor already had the earpieces of his stethoscope in place and, out of habit, warmed the disc between his hands as he took up a position in front of the first hanging body.

The escorts scampered around the doctor, each to his designated prisoner, and quickly unbuttoned the prisoners' shirts to expose their pallid chests. As the escorts held the prisoners steady the doctor moved briskly down the line and listened perfunctorily for a heartbeat. He had heard the prisoners' necks break a few minutes earlier and did not waste any time pronouncing them all dead. He turned on his heel and left.

Upstairs the Warrant Officer spoke to the officers behind him and they followed the doctor out of the gallows building to the admin offices.

The usual procession of doors had to be unlocked to let them through and locked again behind them. They had some paperwork to complete before they could retire to the staff common room for tea or breakfast.

At first none of the men in the pit room or in the gallows chamber moved. The pit room was bare except for seven coffins stacked in the corner, two trolleys and a hose-reel connected to a faucet. It was the same size as the gallows room but had no windows. The dead men hung above the pit and spun slowly on their ropes. Blood, excrement and urine continued to drip into the pit.

The escorts stood in a cluster around the bodies, watching the fluttering limbs.

The Warrant Officer was dismayed at the inaction.

'Roer julle gatte daar onder! Kry hierdie fokkers van die toue af!'

The escorts sprang into action.

Each removed from his breast pocket a name tag and tied it to the big toe of his prisoner. Then they assembled in the corner and put on rubber gloves and Wellingtons. When they were ready a key was thrown down from above and one of the escorts stepped behind the bodies and began to unlock the handcuffs. One by one he threw the handcuffs in a bucket. The other escorts followed him down the line and stripped off the white hoods, shirts and trousers. They dumped everything in the pit. When all the bodies were naked, an escort pulled the hose reel up to the line while his colleagues stepped well out of the way. Then he turned the water on and hosed the bodies down where they hung.

Soon the pit was a mess of soiled clothing and body waste. The man with the hose expertly steered the waste into the drain while another picked up the items of soiled clothing one by one with a stick and placed them in a plastic drum for dispatch to the prison laundry. The escorts stood aside for a moment as the last bit of water swirled into the drain.

In the gallows chamber above, two of the standby warders threaded a length of rope through a pulley attached to the beam overhead and threw one end into the pit room. Then they moved the pulley along the beam until it was directly above the first body. Below two of the escorts moved a heavy wooden trolley over the pit and under the body while another slipped the rope around the body of the prisoner and fastened it around the dead man's chest. As soon as he was ready he stepped back and raised his thumb; the two men above promptly pulled the naked body back into the gallows chamber.

Within a few minutes the prisoner was back where he had started, at eye level with the Warrant Officer in the gallows chamber. There one of the standby warders held the prisoner steady while another struggled with the hanging rope. The noose had cut into the prisoner's neck and the rubber grommet was slippery with blood. After a great deal of swearing and manoeuvring the rope was slipped back over the prisoner's head.

When the prisoner was lowered back into the pit room his head was flopping grotesquely on his chest, his neck muscles stretched and torn and the vertebrae crushed. The two escorts watching from below expertly caught the descending body by the hands and feet and slung it onto the wooden trolley in one movement. They untied the rope around the prisoner's chest and passed it on to the next pair of escorts. As they wheeled the trolley to the stack of coffins in the corner, a second body was already ascending into the gallows chamber. When the first pair of escorts reached the coffins they took down the top one and placed it on the floor. One slid its lid aside while the other hauled the trolley over. Then they unceremoniously tipped the body into the coffin. It landed face down and they left it so. One of them shoved the trolley with his foot towards the pit where the next pair of escorts caught it just in time to receive the second body from above.

Soon the escorts were all working in pairs with assembly line efficiency. In the corner an escort removed the tag from his prisoner's toe and tied it to the handle of the first coffin. His companion used a hammer to drive the screws through the lid.

As the blows rained down, another pair of escorts arrived to tip a second body into its coffin. At the pit the third pair was tying the rope around the chest of their body. With the first prisoner in his coffin, the pair of escorts returned to the pit and took their place under the fourth body.

While the escorts were disposing of the bodies in the pit room the paperwork was being attended to downstairs.

The four officials who had to sign them sat down at a table and passed the documents down the line for signature. The first one was for the prisoner at the head of the line on the trapdoors, Mnuxa Jerome Gcaba:

```
CERTIFICATE OF DEATH

I hereby certify that I have examined the body of
MNUXA JEROME GCABA V3664
who has been executed and that he is dead.


------------------------------
MEDICAL OFFICER

The undersigned declare that on this day
10th of December 1987 in Central Prison, Pretoria
MNUXA JEROME GCABA V3664
was executed.


------------------------------
DEPUTY SHERIFF CHARGED WITH EXECUTIONS

------------------------------
MEDICAL OFFICER

------------------------------
COMMANDING OFFICER

------------------------------
EXECUTIONER

/mo.
```

The Commanding Officer deferred to the Medical Officer, who had to sign twice. The Deputy Sheriff and the Executioner patiently waited their turn.

The Deputy Sheriff Charged with Executions took the batch of signed documents and put them in a folder. The top one was for Gcaba and advised the Court that its order had been carried out:

```
1/4/14 4533
                                    OFFICE OF THE SHERIFF
                                           OF TRANSVAAL
                                      PRIVATE BAG X67
                                              PRETORIA
                                                  0001
                                     10 December 1987

Registrar of the Supreme Court
Private Bag X9014
PIETERMARITZBURG
3200

THE STATE versus MNUXA JEROME GCABA

I beg to inform you that the abovementioned condemned
prisoner who was sentenced to death at SCOTTBURGH
on 12 DECEMBER 1986
was executed today.

The death warrant and certificate of death are en-
closed.



--------------------
SHERIFF OF TRANSVAAL
```

An hour after the trapdoors had dropped their load into the pit room the paperwork in the admin offices was complete and the seven coffins were ready to be taken down to the chapel. The officers went to breakfast with the Sheriff, the Executioner and the Medical Officer. The escorts had time only for a quick cup of tea in their staff room before they had to rush off to their next task.

10

Wierda and I received the trial records of the thirty-two men who were hanged between 26 November and 10 December 1987 from Pierre de Villiers on the second day of the trial, just before the close of the prosecution case. We had to read them at night and during the breaks as we could not afford to lose concentration during the hearing. Side by side the case files stood almost a metre wide.

I looked at the files in the stackers on the floor in my hotel room. What was there in these files that would shed light on the matter at hand?

Was there anything to explain our client's conduct? I wasn't sure that I would find the answer in those files, but I had to read them all.

The first four were hanged on 26 November 1987. I made a note of their names:

> Moatche
> Scheepers
> Wessels
> Mokwena

I also made a list of the officials:

> Executioner
> Head of Pretoria Central Prison
> Head of Maximum Security Prison
> Deputy Sheriff Charged with Executions
> Medical Officer
> Warrant Officer in Charge of Security

There must also have been at least seven warders, with four acting as gallows escorts and three on standby duty, but their names did not appear anywhere in the records Pierre had given me.

I started with Moatche's case. The main documents would tell the story:

Indictment. Statement of facts. List of witnesses.
Post-mortem report. Plans. Photographs.
Judgment. Sentencing reports. Sentencing.
Death warrant.
Sheriff's return. Identification statement. Death certificate.

I read Moatche's case with great care, looking for unusual features. I did not have to search for long.

```
INDICTMENT

1. EDWARD PHATAK TSHUMA of 255 Difateng Section,
Tembisa, a Black male and South African Citizen aged
20 years;
2. SIMON RAMOATSHE MOATCHE of 187 Difateng Section,
Tembisa, a Black male and South African citizen aged
21 years; and
3. JACOB SESING of 300 Difateng Section, Tembisa, a
Black male and South African citizen aged 18 years
are guilty of the crimes of:

COUNT 1: MURDER: IN THAT the accused on or about 19
March 1983 and at or near LAMANDLELA STATION in the
district of KEMPTON PARK unlawfully and intentionally
killed WILLIAM MATUTULE, a Black male.

COUNT 2: ROBBERY WITH AGGRAVATING CIRCUMSTANCES AS
DEFINED IN SECTION 1 OF ACT 51 OF 1977: IN THAT
the accused on or about 19 March 1983 and at or near
LAMANDLELA STATION in the district of KEMPTON PARK
unlawfully assaulted WILLIAM MATUTULE, a Black male,
by stabbing him with knives and then and there by
force and violence took from his person and possession
an unknown amount of money, his property or in his
lawful possession, and thus robbed him of the same.
```

The events of the evening of 19 March 1983 started innocently enough. Tshuma, Moatche, Sesing and Tshuma's female companion, Elizabeth Radebe, were drinking at a party in Tembisa. There they hatched a plan to rob some people. The three men were already armed with knives. They caught a train to Leralla. At Leralla the train stopped before starting the return journey. The foursome stayed on board. They had found no one to rob on the outward journey. Then Mr William Matutule, a working man in his thirties, boarded the train at 21:20.

During the journey Moatche, Tshuma and Sesing went from carriage to carriage searching for a suitable victim. They roughed up a number of passengers but found no one with any money. One potential victim eluded them by running to the front of the train.

When they saw Mr Matutule disembarking at Lamandlela Station a few minutes later, Tshuma, Moatche, Sesing and Elizabeth Radebe followed him. The station was deserted. The three men ran after Matutule while Elizabeth watched from a distance. The men caught Matutule at the stairway of the pedestrian bridge. They demanded money from him. He was unarmed and protested that he had no money. Sesing held him while Tshuma and Moatche went through his pockets. When they found nothing, Tshuma said that they had wasted their time. They then took out their knives and started stabbing Matutule. He tried to escape by running up the steps but he was caught halfway across the pedestrian bridge and dragged down to the station platform. The men continued to stab Matutule indiscriminately and repeatedly. He eventually collapsed and fell down between the platform and the railway line. Matutule died of internal and external bleeding as a result of multiple stab wounds. In the frenzy Tshuma had accidentally stabbed Sesing in the arm.

The three killers left the scene with Elizabeth Radebe and went to another party.

Mr Matutule's body was recovered by the Railway Police just before midnight. The police found a thirty-metre trail of blood from the top of the pedestrian bridge down the steps to a large pool of blood on the platform. The post-mortem report listed eighty-seven stab wounds. Matutule had been in the prime of his life and had been killed for nothing.

The killers were arrested soon after the murder when Tshuma and Radebe's relationship ended in some acrimony and she went to the police and reported what she had witnessed. After their arrest Tshuma and Moatche pointed out relevant places at the scene, which indicated that they had personal knowledge of events and facts only the killers could have known. They also admitted to having stabbed Matutule but put the blame on Sesing who, they said, had stabbed Matutule repeatedly. They claimed that they had inflicted only minor injuries in defence of Sesing.

Sesing was arrested later when he was released from hospital; he had been shot in the leg during an unrelated incident and still had a fresh stab wound in his arm. He claimed from the outset to have an alibi, but the evidence was unable to sustain that defence. His alibi defence contradicted that of Tshuma and Moatche.

On 11 July 1984 the three men were convicted of murder and attempted robbery with aggravating circumstances. The Court found that Tshuma had been the ringleader in the planning and execution of the attack upon Matutule and that each of the accused had probably inflicted an equal number of stab wounds. The Court turned to the question of whether extenuating circumstances were present in respect of the murder conviction.

Tshuma had been almost nineteen, Moatche twenty and Sesing seventeen years old when they killed Matutule. After an extensive review of case law and other authorities with regard to the effect of youthfulness and intoxication on the matter and a discussion of the concept of inherent vice, the Court found that the accused had acted out of inherent vice. They seemed to fit that category of township youth who were described in an Appeal Court judgment as men who stabbed for the sake of stabbing. The Court also found that they had planned the crime carefully and that robbery had been their motive. They had clearly acted in pursuit of a common purpose. Liquor had played no discernible role in their behaviour.

Tshuma and Moatche were both sentenced to death on the murder count and to eight years' imprisonment on the attempted robbery count. Sesing was given fifteen years' imprisonment for the murder and eight years' imprisonment for the attempted robbery. The two terms were to run concurrently.

Tshuma and Moatche's appeal was dismissed and on 28 February 1985 the Department of Justice wrote to say that the State President had declined to grant them clemency.

```
DEPARTMENT OF JUSTICE • DEPARTEMENT VAN JUSTISIE
REPUBLIEK VAN SUID-AFRIKA • REPUBLIC OF SOUTH AF-
RICA

                                    CONFIDENTIAL
                      Veritasgebou/Veritas Buildings
            Privaatsak/Private bag X81, Pretoria, 0001.
                            'Justisie'/'Justice'
                        28 2923 - 146 mej A Muller
                              Verwysing/Reference
                              9/5/4 - 3510 (R/2)
The Registrar of the
Supreme Court of South Africa
Private Bag X8
JOHANNESBURG
2000
                                        1986-02-28


CAPITAL CASE: THE STATE VERSUS (1) EDWARD PHATAK
TSHUMA
(2) SIMON RAMOATHSE MOATCHE: MURDER

The State President has decided not to grant clemency
to the above-named.


...................................
DIRECTOR-GENERAL: JUSTICE
```

By right Moatche and Tshuma should have been hanged within a week, but their families made further representations to the State President. They spent another nineteen months in the death cells before the State President's decision was made known on 20 November 1987. There were two letters. The one advised that in Tshuma's case the State President had decided to commute the death sentence to life imprisonment. The other advised that Moatche had not been granted clemency. No reasons were given for the decision.

Moatche was hanged on 26 November 1987. He was twenty-two years old.

I put the file back in the box and ordered a bottle of red wine, an Allesverloren cabernet sauvignon, from room service. The steward opened the wine and left and I sat down to ponder the vagaries of the legal process.

What can you do with a hopeless case? How do you stand in court with a serious expression on your face and conviction in your voice to tell the Judge that it was a case of self-defence when the dead man had eighty-seven stab wounds? And how does an alibi go down when two of your co-accused tell the Judge under oath that you were with them at the scene? You can't cross-examine entries out of books, fingerprints off a dressing table or bullet holes out of a corpse. The prosecutor must have enjoyed the fiasco at the defence table.

Tshuma and Moatche had come to within a week of being hanged two years earlier, but there had been a stay of execution. Who granted it and why? The files did not disclose these details. The State President must have been advised then that there was no reason to grant either of them clemency. Why then did he subsequently grant clemency to Tshuma but not to Moatche? I could understand why Sesing did not receive a death sentence, on strict legal principle, but the hanging of Moatche seemed almost as random an act as the choice of Mr Matatule as victim.

Did they hang the wrong man? Pierre's note on top of the papers in the file read.

I would drink a lot of wine through the years (though none better than that Allesverloren), but I would never be able to answer that question. I repeated it as I looked at the label on the bottle through my empty glass.

Allesverloren. All is lost.

The prosecution's opening statement was delivered by Sanet Niemand. She was as hard and angular as Wierda was soft and round. Her hair was tied in a bun. She wore no makeup or jewellery. I had sensed some tension between her and Wierda, but on the surface they were polite to each other.

Niemand had stated the facts supporting the prosecution theory coolly, without emotion or argument, reading from a prepared script. The opening statement took less than half an hour. The two prosecutors then took turns to lead the evidence of their few witnesses. James Murray was near my age. He had an ominous calm about him and spoke idiomatic Afrikaans without any trace of an accent. At our first meeting in the robing room I had teased him, asking what a good Scot like him was doing in Pretoria. He'd answered that his ancestors were Scottish missionaries who had fallen in with the local population. He was referring to *my* ancestors, I had thought.

Pierre was seated a few rows behind us. An untidy middle-aged man sat next to him. They were talking like old friends but I thought nothing of it then. Labuschagne's family, his parents and his sister Antoinette, were in the first row behind the dock. Labuschagne sat some distance away from them. Despite Wierda's best efforts Labuschagne would still not allow his parents to see him in the cells. In a dock that could accommodate fifteen people, a dock specially erected for Nelson Mandela's trial in 1964, Leon Labuschagne sat alone, the focus of all the drama unfolding around us.

On that first day I had taken some time to study the spectators. Members of the public had taken their positions at the back of the court according to the side they supported, I thought. Most of the spectators in the public gallery in that half of the court behind the prosecutors were black; the majority of those behind the defence were white.

Some voices were raised during the prosecution's opening statement, and again when photographs of the bodies were produced and handed in as exhibits. Each time Judge van Zyl asked the public to remain calm and to allow the Court to do its job.

In the beginning everyone had expected political grandstanding and rioting spectators, but there was neither. The prosecutors had kept their case simple, and we were keeping a low profile. As for the audience, once they had heard the basic outline of the facts as presented by Niemand, they appeared to lose interest. It seemed that everyone, black and white, had become inured to the pain and drama of a murder. It was as if we had had so much of it that even the killing of seven young men could not hold our attention for more than a day or two.

After the opening statement, the State witnesses came to the witness box in a steady stream and left as quickly as they had come. There were no fireworks and no cross-examination to speak of. We avoided confrontation and we did not seek to justify Labuschagne's actions. We shunned the media and stuck to our plan to reveal only as much of our case as we had to.

During the prosecution case we heard the evidence of a man from the municipal water department about how he had gone up to the reservoir to take the water level and found the bodies in the mud. There were fresh tracks around the bodies, but the bodies were untouched. Various policemen gave evidence about their investigations at the scene, about how they had found the murder weapon, as they called it, sunk into the mud, and how they had traced Labuschagne from the number plate of his bakkie. The key was in the ignition, the policemen told the Court, but the bakkie would not start. The prosecutors were to use this fact against us.

We had offered to admit the post-mortem reports, but instead the District Surgeon was called to give evidence about his findings, no doubt to lay the foundation for an argument that the shootings had been planned and deliberate; in other words, that it had been a cold-blooded execution of the victims. We considered cross-examining him about the execution process at Maximum, but decided against it. We needed to keep our powder dry, and our investigations were in any event still in progress.

Roshnee pointed out to us that we had slipped off the front page of the local newspapers. By the third day we were already on page four. But it would not stay that way. The drama was to come in the defence case.

Wierda had the task of cross-examining the last State witness. When he sat down, James Murray immediately started his re-examination.

We were nearing the end of the prosecution's case. Our strategy had been not to emphasise or compliment any part of the prosecution's evidence, and our cross-examination had been short. In the case of some witnesses we had no questions at all. The result was that after a day and about an hour we were set to start the case for the defence.

Murray was on his feet. Sanet Niemand hardly ever glanced in my direction. She also wrote down every word that was said, even during the staccato exchanges when an objection was made. I assumed that she had done the research for their team and was in charge of the administration of the case. We kept a polite distance from her.

The three figures on the imposing bench watched the last prosecution witness intently. The bench was an ornate work of art, a raised, fully enclosed wood-panelled structure approximately three and a half metres wide and three metres deep. Three high-backed swivel chairs stood side by side under a canopy of even more elaborate woodwork. The canopy was in the shelter of an arch, supported on either side by thick wooden columns. Behind the Judge's chair was the door leading to the Judges' quarters, out of bounds to all but the lawyers and clerks who had legitimate cause to enter the inner sanctum of the court. In front of the chairs was a polished wooden table, about one metre wide and spanning the full width of the bench.

I thought about the progress of the trial thus far.

The prosecution case had been presented with cold and clinical efficiency, without fanfare. James Murray was effective and professional. While treating me with the courtesy demanded by the etiquette of our profession, he quietly went about the business of putting our client on the trapdoors under the ropes. The exhibits he introduced were of the nature of plans and photographs. He was confident enough to allow his Junior to perform some of the important tasks of the trial, and experienced enough to let the evidence speak for itself. Here are the bodies. See the bullet holes in them. Here is the murder weapon. It belongs to the defendant. Look at these photographs. There is the defendant's bakkie next to the bodies. See where the bullets have passed through the bodies and into the side of the minibus. When the defendant's bakkie wouldn't start he was forced to flee on foot.

The post-mortem reports told their own grim tale of the heights and weights of the deceased, of entry and exit wounds and the tracks of the numerous bullets. And they were all fired by the defendant, Murray pointed out repeatedly.

Sanet Niemand led the evidence of the investigating detective, a Detective Warrant Officer. He gave evidence on Labuschagne's arrest and his silence when confronted with his pistol. The policeman produced Labuschagne's statement, but it contained nothing of consequence. The statement was in the policeman's handwriting:

I have been advised of my rights and that I am being charged with seven counts of murder. I decline to make a statement.

Q. Do you want a lawyer?

A. (The accused gave no reply.)

The registrar coughed behind her hand. She wore robes and sat in the anonymity that her uniform provided, directly in front of the Judge in her own domain of wood panelling and red leather. From her slightly elevated position she could face the assembly of people in the court, from the stenographer, whose table stood in front of hers, to the advocates in the first row of seats. The attorneys' table and the dock completed the well of the court. Finally there were the public benches behind the dock and in the gallery above. The media were in a privileged position, occupying the two rows of seats in the jury box. Trial by jury had been abolished because it had become clear that the jury system simply could not work in a society divided by race.

Directly opposite the jury box on the right was the witness box, occupied for the moment by the prosecution's last witness. I had lost interest in him; he could not make our case much worse than it already was. The witness box was enclosed on three sides by the same dark wood panelling that enclosed the bench. Its floor was just slightly raised – twenty centimetres or so – above the carpeted floor so that a witness always stood slightly higher than counsel, perhaps as an indication of their relative importance in the process of arriving at the truth.

My rambling thoughts were interrupted when James Murray informed the Judge that he had no further questions and Judge van Zyl nodded in the direction of the witness. By this time I had got used to the way he controlled his Court with nods and the inclination of his head instead of words. A tap of his pen on his bench pad meant, wait, you are going too fast. He only had to tap once and I knew what to expect. When he took his spectacles off it meant he needed time to think. We had to watch his pen and his eyes to adjust the pace of our questions. I quickly learnt that I would have to keep an eye on him throughout.

'You may step down,' he now said to the witness, 'and you are released from further attendance.'

James Murray had remained standing and announced the close of the prosecution case. 'That is the case for the State, M'Lord and gentlemen Assessors.' Then he sat down.

It was our turn at last, after months of preparation. While I knew the case materials backwards I could still feel some nervous tension in my shoulders. Wierda and I knew that everything we said would be subjected to close scrutiny, that every proposition would be tested, not only by our opponents but by the Judge and also by the media. Every word would have to be weighed and measured to fit exactly into the scheme of the defence we had prepared.

I started tentatively. 'May it please M'Lord and M'Lord's Learned Assessors. We intend to call witnesses and we have an opening address.'

'Yes, carry on.' Judge van Zyl was not wasting any time; his posture said: get on with it.

I placed my trial notebook on the lectern in front of me and adjusted my robes with a tug at the shoulder. It was a nervous habit. I could feel the focus of the spectators shifting to our table.

'This is an extraordinary case,' I opened quietly, 'where the evidence for the prosecution is undisputed and the prosecution's case is, in a way, also the case for the defence. The prosecution has been at pains to show what has happened. The defence will explain why it happened. The prosecution's case has been about the *what* and the *how*. Our case is about the *why*.'

Judge van Zyl and his Assessors did not stir, but they were watching me. There had been so little cross-examination of the prosecution witnesses that they had not seen much of me; I now got the impression that they were observing me very closely. I continued without having to look at my notes.

'This is essentially a case of taboos.' I paused for a moment before I explained. 'First there is the taboo of killing. The killing of a human being is viewed with universal disapproval, and the more brutal the killing, the greater the disapproval with which members of the public view the event and the killer. Multiple killings increase that disapproval to the point where ordinary, right-minded members of society are prepared to cast the killer to the wolves without a trial.'

There was still no reaction from the bench. No one except Niemand was taking notes.

'The second taboo is the taboo against interracial crime. For decades our courts have viewed interracial incidents, especially in crimes of violence, as more serious and have punished their perpetrators more heavily than the norm for similar crimes where race was not an element. And here we have had a killing across the racial divide: the defendant is white, the deceased were all black.

'The third taboo is the taboo against the so-called blackout defence. In strict legal theory it is a defence against the actus reus element, although that principle has not always been expressed clearly in our textbooks and judgments. It could also be a defence against the mens rea element. But we are going to lead evidence that there was no legal act, no act to which the law attaches legal consequences in this case.' I had used old Latin legal terms for the criminal act and for state of mind.

The Judge made a note in his notebook. I waited for him to finish and when he looked up and nodded at me I made sure to engage the two Assessors in eye contact before I resumed.

'M'Lord and gentlemen Assessors, the prosecution has to prove the following elements on a charge of murder.' I used technical terms to list the legal requirements for a conviction on a murder charge. I held up a finger for each element as I spoke: 'Murder is an

> one – unlawful
>
> two – intentional
>
> three – act
>
> four – that causes the death
>
> five – of another human being.'

I told them a second time that our defence was that there had not been a criminal act because Labuschagne lacked criminal capacity.

The Judge shifted in his high-backed chair and when he spoke his tone was charged with incredulity. 'Are you suggesting that there has been no act, when we have seven bodies here?'

He looked sideways at each of his Assessors in turn and said something under his breath. I was sure the reporters nearest to the bench could hear him as clearly as I could. 'Moenie my vertel perdedrolle is vye nie!' I got the message.

I played to the mood of the bench. 'According to case law M'Lord is entitled to be sceptical, as we shall demonstrate to M'Lord and the Learned Assessors when we address the Court on the law during our closing argument.'

When there was no response I carried on, using *we* to include Wierda in the submissions, 'We mentioned the third taboo earlier because it is entirely natural to be sceptical of this defence when the killing has admittedly been committed by the defendant's hand.'

Judge van Zyl intervened. 'You had better explain very carefully what the defence is as I am at a loss to understand how you can say that there was no act when you have admitted that the accused has killed the seven deceased.'

'With respect, M'Lord,' I began, 'in the statement explaining the basis of the defendant's case, which we handed in at the commencement of the trial, we explained that the defendant admits that the deceased were killed by his hand but denies that his actions had been, to quote from the defence statement, *voluntary and conscious*. The issue is whether there has been an act within the requirements of the law, an act which was both a conscious and a voluntary act.'

He intervened again. 'What you have said relates to the defendant's state of mind, not to his physical acts.'

I wanted to pacify him by referring to case law and textbooks dealing with the principle that unconscious and involuntary acts are not punishable, but as I reached for a *Law Report* he stopped me.

'You may assume that I know the law,' he said.

I needed a different angle. Before I could speak again, I heard Wierda's pencil tapping against his teeth. Tap tap tap. I tried not to let it distract me.

'The underlying facts of the events are common cause and were proved by the prosecution's witnesses. May we remind M'Lord and the Learned Assessors of the events of the evening of 10 December 1987, as deposed by the prosecution's witnesses?'

I did not wait for Judge van Zyl to respond to my question. 'We would like to emphasise that the facts of the prosecution's case are also the facts of the case for the defence – the events starting at Saxby Road, the car chase all the way down the Old Johannesburg Road, Jan Smuts Road, down to Magazine Street and up to the reservoir on Magazine Hill. All of those events are common cause. It does not matter whose fault those events were. The events at the reservoir are also not in dispute. Even the brutality of the killings is an essential component of the defence.'

As I spoke I could see the Judge studying the prosecution's exhibit, a photo album.

'It is the very brutality, the savagery with which the deceased were killed,' I continued, 'the scale of the event – seven fit and strong young men killed by a single individual – that calls for closer scrutiny. The ritualistic positions in which the bodies were found is another factor prompting an intensive enquiry. The prosecution has adduced no evidence of a motive and there appears to be none. What we ask for is a rigorous but fair examination of the defence and the defence's evidence in the light of all the circumstances. We ask for no more than that.'

Judge van Zyl took the bait. 'I, um, we intend to do just that. Didn't you say that there is authority to the effect that we should be careful in our scrutiny of the defence evidence in a case like this?'

I caught myself tugging at my robes again. 'This case is about *why* the defendant behaved in the way he did and whether he can be held criminally responsible for what happened that evening. The defence contends that he cannot be held responsible. We intend to lead detailed evidence about the defendant's background, in particular, his work circumstances during the eighteen months before 10 December 1987.'

The Judge looked at the clock and indicated that it was time for the tea adjournment. 'You can tell us about the defendant's background when we return.' Then he rose and left the court through the door immediately behind his chair. The Assessors followed him.

Labuschagne was taken down the stairs to the cells. Members of the public stayed in the courtroom to preserve their seats. Reporters spilled out of the jury box into the corridor, looking for an opportunity to smoke a cigarette while phoning their editors. I left for the robing room with Wierda. I needed some air.

We left our robes in the robing room off the corridor directly behind the courtroom. There were other advocates there and we left quickly. Wierda suggested that we go for a walk on Church Square. 'We can talk there,' he added.

We met Roshnee on the steps and rushed across the street to the Square. We sat down on the steps of the monument in the centre of the park-like grounds. Vagrants had occupied all the park benches. We were in the shade cast by the statue of the last President of the Transvaal Republic, Paul Kruger, affectionately known as Oom Paul. We bought some soft drinks from a street vendor. Wierda and I discussed the remainder of our opening statement, refining it here and there and adding bits that arose from the questions the Judge had asked and the attitude he had exhibited thus far. I scribbled a note to myself in the margin next to the relevant paragraphs of the draft.

'An impressive building, even if it is a bit run down,' I said, twenty minutes later, as we were making our way back to the Palace of Justice for the second session of the day.

'My great-grandfather designed it,' Wierda said with a glow of pride. 'In 1894.'

Crossing the street, we made our way up the steps in front of the building together. Wierda showed me the plaque at the entrance, on the left.

GEBOUDED IN DE JAREN 1896–1899
S WIERDA J MUNRO H V WERKEN AANNEMER

It was an odd combination, a Hollander and a Scot.

I did not stop to notice the elaborate foyers at the entrance as I was already lost in the details of the opening statement.

I took my time when I sketched Labuschagne's history and background; it would eventually become an important component of our attempt to explain the events at the reservoir. I spoke slowly and emphasised the salient features without repeating them and without presenting facts as argument.

I next had to deal with the witnesses to be called to give evidence on behalf of the defence. There was three-quarters of an hour left before the lunch adjournment. On the spur of the moment I decided to depart from the prepared opening statement and to give the Judge and Assessors only the most basic outline of the proposed evidence. I closed my trial notebook and spoke off the cuff.

'The defendant will be called first,' I said. 'The second witness will be his wife, Magda Labuschagne. We intend calling the headmaster of the defendant's high school. Then we intend to call two expert witnesses. First, Dr Marianne Schlebusch, a practising clinical psychologist and lecturer at the University of the Witwatersrand. Dr Schlebusch will say that, in her opinion, when he shot the seven deceased at the reservoir, the defendant's mental processes had broken down to such an extent that he was neither aware of his actions nor in control of them.'

Wierda passed me a note, but I knew what it said and pocketed it unread. I continued without a pause.

'Our last witness will be Professor Leonard Shapiro who teaches Psychiatry at the University of Southern California Medical School and is a forensic expert on the panel of psychiatrists of the United States District Court for the Central District of California. The burden of Professor Shapiro's evidence will be that, after studying the case materials and the several interviews he has conducted with the defendant, he agrees with Miss Schlebusch's opinion.'

The courtroom had become eerily quiet. We had finally disclosed our hand; in the language of bridge we had made our bid. There were a few minutes left before one o'clock. The moment had finally arrived for Leon Labuschagne to talk, to tell his story and to face the consequences.

'M'Lord,' I said, 'we are ready to call the defendant, but we would ask for an indulgence, namely to adjourn for lunch at this stage.'

Judge van Zyl nodded but did not announce the adjournment.

'There is a matter that is of some concern to me,' he said gravely. 'You mentioned that the defendant worked in Maximum Security Prison and that evidence will be given of his work conditions and of events which took place there, am I right?'

I confirmed that that was our intention.

He thought for a while. 'In that case,' he said eventually, 'I do not want any names to be used, not of the officials or the inmates, no one at all unless it cannot be avoided.'

'We shall oblige,' I agreed immediately. It would give the defence greater freedom to make use of the information we had gathered.

Judge van Zyl pointed his spectacles at me. 'And I expect you to ask me for permission before you use anyone's name.'

I agreed again, though it was a promise that would not be easy to keep.

'The Court adjourns until two-fifteen,' said the Judge and we trooped out to the Square for the second time. Before I left I arranged with the cell sergeant to let us into the cells below the courtroom at half-past one to give our client his final briefing.

As we were walking to the robing room, I took Wierda's note from my pocket. *Why are you abandoning our prepared opening statement?*

'A change of tactics,' I said. 'I thought it would be better to leave the explanations for the closing argument.'

Wierda was not convinced. He shook his head in displeasure at my changing course without consulting him. We had spent many hours in his chambers crafting together what we thought was a perfect opening statement, one with a solid mix of logic and emotion, balancing law and fact, evidence and inference, a teasing statement that left the details for later. It was the detail that worried me. Would our witnesses produce the goods?

Roshnee showed no interest in the discussion and, as was her habit, stuck to more practical things. 'Let's get something to eat quickly, we don't have much time.'

We departed promptly and ate our sandwiches in the shade provided by a tree a few yards away from Oom Paul's statue. I took the opportunity to brief Wierda and Roshnee on the second case I had summarised.

V3421 Joseph George Scheepers

12

The indictment charged four young men with robbery with aggravating circumstances, rape and murder. They were Schalk Burger, Joseph Scheepers, Johannes Matthysen and Daniel du Randt. Burger was twenty years old, Scheepers twenty-one, and the other two nineteen. They had robbed Mr Jacob Wessie of his car and other possessions and had raped and murdered his female companion, Miss Ginny Goitseone.

On Friday 1 February 1985 du Randt bought a toy revolver as a present for his younger brother. He still had it with him late that evening when he and Matthysen met Burger and Scheepers outside the Tivoli Hotel in Klerksdorp for a night of drinking and playing darts. When the bar closed at eleven they had no choice but to leave.

Outside Scheepers stopped a passing motorist, Mr Johannes

Mophuting, and demanded that Mophuting take him home. Burger, Matthysen and du Randt followed in Burger's car. Mophuting stopped in front of the police station. Scheepers jumped out and got into Burger's car. He had seen some music cassette tapes in Mophuting's car and at Burger's suggestion they followed Mophuting on his journey home to rob him.

But Mophuting saw them and when he arrived home he locked the doors of his car and sounded his hooter. Scheepers broke the left front window of Mophuting's car with a rock and pointed the toy revolver at him. Mophuting ran away, but his neighbours swarmed to his aid and the four white men fled empty-handed.

As they left Jouberton they came across a BMW car parked next to the road. Mr Jacob Wessie was in the driver's seat and Miss Ginny Goitseone was sitting in the passenger seat. Burger stopped next to the BMW and Scheepers went to Wessie's window, pointed the toy revolver at him and shouted that he was a policeman. He ordered Wessie to open the window and when Wessie opened the driver's window he grabbed the ignition keys. Scheepers said the BMW had been stolen and that he was going to take Wessie to the police station. He ordered Wessie into the back seat and told du Randt to get in behind Miss Goitseone. Scheepers then drove off in Wessie's BMW and Burger and Matthysen followed in Burger's car.

During the journey du Randt had held the toy revolver against Wessie's neck while fondling Miss Goitseone's breasts with his other hand. Scheepers asked du Randt, 'Nou wie gaan met die meisie begin?' Scheepers stopped in a deserted cul-de-sac among some smallholdings about fifteen kilometres away. There Scheepers and Burger subjected Wessie to a prolonged assault, robbed him of his money and removed his car radio-cassette player while du Randt and Matthysen took turns to rape Miss Goitseone. 'Die meisie is lekker,' du Randt said when he returned to the BMW. Scheepers and du Randt tried to force Wessie into the boot of the BMW. Wessie noticed the first three registration letters – DLL – of Burger's car. He pretended to get into the boot but instead suddenly ran off into the dark. He was pursued in vain by Burger, Matthysen and du Randt. They returned to the cars without their captive. They now had a problem. Wessie could identify them and Scheepers' fingerprints were all over the BMW.

Wessie hid behind some bushes and saw the two cars being driven away a short while later. Scheepers, in the presence of Matthysen, had forced Miss Goitseone into the boot of the BMW before driving off. She was still alive.

Some eleven kilometres away they stopped. Burger raised the bonnet of his car and Scheepers sucked some petrol from the fuel supply to the carburettor into his mouth and spat it out on the upholstery of the BMW. He made several trips. At one stage Miss Goitseone was heard to call, 'My baas, my baas!' She was screaming and pleading, but to no avail. Burger started up his car and Scheepers set the BMW alight. The four men drove off in Burger's car and stopped on a bridge. Burger and Scheepers looked back towards the BMW to see whether it had caught alight but they could not see anything from where they were.

Matthysen remonstrated with them, saying that what they had done was murder and that he wanted to have nothing to do with it. Scheepers' response was that Matthysen had also hit Wessie. He added, 'Ek voel fokkol vir die lewe.' After dropping Matthysen at a tearoom near his parents' home and with du Randt sleeping on the back seat, Burger and Scheepers returned to the BMW. They saw that the vehicle had been completely gutted by the fire. They took du Randt home and went their separate ways.

Wessie eventually found his way to the police station. The police found the BMW with Miss Goitseone's charred body in the boot the next day, Saturday 2 February 1985. They had no leads until Matthysen arrived at the police station late the next evening. He handed himself over and told the police what had happened. The others were arrested the next day. Scheepers and Burger had already fled 750 kilometres to Durban and had to be brought all the way back for their trial.

Wessie had suffered numerous injuries and his clothes were covered in blood. Miss Goitseone had died of smoke inhalation or carbon poisoning before her body had been rendered unrecognisable as that of a human being.

On 17 September 1985 the four accused were convicted of robbery with aggravating circumstances. All four were also convicted of rape, with Matthysen and du Randt declared guilty as principal offenders and Burger and Scheepers as accomplices. On the murder charge Burger and Scheepers were convicted while Matthysen and du Randt were found not guilty.

The next day the Court heard evidence and submissions on the question of extenuating circumstances with regard to the murder conviction. A psychiatrist in private practice gave evidence and explained his findings and conclusions. His written reports on Burger and Scheepers were placed before the Court. A State psychiatrist concurred with the findings and conclusions in every respect. The opinion of the psychiatrists was that Burger had not suffered from any mental illness at the time of the examination, nor had he at the time the crimes were committed. Scheepers, on the other hand, was found to suffer from an antisocial personality defect, but no mental defect as contemplated by the law was detected. He was a psychopath.

The Court found no extenuating circumstances and Scheepers and Burger were sentenced to death on the murder charge. On 20 September 1985 the Court reconvened to pass sentence on the remaining charges. For the aggravated robbery on Wessie each of the men was sentenced to twelve years' imprisonment. For the rape Burger and Scheepers were sentenced to death a second time and Matthysen and du Randt each to sixteen years' imprisonment.

Scheepers and Burger appealed. Their death sentences on the rape charge were set aside, but their death sentences on the murder charge were confirmed.

On 20 November 1987 Burger and Scheepers were called from their cells at Maximum Security Prison and the Deputy Sheriff advised them that the State President had extended mercy to Burger but not to Scheepers. Burger was to serve life imprisonment instead and Scheepers was to be hanged on the twenty-sixth.

The night before the execution Scheepers' family launched an application for a stay of execution. The application papers included affidavits by Scheepers and his father. However, the application was hopeless, devoid of merit, and the Judge dismissed it out of hand. The team of lawyers acting for Scheepers turned their pleas for mercy to the State President, but to no avail.

Scheepers was hanged the next day. He was twenty-three years old.

Palace of Justice

13

After the lunch break we rushed back to give Labuschagne a final briefing. We had half an hour before the Court was due to re-assemble. The cell below Court C was damp and uncomfortable. The sergeant in charge of the cells locked us in the cell with Labuschagne and went off to have his lunch.

'Will you please take him through his statement?' I asked Wierda.

I tried to make myself comfortable on one of the wooden benches. For a while I listened as Wierda took Labuschagne through the timeline we had prepared for his evidence. The walls were covered in graffiti. I craned my neck to read some. I quickly dropped any pretence at indifference. A crude gibbet was drawn on the wall above my head, the noose around the letters ANC. A snake-like appendage hanging from the third letter dripped blood onto the floor. Above the noose was a name.

WITKOMMANDO

Adjacent to it a defiant member of Umkhonto we Sizwe had scribbled a manifesto on the wall in imperfect English:

M.K. MANUFESTO
THERE COMES A TIME IN THE LIFE OF EVERY
NATION, WHERE THERE REMAINS ONLY TWO CHOICES,
SUBMIT OR FIGHT, AND THAT TIME HAS COME TO S.A.
WE SHALL NOT SUBMIT, AND WE HAVE NO CHOICE, BUT TO

HIT BACK WITH ALL MEANS WE HAVE IN OUR POWER, IN
DEFFENCE OF OUR PEOPLE, OUR FREEDOM AND OUR FUTURE.
AMANDLA! O'POVU

I walked around to another wall. The names of the accused in a 1977 case were listed under the heading:

NC TERRORIST TRIAL 17/7/77
MOSIMA SEXWALE
NALEDI TSIKI
JACOB MOTAUNG
SIMON MOHLANYANE

There were other names I had never heard. Some names had been partly obliterated by the moss feeding in the damp; others had been defaced by other occupants of the cell. I walked from wall to wall, reading messages from the past. It was plain that a political battle was also being fought here in the cell, mostly by anonymous participants.

More subtle in its power and universal in its application was a passage from the Bible, St James edition. The damp had destroyed the text at the edges.

PSALM 94
SHALL THE THRONE OF INIQUITY HAVE ...
WHICH FRAMETH MISCHIEF BY A LAW
THEY GATHER THEMSELVES TOGETHER ...
THE RIGHTEOUS AND CONDEMN THE INNOCENT ...

It was a wall of political protest and defiance, mostly by black prisoners raging against the white regime, with the odd riposte by a white prisoner. Some light relief was provided by the career criminals, for whom a stay in the cells was merely part of the job, an occupational risk, so to speak, and thus to be endured with fortitude, a bit of cheek and some good humour.

One inmate had taken a sly dig at his lawyer:

GULZMAR
EBRAHIM
WAS HIER VIR ROOF
EN KAR DIEFSTAL EN
HET AGTER SY ADWORKAT
GEGAAN EN SKELDEG GEPLYT
SY VONNIS WAS 9–15 JAAR
TRONKSTRAF SHALOET

Wierda and Labuschagne were working at the table, poring over the papers and concentrating on the job at hand. I studied our client for a moment. A rather serious young man, but given the circumstances, that could be forgiven. The question was, would he let us down when he got into the witness box? Clients always do; that is just one of the hazards of the job. Somehow cases always seemed to go well until the client steps into the witness box; then all the careful stitches in the cloth holding the case together are unravelled one by one.

I wished I was far away from there, perhaps in a nice shipping case with lots of documentary exhibits and fees paid in pounds sterling or US dollars. There was a sobering message for me on another part of the wall, however:

DON'T TALK ABOUT
SHIPS OR SHIPPING

When Wierda had completed the briefing, I called for the cell sergeant. Our brief sojourn in the cell confronted me yet again with the claustrophobia of life in prison. The sergeant followed us into the courtroom up the steps leading into the dock.

The most difficult and unpredictable part of the trial was about to begin.

The Court started promptly at two-fifteen. The defence experts had taken seats at Roshnee's table, directly behind me. Marianne Schlebusch and Dr Shapiro sat ready to observe and to give advice, but for the time being all eyes were on the defendant.

I stood up and announced, 'We call Leon Albert Labuschagne.'

The spectators strained to get a better look at him. For the first time during the trial he had to face those at the back of the court.

The registrar administered the oath.

I started with the first topic in our prepared timeline. It would take at least two days, perhaps three, to cover all the prepared topics, and I started slowly. Labuschagne's eyes darted from left to right, from the bench to me and back to the bench again, but never to the spectators behind me.

'How old are you?'

'Twenty.' He coughed to clear his throat. He had turned twenty a month before the trial.

'Where did you go to school?'

We carried on in that vein for a while, covering his early years and his last two years at school. Labuschagne was patently nervous; how could he not be?

'So what did you decide to do for a career as you approached your final school examinations?'

'I was recruited by the Prisons Service.'

'Why did you join?'

'They said that if I joined the Prisons Service I would not have to go to the army.'

We were fighting a war in Angola and many young men joined the police or Prisons Service to avoid being sent to Angola.

'Once you had joined, where were you posted?'

'The training college in Kroonstad.'

'How did your training go?' It was like pulling teeth, but at least he did not talk too much.

'The training was cut short after three months because of a manpower shortage. I was then posted to Central Prison.'

'How long were you at Central?'

'For about two months.'

'Where did you go from there?'

'I was sent to Maximum Security Prison.'

'How did that come about?' The question called for an explanation and Labuschagne had to do the talking without prompting from me.

'I got into trouble for sleeping when I was on night shift. The Commanding Officer of the prison held a surprise inspection of the prison at four o'clock in the morning. He said I was sleeping on duty and he then transferred me to Maximum as punishment.'

'When did this happen?'

'May, the year before last.' 1986.

'How old were you then?' I asked, although everyone could work it out.

'Seventeen.'

'Did you know what your duties would be in Maximum?'

'No, sir.'

'What was the date of your transfer to Maximum?'

'It was the middle of 1986, towards the end of July.' I looked up from my notes. There was a pause before he corrected himself. 'No, sorry, it was June.'

We were still dealing with background matters, and it would be a tedious and slow affair to get all the evidence before the Court, but it had to be done. We were in for a long afternoon. Judge van Zyl yawned and looked at the clock. I decided to deal with something more dramatic.

'Could you please tell the Court about your first day at Maximum?'

'I reported for duty at seven in the morning on the twenty-third of June 1986. The Warrant Officer took me around the different sections of the prison and told me what my duties would be. He first took me to the administration section next to the Major's office and marked my name on the roster for the day shift. Then he showed me the cells in A Section.' It was a prepared answer.

'What else did the Warrant Officer do?'

'He took me to the Major's office. They told me how important secrecy was. Basically they said that if I should speak to anyone, even my wife, about anything to do with the work or anything that happens inside the prison, I would be fired on the spot. They made me sign a document that said something about official secrets.' Another prepared answer. We had many of them.

'Where was the Major during this induction into prison culture?' I was still keeping my promise not to mention any names.

'I think he was doing the morning roll call in the cell blocks.'

'Where did you go from the Major's office?'

'From there the Warrant Officer took me to A and B sections. he showed me that the black, coloured and indian prisoners were in A Section and the white prisoners in C Section. There was only one prisoner in B Section.'

'What did you do the rest of the day?' I wanted to get to the next day's events before the Judge lost interest.

'I spent the rest of the day with the Warrant Officer. I had to go everywhere with him.'

'Did anything in particular happen that day?' I asked as I made a tick in the margin of the notes in my trial notebook to indicate that the particular subject had been dealt with. There were many topics to cover still before Labuschagne would be handed over for cross-examination.

'In the afternoon ten new prisoners came,' he said. I waited for Labuschagne to continue. He did not need to be asked for every little detail and would have to get used to the idea that the information had to come from him.

'Yes,' I said, slightly impatient.

'The Warrant Officer called me and told me to see how the admin was done when they were taken in.'

'Please tell the Court what the procedures are.'

'There were ten. Two came from Johannesburg, five from Pretoria, two from Cape Town and one from Mossel Bay.' Labuschagne looked at me and then added, 'Do you want their details?'

'In a minute,' I said. 'I'd like to know what you did with them and I want you to remember not to mention any names.'

Labuschagne looked up towards the Judge and Assessors and then said, almost inaudibly, 'We hanged them, sir.'

The Judge leaned across towards the witness box as he intervened. 'Could you say that again? I could not hear you. And remember to speak up.'

Labuschagne glanced nervously at the Judge. 'We hanged them, sir. They are dead.'

I tapped on my trial notebook with my pen.

'No, we'll get to that later,' I said. 'What I want to know is how they were processed on their arrival that day.'

'Oh, okay,' he said. 'They were still in their own clothes. They had their death warrants with them. First we put their fingerprints on the death warrants. Then their details were written in a register and they were given their v-numbers.'

'What is the significance of the v-numbers?'

'Every prisoner in Maximum gets a v-number.'

'What do the v-numbers signify?' the Judge wanted to know.

'The V is for Veroordeelde,' said Labuschagne.

When Judge van Zyl nodded in my direction, I started laying one of the cornerstones of our case. 'How did the new prisoners react or behave during the admission processes?'

'Nervous and afraid. Some cried. I think they thought they were going to be hanged immediately.'

'How were you affected by this?'

'I was also nervous and afraid.' Labuschagne's voice was too low and he had to be reminded to speak up.

'Speak up so that we can hear you, please,' I said. 'Do you have the details of the prisoners who were admitted that day?'

'Yes, sir. It is in the register.'

'Are you referring to the Register of Capital Cases kept by the Chief Registrar of this Court?' I asked.

'Yes, sir.'

I turned slightly to face Judge van Zyl square on. 'M'Lord, I ask leave to place a copy of the register before the witness. The original register is available at the Chief Registrar's office, but since it is in daily use we have decided to make copies instead. I offer to prove the original by calling the registrar if there should be any dispute about the admissibility or correctness of the copy my Learned Junior has prepared. I have copies for M'Lord and the Learned Assessors as well as our Learned Friends.'

When there was no reaction from Judge van Zyl or James Murray I turned towards Wierda and held out my hand. He stood up and took eleven identical lever arch files from Roshnee's desk and handed them to the usher for distribution. All of this took some time.

I waited until the Judge and Assessors had received their sets from the registrar before I continued. 'I have taken the liberty of marking this register, or rather, this copy of the register, as Exhibit G, M'Lord.' Then I turned my attention back to the witness box.

'Is what you have in front of you a copy of the register you referred to earlier?' I asked.

Labuschagne opened the file and after glancing over a few pages nodded. 'Yes.'

'What we have here are eight columns spread over the two facing pages. Is that right?'

'Yes.'

'Each column has its own heading, starting with the first column on the left-hand side of the page: *Serial No, Name, v-no, Place Sentenced, Date, Judge, Outcome* and *Date*.' I followed the columns with my finger and kept one eye on the Judge and his Assessors to make sure that they were following the evidence.

'Yes, that's right,' said Labuschagne without waiting for a question or a prompt.

'Please turn to the page reflecting the admissions on your first day at Maximum, the twenty-third of June 1986.' I waited for him to find the page. When he stopped paging through the file and looked at me again I turned to the Judge and said, 'May I ask if M'Lord has found the page?'

The Judge did a quick check with his Assessors and nodded. 'We've got it. Carry on.'

I returned my attention to Labuschagne. 'Can you confirm the details set out on that page?'

'Yes.' He paused for a moment. 'I was present when they came in.'

I stopped and waited while the Judge, the Assessors and the prosecutors studied the document. Their eyes darted across the rows and columns. One of the Assessors bit his lip. Then he looked at Labuschagne – for the first time, it seemed to me.

SERIAL NO	NAME	V-NO	PLACE SENTENCED	DATE	JUDGE	OUTCOME	DATE
4419	Alfred Tshu-peng	V3550	Johannesburg	23.6.86	O'Donovan	Executed	21.11.86
4420	Elvis Boima	V3551	Johannesburg	23.6.86	O'Donovan	Executed	21.11.86
4421	Selby Magubane	V3552	Pretoria	23.6.86	W Hartzen-berg	Executed	26.11.86
4422	Jonas Malatso	V3553	Pretoria	23.6.86	W Hartzen-berg	Executed	26.11.86
4423	Walter Mtshali	V3554	Pretoria	23.6.86	W Hartzen-berg	Executed	26.11.86
4424	Bafana Muneka	V3555	Pretoria	23.6.86	W Hartzen-berg	Executed	26.11.86
4425	Nicolas Mtshali	V3556	Pretoria	23.6.86	W Hartzen-berg	Executed	26.11.86
4426	Eric Ntsali	V3557	Cape Town	18.6.86	Baker	Executed	5.12.86
4427	Dawid Lourens	V3558	Mossel Bay	13.6.86	Williamson	Executed	03.04.87
4428	John Swarts	V3559	Cape Town	13.6.86	v. Schalkwyk	Executed	25.8.87

Judge van Zyl looked up, my signal to resume.

'Are these the ten prisoners who were admitted on your first day at Maximum?' I asked.

'Yes.'

'Before we move on to other matters, could you tell the Court how well you had got to know these men by the time they were hanged?'

'Very well,' he said.

I left the answer at that for the time being. It was one of the main themes of our case and I would have to explore it in more detail later.

I made eye contact with Labuschagne. 'What did you do with these prisoners after they had been given their v-numbers?'

'We gave them prison clothing and Bibles and short toothbrushes. The admin people took photographs of them. The Warrant Officer then told them the rules. After that we had to take them to their cells.'

'Could you please tell His Lordship and the Learned Assessors what the main rules were that were explained to the prisoners?'

I listened with half an ear as he spoke of supervised visits from their lawyers, their family and their pastors. The prisoners were not allowed to speak to anyone about their treatment in the prison. They could write and receive letters but the letters would be censored. They had to clean their own cells every day before the Major's rounds at ten o'clock. They had to address all warders as sir and had to stand up with their hands by their sides when spoken to by a warder. Under no circumstances were they to make eye contact with a warder. Any breach of these rules would result in a withdrawal of privileges. Their visits could be curtailed, their correspondence would be withheld and in severe cases they could be locked in isolation cells and put on a restricted diet. These were the official punishments, according to Labuschagne.

'Were there unofficial punishments?'

'Yes, sir.' I watched as he swallowed.

It was getting late in the day and we were all tired. I looked at my watch and when I looked up I saw the Judge also looking at the clock.

'To recap then, you were present when these prisoners were admitted and you were present when they were executed later?'

Labuschagne was caught off guard and took a moment to study the list again. 'Yes, I was.'

'How well did you get to know them before they were hanged?'

He swallowed again. 'Very well.' He was not comfortable with this subject, I thought.

'How did that happen?'

'I spent all my time with them.'

'Where were the other warders during those times?' I asked.

'They were in their own sections,' he said. 'Every warder is locked in with the prisoners in his own section.'

It was time to adjourn for the day but I wanted to get a last point in.

'And then, on the appointed day, you took them up to the gallows,' I suggested in a leading question.

The answer was monosyllabic. 'Yes.'

'You stood next to them as the ropes were put over their heads?'

'Yes.' Labuschagne licked his lips. I kept the pace up. He could have a drink of water after I had finished.

'And you went down into the pit and took them off the rope?'

'Yes.'

'And you put them in coffins, took them to the chapel, sat through a funeral service with their relatives and eventually went out and buried them?'

'Yes, and registered their deaths,' he added.

I could not resist the last question.

'You had read the Bible to these men, and then you took them up to be hanged?' It was another leading question but there was no objection.

'Yes.'

During the last few exchanges of questions and answers I had noticed that Judge van Zyl was watching me. I met his eye and asked if it would be convenient to adjourn to the next day.

'Very well,' he said, 'the Court is adjourned until ten tomorrow. The defendant is to remain in custody.' It was a ritual we went through every afternoon at the end of the day's work.

Labuschagne was taken back to his cell. Roshnee went over to speak to his parents. Antoinette Labuschagne and her parents were the last to leave the courtroom. They stood and watched in silence as Labuschagne was escorted down the staircase to Cell 6. I asked Wierda to comfort them and arranged to meet him at his chambers.

Roshnee returned to the hotel. She had to run her practice by telephone and fax machine. Her mother was looking after her children. I had given up trying to keep abreast of events in Durban.

Wierda's secretary brought us coffee as soon as we had sat down.

'What do you want me to do?' Wierda asked from the other side of his desk.

I explained.

'That sounds easy enough,' he said, taking a sip of coffee.

'Maybe, maybe not,' I ventured. I had more experience at this than he did – two cases, Moatche and Scheepers – but he would learn soon enough.

'Where do you want me to start?' asked Wierda, pointing at the file stacker filled with files identical to the ones standing on the floor of my hotel room.

I thought about it for a while. 'Let's do one together and see how it goes.'

'Fine,' he said, 'who's next?'

'Wessels,' I said as I pulled the file from the stacker.

We finished after dark and I badly needed a drink by then.

v3615 Johan Christiaan Wessels   15

Wessels was eighteen years old when, together with three older men – Christo Viljoen, Frederik Swanepoel and Michael Mynhardt – he was charged with two counts of robbery with aggravating circumstances, rape and murder. They had robbed two men and had gang-raped Miss Elizabeth Mokoena before Wessels and Viljoen murdered her.

During the evening of 10 January 1986 Wessels, Viljoen and Swanepoel went to a drive-in cinema in Bethlehem and watched the film *Mad Max* starring Mel Gibson in the title role. They had twenty-four beers and drank most of them there. Afterwards they went to a dance at Loch Athlone. There was an altercation between Viljoen and some other men at the dance. They went to Mynhardt's house where the drinking continued. They had a bottle of Klipdrift brandy with them and Mynhardt served more brandy from his own stock. They told Mynhardt of the trouble Viljoen had had at the dance. Viljoen asked Mynhardt to help them sort out those other men, who were thought to be soldiers from the Army base nearby. They left in Wessels' bakkie to look for them. The bakkie was too small to seat all of them in the front so two of them had to ride in the loading bin.

They had lost track of time at this point, but it must have been near midnight when they left Mynhardt's house. They were looking for trouble. They trawled through various parts of the town frequented by soldiers but could not find any. They were not looking for a specific soldier; any soldier would do for Viljoen's revenge. Eventually they found themselves at the area set aside as a taxi rank and bus stop. They turned their wrath on three innocent people waiting for a bus. They were the deceased, Miss Elizabeth Mokoena, and her two brothers, Mr Lesia Mokoena and Mr Petrus Nkomo.

Mynhardt started by saying that he and his friends were policemen and demanded to see their identity documents. The two men had theirs but their sister did not. Mynhardt said she should be taken to the police station. They forced Miss Mokoena into the loading bin of the bakkie and they drove off. Viljoen was driving, Mynhardt sat in the cab with him and Wessels and Swanepoel rode at the back with Mokoena. Mokoena's brothers were left at the bus stop. During the ride Wessels kicked Mokoena in the face for no reason. She pleaded with them. They drove to Loch Athlone on the Fouriesburg road. Viljoen stopped the bakkie at a secluded spot.

Mynhardt told Miss Mokoena to remove her clothes and she complied. Mynhardt then raped her. There was more drinking; they still had some of the Klipdrift and a litre of Coca-Cola left. Viljoen and Swanepoel then followed Mynhardt in raping the woman. Having done so they spurred Wessels on, calling him chicken. Finally he too then raped Miss Mokoena. When he had finished she said she was going to the police and got up. Wessels hit her on the back of her head with the empty Coca-Cola bottle. She was left there in a semi-conscious state as they drove off.

Mynhardt had to be back at work at six a.m. and asked them to take him home. They left him at his house. Wessels insisted on returning to the scene. They found Miss Mokoena on her knees, having recovered sufficiently from her ordeal to get up and to start dressing herself.

Wessels took a fishing knife from the glove box of the bakkie. Swanepoel told him not to stab her and tried to stop his friend, but Wessels ignored him. He walked over to Miss Mokoena and stabbed her six times, though one stab wound in her back was sufficiently mortal on its own, having punctured a lung. He then tried to cut her throat.

When they realised that she was still not dead Viljoen drove the bakkie over her. However, he failed to inflict any further injury because he had driven over her lengthwise, straddling her with the wheels. Wessels then took charge and drove over her twice, forwards and backwards, making sure that the wheels went over her each time.

They drove back to town. On the way Wessels ordered Viljoen to stop and he threw the knife into a pond. Having eventually gone their separate ways both went to bed.

Miss Mokoena's partly dressed body was discovered late in the afternoon. She was lying on her back with her left hand across her breast and her right arm raised, fist clenched. Some items of clothing were lying nearby. The cause of death was established to be bleeding and a collapsed lung.

On 16 January 1986 the four men surrendered themselves to the Bethlehem police. At their trial they raised three principal defences. They contended that they were so drunk that they could not form the requisite intent to rape and, in any event, alleged that Miss Mokoena had consented to intercourse. As far as the murder charge was concerned, Mynhardt's defence was that he had nothing to do with it; he had remained at his home when the other three went back to the scene. Swanepoel's defence was that he too had had nothing to do with the killing and that he even tried to stop Wessels from killing Miss Mokoena. Wessels and Viljoen contended that they had been too drunk to form the intention to kill. Viljoen had an additional defence: that his actions had not contributed in any way to Miss Mokoena's death.

The Court's verdict was that all four accused were not guilty on the robbery charges. On the rape charge all four were convicted. On the murder charge Wessels and Viljoen were convicted and Swanepoel and Mynhardt were acquitted.

Counsel for Wessels submitted that three circumstances separately and cumulatively constituted extenuating circumstances: (a) the fact that Wessels had been only eighteen years and four months old at the time, (b) his susceptibility to the influence of others, and (c) the degree of intoxication. In Viljoen's case, his lesser degree of participation, his relative youthfulness and the degree of intoxication were advanced as extenuating circumstances.

The Court concluded that extenuating circumstances had not been proved with regard to Wessels. In Viljoen's case, however, the Court found that extenuating circumstances were present in his youthfulness, the fact that he had acted on the impulse of the moment, that he had not physically caused Miss Mokoena's death, and that he had not been shown to have acted out of inherent wickedness.

On 2 October 1986 Wessels was sentenced to death and Viljoen to nine years' imprisonment. Each of the four accused was sentenced to eight years' imprisonment on the rape charge.

Wessels was twenty years old when he followed Scheepers onto the trapdoors.

Wierda and I made detailed notes about this case, mostly in the form of questions that had formed in our minds as we read the judgments and the submissions. We knew from what Labuschagne had told us that he had become attached to Wessels and we had to find a way to use that in his defence. What did the four men plot and discuss before they went to the police station to surrender themselves? Who had made the decision to surrender, to tell the police what had happened? Was the full truth ever told in Court, or was that a sanitised version put together to protect some of the others?

I also thought about Scheepers. There seemed to be no real basis for a comparison between him and Wessels. Scheepers had been the ringleader, a five-star psychopath, cruel, calculating and unrepentant. Wessels, on the other hand, appeared to have been a quiet, unassuming and withdrawn young man, a boy still on the verge of manhood. He had to be encouraged at the scene to participate in the rape of Miss Mokoena. The three other men were the leaders of the pack at that time and they were all older. Was Wessels trying to prove something to them? What turned Wessels into the leader when he returned to the scene with Viljoen? Whose idea had it been to return to the scene and kill Mokoena? When was that decision made?

I needed to understand why Wessels and the others had killed. What made them kill?

There was an obvious parallel between Wessels and Labuschagne, two young men from good homes who had started out as meek and well mannered but ended up killing. Was there a gang mentality in both cases? Did the teamwork of the hanging process turn Labuschagne into a killer even when on his own? The trial would provide some answers, but not clear answers.

By six o'clock we had run out of ideas and energy, and Wierda had a young family to tend, so we wrapped it up for the day. I called home and asked Liesl how the boys were. 'As usual,' she said, 'fighting half the time and playing together the other half.'

At least things were normal back at home.

Palace of Justice

16

I phoned my sister from Wierda's chambers.

'Annelise, are you going to invite me to dinner?'

'Yes,' she said, 'come over now and you and Pierre can do a braai. We have some nice warthog steaks and a fillet in the fridge.'

'Get the red wine out,' I said, 'I'll be there in ten minutes.'

Wierda dropped me off on his way home. I was still in my suit.

Pierre looked relaxed within the boundaries of his house and garden,

I thought. But as soon as he got to the other side of the fence he became restless and distressed, Annelise had told me.

I sat in Pierre's lapa and watched as he put the fire together with leadwood logs split into quarters. The coals would glow deep into the night. The lapa was built in the traditional African style, a low mud-brick wall with a wide gap for an entrance and a wavy thatched roof on creosote poles for privacy and protection from the sun. The braai was built into the outside wall of the lapa, with the thatch curving around well away from the flames.

I don't think I have ever seen a man with such strong and blond hair as Pierre's. His hair wasn't just blond, it was white, and it was thick and strong. Combined with his tanned skin and light-blue eyes his hair created a startling effect. I wouldn't like to get into a scrap with him.

Pierre didn't say much and I had a tough time making conversation. Some subjects were out of bounds but I felt I had to bring the conversation round to one that was of immediate interest to me.

'Pierre, tell me how it feels to be shot at,' I asked gingerly.

He stood up and came over to me. Without a word he took the wine glass from my hand and refilled it. I took a deep draught from the glass.

'It is better to shoot first,' Pierre said. He was looking into the fire.

'Even then, how does it feel when they shoot back?' I insisted.

'Shooting someone and being shot at are equally bad. The one is no better than the other.'

I knew he had killed in the war in Angola. I knew also that he never spoke about it, but I had to take the risk nevertheless.

'What does it feel like to kill someone?' I asked.

He stood bent over at the fire and looked at me over the curve of his shoulder. After a very long silence in which he held my gaze he said, 'You've asked me this before and I told you no one ever talks about it. That includes me.'

I knew I had to break through now or I would never get the door open.

'I know that,' I answered, 'but Pierre, please. I'm fighting for a man's life here. It is the opposite of killing. And I need to know what only you can tell me.'

'Why me?'

'Because I trust you. And because you can trust me.'

Then my instincts told me to go straight at him. 'Pierre, what is the worst killing you have ever done? Tell me.'

He pottered around the fire for a long time. I sipped my wine and watched. He wasn't doing anything specific or constructive; he was playing for time. Eventually I decided that the subject was too uncomfortable and that he was not going to answer. Annelise called me to fetch the meat from the kitchen. I was reluctant to leave the lapa and stood up slowly.

As I walked past Pierre, he said softly, his voice dropping, 'When I had to shoot a woman.'

I stopped in my tracks. 'When you did what?'

He repeated, louder, 'When I had to shoot a woman. That was the worst.'

I called to Annelise that I'd be there in a minute and sat down again, closer to Pierre.

'Can you talk about it?' I asked.

'No.'

He changed the subject, making small talk that continued after I'd fetched the meat until Annelise and the children came out to join us.

I renewed my attack on his reticence after we had eaten and Annelise and the children had left the lapa again. 'Pierre, how long have we known each other?'

He was looking up at the stars without answering me. No answer was needed because we had known each other from the time he was still at university and courting my sister. Now their children were in school already.

'You are going to have to talk to someone some time, and it might as well be me.'

He was obstinate. 'What if I don't want to talk?' he said with a note of belligerence.

'Ag kak, man!' I said.

He stirred the embers with the barbecue tongs. 'No really. What if I just don't want to talk?'

I had only one card and I'd already played it. 'What if I need help and only you can provide it?'

He did not look up from the fire. 'I am not ready to tell the whole story, and it might get you into trouble if they find out that I've told you.'

'Just tell me what you can, and let's take it from there.'

He started with a blunt statement.

'I'm not mad.'

I nodded. That much I knew.

Pierre dropped me off at the hotel much later, but there was still time to read another case and to make a summary of the salient facts. This time I was forewarned and ordered a bottle in advance. The hotel sent up an unremarkable Nederburg.

v3695 Jim Kgethang Mokwena

17

Mokwena faced four charges, two counts of murder and one each of robbery with aggravating circumstances and rape. He had robbed Mr and Mrs Dercksen on their smallholding, raped Mrs Dercksen and killed them both.

The Derckens were a retired couple who lived in the Bredell section outside Kempton Park. They kept much to themselves and the highlight of their week was Sunday afternoon when their sons and daughters came to visit with the couple's grandchildren. They kept a few animals, a milk cow and its calf, a heifer, some fowls and two dogs. At the time of his death Mr Dercksen was seventy-four years old and Mrs Dercksen sixty-nine.

Their daughter and son-in-law, Jan Venter, had visited them on Sunday 16 March 1986. Venter had spoken to the elderly couple the following Wednesday evening when they had telephoned to wish him a happy birthday. The Venters received their weekly milk supply from Mr

Dercksen; that was one of the reasons for their regular Sunday visits. When Venter arrived at the smallholding in the late afternoon of the next Sunday, 23 March, he noticed immediately that there was something wrong. The gate was hanging askew, its bottom hinge dislodged. A tree in the privet lane was broken. He found a short note written by one of the Dercksens' daughters pinned to the back door, to the effect that she had been there earlier in the afternoon but found her parents were away. On his arrival the cows had come running towards him and on closer inspection it became obvious that they had been without water for days. Venter immediately watered them. Then he noticed that the shed was locked, something his father-in-law had never done. A terrible smell emanated from the shed. One of the Dercksens' sons arrived and he and Venter forced entry into the shed. They found Mr Dercksen's body on the floor of the shed, partly covered by grass. A wire ligature was tied tightly around his neck. The body was already in an advanced state of decomposition.

Shocked by what they had found they started looking for Mrs Dercksen. They broke into the house and found that the telephone line had been cut. There were signs that someone other than the Dercksens had been in the house for some time. A suitcase packed with Mrs Dercksen's clothing was found in the bedroom. In the meantime more members of the family had arrived at the smallholding. Since they could not alert the police by telephone, they sent someone to the police station while others continued their frantic search for Mrs Dercksen. Someone spotted an area of recently disturbed ground near the cowshed. In that shallow grave they found Mrs Dercksen's body, no more than twelve metres from where her husband's body lay.

What happened to the Dercksens between Wednesday 19 March and Saturday 22 March 1986 was subsequently recounted by Mokwena:

I was arrested today and have made a mess. I have killed people. I found them at the house. I went into the house in the morning. I found the man at the cowshed. I grabbed him around the waist with my arms. I then picked up a rock and hit him with it while he was lying on the ground. He was bleeding. I then took a piece of wire from my pocket and tied it around his neck. After that I took grass and placed it on him. Then I took the lock and locked the cowshed. I walked away.

I then came across a white woman. She was afraid. I called her. She ran away. I prevented her from fleeing. I tripped her and she fell down. I pulled her to the house and locked the door.

I asked her where the money was and she kept quiet. I was sitting on top of her at this stage. I was holding her hands. I asked her again and she remained quiet. Then I throttled her. After I had throttled her, I had sexual intercourse with her. She held onto my body while I was lying on top of her. I then throttled her. She was stronger than I. She held onto my clothes. I hit her with my fists.

I had a rope in my pocket. I took it out and tied it around her neck. I let go of her for a while and she took a deep breath. She screamed. When I heard her screaming, I pulled the rope tighter. At this stage I put my foot on her and pulled the rope tighter. I then noticed that she had no strength left and her hands became limp. I pulled her under the bed. I lowered the blankets on the bed to the floor so that she could not be seen.

I then searched the wardrobe and removed some clothing that I put on the floor. There were jackets and dresses. I found a firearm in a pillowcase. There were two firearms; a big one and a small one. I planned to sell them but decided against that. I put the big one aside under the mattress. I took the small firearm to another room and put it under a pillow. I turned the television on. At that stage I made some porridge. I slaughtered a fowl and cooked it. I then watched some television.

I went to pack some clothing in a suitcase. While I was busy doing that, the dog barked and I went outside. I fed the dog. I went to the car as I wanted to drive it. I started it. The car could only go forward and I decided not to drive it because I would be arrested. I went to the other car and opened the hood. The battery was present but a certain wire had been cut. I looked for some wire and repaired the connection. I tried to start the car but it would not start. I then left it.

I went back into the house. I took the wheelbarrow and loaded the woman in it and went and buried her. I took the television set and went to sell it. I also sold the clothing at Tembisa. After selling these items, I went back to the house. I took some suitcases and sold them at Bredell. I stayed at the house the whole Saturday. I left early on the Sunday morning. In the afternoon I saw a car and returned. When I saw the car I ran away.

I later heard they were looking for me, but they did not tell me that. I then took other things there. The car was gone then. I then took these trousers, socks and shoes I'm wearing now. (Brown trousers, brown socks and brown shoes.) I took two blankets and went and sold them. I put my own shoes around the corner of the house. I burned my own trousers. I left my shirt in the toilet. I then put on another shirt. I decided to leave because I was afraid I would be caught. I locked the house and threw the key through the window.

I rambled about the smallholdings looking for liquor. The money ran out and I decided to look for work. I was thinking that I had done a strange thing. I looked for work at a certain Italian's place. That was the Wednesday. I encountered his wife and children. They ordered me to stop. I was afraid they would call the police. An old woman said I should come the next day. Then I came across the detectives. They were driving a white car. I thought they were looking for me but they drove past. I saw them going in at the Italian's place. I left and asked for a place to sleep. I slept.

The next day I went to the Italian. I went into an African woman's room. The Italian came and asked me if I was the one looking for work. I said yes. He left me and walked away. Then some other people came there and arrested me. I went with them and asked what I had done. I was afraid to tell them. I thought they were going to hit me. At the police station they said I must just tell the truth, they won't hit me. I said I would and told only the truth. A photograph had been taken of me. They asked if I was the person in the photograph. I said the photograph wasn't clear.

Then I was brought here. That is all.

On 16 February 1987 the Court convicted Mokwena on all four counts and imposed the death sentence on each of the murder charges, and ten years' imprisonment on each of the robbery and rape counts.

Mokwena was hanged with Moatche, Scheepers and Wessels on 26 November 1987. He was twenty-seven years old.

I tried to make sense of the four cases I had read.

What did these men have in common? Was there a pattern? I listed similarities and distinctions in my mind. Had there been mistakes in the tactics adopted by defence counsel in those trials and could Wierda and I avoid making them?

Moatche, Scheepers and Wessels had killed in gangs.

They were young men, in their late teens or very early twenties.

Wessels, I thought, had been quite drunk, but not so Moatche and Scheepers, and Mokwena had been stone cold sober.

Mokwena was a loner, but like the others he was a young man.

Scheepers, Wessels and Mokwena had also raped their victims. In each case the rape was across the racial divide. Scheepers and Wessels, white men, had raped African women. Mokwena, an African man, had raped a white woman.

I thought about motives.

Greed was present in the case of both Moatche and Mokwena.

And what about killing simply to avoid detection? Undoubtedly Scheepers and Wessels had done so. Mokwena also admitted as much.

It was more difficult to find a motive in the rape cases. What motive could a man have for rape?

Rape is a crime of violence, my professor had said, it does not belong in the chapter dealing with sexual offences. He was talking about his own book on criminal law.

If the professor was right, then Scheepers, Wessels and Mokwena were involved in some power play when they raped and killed their victims. I also thought about the apparent desire in all of these men to confess their crimes. Why would anyone in their position want to confess as soon as they are confronted by authority? Mynhardt had even gone to surrender himself at the police station and so had Wessels and his friends. Mokwena had made no real effort to escape.

In the end nothing made complete sense, but the one factor that stood out above all others was the utter contempt these men had for the lives of their victims. They were so bent on killing that they did not pay much heed to the danger to their own lives either.

It wasn't easy to work up any sympathy for the killers, but I worried that Labuschagne would soon join them in the registers.

DAY TWO

Defence: 5 October 1988
Execution: 3 December 1987

v3473 Kanton Klassop
v3564 Willy Jacob Mpipi
v3565 Johannes Mohapi
v3574 Johannes Stefanus Delport
v3680 Jomyt Mbele
v3681 Case Rabutla
v3682 Clifton Phaswa

18

The hanged men's relatives were escorted into the chapel as a gang of prisoners were let into A1 Section to clean the cells of the Pot and to gather the dead men's belongings. The cleaning gang considered themselves lucky as they were allowed to keep any consumables they found, such as a bit of tobacco, if they were lucky, or an unopened packet of biscuits. Prison gear like shoes and socks, underwear and pyjamas would be sent to the laundry to be recycled and issued to the next intake. Personal belongings would be bundled up and given to the relatives after the funeral service.

The chapel formed the hub linking the two wings of B Section and was situated in the shadow of the building housing the gallows and the pit.

> Nearer my God to Thee
> Nearer to Thee

The escorts sat in the back pews and sang and prayed with the bereaved, asking for peace in the afterlife, for love in the present one, and for salvation for those who had done what they had done. There was some sobbing, but for the most part the tears had been shed long before, during lonely nights in distant parts when the relatives of the condemned men had thought of their loved ones and had waited for this awful day to arrive. That day had now arrived in full. In a way it granted the relatives release, it freed them to think of happier times long gone when their sons and brothers were children doing the silly things that boys do to catch a parent's eye or to amuse a sibling.

The coffins lay side by side in front of the pews with name tags hanging from the handles and modest wreaths resting on the plain wooden lids. They took up the entire width of the room. The plain nondenominational chapel was full, with an escort and two relatives for each of the hanged men.

The solitary prisoner in the cell adjacent to the chapel could hear every note of the hymns and every word spoken by the parson. In fact, he could easily have led the sermon himself, having heard it so many times since he was transferred here when Maximum first opened its doors to receive the condemned. The admin staff in their offices in B Section preferred not to hear the inevitable crying and wailing and had retired to their common room for tea and biscuits as soon as the sermon began. For them these men would cease to exist as soon as the administrative processes were completed and their photographs were removed from the office wall.

There were two representatives of each family at the service and more family members were waiting in the parking area outside the main entrance. Trains from distant parts of the country had brought them here. The Department of Justice had paid for their tickets and for their overnight stay in cheap hotels. For most of them the train ride and the stay in a hotel were novel experiences. The train from Cape Town had taken two days to cover the one thousand eight hundred kilometres; the distance from the lower South Coast of Natal was only eight hundred kilometres but the journey had taken equally long as the elderly Zulu relatives of the condemned men had to catch a minibus from a distant rural area to Port Shepstone where they had to wait for the train to Durban, and then had to wait for the Johannesburg train that departed only the following day. Those who had come from the East Rand were used to train travel and had taken suburban metro trains and buses earlier in the morning.

The seven escorts sat in the back pews; they had to keep an eye on the coffins as much as on the visitors. The parson rambled on in English though none of those present, neither the visitors nor the escorts, was English speaking. God had forgiven these men, he declared, but no one believed him. The escorts had witnessed the manner of death and had seen the broken bodies. When the parson called for everyone to stand in prayer the escorts rose and bowed their heads with the families of the men they had helped to kill and then sang the last hymn with them.

The parson finally brought the proceedings to a close and the bereaved filed past, hands stroking the coffins in a final moment of intimacy.

In the main foyer an administration officer handed each family a small parcel containing the humble personal possessions of their departed relative, a Bible perhaps, and a few letters, the record of an appeal or a petition to the State President begging for mercy. The admin officer explained, through a warder acting as interpreter, that death certificates would be posted in a week's time, and that the family could apply for details of the grave number and site after five years.

Every item had to be signed for in the register.

The visitors were made to march to the exit at the main entrance in a column of two's, a posse of warders escorting them to the gate, the rifles on the guard towers aimed at them.

They comforted each other in the parking lot. Eventually the visitors left as quietly as they had come to this place, as mystified and bewildered as they had been when their sons were arrested and later sentenced to die. They were left to wonder if this was the way things were always destined to be, and never to know the answer. The hymn played over and over in their ears and would haunt them for a long time to come:

Nearer my God to Thee
Nearer to Thee

V3473 Kanton Klassop

19

Kanton Klassop was thirty years old when he faced charges of murder, rape, robbery with aggravating circumstances, two counts of housebreaking with theft, and arson. He insisted on conducting his own defence.

The events started on 11 March 1985 when the Smith family of Port Alfred left their home early in the morning. Mr and Mrs Smith went to work and their daughter went to school. When they returned later in the day they found that someone had broken into their house and had stolen some of their possessions. The burglar had smashed a window to gain entry. They reported the matter to the police and gave them a list of the stolen items.

On the morning of Friday 12 July 1985 Mrs Dorothy Gilder left for work. Her fifty-five-year-old domestic assistant, Mrs Girley Evelyn Ndzube, was left in charge of the house and was to engage in her usual household duties. Mrs Ndzube was to leave the key in a special hiding place when she had finished. However, when Mrs Gilder returned home in the late afternoon she found the house locked and the key not in its place. The kitchen window was open. Mrs Gilder called the neighbour's gardener and the young man climbed through the open window to unlock the doors. He found Mrs Ndzube's body on the floor in the kitchen. They called the police. There were signs of a violent struggle just inside the front door. The house had been ransacked.

Mrs Ndzube's body had been placed with her legs apart and a jersey and a brick over her private parts. A khaki jacket and a towel covered her head. When these were removed, she was seen to have suffered a number of chop-like blows of such severe force that the left side of her face and head was shattered. The blows had penetrated her skull and brain and completely destroyed the left eye and its socket. There was a pool of blood under her head. There were also signs that a ligature of some sort had been tied through her mouth and around the back of her head. There were injuries to her neck consistent with strangulation.

There were signs that the killer had prepared a meal for himself in the kitchen while his victim lay a few feet away.

The police gathered evidence from the scene. They found identifiable fingerprints on a powder-box on the dressing table in the bedroom, and on a cake tin, a wine carton and the bread knife in the kitchen. All of these items belonged to Mrs Gilder and had been in the house earlier in the day when she had left for work. They took blood samples and the pathologist took vaginal swabs and scrapings from under Mrs Ndzube's fingernails. These would later prove to be inconclusive.

The next day Mrs Gilder and some family members cleaned the house. Her son-in-law found the murder weapon under the bed in Mrs Gilder's bedroom. It was a heavy meat cleaver. Tied to its handle was a school tie taken from the Smith's house on 11 March. Blood traces on the cleaver matched Mrs Ndzube's blood type. Mrs Gilder found that some items were missing from the house; these included a rare torch and siren combination her son-in-law had given her for use in case of an emergency.

On 13 July 1985 the Smith family returned from an outing and found that their house had been broken into a second time. Various items including foodstuffs, bedding and crockery had been taken. Fires had been started in two separate places in the house and had caused some damage but had somehow been extinguished. Outside the broken window they found a torch and siren combination that did not belong to them. They again made a list and reported the matter to the police. The police took possession of the torch. Mrs Gilder and her son-in-law were able to identify it as the one that had been taken from her house the previous day.

Klassop was arrested on 16 July 1985. He was living in the wild in a shelter behind some bushes although he also had a room at his mother's house.

Klassop had no answer to the circumstantial evidence. His finger-prints matched those taken at the scene of the murder. A number of items taken from the Smiths' house during the two burglaries had been found in his possession. The explanations he gave were demonstrably false in a number of respects.

The evidence suggested that Klassop must have entered Mrs Gilder's house through the front door. Mrs Ndzube must have resisted him as signs of a violent struggle were found just inside the front door. Klassop was armed with the meat cleaver. He had carried it to the scene tied around his waist with the tie he had previously stolen from the Smiths. It could easily be concealed under his shirt or coat in that manner. The struggle had continued towards the kitchen. There Klassop put the tie around Mrs Ndzube's face to overpower her and to stop her from calling for help. He then struck Mrs Ndzube with a brick and with the meat cleaver until she was dead.

Klassop then searched the house and prepared to take a number of items with him. In the process he handled the items on which his finger-prints were subsequently detected. He took some food and ate some of it in the kitchen and the rest in the bedroom. Before he left he wiped the blade of the meat cleaver and threw it under the bed. He left the house after taking more food, a radio and tape combination, a towel and Mrs Gilder's torch. There were indications that he had been disturbed before he could gather everything he had wanted to take. Some things were found wrapped in a bedspread in the bedroom. He had finished some wine too; the empty container was also found under the bed. The next day Klassop took the torch to the Smith's house when he went to burgle it for the second time. He left the torch under the window by mistake.

The Court acquitted Klassop on the rape count but convicted him as charged on the other counts. Klassop admitted to a long list of previous convictions. He was a serial burglar. All his recorded crimes had been committed in Port Alfred. The local police must have known him well.

There were no extenuating circumstances. The Judge sentenced him to death on the murder count, to twelve years' imprisonment on the robbery count, to three years on each of the housebreaking counts, and to three years on the arson count.

Klassop arrived in Pretoria on 11 February 1986. Six weeks later he changed his mind about legal representation. It would take nineteen months before his final appeal was rejected.

He was hanged on 3 December 1987. He was recorded as being thirty-two years old, although his criminal record suggested that he might well have been a few years older than that.

Palace of Justice

20

The Court started on the stroke of ten. Judge van Zyl and his Assessors took their seats after the officials and the legal teams all bowed to them. The registrar reminded Labuschagne that he was still under his former oath. I muttered the customary 'May it please M'Lord' and turned to face the witness box squarely.

We needed to place more of the dreary background material before the Court, but the day would include some contentious evidence about the prison layout and routine. Wierda and I had anticipated some resistance to our next line of questioning and I needed to introduce the topic carefully.

'I need to discuss with you the daily routine of the prisoners so far as you were involved. I am going to start with ordinary days; we can deal with your activities on execution days and on days immediately before execution days later.'

Labuschagne nodded. I waited a moment for an objection but there was no movement from James Murray and the Judge did not stir either.

'What was the daily routine in Maximum?' I asked.

Labuschagne looked refreshed after his night in the cells. He wore a dark suit, a clean white shirt and a black tie. The shirt was a size too big and the tie drew the points of the collar together, almost completely hiding the knot at his throat.

'It starts with the bell at six,' he said. 'The prisoners have to get up then, dress in their day uniforms and tidy their cells. They have to wait in their cells until seven. At that time the day-shift warders come on duty and do the roll call.'

'What duties did you perform during that hour?' I asked. I wanted the evidence to concentrate not so much on the prisoners but on a warder's activities.

'It depends on your duty allocation for the day. You stand at a door with its key and let people in and out, or you stand around in the sections. Every time a prisoner moves to another place you have to search him on this side and they search him on that side. Apart from that there is nothing to do.'

The answer was incomplete and I had to prod him a little. 'And what would you be doing during that time if you had been posted to one of the guard towers or to the catwalks above the cells?'

He frowned before he spoke. 'There is nothing to do in the guard towers. You just sit there with your rifle and wait for your shift to end. On the catwalks you have to patrol.'

I glanced at Judge van Zyl. He was watching Labuschagne without taking notes. Before I could speak again, Labuschagne said, 'That's about it. There is nothing much to do on those days.' He shrugged his shoulders as he said it.

'Could you describe the general layout of the place, please?' I asked.

Murray was caught off guard and his objection came belatedly. 'With respect, M'Lord, the layout of the prison is not relevant to any issue in the case.'

'I would have thought so myself,' said the Judge before I could respond. I took a moment before I answered.

'The defence centres on the defendant's state of mind at the time of the events at the reservoir. The prison environment is relevant to that. It is important for a proper understanding of the defence case to know what happened to him in the different parts of the prison. We do not intend to compromise the security of the prison.'

Judge van Zyl did not bother to make a ruling. 'Carry on,' he said.

I repeated the question. We'd received a detailed description on the interior of the prison.

there were three cellblocks, A, B and C sections.

Most prisoners were in A Section, which had three blocks or wings. There were about fifty-five single cells in each wing of A Section and about half a dozen communal cells. Each of the communal cells accommodated about five men. Each block also had a padded soundproof isolation cell where they put troublesome prisoners. The individual cells were about two metres by three, with a steel door. At about head height there was a grille with steel bars in each door. Every cell had a wooden bunk fixed to the wall and a wooden flap serving as a table. There was a toilet and a radio speaker mounted on the wall. The catwalk where the warders did their rounds was above the cells and protruded some distance over the cell so that the warder on the catwalk could look down into the cell. There was a barred window between the cell and the catwalk, quite high up.

The Judge looked down at James Murray and asked, 'Are we going to have an inspection of the prison?'

'Not as far as I know,' said Murray, half rising from his seat and glancing in my direction.

'We think it would be very helpful, M'Lord,' I said. 'It is crucial to the defence that the Court should be aware of the atmosphere that prevails in the prison. It may also be helpful for the Court to see the various parts of the prison where the defendant worked and where important events occurred.'

'Well, we might have to inspect the prison in order to follow the evidence in any event,' the Judge explained.

Murray was not convinced. 'Could we perhaps present Your Lordship with a plan of the prison and perhaps some photographs?' Niemand handed him a note.

'On second thought, M'Lord,' Murray said quickly after reading it, 'it may not be a good idea to distribute plans and photographs of the prison. May I take the matter up with the authorities during the next adjournment and advise M'Lord of their attitude?'

'You may carry on,' the Judge said, nodding in my direction. 'We may have to reconsider the issue later depending on how the evidence develops.'

I rose to my feet and placed my trial notebook back on the lectern.

'Mr Labuschagne, we were dealing with the routine in the prison and you have mentioned the roll call at seven. Who conducted the roll call and how was it done?' I asked.

None of the important details of the warders' confinement with the prisoners had been exposed during the prosecution evidence earlier and I wanted to show the Court how boring their existence was on days when no hangings were scheduled compared to the high drama of hanging days. It was either boredom or high anxiety.

The Judge suddenly leaned forward. 'Has there ever been a case where someone was missing?' he asked. He continued before anyone could respond. 'Didn't Vontsteen get out?'

'Sir, that happened long ago. The Warrant Officer said only two men ever escaped and he said they had been allowed to escape by corrupt warders.'

We must have looked doubtful, for Labuschagne added, 'You can't escape from there unless they let you out. They would have to unlock about six or seven different grilles or doors for you. Every door has a warder with a key. You can't get from the cell to the catwalk and any prisoner in that space will be shot immediately. The warders in the guard towers have orders to shoot anyone in the yard that is not with a warder.'

The Judge was intrigued by this. 'So the only way a prisoner can leave the prison is if he is released through the front guardhouse or if he goes through the gallows chamber?'

Labuschagne disagreed. 'Four were shot trying to escape, and there have been suicides.'

Wierda came to life next to me and slipped me one of the registers. It was opened at a page in 1962. I did not have a chance to look at the details.

'How do you know this?' the Judge wanted to know.

'It is in the registers. And we often spoke about it.'

I asked Labuschagne to deal with the issue of the keys.

The keys to the cell were locked in the safe at night. Only the Warrant Officer could open the safe between lock-down at night and roll call in the morning. He alone carried the keys to the safe.

One of the Assessors sought the Judge's attention. After a whispered conference between them the Judge turned to the witness box and asked, 'But what would you do if there was a fire?'

'If there is a fire in one of the cells we can put it out from above, from the catwalk. But we cannot get into the cell without the key.' Labuschagne was speaking in the present tense but I was more interested in the past.

'What were your duties after the roll call?' I asked him.

He spoke quickly, reciting the relevant details as if he were a tour guide. The cells were unlocked at quarter-past seven. When the prisoners came out of their cells, they were searched. They went to the showers in batches of about eleven. They were searched before and after they had their showers. Each batch had five minutes for this. Then it was back to the cells for them. They were expected to spend the day reading their

Bibles. They had breakfast in their cells, porridge and coffee, at about eight o'clock. After that there was a medicine round. A medic came around asking if anyone needed medicine and handed out sleeping pills. The Major did an inspection round at ten o'clock and saw every prisoner every day.

'What arrangements were made for the prisoners to get some exercise?' I asked.

The prisoners were allowed to exercise in the hall after the inspection round. They were allowed to walk but not to run or do exercises. At the end of each block of A Section was an exercise yard. Prisoners were taken there in small groups with two warders to each prisoner. They were searched going out and again coming in. Outside they were allowed to walk in a circle for an hour a day.

'Were you involved in that?' I asked Labuschagne.

'Yes, sir.'

'So what do you do during the hour that they exercise?'

He sighed. 'You stand and watch.'

I changed the subject. 'What about visitors? Are the prisoners allowed to receive visits?'

'Yes, if they have not been stripped of privileges. Visiting is from nine till eleven in the morning and again from two to three in the ... '

'For what reasons could they be stripped of privileges?' I interrupted without an apology.

He returned to the theme. 'We search them before they enter the visiting room, the prisoners and the visitors. Then we search the prisoners again when we take them back to their cells.'

'Yes,' I said as if the searching did not matter, 'but what about the loss of privileges? What offences could trigger a loss of privileges?'

He rattled off the Warrant Officer's rules. 'No talking between five-thirty in the morning and five-thirty in the evening. No talking in the showers. No swearing at warders. No touching a warder. No running. Stand still when spoken to and look at the ground ...' He paused for a moment. 'There were lots of other rules.'

'And what did you do during a visit by their family or lawyer?'

'You watch and listen.'

I suggested a new topic. 'Tell us about the routine for the rest of the day, from eleven onwards.'

Labuschagne spoke about a cleaning squad moving around polishing floors, with the warders watching. Everything had to be done in absolute silence. Lunch was the main meal and was served between twelve and one. Supper was at three-thirty.

I decided to cut the evidence short. 'What duties did you have to perform while the prisoners were going about cleaning the place or having their meals?'

'We watch.'

'During all of this, from sunrise until after supper, did anyone in the sections speak?'

Labuschagne looked up in surprise. 'There is no talking from sunrise to sunset.'

I feigned ignorance. 'Do you mean there was no talking by the prisoners?'

'No,' he said. 'The warders too. We are not allowed to speak to the prisoners except to give them orders or to help them with their Bible study.'

'Did you say the prisoners got their supper at three-thirty in the afternoon?' I asked.

'Yes, the day shift goes out at four and by that time supper has to be over and the prison in lock-down for a roll call.'

'Please continue. What happens after supper?'

Judge van Zyl intervened without a glance in my direction. 'What's all this searching about? How many times a day *do* you search the prisoners?'

'We search them every time they come out of their cells and every time they go back in.'

'Well tell me, how many times would that be in an ordinary day?'

Labuschagne thought about it for a while. 'It could be between twelve and twenty times, depending on whether there is a visit or a haircut.'

The Judge nodded in my direction, so I took over again.

'And after the day shift has gone, what happens then?' I was interested in the nights.

'The prisoners are locked in their cells and may write and read. They can get reading material from the library or buy their own from the tuck shop. After five-thirty they may talk but the bell rings for bedtime at eight o'clock. Then they have to be in their beds.'

'What time is lights out?' I asked with an eye on the Judge.

'Oh, come on!' said the Judge from the back of his chair. 'Everyone knows they never turn the lights off in that place.'

I did not wait for an answer.

'How did you participate or to what extent did you participate in the daily activities of the prisoners?' I needed to stress an important aspect of the defence case.

'Well,' he said and bit his lip, 'I'm with them all day.'

'Could you elaborate on that, please?' I asked. Why did I have to drag it out of him? 'Tell the Court about the things you did with the prisoners.' I let the ambiguous question hang in the air.

'I am with them all the time. I sometimes help them read the Bible. I speak to some of them during the evening shifts when they are allowed to talk, but that is all. Most of the time I just stand and watch.' His recital was as boring as his shifts on non-hanging days must have been.

It was a game of watching and waiting.

'How well did you get to know them then?' I asked.

There was no pause. 'By the time we hang them we know them very well.'

Were we still in different tenses. The thought crossed my mind that by using the present tense Labuschagne was dissociating from the past. It was time for a break. Before I could ask my next question the Judge asked, 'Would this be a convenient stage to take the short adjournment?'

He looked surprised when I did not immediately agree. 'I wonder, M'Lord, if we could perhaps deal with one more topic? It should take no longer than five minutes.'

He nodded. I wanted to strike a solid blow before the tea break.

'What happened just before you came off duty on your *first day* in Maximum?'

Labuschagne took a deep breath before he answered. 'The Warrant Officer asked me to come with him. He took me to A1 Section. There were seven prisoners there. He told me to look in through the small window. I looked inside. Pick one, he said. I did not understand what he meant. He said, Pick one, because you are going to escort one of them when we hang them tomorrow. I said no, I'd rather that he just give me one, but he said it was tradition that the new boy had to pick one. I said I would take the first one. Then he said that it wasn't such a good idea to take the first one for my first hanging, as I would have to learn what to do by watching what the other escorts did. He said, Take the last one. I said that was okay, but I did not know which of them was the last one. He told me to be at his office at six o'clock the next morning. He said that the escorts had to come in early on hanging days.' This was one of the prepared answers and he gave it well.

It was time to finish off this topic.

'Did he tell you what you were to do the next day?' I asked.

'No, he said I must watch the others.'

'Did he show you where the gallows chamber was and what you had to do there?'

'No.'

I turned to the Judge. 'We are ready to take the adjournment now, M'Lord.'

The courtroom had become very quiet; there was none of the usual shuffling and sniffing or coughing.

What a job! What a first day! I wanted them to think. And what a second day to look forward to!

Judge van Zyl looked at me for a long time before he said, 'The Court adjourns for half an hour.' Then he rose abruptly and left.

In the robing room I looked at the page in the register Wierda had moved under my nose during the evidence. There were post-it notes against four names:

NO	DATE	NAME OF PRISONER	JUDGE	PLACE	OUTCOME	DATE
1163	27.4.62	Philemon Mhlungu	Kennedy	Durban	Fatally shot in attempt to escape	30.9.62
1166	27.4.62	Titus Malinga	Kennedy	Durban	Fatally shot in attempt to escape	30.9.62
1196	14/6/62	Sam Ndlovu	Snyman	Johannesburg	Fatally shot in attempt to escape (Died 2/10/62)	30.9.62
1219	25/8/62	Robert Shangase	Caney	Durban	Fatally shot in attempt to escape	30.9.62

These four at least did not go without a fight. I closed the register and decided after tea to ask Labuschagne to talk about the use of violence by warders and resistance from prisoners.

The robing room was deserted. I was stiff from standing for the past hour and more. I sat on the table, swinging my legs and turning my torso from side to side to relax the strained muscles. Wierda asked if I was ready to discuss the next case. I was.

He opened his notes and handed me a copy of the indictment. 'This was a cell murder case,' he said. 'It happened in Leeuwkop.'

There was nothing to it, a cell murder. Everyone in the profession knew that no power on this planet could save a man who has killed another prisoner.

I had been to Leeuwkop many years earlier. I remembered that visit too. I had been on a prosecutors' training course in Pretoria. Our instructors had taken us to Leeuwkop to see where those we had prosecuted would go after they had received their sentences. I read the indictment and as Wierda spoke the smell of Leeuwkop came back to me: soap, wax polish, Brasso, sweat and stale tobacco – not from cigarettes but pipe tobacco smoked in rolled brown paper.

I didn't know it then but what I had thought was the sweet smell of the oily brown paper was the smell of cannabis oil, the soporific of the prisoner.

v3564 Willy Jacob Mpipi
v3565 Johannes Mohapi

Five men were charged with the murder of their cell mate in Leeuwkop Prison, situated between Johannesburg and Pretoria. They were Willy Mpipi, Johannes Mohapi, Ben Wesie, Jabulani Dube and Daniel Koopa. Mpipi and Mohapi were in their mid-forties, the others in their early thirties. They had killed Johannes Modise during the night of 18 December 1984.

This had happened in Cell 4 of c Section in Leeuwkop Prison. c Section is the maximum-security section of Leeuwkop. At six o'clock in the evening of 18 December 1984 eighteen long-term prisoners were locked in Cell 4 for the night. These men had been in prison so long that it had become their natural habitat. Almost all of them were members of prison gangs. Within the militaristic subculture of a gang there were ordinary members and officers of different ranks. Mohapi was a senior officer in the Big Fives gang, the Big Boss, or President, of the gang. His co-accused were all members of the Air Force 3 gang. Mpipi was a *colonel*, Dube was a *chief inspector* and the other two were ordinary *airmen*. There were also members of the 26s, the 28s and the Air Force 4 gang in the cell. Prisoners belonged to gangs for protection and survival. The price they paid for this protection was unquestioning loyalty to the gang and absolute obedience to the gang leaders.

The deceased, Johannes Modise, was placed in Cell 4 for the first time that afternoon. He was only twenty-two years old and had become Mohapi's personal sex slave. Modise had tried to leave the 28s. The punishment for leaving or attempting to leave is often death, slowly and brutally meted out in front of as many other inmates as possible, for maximum deterrent effect. When Mohapi learned of Modise's defection, he arranged for Modise to be transferred to Cell 4. It is not clear why he plotted to kill Modise for defecting from the 28s.

Shortly after six o'clock, after the cell had been locked for the night a gang meeting, or a skumba, was called for the members of the Air Force 3 gang and Mohapi of the Big Fives. The meeting was attended by Mpipi, Wesie, Dube, Koopa and Mohapi. At the time of the meeting Wesie, a common soldier in the Air Force 3 gang, was in trouble of his own. He had warned another prisoner, Thomas Mathebula, that he was about to be killed by the Air Force 3 gang and Mathebula, thus forewarned, had made arrangements to be transferred to another cell. Mathebula's crime had been to obliterate his Air Force 3 gang tattoo on the inside of his arm and replace it with that of another gang. Because of his betrayal, Wesie was given a choice: he would be killed unless he played his part in killing Modise.

The plan was simple. Modise was to be called over and would then be killed. Mpipi would grab him by the neck and Wesie was to hold his legs.

Mpipi called Modise over. He had chosen the spot very carefully: that small area against the door where they would be out of the sight of the warders on the catwalk. He asked Modise to sit down and as he did so Mpipi and Wesie grabbed him as planned. Mohapi, Dube and Koopa then trampled Modise until he no longer moved. Then Mpipi and Wesie also trampled him. Mpipi then called another inmate to come over and told him to make a bed for Modise. Mpipi and Mohapi laid Modise's lifeless body on it.

When the bell rang at seven o'clock, signalling bedtime, Mpipi heard some noises from the deceased's bed and went over and lifted the blanket, exposing Modise's upper body. Mpipi called Wesie over and said, 'The dog is still alive.' A death rattle escaped Modise's throat. Mpipi ordered Wesie to stomp on Modise's neck, which he did. Mpipi then ordered Wesie back to his bed and Wesie complied.

A while later Modise's death rattle started again. This time Mohapi came over to Mpipi, who took a belt from another inmate and said to Dube that they were going to strangle Modise with it. Dube said, 'No, don't do it,' but Mpipi paid him no heed and Mohapi and he went on to strangle Modise with the belt. Mohapi then lay down next to the body and slept.

The killing had taken almost an hour. The next morning Mohapi took the bloodstained belt from Modise's neck and handed it to Koopa. They flushed it down the toilet after Koopa had cut it up with a razor blade.

When the cell was unlocked for breakfast, Warrant Officer Mkatshwa immediately asked why the deceased was not up. Mpipi said that Modise had sworn at him. Mkatshwa asked if that was reason enough to kill a man. There was no reply. He then asked the prisoners in the cell who had taken part in the killing to step aside and to hand over their prison tickets. Each prisoner had a ticket with his name, prison number and date of release. In prison this served as an identity document. The five accused stepped aside and handed over their tickets. In the culture of the prison, this was as unequivocal an admission of guilt as the circumstances allowed.

They were later formally arrested and taken to court for a first appearance.

The post-mortem examination on Modise's body revealed an inordinately large number of injuries. He had not died easily or quickly. He had suffered multiple injuries, spread across the face and head, his neck and his upper torso. Internal injuries corresponded with the external signs of trauma. There were eleven separate injuries to the face and head alone, to the left and right cheekbones, above the left eye, both eye sockets and both sides of the face, to the left ear, lower jaw, both sides of the neck, and to the throat extending into the chest area below the neck. Internally there were large amounts of blood in the muscles of the chest and all the strap muscles on the right side. There was severe internal bruising of the muscles of the neck and of the back. There was a swelling of the brain. The lungs were filled with blood and the muscles of the heart were bruised. The liver was congested with blood and the left kidney showed some bruising.

The trial was a farce, a condition into which many trials involving prison gangs and cell murders degenerate. Wesie raised the defence of coercion. He pleaded that he had been forced to participate in the attack on the deceased. The test for this defence to succeed was whether the evil threatened to the person who claimed coercion as an excuse for killing weighed up equally to the evil done. There was good legal precedent for this principle.

The Court found Wesie's evidence to be true in substance and found him not guilty on the basis that he had acted under coercion. The other four accused were convicted, Mpipi and Mohapi of murder and Dube and Koopa of assault with intent to do grievous bodily harm.

Each of the men had a long list of prior convictions. Each of them had previously been convicted of offences involving serious violence. Mpipi, Mohapi and Dube had killed before. Mohapi had been previously sentenced for trampling a fellow prisoner to death, and was serving that very sentence when he participated in Modise's murder. Mpipi had previously kicked a man to death in the cells. Dube had twice been convicted of murder; the second had been a cell murder.

The Judge sentenced Mpipi and Mohapi to death as there were no extenuating circumstances. Dube and Koopa received two years' imprisonment each for assault with intent to do grievous bodily harm.

On 27 November 1987 Mpipi and Mohapi were informed by the Sheriff that they were to be hanged on 3 December 1987.

They had been in the death cells for a year and four months. Mpipi was forty-eight years old and Mohapi forty-nine.

There was still some time left before we had to be back in court. I asked Wierda, 'Do the judges in this division regard being sworn at as sufficient provocation to constitute an extenuating circumstance?' I was grasping at straws. In my division it would count for nothing.

'Why are you so concerned about these people?' he asked with a sweep of his arm. 'There is nothing you can do except getting rid of them for good.'

I was staring in the distance and did not concentrate on Wierda's words.

'They kill even in prison,' Wierda continued, speaking more to Roshnee than to me, as we were making our way back to court. 'You can see that prison is no deterrent to them and no safeguard for us.'

I did not know what to say and Roshnee had given up arguing with Wierda. We crossed the street in silence, but the case had planted a seed of hope in my mind. The decision on the absence of extenuating circumstances in the prison murder case had been a majority decision, which meant that either the Judge or one of the Assessors had felt that the conditions in the prison were so degrading and inhuman that the actions of the killers were, from a moral point of view, less blameworthy. I immediately decided to concentrate our efforts even more on the special circumstances prevailing in Maximum, but I was not sure how Judge J P van Zyl would react to that.

According to his record of previous convictions Koopa had stood trial in c Court at the Palace of Justice in 1981. I remembered graffiti with his name on the wall in Cell 6 but I would have had to revisit the cell to recall its detail:

DANIEL KOOPA WAS HERE
DANIEL KOOPA
3/9/81 = 19 YEARS
6-10-81 = 29 YEARS
TOTAL = 48 YEARS

When we were seated at the defence table waiting for the Judge and his Assessors to make their entrance I asked Wierda to remind me to concentrate more on the Assessors. Anonymous though they were – I had forgotten their names as soon as we had left the Judge's chambers after the introductions of the first day – they could swing a decision in our favour, or against us should we have persuaded the Judge but not them. Their votes carried exactly the same weight as that of the Judge on questions of fact. Winning 2–1 would be good enough for us, and it did not matter how the majority was made up.

Palace of Justice

22

'Tell us in your own words what happened the second day after your arrival at Maximum Security Prison, Mr Labuschagne. Start from the time you went on duty.'

Labuschagne squared up.

'I was there just before six. The Warrant Officer inspected us in the passage. He put me fourth in the line. He told us to follow him. He went into A1 Section. He unlocked the cells one by one. Each of us stood at the door of our prisoner's cell. The Warrant Officer came and stood next to me. He told my prisoner to dress in his day clothes but without shoes or underpants. When the prisoners were dressed they came out and we lined up behind the Warrant Officer. He told me to take my prisoner by the arm and to follow. We came to the table in the passage.'

So far he was following Wierda's instructions, but I still expected him to let us down.

We were into the second day of the defence case and I would have expected James Murray and Sanet Niemand to have prepared overnight to counter what we had produced and to prepare themes for their cross-examination. They were both working with their heads down, scribbling furiously as the evidence was given. Apart from saying good morning we had not exchanged any words.

There was a man sitting in the row behind the prosecutors whom I had not previously seen. He looked like a policeman, tough and hard, with his jaw set square and with strong, thick-fingered hands. He had not taken an overt part in the proceedings, although Murray and Niemand spoke to him from time to time. I thought that he might be a prosecution expert, someone who would be called to rebut the evidence of the defence experts. I decided to keep an eye on him.

'What happened there outside the office?' I asked Labuschagne.

'The prisoners were fingerprinted. They also checked their photographs.'

'Could you look at the register and give us the v-numbers of the prisoners? Don't mention their names,' I cautioned.

'Yes.' Labuschagne read the numbers quickly.

I looked up at the bench. 'M'Lord, we have prepared an extract from the different pages of Exhibit G. I ask leave to hand up a copy.'

Judge van Zyl merely nodded and I handed copies of the list to the usher. He went round to the prosecutors and the registrar and handed them out.

SE-RIAL NO	NAME	V-NO	PLACE SENTENCED	DATE	JUDGE	OUT-COME	DATE
4299	Willem Scheepers	V3430	Grahamstown	29.10.85	Cloete	Executed	24.6.86
4300	Matthews Maluleka	V3431	Johannesburg	31.10.85	Heyns	Executed	24.6.86
4316	Zathini Mduduzi Shange	V3447	Durban	29.11.85	Shearer	Executed	24.6.86
4317	Aaron Mzamo Mhlungu	V3448	Durban	29.11.85	Shearer	Executed	24.6.86
4319	Lawrence Tuntubela	V3450	Cape Town	29.11.85	Van den Heever	Executed	24.6.86
4320	Hendrik Fielies	V3451	Cape Town	29.11.85	Van den Heever	Executed	24.6.86
4333	Anthony Fredericks	V3464	Cape Town	18.10.85	Lategan	Executed	24.6.86

I waited while Judge van Zyl and his Assessors read the extract. When the Judge looked up from the page and nodded, I turned my attention back to the witness box.

'Mr Labuschagne, could we return to the events in the passage outside the office? What did you do after the fingerprinting had been completed?'

'We took them to the chapel and they had a church service. After the service we lined them up and handcuffed their hands behind their backs. I just did what the others did. The Warrant Officer walked with us and checked everything and gave orders. The Sheriff came up too. We went up the stairs to the first room before the gallows. I just followed the others. The prisoners were difficult and we had to push and drag some of them to get them to the top floor. At the top we put them in a line against the wall. The Warrant Officer told them to turn and face him and he checked their photographs again. The Sheriff asked them if they had last statements or requests and he made notes. Then we took them through to the gallows room.'

It was necessary to make some of the main points of the defence case in a more dramatic fashion and I broke the chronology of events to achieve that.

'Had you been up to the gallows room previously?' I asked.

'No.'

'Had you received any training for what you were about to do?'

'No.'

'Had you been screened or assessed in any way to ensure that you were suitable for the job you were about to do?'

'No.' He shook his head.

'Were you given any choice with regard to the question of whether you were willing to do this work or not?'

Labuschagne looked puzzled. 'No,' he said finally.

'How many days had you worked there when you were called upon to help hang these men?'

'One.' His voice was tight.

I kept up the pressure. 'Please describe your reaction, your feelings, how you felt when you entered the gallows room.'

Labuschagne looked up at the crest above the canopy over the bench. All eyes were on him. The Judge had put his pen down and the two Assessors were watching Labuschagne in identical poses, their heads inclined slightly backwards. Judge van Zyl was leaning into his chair.

Labuschagne's sigh could be heard in the public gallery. His knuckles were white on the front of the witness box. He spoke softly.

'The ropes were right there at about eye level. That's what I saw first as we walked in. When I looked down I saw the little feet painted on the trapdoors. Then I tried to look away but the ropes were right next to my face. I felt my prisoner shiver in my hand. He walked slower. They all slowed down. I felt dizzy. Then the man behind me bumped into me and I had to keep walking forward. I walked my prisoner further onto the trapdoors. Then we stopped again.'

He stopped speaking and I decided to help him a little.

'Take your time,' I suggested. 'Speak when you feel ready.'

He stood completely still. I thought of the demons that had to be raging inside him. I found that I had synchronised my breathing with his, taking deep breaths and exhaling slowly. We stood like that for a minute or more. When he spoke again his voice had dropped to hardly more than a whisper but the Judge did not have to ask him to speak up. The courtroom was absolutely silent.

'I was right next to one of the ropes. I could smell it. It was like a wet doormat. It was frayed. I tried not to look but it was there, right in my face. I couldn't hear anything except a rushing noise in my ears. Everything was hazy. I felt the whole of my left arm shaking. I don't know if it was the prisoner shaking like that or whether it was me.'

Labuschagne demonstrated with his arm, as if holding onto his imaginary prisoner.

'A man came moving up the line from the back, on the left side. I was afraid. When the man stood next to my prisoner he put the rope around the prisoner's neck and pulled the white hood down over his face. Then he went to the ones in front. It felt as if my prisoner was falling and I held him tighter.'

We waited for him to continue. I wanted him to tell as much of his story in his own words and at his own pace as he could.

'Suddenly there was a loud noise and he just disappeared. The one moment I was holding onto him and the next he was gone. I felt as if I was falling too. I fell against the rail and held on.'

I intervened. 'How did you experience the execution from that moment on?'

Labuschagne spoke fast. 'I saw his head just below my feet, with all the others. They were hanging there and turning. I looked up and saw everyone looking at me. The other warders and the Warrant Officer were looking at me and they were smiling. I looked down again but there were the prisoners, turning on the ropes and with the white hoods over their heads. Their heads were pointing to the side, the right side, at an angle. I couldn't look anymore. The Warrant Officer came up to me. You'll be okay, he said. Don't look down. Just breathe deeply and relax for a moment. I tried but I was wheezing. The air was trapped in me. Then the Warrant Officer said, Don't hold on so tight the next time or he'll pull you down with him. And then you'll look stupid and he won't be dead. The others were looking at me. They were laughing.'

Labuschagne had paled visibly during this account. He stood with his head bowed low, heaving deeply. 'It was hard,' he added, shaking his head. 'It was hard.'

I did not give him a breather. 'Did anyone speak to you after that, to offer you advice or counselling or anything like that?'

'No.'

'No one at all?' I asked.

'No, sir, no one.'

'What about the Warrant Officer, or the Major?' I ventured.

He thought about it. He exchanged glances with the man sitting behind the prosecutors. 'No one said anything, sir.'

'What else did the Warrant Officer have to say to you at that time?'

Labuschagne turned slightly away towards the Assessor nearest to him and looked him in the eye as he spoke. 'He told me that I would be doing that job two or three times every two weeks, and that he had other jobs for me. He again said that I should not hold onto the prisoner so tightly as I might be pulled down with him. He also said that if I were to take some of the prisoner's weight the drop calculations would be nullified.'

'No,' I said. 'I think you might have misunderstood my question. I want to know whether anyone said anything about how the execution might have affected you and whether you needed any help or counselling.'

'No, sir.'

Wierda passed me a note: *He is not ready to deal with what happened in the pit room.*

Wierda sat with his pencil between his teeth.

I turned my attention back to the witness box. Labuschagne was as pale as a sheet. I gave him time to recover, to take a sip of water, but then I couldn't wait longer and asked, 'Did you eventually find out what other jobs the Warrant Officer had for you?'

'He told me to service and check the gallows equipment and later taught me how to do the drop calculations for him.'

'We can deal with that later,' I suggested. 'I would like you to tell the Court how you coped in the beginning with the new job and your new duties.'

'Do you mean the hangings?' Labuschagne asked.

I nodded.

'Well, I got used to the work after a while, a month or so, the hangings, the cleaning up and the burials. But some hangings were worse than others.'

'Can you give examples? I mean of hangings that were worse than others.'

'Yes. The first one was when we had to hang a father and son together, in October. I heard that they had killed the old man's father. They were in c Section. And on the same day we hanged two brothers, also from c Section.'

Wierda gave me the places in the register:

v3367 John Steytler
v3368 William Steytler
v3320 Johannes Nel
v3321 Willem Nel

'Were you ever involved in the hanging of a woman?' I asked, thinking of what Pierre de Villiers had told me.

Labuschagne answered with a nod and reached for the glass. It was empty and I waited as the usher filled it. I watched as he drank.

'Tell the Court about it,' I said. I kept the question deliberately vague. I wanted him to give the details that had left an impression on his mind, and I wanted the Judge and the Assessors to imagine an eighteen-year-old involved in such a macabre ritual.

'In December we had to hang a woman. The women are not kept at Maximum. They come in for their v-numbers and then they go to the women's section of Central. She was brought over early in the morning. Women are always hanged separately. We hanged them at about twenty to seven and the men at seven o'clock. She came in and …'

Labuschagne froze in mid-sentence. I waited for him.

'The matrons from Central pleaded with us to take her up. They were crying with her. The Warrant Officer told them to wait in his office and we had to take her up, but we did not go down into the pit room. The doctor went alone and then the matrons from Central came in and took over. They had to be quick because we still had to hang some men after that, I remember, and we had to pull the trapdoors up again and set them for the next drop. I had to bury the woman later that day in a different cemetery from where the men were buried.'

I had busied myself with the register and looked up when Labuschagne added, 'I don't know what to say.'

The entry in the register did not tell the full story either:

SERIAL NO.	NAME	V- NO.	PLACE SENTENCED	DATE	JUDGE	OUT-COME	DATE
4397	Roos de Vos	V3528	Springs	30.5.86	Stegmann	Executed	12.12.86

'Which hangings were the worst for you, speaking generally?' I asked, as if one hanging could be better than another.

'When we have to hang more than one.'

The Judge intervened. 'What is the most you've had to hang in a day?'

'Eight.' When no one reacted, Labuschagne went on. 'We take one up first and then the other seven.'

'What was the problem you experienced with the multiple hangings?' I asked.

'If one of them starts crying or wailing, they all start. And then you can't stop them. And then we have to carry them up.'

'What other problems did you have?'

'It was difficult to hang prisoners who were my age or my father's age,' he said.

He hadn't answered the question, but I had decided to change topics in any event. I could introduce the pit room evidence later.

'What was the prison policy with regard to the use of violence to restrain or discipline prisoners?'

Labuschagne lowered his eyes before he answered. 'We use violence when we have to.'

'How was that policy implemented?'

'We start with the new ones. We make the prisoners strip down naked and search them. All their personal stuff is taken away and they get prison garb – trousers, shirt, socks, shoes without laces, underpants and pyjamas.'

He was stalling, I thought, so I interrupted and asked, 'No, we went through this yesterday. Please return to the issue of violence. I want you to tell the Court about that.'

He did not answer.

'Were you given any specific instructions about how you were to deal with the prisoners?' I asked.

This time Labuschagne was more forthcoming.

'Yes. The Warrant Officer said that the only language these prisoners understood was violence. They had committed violent offences. They didn't feel anything for anybody. He warned me always to be alert when the prisoners were out of their cells and to have another warder with me at all times.' I thought I saw him glance at the man sitting behind the two prosecutors again.

'What did you understand the Warrant Officer to mean when he said these prisoners understood only violence?'

Now he looked openly at the man behind the prosecutors. 'He said if a prisoner stepped out of line I should knock him down there and then. We had to break them in quickly or we would always have trouble with them. I asked him to give me examples and he said that if a prisoner did not stand up when I spoke to him I should kick him in the face where he sat. And if a prisoner spoke to me without calling me sir I should hit him. I could use my fists or a baton, he didn't care what injuries the prisoner got. He said it would make it a lot easier for everyone if all the warders treated the prisoners the same. Then we can all walk around in our prison without any fear of being attacked. He said that we had to prepare the prisoners for the day of their hanging. He said they had to get used to following orders, because we want them to walk to the gallows without any trouble. He told me to watch what the other warders did and follow their example.'

'Did you have any questions about anything that might not have been clear to you?'

'Yes, sir. I asked the Warrant Officer if I wouldn't get into trouble if I hit a prisoner. He said that there's no such thing as assault on a prisoner, it doesn't exist in a prison's vocabulary. He said we only act in self-defence or to prevent violence between prisoners or to stop escapes. He said we all stand together. He said there are four rules. First, the prisoner is always wrong. Second, warders do not rat on each other. Third, always go to the assistance of another warder when he's in trouble. Last rule, keep your mouth shut.'

'And how did you implement the prison policy with regard to the prisoners?'

Labuschagne looked at me reproachfully, but I had a job to do even if it displayed him in a bad light.

'We had to pay special attention to the new arrivals. They had to be broken in before they could get into bad habits. They had to learn the prison culture.'

'What culture are you referring to?'

'To obey orders.'

Wierda and I had a long list of examples but I decided to leave the rest to the imagination.

'Tell the Court how you dealt with difficult prisoners.' I caught myself tugging at the shoulder of my robes again. I glanced at the Judge. He was watching Labuschagne intently now. Did he, like me, sense that we were not getting the whole truth?

'Well, as I said, we were very rough with them the first few days after they arrived. We had to break them in quickly. Then we would keep up the pressure until they went into the Pot.'

'Did it always work like that, with all the prisoners you had to hang?'

'No.' I waited for more information but Labuschagne just stood there looking at me. Perhaps he was taking Wierda's instruction not to volunteer information too seriously.

'In what way did some prisoners behave differently?'

There was no answer.

'Let's talk about those who were difficult on arrival,' I suggested. 'Give us an example of such a case and how you dealt with him.'

Labuschagne did not answer immediately. 'There was a terrorist who gave us trouble. He wouldn't look down when we said not to make eye contact. He walked slowly when we said walk faster. He ran when we said slow down. He spoke when we said shut up and when we asked him something he refused to answer. He even threw ...' He was looking for the right word. 'He threw shit at some of the warders.' Labuschagne didn't have a softer word.

He looked at me and I nodded for him to continue.

'When the next round of hangings came up the Warrant Officer called him out and put him in the Pot with the others. He even took his weight and his neck measurements. The prisoner said that he still had an appeal pending. The Warrant Officer said the appeal had been dismissed. The man said he wanted to see his lawyer. The Warrant Officer said his lawyer was overseas. He put him in the centre of the cells in the Pot, right in the middle of the singing and crying and praying. For the whole six days we treated him like the other prisoners in the Pot, except we did not allow him to receive any visitors. We took his order for his last meal, just like we did with the others, and gave it to him to eat the night before the execution. The next morning we lined up behind the Warrant Officer. He opened the cell doors one by one and called them out. Dit is tyd! Trek jou dagklere aan, geen onderbroek, skoene of kouse nie.

'The Warrant Officer went into the cell. I was escorting the prisoner in the cell directly across and saw the man sitting on the bed, dressed and wearing his prison shoes.

'The Warrant Officer said, Uit met jou skoene! Then he stood and watched as the man took his shoes off. I watched. He was very pale and moved slowly. Then we took all of them into the passage where their fingerprints had to be taken. Then the Warrant Officer pulled him out of the line and took him to the section chapel.

'The Warrant Officer told us to wait. He went back in and I heard him say to the prisoner, Sit jou hande hier, teen die muur, palms oop, vingers uit. En bly hier tot ek sê jy mag roer. Verstaan? We then moved through to the main chapel with the others.

'Later, after we had cleaned up in the pit room and had taken the coffins to the main chapel, the Warrant Officer called me and we went back to the chapel in A1. The prisoner was still standing there with his palms against the wall. His eyes were red and puffy. He was shaking. His pants were wet. Het jy gevoel? asked the Warrant Officer. The man nodded. Presies sewe-uur? the Warrant Officer said. Yes, said the prisoner. Then the Warrant Officer told me, Vat hom terug na sy sel toe. And when we were ready to go, he said to the prisoner, Ek wil nie weer kak van jou hê nie, verstaan? We never had any trouble with him again.'

Judge van Zyl stepped in. 'I trust this is going somewhere,' he said. 'This is a murder trial.'

'Indeed, M'Lord,' I said. 'We intend to lead expert evidence about the effect of the culture of violence on the breakdown of the defendant's psyche to explain the events at the reservoir.'

'Go ahead,' said the Judge, 'but remember to keep the prisoners' names out of it.'

'As M'Lord pleases,' I acknowledged. 'You heard that,' I said to Labuschagne. 'Don't mention the prisoners' names in your evidence, unless I ask you to.'

I waited for him to nod.

'Were there any other cases like that?' I asked.

'Yes, there was a white murderer who had shot some black people. He needed to be broken in too.'

Before Labuschagne could explain, James Murray objected. 'M'Lord, do we really have to listen to more of this?'

The Judge stopped me as I was about to reply. 'Yes, I agree, one is enough. Move on, will you?' he said. I had to acknowledge the ruling.

'As M'Lord pleases,' I said and turned to Labuschagne. 'What was the idea with all this violence and intimidation?'

'Sir, the idea was that we had to soften them so that we could get them up the staircase to the gallows chamber and onto the trapdoors with their feet on the marks.'

Judge van Zyl looked up from his notes when Labuschagne stopped. I pretended to be preoccupied with something in the brief. After a pause the Judge asked, 'What was your own attitude to this culture of violence you have described?'

It took a long time before he answered. 'I don't know what to say. I did what I was told.'

I took control of the questioning again. 'How did the prisoners behave, generally speaking?'

'Most of them behaved, but some of them were difficult.'

'How were they difficult? Give us examples please, and tell us how you dealt with them,' I asked.

'Some go berserk and we put them in isolation. When they fight we break it up.'

'What is the worst experience you had with a prisoner who went berserk?'

He thought for a while. 'When a prisoner rushed at me and smeared … uh … shit on me.'

'What happened to the prisoner?'

'He was put in the padded cell for a week.'

'How did this incident affect you?' I had to ask.

Labuschagne shrugged. 'It was tense in there.'

'I'll return to the matters you have mentioned later, the suicides and the shooting, but for the moment I would like to ask you how the violence affected you, as far as you are or were able to see that yourself.'

'I don't know what to say.' Then, after another pause, 'Do you mean in the beginning or at the end?'

'I mean in the last six months or so, the last six months, say, before the tenth of December 1987.'

'I don't know what to say,' he said for the third time.

I stood still, facing our client, and asked softly, 'Did you at any time sense or feel that something was not right?'

He spoke for a long time; we had been through this three or four times in our preparation. I picked listlessly through one of the registers as he spoke. I found that twenty-two prisoners had been hanged on one day thirty years earlier. I scanned their Zulu names:

Mandolozana Ndaba, Matshweshu Mdluli, Bhobolwana Mdluli, Kamu Hlongwane, Mganda Mdladla, Mhlonzana Mdluli, Mgolobane Dlamini, Nhlangwini Hlongwane, Xhegu Mbhatha, Tlela Dlamini,

Dlayedwa Hlongwane, Magangweni Kubheka, Nsingisi Mthembu, Mdolomane Hlongwane, Mshudeki Mhembu, Babalane Hlongwane, Nhlansi Hlongwane, Ndoboka Mdluli, Hambawodwa Mdladla, Mantongomane Mdluli, Mbulali Mdluli, Mandlakayise Nzimande, Jubhela Mahlobo.

Twenty-three of them, all condemned by Judge Kennedy in Pietermaritzburg on the same day, 9 August 1956. And all executed on 21 March the following year – all except Mandlakayise Nzimande, whose appeal succeeded and who was released four months later, on 3 August 1957.

I tried to imagine the scene. The place must have been like an abattoir. The logistical arrangements must have approached those of a small military operation. If for seven condemned the chapel was crammed I couldn't see how twenty-two coffins and all the relatives, two per prisoner, could have fitted into the chapel for the traditional funeral service.

Nuremberg could have had nothing on this scale, not even with the spectre and spectacle of Von Ribbentrop twitching and turning on the rope for more than a quarter of an hour as a result of the incompetence of the Executioner.

The image of an abattoir kindled an idea at the back of my mind. I closed my eyes and stood very still, waiting for the mist to clear. It did soon enough. Labuschagne was still explaining something to the Judge, but I was not concentrating. Something Marianne Schlebusch, our forensic psychologist, had said reared up from my subconscious.

A small minority of people suffer mental breakdown after one traumatic experience. But only a very small minority do not suffer mental breakdown after prolonged exposure to trauma.

I thought of Leon Labuschagne, seventeen or eighteen years old, and his descent into the abyss. They might have hanged twenty-two men in one day way back in 1957, but that was one traumatic event. And the register did not disclose any other multiple hangings that year. But Leon Labuschagne had been exposed to multiple hangings on numerous occasions, and then, with the respite that the December holidays were to bring, the trauma escalated in weight and frequency. It was as if the system wanted to deal him a crushing series of blows:

> four on 26 November
> seven on 3 December
> seven on 8 December
> seven on 9 December
> seven on 10 December
> Take that, Leon! Smack smack smack!

I was still staring at the register when the Judge announced that we would have a half-hour adjournment. He said he had to sentence someone in the adjacent court. I wondered if it was to be a death sentence.

We went for a walk on the Square. My mind was elsewhere while Wierda recited the facts of the Delport case to Roshnee. I did not know what to make of the case. He had confessed openly and then tried to retract. He did nothing realistic to get away from the scene. In fact, he went looking for the body of his victim. It is almost as if he was so ashamed of what he had done that he co-operated with the police in order to expedite his execution. It was only when a lawyer looked at his case – the attorney must have been as baffled as I was, thinking that insanity could be the only defence – that Delport tried to retract his confession and started to put up a struggle for his own life.

It was not a happy conclusion for me to draw.

Do we, as lawyers, try to save our clients' lives when they have decided to give them up? My own client had given every indication of having surrendered, of being quite content to receive any sentence the Court administered.

What then was I doing here, reading these cases?

Delport faced three charges in the High Court. He had indecently assaulted and murdered a four-year-old girl, Charmaine Opperman, in a
small town called Frankfort.

Frankfort is an hour's drive south of Johannesburg. The Wilge River
flows through the town and on its banks there is a popular recreation
area. Delport arrived here looking for work. After finding a position at a
local firm of panel beaters, he moved in with a Mrs Elizabeth Opperman
and her family, which included two small children, both girls. Within
a week, on Sunday 20 October 1985, Delport asked Mrs Opperman if
he could take her youngest daughter, Charmaine, to church with him.
Charmaine was four years old. An arrangement was made that Delport
and Charmaine would be taken to church by Gideon van Heerden, Mrs
Opperman's companion, who would also fetch them after the service, at
noon. When van Heerden returned at twelve to fetch them as arranged
they were not there. He returned home thinking that Delport and
Charmaine might have walked home.

The pastor's wife, Mrs Thalita de Beer, saw Delport leaving the church
at about eleven-thirty. He gave her a false name when she asked if he had
recently moved to Frankfort. A Mrs Henning, who lived near the river,
was at home at this time. Her dog started barking uncontrollably at about
a quarter to twelve. She went outside to investigate and saw Delport and
Charmaine walking in the direction of the river. About fifteen minutes
later she heard a small child scream and wail. Then the crying stopped
abruptly. The crying had come from the direction of the river. At half
past twelve a seventeen-year-old schoolboy, Frederic Buys, walked past
Delport who was sleeping at the foot of the steps leading down to the
picnic area at the river's edge. A hymn book lay on the steps next to
him. He saw Delport still lying in the same place later in the afternoon,
at about three o'clock. Frederic saw Delport leave at about four o'clock
and return within minutes with Mrs Opperman and Mr van Heerden.
They were looking for Charmaine.

Delport, of course, knew what had happened to Charmaine, but he feigned complete ignorance.

Charmaine's body was found only on Thursday 24 October, more than twelve kilometres downstream.

Major G R Viljoen of the Benoni Murder and Robbery Unit arrived in Frankfort to take over the investigation. Delport had already been brought in for questioning. To the policeman's surprise, Delport spontaneously offered to take him to the river and to point out what had happened there.

Delport said that he wanted to 'get this thing' behind him. He made a complete confession to Major Viljoen, saying, 'I am so ashamed about this business.' Pointing to a spot on the grassy bank between the river and the foot of the steps leading down from an upper picnic area, he told Major Viljoen, 'We came down here, and she and I came and sat here. She went to the toilet first and came and lay down here next to me. I first started playing with her with my hand. She then said, No Grandpa, don't. Then I raped her from behind. I could not get in properly in front. She cried too much, Stop! and screamed.' Then he added, 'I forgot something. There was a yellow plastic bag here. I made her lie on it. I took her by her shoulder and leg and threw her in here. After that I sat here below and washed myself. Then I dressed and pretended to be sleeping. I was not really asleep.'

The pathologist performed a post-mortem examination on Charmaine's body on 25 October 1985. He determined that the cause of death was drowning. He found a number of injuries consistent with Delport's confession to Major Viljoen.

Before the Magistrate Delport pleaded guilty to murder and rape but said that it had not been his intention to kill Charmaine. The Magistrate's questioning turned to the rape charge. The questions and answers were recorded:

Q. On 20.10.85 were you at the Wilge River Municipal Grounds, Frankfort?
A. Yes.
Q. Who was there with you?
A. Charmaine Opperman.

Q. Is she a girl?

A. Yes.

Q. How old was she?

A. Between 4 and 5 years old.

Q. Did you assault her?

A. Yes.

Q. How?

A. I first, from behind …

Q. Did you have intercourse with her?

A. Yes.

Q. How many times?

A. It was one process.

Q. Did you have any right to do so?

A. No.

Q. Was there any penetration?

A. Yes.

Two experienced psychiatrists reported to the Court that Delport had not been suffering from any form of mental illness or defect at the time of evaluation and that at the time of the offences he had the capacity to understand the unlawfulness of his actions and to act in accordance with that understanding.

The Court found Delport guilty on the murder charge and the charge of indecent assault but acquitted him on the rape charge.

On 28 August 1986 the Court sentenced Delport to ten years' imprisonment on the indecent assault charge and imposed the death sentence on the murder charge. He was hanged on 3 December 1987. He had spent just over a year and three months in the death cells and was forty-nine years old.

Palace of Justice

Palace of Justice

24

The Palace of Justice dominated the atmosphere of the Square. We were sitting on the steps under Oom Paul's statue. I sought a diversion.

'Tell me about this building your great-grandfather designed,' I said to Wierda, looking over my shoulder at the Palace of Justice. 'What style is that, Neo-Gothic, Neo-Renaissance, Neo-Baroque or just Nineteenth Century Eclectic?' I did not mention that I had picked building styles at random from one of my son's Art History assignments.

Wierda stood up and faced the building directly. It sat in splendid sunshine under a clear blue sky, the row of trees in front of it already in their finest greenery. Spring is a good season to be in Pretoria. The temperature was in the mid-twenties, not too warm to wear a full suit in the sun, and there was just the gentlest of breezes. Pretorians of all hues were lazing about on the Square. Some tourists were taking photographs.

'Well, it is said to be in the Italian Renaissance style,' said Wierda.

'What makes it Italian Renaissance?' Roshnee asked. 'It looks just like the City Hall in Durban. The same grey stone masonry and the corners with those blocks that look like sentinels. Isn't that rather British?'

Wierda stood up, his half-finished cool drink forgotten for the moment. 'The English had nothing to do with the design of the building. It was almost complete by the time they occupied Pretoria in 1900.'

'That only tells us the building isn't English,' I grumbled. 'But what makes it Italian Renaissance?'

Wierda sighed. 'Come and stand here and I'll show you,' he ordered with sudden authority.

'Look at the building,' he commanded. Having asked the question I now had no choice but to get up for a lecture.

Wierda pointed as he spoke. 'See the symmetry in the design of the facade. See how the eye is drawn from the corners of the building towards the centre and then up to the two towers and how the dome is set slightly back between them? Note how the smaller columns support the brickwork of the first and second floors and appear to extend further upwards to the spires on the roof? See how every feature forces the eye inward towards the main entrance and upwards from there to the dome?'

Roshnee and I dutifully followed the finger pointing to the features mentioned. We looked from side to side and up and down as instructed.

Wierda then scrambled higher up the steps of the monument and stood at the top at Oom Paul's left hand. 'Come up here so you can see over those trees.'

He barely waited for us to join him at the top of the steps before he continued. 'Look at the lines of the columns at the centre. They are supported by those huge stone arches between the two towers and point straight up to the dome, which is the centrepiece of the whole design. Every feature of the design is meant to draw your attention to the dome. When we are back inside the building I'll show you that this idea is also at the core of the interior design. In its design this building dates back to the late sixteenth or early seventeenth century.'

'Well, that would make it Late Renaissance, wouldn't it?' I suggested.

Wierda got off his perch and pointed at the building again.

'There is so much in the design of this building, it would take days for me to point out all the features that make it Italian Renaissance. When you look at the Palace from here you can see how the two wings spread out from the central block. Note the symmetry. It is the symmetry that pleases the eye. The symmetry of this building is accentuated by the portico with its columns and the pediment across the front of the central block.'

'Oh, you mean that low-pitched thing there?' I pointed with my reading glasses. 'I thought a pediment had something to do with feet.'

Wierda shook his head. The look on his face said it all. 'Total philistines,' he muttered.

'Come on down and finish your sandwich,' I said. 'We are due back in court in ten minutes.'

'No,' he said, 'I'll make you a sketch.' He took his pad and with a few quick strokes of his pen produced a sketch. As I looked from the sketch to the building the thought crossed my mind that the blood of the architect who had designed the Palace was flowing in the veins of the young man next to me.

Wierda's enthusiasm was contagious and I was to find myself unable to look at the Palace again without wondering about its lines, the angles, the proportions and the mixture of materials. The classical portico, now that I understood what it was, did indeed lend an appearance of timeless grandeur and elegance to the Palace.

I wondered also whether art was supposed to be about peace and harmony. Wierda had made the Palace look so peaceful, but inside its pleasing exterior was Court c, a place of pain and conflict and fear and death, and we were walking slowly back to it.

We took our places and I turned to a new section in my trial notebook.

'All right, Mr Labuschagne, let's deal with the servicing of the equipment first. Could you please tell the Court what duties you had in this regard?'

Labuschagne explained that he was given these tasks because he was the new boy.

He had to clean and prepare the gallows room. The cleaning started at the staircase from the ground floor up. There were fifty-four steps going up two storeys with railings on the left and right of the stairs. The stairs and railings had to be wiped down. He had to sweep and clean the two rooms at the top. There was often urine and excrement on the stairs and in the anterooms. In the gallows room he had to clean the windows and all the equipment had to be serviced.

He had to take the ropes off the beam and clean them.

I asked him what he did with the ropes.

'I would wipe and coil them and put them in the wardrobe,' he said.

'Tell the Court about servicing the gallows, but keep it short, please.'

'I had to check everything. I had to pull the trapdoors up and lock them into position. I put the safety pin in and cleaned the lever and oiled the moving parts. I went down to the pit room to clean and oil the underside of the trapdoors. I checked the stopper bags and if they were broken I had to repair them.'

When he stopped speaking, I asked, 'Did anyone assist you with this work?'

'No, sir.'

'Why not?' I asked, though I knew why.

Labuschagne looked down and mumbled inaudibly.

I gripped the lectern more tightly. This was an important piece of evidence. I raised my voice slightly. 'I beg your pardon,' I said, 'I couldn't hear your last answer. Would you please speak up?'

Judge van Zyl shook his head slightly; perhaps he had heard the answer the first time.

I continued. 'Why did no one want to work in that room?'

Labuschagne hesitated more. Then, still looking down at the microphone in front of him, he answered simply, 'Because there are ghosts there.'

For the second time in minutes silence fell over the Court. I stood motionless as I waited for Labuschagne to look at me. He was staring at a point on the registrar's table. I waited until he looked up and found my eyes.

'Tell the Court about the ghosts in that room.'

Labuschagne took a half step away from the microphone as if it was itself a ghost he'd suddenly seen before him.

'There are ghosts there,' he said again. 'I've seen them. Everyone has seen them.'

'Tell us about the ghosts,' I said.

Labuschagne looked from me to the Judge.

'I saw it for myself. The first time I was working on the stopper bags, I was sewing a bag together again and I felt the hair on my arms rise and someone blowing cold air in my face. I saw something or someone, in the corner of my eye. I looked in that direction, but there was nothing. But as soon as I looked down at the bag it was there again, in the corner of my eye, moving across the room. I looked up, but it was gone again. I worked out that it could not be faced directly. But it was definitely there, and it moved across the room, sometimes from left to right and sometimes in the other direction.'

'Did you do anything about what you had seen?' I asked.

'No, sir. I thought they would think I was chicken, but we all knew the ghosts were there. Everyone talked about it.'

Judge van Zyl stirred and, when I hesitated, asked, 'Did you see the ghost before or after you had heard the other warders talking about it?'

'I saw the ghosts many times before I heard. And the prisoners in C Section complained that someone was gliding along the catwalk and was keeping them awake. So we checked the whole section, but we could see nothing.'

The Judge sat back in his chair again, indicating that I could continue. 'So what did you make of what you had seen?' I asked.

'Well, I started thinking about that room. I thought about the people who had been hanged there since the prison had been built. I became worried that some of them could have been innocent, maybe, or perhaps hadn't deserved to die. I prayed more and I went to church more often. Then I found that I was no longer scared. I could work in that room without fear. There was nothing a ghost could do to me. I just carried on with my work.'

'What else did you have to do with regard to the maintenance and servicing of the gallows equipment?'

Labuschagne thought about the question. 'No, I think that was all. We always cleaned the pit room immediately after a hanging, so I had nothing to do there.'

'So what was left for the Executioner to do before an execution?'

'He tied the ropes to the beam according to the drops we had calculated, the length of the drop for each prisoner, and then he just waited for the prisoners.'

'Did you say the length of the drop *we* had calculated?' I asked.

'Yes, sir. We took the measurements and I did the drop calculations.'

'Why were you doing that?'

'The Warrant Officer said I had matric maths and could do it; he showed me how. He gave me an old circular and this circular set out how to calculate the length of the drop for each prisoner.'

'What calculations did you have to make?' I realised that the question was not exactly as I had intended and I had to correct myself quickly. 'Or rather, how did you calculate the drop?'

'Well, we took the weight, height and neck size of the prisoner. Then I would look at the table and find the correct drop for the prisoner's weight. I would then work out the precise length of each rope for the prisoners to be hanged and give them to the Warrant Officer. In the beginning he double-checked my drops but later he simply passed them on to the Hangman. In the morning he tied the ropes to the beam.'

The Assessor on the right whispered something to the Judge.

'I did not quite follow how you calculated the drop and I think one of my Assessors has the same difficulty,' said the Judge. 'Could you please explain again but take it slowly, step by step.'

'Can I use the table?' Labuschagne looked at the Judge, but I answered him with a question.

'Do you have it with you?'

'Have your counsel seen it?' asked the Judge.

'Yes, sir.'

Judge van Zyl conferred briefly with his Assessors. 'Then you may use the table. Are there copies for us?'

I held them up in my hand and the usher came across and took them. Then he handed all but two to the registrar and gave those to the two prosecutors. James Murray looked at me questioningly. I shrugged. I had not intended to lead this evidence, but if the Judge and Assessors were interested they should have it.

The Judge and Assessors studied the document briefly before the Judge nodded, 'Proceed.'

'As M'Lord pleases,' I said. 'I'll mark this Exhibit н.'

'Please explain to us, using this table, how the drop was calculated. Go slowly, step by step.'

Labuschagne picked up the two sheets constituting the Table of Drops and studied it for a moment. Pointing at the table, he spoke with the authority of a man familiar with the details. 'For the weights within the scale of the table, we used the drops set out there.' His voice gained strength. 'For weights off the table, for example, men weighing more than two hundred and ten pounds, we did the calculation according to the formula. We often had men over two hundred and ten, and then we used the formula. You divide eight hundred and forty foot-pounds by the weight of the prisoner and his clothing. That gives the distance the prisoner has to fall. The length of the rope has to be the distance from the shackle on the beam to the prisoner's neck plus the length of the drop.'

He looked up to find everyone studying the table.

EXHIBIT H
EXECUTIONS: – TABLE OF DROPS (APRIL 1892)

The length of the drop may usually be calculated by dividing 840 foot-pounds by the weight of the culprit and his clothing in pounds, which will give the length of the drop in feet, but no drop should exceed 8 feet. Thus a person weighing 140 pounds in his clothing will require a drop of 840 divided by 140 = 6 feet. The following Table is calculated on this basis up to the weight of 210 pounds: –

TABLE OF DROPS

WEIGHT OF THE PRISONER IN HIS CLOTHES	LENGTH OF THE DROP	WEIGHT OF THE PRISONER IN HIS CLOTHES	LENGTH OF THE DROP	WEIGHT OF THE PRISONER IN HIS CLOTHES	LENGTH OF THE DROP
LBS.	FT. INS.	LBS.	FT. INS.	LBS.	FT. INS.
105 and under	8 0	127 and under	6 7	163 and under	5 2
106 "	7 11	128 "	6 6	165 "	5 1
107 "	7 10	130 "	6 5	168 "	5 0
108 "	7 9	132 "	6 4	170 "	4 11
109 "	7 8	134 "	6 3	173 "	4 10
110 "	7 7	136 "	6 2	177 "	4 9
112 "	7 6	138 "	6 1	180 "	4 8
113 "	7 5	140 "	6 0	183 "	4 7
114 "	7 4	142 "	5 11	186 "	4 6
115 "	7 3	144 "	5 10	189 "	4 5
117 "	7 2	146 "	5 9	193 "	4 4
118 "	7 1	148 "	5 8	197 "	4 3
120 "	7 0	150 "	5 7	201 "	4 2
121 "	6 11	152 "	5 6	205 "	4 1
123 "	6 10	155 "	5 5	210 "	4 0
124 "	6 9	157 "	5 4		
126 "	6 8	160 "	5 3		

When from any special reason such as a diseased condition of the neck of the culprit, the Governor and Medical Officer think that there should be a departure from this Table, they may inform the Executioner, and advise him as to the length of the drop which should be given in that particular case.

'Did you ever depart from the formula or the drops as indicated by the table?'

The answer came quickly. 'Yes, when the prisoner was very thin or had been caught exercising his neck muscles. Then we added about three inches.'

I looked up at the Judge and asked, 'Would this be a convenient time for the adjournment, M'Lord?'

Judge van Zyl looked at the clock. 'Is it time already? Yes, we'll take the adjournment now. I'd like to see senior counsel in chambers.'

I joined James Murray at the door and we followed the usher to the Judge's chambers.

'Have you finalised the arrangements for the inspection in loco?' the Judge asked as soon as we arrived. He was looking at Murray. I wondered why, because the prosecution's case had been closed and it was the defence's prerogative to ask for an inspection now. I said nothing, however. I could always argue later that the Court had instigated the inspection. Or the prosecution.

'Yes, Judge,' said Murray. 'We are expected at the main entrance at two-fifteen. The Head of Maximum will give us a tour. It should take about two hours.'

'Very well, I'll go in my own car and take the registrar and my Assessors with me. Does the defendant have to be present?' Judge van Zyl turned his attention to me.

'We don't need him to be there,' I said.

'Do you need him there?' the Judge asked Murray.

'No, thank you, Judge,' was the response.

'See you there then.'

We walked back to the courtroom to collect the materials we would need during the inspection. I found Wierda and we went to the robing room to change into our suits.

We worked through the next case in the coffee shop near Wierda's chambers. Roshnee announced that she would not accompany us on the inspection.

v3680 Jomyt Mbele
v3681 Case Rabutla
v3682 Clifton Phaswa

25

Mbele, Rabutla and Phaswa were prosecuted on three counts: murder, rape and abduction. They had murdered Mr Joseph Mashiloane, a truck driver, and had abducted and raped Miss Sarah Ngobeni. Each of the charges carried the death sentence.

The deceased, Mr Joseph Mashiloane, was a forty-eight-year-old truck driver. He was en route to Phalaborwa with a consignment of goods and decided to break his journey at Duiwelskloof. He met Miss Ngobeni at a tearoom on the evening of 21 July 1985. She agreed to spend the night with him in his truck. He parked it next to the road near the Sekgopo Township.

At the same time Mbele, Rabutla and Phaswa met at Turfloop, some sixty kilometres away, and started an evening of drinking and driving around. They travelled in Rabutla's minibus and, after a visit to a beer hall in Kgapane, they drove towards Pietersburg and came across Mashiloane's truck. Phaswa told Rabutla to stop.

Rabutla stopped the minibus about forty metres from the truck and the three men approached the truck in the dark. Mashiloane and Ngobeni were sleeping. Phaswa went to the truck and called the other two over. He then broke the window of the truck and he and Mbele climbed into the truck. Phaswa had a knife. Mashiloane asked them, 'What are you doing?' One of them said, 'Don't talk to us.' Phaswa or Mbele stabbed Mashiloane repeatedly and virtually cut his throat.

Rabutla then pulled Miss Ngobeni from the truck and forced her into the back of the minibus. He raped her while Phaswa and Mbele were still engaged at the truck. When they returned from the truck, Mbele drove the minibus away from the scene. The minibus broke down twice on the way to Pietersburg, but each time Rabutla somehow managed to repair it. Rabutla took the wheel after the first breakdown. During the journey Mbele and Phaswa took turns to rape Miss Ngobeni. Eventually they stopped at a petrol filling station on the outskirts of Pietersburg early in the morning. Mbele accompanied Ngobeni to the toilets, but she refused to get back into the minibus. She started complaining to the pump attendants, saying that she had been raped and that the men had killed a truck driver. The three men drove off quickly in the minibus, leaving her there.

Mr Mashiloane's body was found in his truck early on 22 July 1985. The cause of death was cerebral hypoxia caused by the perforation of the main arteries to the brain. There were numerous injuries, including seven stab wounds, most having been inflicted to his back and neck. One stab wound had cut through the carotid artery. Another had penetrated the right lung. Two other stab wounds had penetrated the liver. The weapon must have been at least eleven centimetres long. The stab wound cutting through the carotid would have caused Mr Mashiloane to lose consciousness immediately. The stab wounds to the lower back alone would have caused death, had Mr Mashiloane not already received the wound severing the carotid.

The Court found that Mbele, Rabutla and Phaswa had decided in advance to find a woman with whom they could have sexual intercourse. When Phaswa found that there was a woman in the truck, he called Rabutla and Mbele over and they decided to get rid of Mr Mashiloane. So they killed him and abducted Miss Ngobeni with the intention of raping her. The Court found that they had acted with a common purpose in respect of all three counts and convicted them.

The Judge passed a double death sentence on the murder and rape counts and sentenced each of them to three years' imprisonment on the kidnapping charge.

On 27 November 1987 Mbele, Rabutla and Phaswa were informed that they were to be hanged the next week. On Friday 3 December they were hanged.

They had spent ten months in the death cells. Rabutla was twenty-one years old, Phaswa thirty-two and Mbele thirty-five.

Again I looked for common features.

Klassop was a loner, as Mokwena had been, and was after material gain.

Mpipi and Mohapi had killed in a gang, and so had Mbele, Rabutla and Phaswa, and, of course, Moatche, Scheepers and Wessels.

Delport was in a category of his own, defying reliable analysis other than that he was a paedophile.

Rabutla was a young man, hardly an adult. The extreme youth of these men was beginning to show a pattern.

And Leon Labuschagne fitted the pattern.

But there were some older men too, like Delport, Mpipi, Mohapi and Klassop.

Delport had killed to avoid detection. This was also beginning to emerge as a pattern. For the others the killings were done almost matter of factly, with no obvious motive except the pursuit of their crimes.

Maximum Security Prison

26

I watched from the passenger seat as Wierda drove us to Maximum.

Maximum Security Prison was part of Pretoria Central Prison. We entered the complex from Potgieter Street. A high fence surrounded the whole complex. The road ended abruptly in a jacaranda-lined parking lot in front of a gate in a concrete wall. In front of us were two heavy steel gates on rollers. The entrance consisted of a small building with the usual security apparatus: a metal detector through which visitors had to pass and an x-ray machine for their belongings. I stood at the gate looking at the aerial photograph Wierda had obtained from the municipal offices. Wierda offered me a sketch plan he had prepared from it, with some of the detail filled in during his sessions with our client.

'We might be able to hand this in as an exhibit,' he suggested. I could not see the Judge agreeing to that, but took it from him nevertheless.

Wierda's sketch was line perfect. He must have used drawing instruments – yet another expression of the architect's genes in his blood line. My instincts told me that it might be an offence to make or publish a sketch of the prison and I quickly hid Wierda's effort in among the sheets of my writing pad.

It took a while for us to be signed in at the front guardhouse. A warder told us to stay together and ushered us towards an officer in a drab olive-green uniform waiting for us. A grey concrete wall, easily six metres high, came into view. The buildings were well away from the wall. I turned to take a good look at the surroundings.

Above the checkpoint was a guard tower. I counted five of them altogether, each consisting of an eight-metre-high red-brick structure, about four metres square at the base, with a sheltered guardhouse on top. The guards on the towers had their rifles pointed at us. I realised that their job was to prevent escape, not an invasion. They were all facing inwards. There were security lights on thirty-metre steel posts near each tower. I remembered from Wierda's sketch that the complex was laid out in a pentagon of uneven angles and sides.

The warder introduced us to the Major. The Major would not let the women in and the Judge's registrar and Sanet Niemand left in one of the cars. Niemand was fuming, but she left without looking back after James Murray had whispered something to her behind his hand.

'This is the most secure prison in South Africa,' the Major began after the women had left. 'We intend to keep it so. So we will not allow any photographs to be taken, and you will not be allowed to speak to any of the prisoners or staff once we are inside. Is that clearly understood?'

We stood squinting at the Major in the blazing sun. I wondered how Judge van Zyl felt taking orders from the Major, but the Judge stood in anonymity amongst us. In his suit he looked like any other lawyer.

The Major insisted on an audible answer. 'Is that clearly understood?' he asked a second time, in a firmer tone.

'Yes,' some muttered.

'Yes, sir,' said Wierda. He stopped just short of saluting.

'May we take notes, sir?' Wierda asked with some cheek.

'Yes, but you are not allowed to make any drawings of the prison. That would compromise our security arrangements and it is a crime in any event.'

Wierda stole a glance at me and I glared at him. What would happen if we were searched on the way out? I could claim professional privilege, but it would be embarrassing if the Judge did not agree.

'Stay in this group, with these warders,' said the Major. 'If you stray off on your own the men on the towers will shoot you. Be careful.'

Half a dozen warders had quietly joined our little mission.

The Major spoke about the prison and its history but I quickly lost concentration. I heard the rustle of running water and birdsong behind us. There was a park-like garden between the wall and the first buildings and I turned to look at it. I don't know why I was afraid of the Major.

The garden consisted of rocky ponds surrounded by indigenous trees, shrubs and plants. There were some goldfish in the ponds. Birds fluttered in the branches overhead. I saw a number of different species of birds. I recognised at least five, a lilac-breasted roller, marico sunbirds, blue waxbills, a pair of red-eyed ring-necked doves and some red-faced mousebirds. On the ground I saw a tortoise, a steenbok, a pair of rabbits and some common ground lizards. A blue-headed tree agama scratched its way up the rough bark of a tree. I gazed in amazement. In this place of death there was also an abundance of butterflies, dragonflies and wasps. I knew that steenbok were nocturnal animals. This one stood in the shade, as if in a daze, looking at us with large unseeing eyes. Even this lush artificial paradise without predators was a prison, trapping this daintiest of all the antelope and buck of the bush in a foreign time zone.

I felt uneasy, and when I looked up, I saw a rifle pointed at me from the tower above the main gate. I realised that I had been left behind. The others were already near the steps leading up to wooden doors at the main entrance to the buildings and I rushed to join them at the door. From what I could remember of Wierda's sketch we were now at the main door. I resisted the impulse to check the sketch as I went up the steps; I would have to confirm the details later when we got back to Wierda's chambers.

At the top of the steps was a heavy wooden door with steel reinforcing and a peephole at eye level. The Major knocked, prompting a warder to look at us through the peephole. Even the Major had to be checked in, it seemed. They let us in one by one, subjecting each of us to a cold silent scrutiny that raised the level of my unease sharply.

The warder slammed the door shut and locked it behind us when we were all inside. We were in a foyer of sorts now and were quickly taken through to the next section, which I remembered from Wierda's useful sketch. There were no windows and it was difficult to maintain my orientation. Straight ahead were three steel grille gates leading from the foyer to A, B and C sections respectively, the Major said. The gate to A Section was on the right. We were to visit that section first.

The place smelled just like Leeuwkop as I remembered it, only worse, with the unmistakable odour of fear added to the mix of tobacco, unwashed bodies, steel and concrete.

The prison had been placed in lock-down mode for our visit. The mood was sombre and heavy. The place was very quiet; our footsteps and the clanging of keys in locks were the only sounds. The Major spoke softly, as if we were in a hospital for the terminally ill, the parade-ground voice he had used outside at the gate subdued inside. The place did, in a way, feel like a hospital with its muted colours and uniform fittings and furniture. Instead of general wards, single rooms and beds, the prison had sections, cells and bunks. I thought, grimly, that I knew the operating theatre was elsewhere on Wierda's sketch.

Without prior orientation from the sketch I would have been quickly lost in the maze of passages and doors. The outside world had ceased to exist; there was no natural light and the colours were all shades of grey under harsh electric lights. There was a humming noise that I imagined was the outside world held at bay, but it could have been the prison's generator. We never heard a prisoner speak and, apart from the Major, none of the prison staff uttered a word. It struck me that no one even coughed; it was as if the whole place was holding its breath.

In all my life I had never felt so completely lost.

Wierda tried to take notes, but the Major reminded him gruffly that he was not to make any sketches. Wierda elbowed me in the ribs and whispered that he would do so afterwards. And indeed, he and I were subsequently able to reconstruct precisely where we had been and what we had seen simply by using his updated sketch.

We were taken from the foyer into a passage separating A and B sections from each other. The passage ran north-south, and was perhaps thirty-five to forty paces long. Three steel grille doors on the right opened into A1, A2 AND A3 sections respectively. Some doors on the left side of the passage led into administration offices in B Section. Our attention was drawn to a small table in the passage.

'This is where the prisoners' fingerprints are taken on the morning of an execution,' the Major said.

The table was more or less opposite the Warrant Officer's office.

We had heard a good deal about the Warrant Officer from Labuschagne. I looked into the office but its occupant was absent. From what Labuschagne had told us this man held a special position, namely that of Warrant Officer in Charge of Security. This was a misnomer, according to Labuschagne. The Warrant Officer was really the man in charge of executions.

The Major continued with his tour. We would only be shown A1, he said, because A2 and A3 were virtually the same.

Inside A1 there was a long central passage ahead of us, at least sixty paces long, with steel doors on either side of the passage and a catwalk above it. The first room on the left was arranged and furnished as a chapel. Directly opposite the chapel was an office. There was a steel door to the bathroom. The rest of the section consisted of cells.

There were communal cells, an isolation cell and ordinary single cells. The single cells were about two metres wide by three metres long. The Major asked the warder with the keys to unlock the cell. He showed us that the isolation cell had been equipped with sound-muting materials and a window of soundproof glass. The cell had claustrophobia written all over every feature.

On leaving the section through a steel door at the end of the passage we found ourselves in a small exercise yard, about ten metres by twenty, enclosed by its own wall.

I breathed easier outside, relishing the smell of a solitary orange tree in the exercise yard mixed with the smell of dust; relief, such as it was, from the nauseating smell we'd left behind. The outer concrete walls of the complex were too high for me to see anything beyond their grey confines but I was able to work out where we were by reference to the sun and the guard towers which, according to Wierda's sketch, were at the south-western and north-western corners. I looked up to see if the hillside from which Wierda and I had looked down on the prison months earlier was visible but the walls were too high. Even outside the cell-blocks the free world was obliterated. I remembered the vagrant who had scared me senseless and wondered if he was back on the hill, looking down at the complex but unable to see anything inside. What would he think of the place if he knew what the function of these buildings was? How much would he appreciate his miserable existence, his freedom, if he knew? Was he the one who had left tracks around the bodies and left without touching them?

Back inside I felt eyes on me and when I looked up there was a warder in shorts on the catwalk. He was barefoot and without a shirt. His chest glistened with sweat. He held a rifle in his hands, at the ready, pointing it straight at me. I followed the Major to the end of the passage without looking back. There was an itch between my shoulder blades, but I resisted the impulse to scratch.

We trooped past the chapel; it was cold and formal like the rest of the prison. Behind the Major we climbed up the steps to the gallows chamber. I could smell the hemp of the ropes hanging on hooks attached to the wall of the gallows chamber, but they were not hanging ropes. Everyone was suddenly in a hurry. Wierda stepped onto the trapdoors and placed his feet in the painted footmarks. The Major gave him a hard stare, but Wierda was oblivious to that. He inspected the mechanism of the lever and its clutch in the greatest detail. I noticed Judge van Zyl taking his time to do the same. He held a whispered conversation with Wierda, who nodded from time to time. I stood to one side, watching. The two Assessors stood side by side, their hands clasped in front of them like funeral directors.

The pit room below was stark and smelled damp. It looked as if it had recently been rinsed with water and detergent. From underneath the mechanism of the trapdoors could be seen more clearly. Wierda again inspected every component, prodding the stopper bags with his fist. Here, I noticed, was the only colour other than grey or brown in the building. The steel parts of the gallows machine had been painted a bright blue. Wierda pointed at the sliding mechanism that would release the trapdoors, Judge van Zyl taking in every detail, as thick as thieves with Wierda in this pursuit. The artificial lighting in the windowless room made us all look sick, a yellowish hue on every face and on every surface.

I found myself next to James Murray. I knew that he disapproved of my tactics, but he knew as well as I did what we had to do. It was dirty work but we were both trapped in it by our respective duties, his even more onerous than mine. My conduct was defined by my duty to the Court and to my client. The prosecutor's duty was to ensure that justice was done. We stood side by side, looking into the drain in the pit. I walked with him to the next room.

There we found autopsy tables and refrigerators. There was a stack of coffins in the corner waiting for the next batch of executions. Everything was spick and span, as spotless as military barracks, but with the smell of the operating theatre of a hospital.

'We don't use the autopsy room anymore,' said the Major. 'There is no need to determine the cause of death because we know it in advance and there is a doctor present when death occurs.'

He must have noticed the sceptical look on my face; everything was just too organised for the room and its equipment not to be in use. 'Well,' he said, 'from time to time we have one of the professors from the medical school to conduct an autopsy and then we allow a class of their students to witness it.' He looked uneasy as he spoke, apologetic perhaps. 'And sometimes, when we have a suicide, the District Surgeon may do the autopsy here too.'

The warders had laid on tea and biscuits for us in their common room and we could not refuse. We sipped guiltily at the sweet brew while we made polite small talk. One of the Assessors mentioned the rugby and speculated on the outcome of the Currie Cup final. The biscuits were dry in my mouth. We left the main section of the prison with the clanging of the doors and the rattle of heavy keys still ringing in our ears. A troop of warders accompanied us to the main gate. We stayed close to them.

We were made to sign out again at the front guardhouse. The warder on duty smelled like the prison – of sweat, fear and cheap tobacco.

It was good to be out in the open air again. The air smelled sweet with the perfume of the jacaranda flowers. I heard a faint tune and African voices behind us as I walked with Wierda to his car.

Kumbaya, my Lord
Kumbaya

Judge van Zyl walked away with the rest of us. 'I'll see you back in court tomorrow at ten,' he said.

DAY THREE

Defence: 6 October 1988
Execution: 8 December 1987

v3506 Ishmael Mokone Marotholi
v3507 Zacharia Molefi Kodisang
v3508 Richard Busakwe
v3747 Stanley Allen Hansen
v3768 Nicholas Prins
v3769 Sizwe Goodchild Leve
v3770 Stanley Smit

By the time the escorts had returned after seeing the relatives out the death notification forms had been completed by the admin office. One coloured and six black men had been hanged, so the deaths had to be registered at two different Home Affairs offices in the city.

The escorts engaged in a game of paper, rock, scissors; the losers would be the two who had to register the deaths and the winners would join them later for the burial detail. The game ended quickly and the losers collected their documents. They checked them cursorily. The cause of death in each case was stated as *Judicial Execution*.

The two escorts departed together in a prison car. They were well known at the Home Affairs departments and were given preferential treatment. At the first office they went to the front of the queue and were admitted to a back office with a window and a red carpet where a supervisor occupied the desk.

'How many do you have today?'

'Six,' said the escorts in unison.

Within half an hour the department's records had been amended to record the deaths of the six men and the escorts left with their certificates for the second office they had to visit. There they had only one death to register: Willem Maarman's. Back at Maximum they handed in the certificates to admin and set off with the other escorts on the next leg of their mission.

At the chapel they collected the coffins and manoeuvred them through the passages to the garage behind the gallows building. Two minibuses were waiting there. They quickly sorted the coffins according to the race of the occupants and loaded them in the minibuses. Just as there were two Home Affairs offices for the registration of the deaths, so there were two cemeteries for the bodies. One would go to Eersterus Cemetery and the other six to Mamelodi.

The prison had only one minibus with panelled windows for the purpose and they had had to rent another from an undertaker, whose assistant was to drive the coffins to Mamelodi. With six coffins loaded in the minibus there was no space for a second escort and, after playing paper, rock, scissors again, only one escort accompanied the bodies to Mamelodi. He was heading for a nightmare of a different kind.

On the way to the cemetery a car approaching from the right failed to stop at the red light. Its brakes must have failed, for it didn't stop even when the undertaker's minibus drove through the green light, right into its way. A perfectly executed ballet followed. The errant car lurched to the right as the minibus veered left just enough for the two vehicles to touch sides for half a second, and for the two drivers to recognise mutual fear in the short time they had eye contact before the car went on its way and the minibus spun out of control into the parking lot of a shopping centre.

Coffins crashed about the minibus, spilling their contents. By the time the minibus came to a halt, its interior was a mess of planks and mutilated naked bodies. The undertaker's driver took one look and ran away, leaving his door open, the minibus idling and the prison warder on his own in the disarray.

At Eersterus the two escorts paid a passer-by to fill in the grave for them. They made themselves at home under a tree and smoked one cigarette after another. The body underground would still have been warm when they left. They were back at Maximum in time for lunch.

It was a different story at the other cemetery. Long after midday the lone man at Mamelodi was still struggling with his rickety load of coffins. When he had arrived the graveyard was deserted. It was midsummer and hot; swirls of wind chased red dust devils across the flat expanse of untended soil.

He dragged the first coffin by its front end and slid it out the back of the minibus. When the rear end of the coffin fell to the ground, the lid, hastily nailed back after the near accident, popped open again and fell off. The escort refastened the lid with a few blows of his shoe and picked up the front end of the coffin a second time. By the time he had dragged the coffin to the open grave a few yards away he was sweating profusely. He stopped next to the fresh mound of soil and pondered the best way to get the coffin into the grave.

Still bent over the front end of the coffin he half turned to look into the shade below. This was a job usually done by two men, now he had to find a way of doing it on his own. He decided to slide the coffin across so that its front end protruded over the edge of the grave. First he pushed the coffin over and then jumped into the grave. He grunted with the effort as he pulled the coffin over further and further until its back end was right on the grave's edge. Then he gave it a final tug and stepped back, but there was insufficient space behind him and he was trapped when the coffin crashed six feet down into the hole and fell against his shins.

A cloud of dust rose from the grave and when it had settled he saw that the cheap coffin had disintegrated; its occupant lay on his side, an arm flung wide. Oblivious of the blood seeping from the abrasions on his legs he scrambled out of the grave, crawling like a spider with his hands and feet in the earth. Streams of sweat traced white lines in the dust on his face.

He struggled with each coffin in turn, dragging them from the minibus and across to the allocated graves. Five more times he disappeared into the shady hollow of a grave, getting dirtier with each drop until he was as red as the soil, with sand under his fingernails and clinging to his scalp. He did not bother to put any of the coffins and bodies together again, leaving them as they had landed, in a mess of planks and limbs.

Filling in the graves on his own took yet more time and greater physical effort, and he became progressively more dehydrated. His throat was parched as he toiled, shovelling soil into the graves.

It was late afternoon before he arrived back at Maximum. He returned dog-tired, incoherent with dehydration and with a pounding headache, only to be mocked by his fellow escorts and castigated by the Warrant Officer for having taken so long to complete the job.

28

Judge van Zyl broke with tradition and announced that he would not be producing a sketch plan of the prison to incorporate in the record of the trial what we had observed of the various sections of Maximum Security Prison. 'We all know what we have seen, and I am not going to compromise the security of the prison.' He ignored the fact that any member of the public could pick up a copy of the aerial photograph from the municipal offices around the corner.

Labuschagne's family were sitting in the front row immediately behind the wooden barrier between the well of the court and the public section, on the defence side. His sister Antoinette sat between their parents. I wondered what went through her mind as she watched her brother admitting to the things he had done. Antoinette had attended every session so far. It reminded me of my grandmother's wisdom: a sister's loyalty knows no bounds.

One of the spectators on the balcony coughed and I looked up. A row of faces looked down on us. I wondered about them as they must have wondered about us. What did they think of us? Did they see us as gladiators or as monks, dressed in secret robes and engaged in a strange, ritualistic duel? I imagined I could feel their hostile gaze on the thinning spot at the crown of my head. I hoped that they had been properly searched at the entrance. Who were these people? Were they capable of killing? What business did they have here? It was, after all, a work day.

Judge van Zyl interrupted my thoughts. 'Are counsel in agreement with the details I mentioned to them in chambers?' he asked.

James Murray and I stood up and faced the bench. We exchanged a glance and then spoke at the same time. 'We are, M'Lord.'

'I will read my observations into the record then.' The Judge turned the page and continued recording the Court's observations during the inspection. I had to concentrate because everything recorded in this fashion would become evidence in the case.

'The different sections of the prison will be described here in the order that we inspected them yesterday. C Section and the kitchen do not feature in the evidence and will be ignored. Special features pointed out by counsel will be described in detail. Where necessary I shall endeavour to give my own impressions of the atmosphere of the prison.'

The Judge paused for a moment when the Assessor on his left tugged lightly at the sleeve of his robe. They had a quick, whispered conversation. The Assessor pointed at Labuschagne, who was standing in the witness box. The Judge spoke directly to him.

'There's no reason for you to stand through all of this. I'm sorry, I should have noticed earlier. You may return to the dock and sit down until we have finished recording the Court's observations at the inspection in loco.'

Labuschagne stepped out of the witness box and walked around the prosecutors' end of the table to the door in the dock. For a moment he faced the spectators in the gallery behind the dock. He briefly made eye contact with his parents, but immediately lowered his gaze, turned and sat down.

The Judge resumed, and spoke for a long time before he concluded. 'That completes our observations with regard to Section A1, with the exception of the atmosphere. We were there for about half an hour, from about two o'clock, and it was very quiet during the whole of that time. The prisoners were in their cells. The doors were locked. The only movement or sound was that of the guard on the catwalk; he came around every so often.'

Wierda slipped me another sketch. He must have made it overnight. It showed A Section in fine detail but we would not be able to use it.

So this was Wierda's escape, I thought. While I was looking at the sights and features of Pretoria to take my mind off the case, he was making sketches.

I was looking at his sketch, my thoughts elsewhere, when the Judge asked, 'Is there anything counsel would like to add to the observations I have recorded thus far?'

I spoke first. 'We have nothing to add, M'Lord.'

Murray had nothing to add either.

'I turn now to describe B section and, so far as it may be relevant, C Section.'

I studied Wierda's work more carefully as the Judge read more of his observations into the record. This was Labuschagne's place of work, the place where the agony of the Pot was felt most keenly. The sketch reduced all of that to a few strokes of a pen on a page.

I vaguely heard the Judge say, 'There is another door in the chapel that takes one into the main passage of B Section. B Section, like A1 Section, consists of a passage with a catwalk overhead, and steel doors on either side.'

Wierda handed me yet another sketch, of B and C section. He had near perfect recall.

The Judge droned on about B and C sections and concluded, 'It remains for me to record the details of our observations in that part of the complex described as the gallows building. I'll record those details after the long adjournment.'

Then he turned to me. 'Would the defence be able to continue with the examination-in-chief of the defendant in the meantime?'

I stood. 'Indeed, M'Lord, we are ready.'

'You may proceed then.'

I motioned to Labuschagne to return to the witness box. The registrar stood up and reminded him that he was still under oath. Labuschagne nodded. We settled down for the session.

I made room for my notebook and adjusted my reading glasses. I could feel in my voice that the stress of the trial was beginning to take its toll. My voice had dropped half an octave as it always does under stress. The examination-in-chief had now already taken more than a day. When the Judge caught my eye I nodded and continued.

'Mr Labuschagne, let's move on to what happened during the three weeks from the twentieth of November to the tenth of December 1987. How did you experience those three weeks, as a whole?'

He was ready and spoke immediately. 'We were very busy. There was never a day's rest. It felt as if we were emptying the place, but as fast as we carried coffins out through the garage they were processing new arrivals at reception. It was like a conveyor belt.' That sounded rehearsed.

'Can you recall the numbers involved?' I asked, knowing well that he had memorised the details.

'Yes, sir.' He opened the register in preparation for the next question.

'Could you give the Court an idea of the numbers involved, please?'

'Yes. We had been quiet the first half of November. We hanged three on the sixth and another one on the twentieth. Between the twenty-sixth November and the tenth December we had to hang thirty-two. We hanged four on the twenty-sixth November and then seven on the third, seven on the eighth, another seven on the ninth and the last seven on the tenth.'

I held my hand up to indicate that I wanted to interrupt.

'Were you present at any of those executions in November and December?' I knew the answer, of course, but the Court needed to hear it from Labuschagne's mouth.

He looked at me. 'I was an escort at every execution in 1987.'

'So how many executions did you attend during the year then?'

He thought for a while. 'About twenty-five to thirty.'

'Please continue. What else happened during that period, from the twentieth until your arrest?' I realised my question was too vague to make sense. 'Tell the Court about the arrivals and departures from the prison. Take your time and use the register to refresh your memory.'

Labuschagne took his time before he answered. 'Two prisoners came off the rope on the twentieth and transferred out.'

I had to interrupt. 'What do you mean by *came off the rope*?'

'That's what we said when someone won an appeal or got a reprieve. The ones waiting under sentence of death we said were on the rope, and the others came off the rope.'

I asked him to continue. 'So what happened to the ones who were reprieved?'

Labuschagne checked the register before he answered. 'Some warders came across from Central and took them away. On the twenty-third we let two more out as they were found not guilty on appeal. We took them to the gate and handed them over to their lawyers or their family. On the thirtieth five more were found not guilty on appeal and we let them go too. On the same day three others were reprieved. They were transferred to Central. On the first of December another one was found not guilty on appeal. He had been under a double death sentence; we took him out through the guardhouse at the front gate. He didn't want to wait for his family to come and pick him up, so we took him to the main control boom at Potgieter Street and let him go. He just walked down the street.'

Labuschagne concentrated on the register, turning from page to page where we had stuck notes to guide him to the relevant parts quickly. 'The same day another one's sentence was changed to twelve years and he was taken away to Central. On the tenth one prisoner died of natural causes. I can't remember the details because I was involved in escort duties.'

'What about new arrivals?' I asked. 'How many were there in that time?'

'Thirty-two or thirty-three came in between the first of November and the tenth of December.'

As I was about to ask another question the Judge intervened. 'Are all these details apparent from the register, what is it, Exhibit G?'

Wierda handed me our next set of exhibits and I held them up. 'We have taken the liberty of transcribing the relevant entries in the register, M'Lord. It would facilitate not only the examination-in-chief but also the Court's ability to follow the evidence without having to take detailed notes at the same time. May we hand that up to assist M'Lord and the Learned Assessors?'

'Yes, thank you.'

The usher handed the sheets around. When Judge van Zyl had taken a perfunctory look at his copy, he asked, 'We don't have to give this a new exhibit number, do we? It is merely a transcript of what is in the register?'

The registrar shook her head. It was her function to keep track of the exhibits.

'There are two qualifications, however, M'Lord,' I said. 'We have excluded from the transcript any entries that were made after the tenth of December because we want to maintain the situation as it was up to that date. And we have not listed the new arrivals the defendant has mentioned. This is an *exit* list. The admissions after the tenth of December are not relevant to this case because the defendant never got to know them.'

I waited for Judge van Zyl to make eye contact or to give me the nod to continue, and then decided to hammer the point home a little less subtly.

'The prisoners on this list are the ones who, one way or the other, left the prison during those last six weeks. They are the ones whom the defendant had got to know so well during their stay, or should I say, *his* stay in Maximum.'

The Judge nodded as I spoke, but he was concentrating on the list.

'I don't like the idea of the names being used here,' Judge van Zyl said, 'but it is a public record, isn't it?' He did not wait for an answer. 'Give us a moment to read the details.' He adjusted his spectacles and read the extract slowly.

I watched his eyes dart from column to column. As he read, a grim look spread across his features.

Wierda's pencil went *tap tap tap* against his teeth and I put my hand on his arm to stop him.

EXTRACT FROM EXHIBIT G

NAME	V-NO	PLACE SENTENCED	DATE	JUDGE	OUTCOME	DATE
Edward Phatack Tshuma	V3207	Johannesburg	28/8/84	Vermooten	Commuted to life imprisonment	20/11/87
Simon R Moatche	V3208	Johannesburg	28/8/84	Vermooten	Executed	26/11/87
Michael Mfeka	V3410	Durban	6/9/85	Broome	Commuted to 20 years' imprisonment	30/11/87
Schalk Johannes Burger	V3420	Klerksdorp	19-20/9/85	Schabort	Commuted to life imprisonment	20/11/97
Joseph George Scheepers	V3421	Klerksdorp	19-20/9/85	Schabort	Executed	26/11/87
Kanton Klassop	V3473	Grahamstown	10/2/86	Mullins	Executed	3/12/87
Ishmael Mokone Marotholi	V3506	Bloemfontein	9/5/86	Edeling	Executed	8/12/87
Zacharia Molefi Kodisang	V3507	Bloemfontein	9/5/86	Edeling	Executed	8/12/87
Richard Busakwe	V3508	Bloemfontein	9/5/86	Edeling	Executed	8/12/87
Keta Richard Mkhatyiwa	V3520	Johannesburg	23/5/86	Vermooten	Appeal succeeds; not guilty, disch. on both counts	1/12/87
Khuselo Selby Mbambani	V3541	Cape Town	3/6/86	Nel	Executed	10/12/87
Willy Jacob Mpipi	V3564	Johannesburg	29/7/86	Vermooten	Executed	3/12/87
Johannes Mohapi	V3565	Johannesburg	29/7/86	Vermooten	Executed	3/12/87
Johannes Stefanus Delport	V3574	Bloemfontein	28/8/86	Hattingh	Executed	3/12/87
Jacobus Wynand Bosman	V3575	Johannesburg	28/8/86	Vermooten	Commuted to 15 years' imprisonment	30/11/87

Annele Booi	V3602	Bloemfontein	11/9/86	Edeling	Appeal succeeds; conviction and sentence set aside	30/11/87
Abel Moeketsi	V3603	Bloemfontein	11/9/86	Edeling	Appeal succeeds; conviction and sentence set aside	30/11/87
David Tswele	V3604	Bloemfontein	11/9/86	Edeling	Appeal succeeds; conviction and sentence set aside	30/11/87
Government Sogelle	V3605	Bloemfontein	11/9/86	Edeling	Appeal succeeds; conviction and sentence set aside	30/11/87
Monde Nose	V3606	Bloemfontein	11/9/86	Edeling	Appeal succeeds; conviction and sentence set aside	30/11/87
Mncedisi Stamalatyi Khongwana	V3614	Grahamstown	26/9/86	Jansen	Appeal succeeds; death sentences set aside and replaced with 12 years impr.	1/12/87
Johan Christiaan Wessels	V3615	Bloemfontein	2/10/86	Smuts	Executed	26/11/87
Jerome Debishire	V3621	Johannesburg	17/10/86	Stegmann	Appeal succeeds; conviction and sentence set aside	23/11/87
James Dladla	V3623	Johannesburg	17/10/86	Stegmann	Appeal succeeds; conviction and sentence set aside	23/11/87

William Harris	V3625	Cape Town	8/10/86	Van den Heever	Executed	9/12/87
Brian Meiring	V3626	Cape Town	8/10/86	Van den Heever	Executed	9/12/87
Christoffel Michaels	V3627	Cape Town	8/10/86	Van den Heever	Executed	9/12/87
Herold Japhta	V3628	Cape Town	8/10/86	Van den Heever	Executed	9/12/87
Jan Swartbooi	V3629	Cape Town	8/10/86	Van den Heever	Executed	9/12/87
Pieter Botha	V3630	Cape Town	8/10/86	Van den Heever	Executed	9/12/87
Anthony Morgan	V3631	Cape Town	8/10/86	Van den Heever	Executed	9/12/87
Gerald Zibanile Njilo	V3636	Scottburg	31/10/86	Law	Executed	6/11/87
Joseph Gcabashe	V3663	Scottburg	12/12/86	Broome	Executed	10/12/87
Mnuxa Jerome Gcaba	V3664	Scottburg	12/12/86	Broome	Executed	10/12/87
Jomyt Mbele	V3680	Tzaneen	29/1/87	Curlewis	Executed	3/12/87
Case Rabutla	V3681	Tzaneen	29/1/87	Curlewis	Executed	3/12/87
Clifton Phaswa	V3682	Tzaneen	29/1/87	Curlewis	Executed	3/12/87
Jim Kgethang Mokwena	V3695	Johannesburg	27/2/87	Vermooten	Executed	26/11/87
Mlungisi Luphondo	V3705	Grahamstown	5/3/87	Cloete	Executed	6/11/87
Siphiwo Mjuza	V3721	Cape Town	6/3/87	Lategan	Executed	10/12/87
Stanley Allen Hansen	V3747	Swellendam	8/5/87	Friedman	Executed	8/12/87
John Louw	V3748	Cape Town	8/5/87	Tebbutt	Executed	20/11/87
Andries Njele	V3752	Johannesburg	20/5/87	De Klerk	Executed	10/12/87
David Mkumbeni	V3753	Johannesburg	20/5/87	De Klerk	Executed	10/12/87
Nicholas Phopho Khupula	V3767	Johannesburg	12/6/87	Van Dyk	Executed	5/11/87
Nicolas Prins	V3768	Cape Town	9/6/87	Williamson	Executed	8/12/87
Sizwe Goodchild Leve	V3769	Cape Town	27/5/87	Nel	Executed	8/12/87
Stanley Smit	V3770	Cape Town	5/6/87	Munnik	Executed	8/12/87

Willem Maarman	V3771	Cape Town	4/6/87	Van Heerden	Executed	10/12/87
Whanto Silinga	V3793	Port Alfred	24/6/87	Kroon	Died of natural causes	10/12/87
Zinakile Matshisi	V3817	Potchef-stroom	20/8/87	Hartzen-berg	Commuted to 15 years' imprisonment	30/11/87

When he had finished reading, the Judge slowly put the schedule down on the bench. He put his hands under his chin and leaned on his fists, elbows on the table, and rocked slowly. I waited for him to make eye contact, the signal that I could resume the examination-in-chief, but still he gave no sign that he was ready.

At last he leaned forward and spoke under his breath. 'They gave them four for the first three weeks of the month, and then they gave them thirty-two for the next two. What were they thinking?'

Labuschagne answered, even though the question must have been rhetorical and not meant for his ears. 'I don't know, sir. We asked the Major what was going on. He said that the Minister of Justice had been too busy with other things to sign the documents.'

James Murray was quickly on his feet to object, but Judge van Zyl stopped him. 'I did not intend to ask a question.' I was still standing. 'Carry on,' he said.

I muttered the usual, 'As M'Lord pleases.'

'Mr Labuschagne, could you please tell the Court what happened on the twentieth of November?'

'Just a moment,' said the Judge. He still had the sheet we had given him in his hand. 'Did you say that there were thirty-three new admissions in the six weeks before the tenth December and another nine after that, to the seventeenth?'

The question was directed at me. 'Indeed, M'Lord. This is an exit list.'

The magnitude of the operations at Maximum was beginning to filter through at last.

Labuschagne stood upright, in the fashion of a soldier, with his hands resting on the wooden sides of the witness box and his face raised to meet the scrutiny of the Judge, apparently at ease with the subject matter of the questioning.

Look up at the Judge. Watch his pen. Stop when you see him taking a note. When he stops writing, carry on. Don't be in a hurry.

I repeated my question. 'What happened on the twentieth of November last year?'

'We first had a hanging and then we had to take six prisoners to the office. We told them to pack their stuff and took them to the office.'

I turned to the bench before I spoke again. 'M'Lord, we are going to have to start using names from here on.'

The Judge pondered the issue for a while and then, after conferring briefly with his Assessors, said, 'Be careful how you do it.'

'As M'Lord pleases.'

'What are the names of the prisoners you took to the office?'

Labuschagne did not have to look at the register. 'We took Tshuma, Moatche, Burger, Scheepers, Wessels and Mokwena.'

I saw some movement at the prosecution table and hesitated before I asked the next question. Sanet Niemand was talking to the man sitting behind her. I had forgotten about him.

'So what happened at the office?' I asked, keeping an eye on the prosecution table. The discussion became more animated. James Murray rose to object. I sat down quickly.

'We object to this evidence,' he said as soon as he was on his feet. 'It is not relevant to any issue at this trial. It also deals with matters that are protected by public interest privilege.'

I was ready as soon as he sat down. Wierda and I had prepared for every possible objection, including this one. I had the law and our argument ready and knew that an experienced judge would give us free rein in a case like this.

'We submit firstly,' I argued, 'that the evidence is relevant to the defendant's state of mind. Any event that took place in the days preceding the events of the tenth of December last year and that had or might have had an effect on the defendant's state of mind as it was at the time is relevant. Secondly, we submit that the privilege claimed by the prosecution does not cover this situation but cases where the identity of an informer needs to be protected. We would suggest that Your Lordship should allow the evidence to be presented on a provisional basis. The Court may determine its relevance and admissibility at the end of the case when all the other evidence has been led and the importance of this evidence has been explained by the expert witnesses we intend to call.'

Judge van Zyl pondered the matter. I was afraid that he would rule against us and added, 'We have to use the names, M'Lord. To the defendant these were real people, not just numbers as they might be to us.'

He made his ruling immediately. 'I'll allow the evidence provisionally.'

I repeated the question. 'Mr Labuschagne, I asked you to tell the Court what happened at that meeting when you took the six prisoners to the office on the twentieth of November.'

Labuschagne shifted uncomfortably in the witness box. Something had unsettled him. Perhaps it was the man behind the prosecutors.

'What happened?' I asked again.

'The Sheriff read them their letters and told them what was going to happen.'

While Labuschagne was answering I whispered to Wierda, 'Who's the man behind the prosecutors?'

Wierda leaned back to see behind me, and then he scribbled on a piece of paper: *The Warrant Officer.*

'What did the State President decide to do in these cases?' I asked Labuschagne. I took a closer look at the Warrant Officer: brown suit, late forties, military bearing, closely cropped hair, thinning on top. Ruddy complexion of an alcoholic. Broad, strong hands. Otherwise anyone's uncle.

I turned to listen to the answer.

'Tshuma and Burger were reprieved and the other four were going to be hanged.'

'What did the Sheriff do after reading these letters?'

Labuschagne again glanced at the Warrant Officer before he spoke. 'He dealt with each prisoner separately. We took them into the office one by one. He told the four they were to be hanged on the twenty-sixth.'

'What became of the prisoners after that?'

'The admin people took over and asked the ones to be hanged for the details of their relatives so that they could be informed. They then sent them tickets to come for a final visit and for the funeral service.'

That did not account for Tshuma and Burger. Labuschagne must have read my thoughts and added, 'The other two were transferred out to Central.'

'What did you do with the other four?' I pressed on.

'We took their measurements.' Labuschagne used *we*, hiding in the collective. I suppose I would have been slow to admit my involvement if I had been in his shoes.

'The Warrant Officer and I took them,' he added when I was slow with my next question.

'What measurements did you take?' I hurried the questions so that he wouldn't have time for intrigue or scheming before answering.

'We first weighed them without their shoes. The Warrant Officer wrote down their weight. I measured their height, from the floor up to behind the ear. Then I measured their necks.'

I decided to test him. 'How did it feel, measuring their necks, when you had known them for so long?'

Labuschagne gave a gruff, angry answer. 'I felt nothing.'

I let him off the hook. 'What happened after these tasks had been completed?'

'We took Moatche and Mokwena to the Pot in A1. Wessels and Scheepers were taken back to C Section.'

'Did anything unusual happen on the way to the Pot?'

'Yes.' He looked at me and, when I did not follow up on his answer, continued on his own. 'Moatche asked me why he was going to be hanged if Tshuma had been reprieved. He said the whole thing had been Tshuma's idea, to rob passengers on the train. I told him I did not know, but it was the same for Burger and Scheepers. One was reprieved and the other one was to be hanged.'

'What did you do as a result of that conversation?'

'I went to our archives section and I read Moatche's case record. And after that I started reading some of the others. I tried to work out why some were reprieved and some were not. But I just got confused. It did not make much sense to me.'

'What duties did you perform after lodging those men in the Pot?'

'We went back to our normal duties, guarding the prisoners, taking them for family visits and so on. In the Pot they could talk and sing and we read the Bible with them and tried to keep them calm.' There was a pause. 'And we serviced the gallows equipment.'

It was time for the tea break. 'Would this be a convenient time, M'Lord?' I asked, and inclined my head towards the clock.

The Judge glanced up from his papers and said, 'Yes. The Court will adjourn for half an hour.'

It had started raining, so we walked around in the atrium. Round and round we went, with Wierda alternatively telling me about the next case and the features of the building.

The central atrium was about sixty metres long and thirty wide. A very large copper chandelier hung directly under the cupola. I calculated that there were a hundred and twelve marble columns in the atrium; they formed a natural pathway along the outer perimeter and in two places their placement created passages across. Wierda and I traipsed along these paths on marble tiles of black, grey, ivory, red and brown. Heavy wooden benches were arranged between the columns as public seating and Wierda and I eventually sat down under an alcove with a bust of E J P Jorissen, the Transvaal Republic's Secretary of Justice and a contemporary of Wierda's great-grandfather.

I leaned back against the wall and stretched my legs. There was some intricate relief work on the ceiling at least fifteen metres above the floor: a boy and a girl sitting back to back with a globe on a pedestal between them. The girl held an open book, ready with her pen to record the verdict; the boy held the scales of justice and was checking whether they were in balance.

Knowledge and Justice.

Law and Equity.

I wondered if we could make them coincide in our case, but in the relief above our heads they were facing away from each other.

V3506 Ishmael Mokone Marotholi
V3507 Zacharia Molefi Kodisang
V3508 Richard Busakwe

29

Marotholi, Kodisang and Busakwe had broken into the home of Mr Johannes Marx and killed him. They faced one charge of housebreaking with intent to rob with aggravating circumstances and a charge of murder. Both were capital offences.

Mr Marx was sixty-nine years old, a retired man who lived alone at his home in Odendaalsrus, a generally quiet gold-mining town in the northwest of the Orange Free State. On Friday 25 October 1985 he visited his brother at the latter's barbershop in the town and spent half an hour talking to his son, also named Johannes Marx, from about five o'clock in the afternoon. Then he went home. The next morning at about seven-thirty his domestic employee, Mrs Maria Mateboha, arrived for work but found the house locked and her employer's Toyota Corolla sedan missing from the garage. She assumed Mr Marx had gone to town and, after waiting for a while, she went to the barbershop. When she saw only the deceased's brother there, she assumed Mr Marx had gone somewhere without remembering to tell her. She went home.

Later the same morning Johannes Marx junior went to visit his father and found his body on the bathroom floor and that of his dog on top of him. His father's body had been splashed or painted with a silvery paint. His hands were tied behind his back and two belts bound his legs together, one at the knees and the other around the ankles. A pair of socks had been stuffed into his mouth and tied around his lower jaw.

The house had been ransacked and numerous items were missing. A strange message had been painted on the passage wall:

ONCE MORE AGAIN

During the post-mortem examination it was noted that there were a number of lacerations of the deceased's scalp. There was bruising around the lacerations. Four of the lacerations overlay linear fractures of the skull, causing bleeding in many areas of brain tissue. There were multiple injuries mainly of the nature of bruises and abrasions on the deceased's right shin and thigh, right shoulder, forearm and chest. He had injuries consistent with being burnt with boiling water or paint thinners on his chest, abdomen and right thigh. The cause of death was determined to be bleeding throughout the brain.

The murder weapon was a carpenter's file weighing almost a kilogram and about forty centimetres long. The police recovered it from a wardrobe in the ironing room of the house.

The three accused were linked to these crimes and the crime scene by circumstantial evidence and by their own admissions and confessions to the local Magistrate. In these statements they admitted participating in the events that led to Mr Marx's death. The three men were unemployed and out of money. They knew that Mr Marx was living on his own. They planned days ahead to rob him. Marotholi drew a sketch plan of the house and showed it to the others. They waited for the domestic and the gardener to leave before they approached the house.

Kodisang's statement bears the closest relationship to the facts accepted by the Court. According to Kodisang, the events unfolded as follows:

Mokone went in. After a while Richard and I followed him. When we got there we found that he had already tied the dog to a pole with a rope. We went into the ironing room. Its door was open. The door between the ironing room and the kitchen was locked. Mokone broke the door handle with a file. Then he pushed a sheet of newspaper under the door and pushed the key through with a piece of wire until it fell on the newspaper. We then pulled the newspaper back and the key protruded under the door [...] We went in. However, the door leading to the lounge was also locked. Mokone went out again and went to the old man's bedroom window. The top part of the window was partly open. He unscrewed the burglar guard with a knife [...] He then went in and opened the door for us [...]

We went and sat in the dining room to wait for the deceased [...] After a while we heard the deceased's car arrive. We pulled masks over our heads. Mokone and I stood in the passage behind the lounge door. Richard went into the room opposite the deceased's bedroom. When the deceased entered, Mokone grabbed hold of him and clamped his hand over his mouth. The deceased pulled a firearm from a holster in the front of his pants. I grabbed the hand with the firearm.

I had a file and hit the deceased with it on his head twice. Richard arrived and also started hitting the deceased with the file [...] Richard then stuffed a handkerchief in the deceased's mouth. The deceased fell down and Richard covered his head with a carpet [...] I tied the deceased's arms behind his back with a rope and his legs with a belt.

I took the pistol and went and stood at the kitchen window to check if I could see anyone. Mokone had given me the order; he said I was more scared than they were. While I was standing there, Mokone called me and said I had to help open a can of paint ... I stirred the paint with a bread knife to mix it well.

At this stage the deceased was still alive. Mokone and Richard carried the deceased to the bathroom and laid him down next to the bath. Mokone poured paint on the floor. Richard started painting over the blood splashes on the walls. He poured the paint over the deceased. The deceased was still alive. Richard took a paintbrush and started painting the deceased's head. Richard painted the wardrobes and mirrors with the remaining paint. He said he was painting over the fingerprints.

At that stage we searched the deceased [...] and found keys in his trouser pocket. Mokone [...] unlocked a wardrobe in the deceased's bedroom. Mokone found boxes containing cuff links as well as an electric shaver. In another container we found bullets, watches and bracelets. I took the five bullets and a silver watch […] Richard also took a watch. Mokone took all the other goods we had found and put them in a suitcase. Mokone also found handkerchiefs belonging to the deceased and put one pair of shoes in the suitcase.

Richard also took a pair of shoes. Richard also took the waistcoat he is still wearing. Because it was slightly cold, Mokone put on a white pair of overalls of the deceased. I put on a grey jacket of the deceased. Mokone also took a mouth organ and a guitar. In the dining room Richard took a box with gold knives, spoons and forks. Mokone furthermore took two and a half dozen eggs. There were dried fruit rolls in the refrigerator. I took one, broke a piece off and gave it to Richard. Mokone took the other one. We put everything we had taken on the dining room table.

It was then about half-past six. We decided to wait until it was dark so that we could take the deceased's car. I found five rand fifty in the deceased's possession. I sent Richard to the café to buy each of us a packet of cigarettes. When he returned I was busy drinking a litre of milk. Richard took a spoon and spooned peanut butter from a bottle and ate it […]

Mokone went to fetch the dog. He throttled the dog with a rope but the dog wouldn't die. Richard took the paint and poured it into the dog's mouth. However, it still would not die. Mokone thereupon took an axe and chopped the dog. When the dog's tongue protruded he said, 'Yes, now it is dying,' and threw the dog on the deceased's legs. I don't know if the deceased was still alive at this time.

The deceased had spoken only once. He said, 'Did you come to take my car?' […] we decided to flee with the car. While we were fleeing we sold spoons, forks and knives as well as a few of the handkerchiefs. In Carletonville we ran out of petrol. I tried to sell the firearm at a service station. While I was busy trying to sell the firearm the police arrived and arrested me.

I took the police to Richard and Mokone. There was nothing else

I could do because I was homesick. My parents did not know where I was, because I had not told them that I was leaving. I end here.

The evidence was overwhelming. The Court unanimously convicted all three of them on both charges and they received double death sentences on 9 May 1986. Leave to appeal was refused.

They went to the gallows on 8 December 1987 after having spent nineteen months in the death cells. Marotholi was twenty-two, Kodisang twenty-three and Busakwe twenty-one years old.

People started streaming past us to get back into court.

'What do you think happened there?' I asked Wierda as we moved down the passage towards the door on our side of the court. 'Why would they confess so readily?'

Neither Wierda nor Roshnee answered.

'And why did they kill the old man? Couldn't they just have tied him up and driven off in his car? Why did they have to pour paint over him? And why did they kill the dog?'

Wierda, as usual, adopted a sceptical approach – a realistic approach, he would have said. 'They were evil, that's what. Nothing they did can be explained by applying reason to it. They were evil, and their bizarre message on the wall can make sense only to them.'

We had become so engrossed in our discussion that I had forgotten that it was raining outside. When we walked into the courtroom, rain was pelting down on the skylights above our heads and the usher had turned on the lights. A few lights flickered weakly and we completed the morning's proceedings in poor light.

The matter-of-fact manner in which Kodisang had described the murder of Mr Marx persuaded me to present our case with greater emphasis on its emotive aspects.

30

I wasted no time as we had a long session ahead, an hour and a half, eleven-thirty to one o'clock.

'What is the daily procedure in the Pot? Or rather, how does the routine in the Pot differ from the ordinary daily routine?' I asked Labuschagne as soon as everyone had settled down.

He focused his eyes on the wood panelling behind the Judge's chair. I surreptitiously watched the Warrant Officer. He did not look at Labuschagne, even though the witness box was barely three metres away. The Warrant Officer kept his eyes fixed on his hands on the table in front of him.

Labuschagne started slowly but picked up speed.

The prisoners were allowed to have only the minimum of their possessions with them in the Pot, like their clothing, pyjamas, Bible and writing materials. They were locked up in single cells. They were taken to the showers individually, each accompanied by two warders. They were taken to the exercise yard individually, each accompanied by three warders at least. If they wanted to go to the chapel, they were again taken individually, accompanied by at least two warders. They could receive visits from their family. All visits were monitored.

When he had finished, Labuschagne looked at me. 'That's about all I can think of. They spend most of the time reading their Bibles and praying.'

'Did the warders deal with the prisoners in the Pot differently from the way they dealt with the other prisoners?' I asked.

'We had to watch them to make sure they didn't commit suicide.'

The Judge intervened. 'Were there ever any suicides?'

Labuschagne nodded. 'Two.'

'How is that possible?' asked the Judge. 'I thought you said there is always a man on the catwalk doing rounds and that you watched the prisoners around the clock, twenty-four hours a day, and that the lights were never switched off. And from what I was given to understand earlier the prisoners were not permitted to have any items they could use to kill themselves in their cells. So how could it possibly happen, under your nose, so to speak?'

'The one hanged himself and the other one cut his wrists.'

'That's my point,' said the Judge. 'Hanging yourself takes some time. And the prisoner must have had something to cut his wrists with, mustn't he?'

'Sir, can I explain what happened?' Labuschagne took the Judge's questions as criticism and became defensive. 'I was … I can explain exactly how it happened.'

He then stopped himself as he must have remembered our instruction not to volunteer information. He waited for the Judge.

'Go ahead,' said Judge van Zyl, off on a frolic of his own. I could only watch.

Labuschagne picked up the register and turned to the right page. 'The first one was Bongiane Israel Mbele, v3325,' he said, tracing the details in the register with his finger. 'He had come in with two other prisoners who had been sentenced to death together. They were called out to meet the Sheriff. I remember it very well because we called out four white men the same day, a father and son and two who were brothers. We called out seven. The other two in Mbele's case got twenty years. Mbele and the four whites were told they would be going up the next week. We took Mbele's fingerprints and his measurements and then put him in the Pot. On the way there he fought with us. We had to force him into the cell. I went off duty at four o'clock. That night he hanged himself behind the door. He used his pyjamas and one of his socks to make a rope and put a towel through the bars on the cell door. The night shift found him dead.'

He looked around the court before he continued at his own pace.

'They couldn't get in, because the Warrant Officer had the keys. One of the warders used a screwdriver to cut the towel through the bars. Mbele fell to the ground, dead. The key and the medic arrived only much later. But there was nothing anyone could do.'

Judge van Zyl nodded for Labuschagne to continue.

'There was an inquiry. The Warrant Officer accused everyone of sleep-ing on the job. He put the nightshift on the duty roster for the guard towers. The Major and the Warrant Officer also blamed the day shift. First they said that he could not have hanged himself like that. He had to have had help, or maybe we even killed him ourselves. But we pointed out that he was alive when the cells were locked after dinner and that we could not get into his cell without the key. Later they said that the District Surgeon had found strange injuries to his abdomen. They said the day shift had trampled on him and jumped on him.'

Judge van Zyl took this in without making notes. Then he asked, 'What makes you remember this so well?'

'The reason I remember is that I was one of the warders blamed for it. We were also one short on the gallows when the four white men went up, I remember that well. We had to explain why to the Sheriff. And we also had to go to the Magistrates' Court for a formal inquest.'

'Tell us about the other suicide, but keep it brief, please.' I had to stand and watch as the Judge went down an avenue that was not part of the defence case.

'Yes, sir,' said Labuschagne. He paged through the register and put his finger on an entry. 'This is the one. It was Frikkie Muller, v3666. We called him out on 7 August last year. He was going up on the fourteenth. We took his weight and everything and put him in the Pot. They told us to watch him carefully, because he had already tried to commit suicide twice before. He had also told us many times, Julle sallie vir my kry nie. Frikkie Muller is te slim vir julle, my Kroon. The first time he cut his wrists with a piece of wire, but we caught him in time. The second time he tried with a nail in the handle of his toothbrush but we found him in time again. Each time he recovered. Then he tried it again on the twelfth. We got the medics out, they stitched him up and we put him in a straitjacket. This time he had taken a nail from his shoe and melted the end of a ballpoint pen and stuck the nail in it.

'During the night he tore the straitjacket and pulled the stitches out. The Warrant Officer gave him some water to drink and put him back in the straitjacket. He kept screaming that he would kill himself if he got out. The next morning the Warrant Officer and the Major took the straitjacket off and spoke to him and they gave him oxygen, but he died.'

227

Wierda was tapping his pencil against his teeth again. I felt my jaw tightening. Labuschagne continued, but I did not really listen. I was looking for a way to use this evidence in the defence argument.

'We then searched his cell again and found a message in his shoe,' said Labuschagne. 'There was a drawing of a coffin and the words *Dood is Muller* written in ink on the inner sole of his shoe. This time the Warrant Officer did not say anything. He was the one looking after the prisoner during the night so he couldn't blame us for what had happened.'

I had stood motionless during the questioning by Judge van Zyl. After a while the Judge nodded in my direction. I took a deep breath. Up to this point I had been at pains to control the flow of information very strictly by asking closed questions that called for short, direct answers. The next topic could not be dealt with in that fashion if Labuschagne's personal anguish was to be displayed to the Court.

I thought I could see a way to use the suicide to advance the defence. 'How well had you known this prisoner, Frikkie Muller?' I asked.

'Very well.'

'How did that happen?'

'I had to help him read his Bible.'

'How did you feel when he died?'

The question caught him off guard. 'We hadn't finished the last Bible lesson. And we had already prepared his rope.'

'You read the Bible with him, and you prepared the rope for his execution?'

There was no answer and I changed the topic. 'What happened during the week of the twenty-third November?' I asked. The question was deliberately vague.

Labuschagne looked slightly perplexed. 'Do you mean at work?' he asked.

'At work and at home,' I explained.

He started slowly, looking at me from time to time as he spoke. 'It started that weekend. We went out on the Friday evening. We got into a fight with some soldiers. They were drunk. I can't remember how it started, but what I know is that we were looking for a fight. I must have passed out, because I came to on the front steps at my house. Magda – my wife – was wiping blood from my face. I was sick on the steps. She washed me and put me in bed. The next morning I saw that she had not slept in our bed and she told me she was going to leave me and take our daughter with her. She said she couldn't live like that.

'She accused me of things.'

'Such as what?' I asked.

There was a moment's hesitation. 'She said I had lost interest in her and that I did not love her anymore. While we were arguing her father and two brothers arrived. They said they had come to fetch Magda and Esmè and that she was going to live with them. I told them to leave. I got into a tussle with her brothers. Magda walked out of the house with our child. She sat in the back of her dad's car and wouldn't get out.'

Labuschagne stopped talking and stood head down looking in front of him.

'What did she do then?'

Tears welled up in his eyes. 'They left.'

'What was the last thing you saw as they were leaving?'

He mumbled the response through his sobs. 'Esmè's face through the car window.'

It was a cliché but effective and I waited a moment for the image to linger. But I needed more detail.

'How had you treated them before they left?'

Judge van Zyl watched Labuschagne intently as he answered. He was still crying. 'I was bad.'

I stood still. I still wanted more.

'Very badly,' he said. 'I was bad.'

I thought he would tell us more but he clammed up. I decided to leave the matter there. We could get the detail from his wife, even if she proved to be a reluctant witness.

'What did you do when they had left?' I asked when he looked back at me again.

'I went there Sunday and Monday evening and asked her to come back, but her father wouldn't let me in. When I tried to telephone, they put the phone down. They wouldn't even allow me to hold my daughter.'

'How did this affect you at work?'

'I can't remember.'

'How did the week progress? Tell the Court what happened at work and what happened in your personal life. Start with the Tuesday afternoon. What happened that Tuesday afternoon when you came off duty?'

'There was a man standing in the parking lot outside the front guardhouse. When I got to my bakkie he asked who I was and when I told him he gave me some documents. He said he was a Deputy Sheriff and that he was serving me with an interdict. He said I was not to come anywhere near my wife and daughter and if I broke the terms of the interdict I would go to jail. He said I was not to visit or phone. I was not to talk to them except through their lawyer. I asked him how I could speak to my child through a lawyer and he said I must get my own lawyer; he was not there to give me legal advice. Then he threw the documents in the back of the bakkie and walked off.'

'How did you feel after that episode?' I asked. This was one of our prepared questions but he was not helpful with his reply at first.

'I don't know.' When he realised I was not satisfied with the answer he added, 'I did not know what to do.'

I put it to him bluntly, 'Did you seek advice?'

'I had no one to talk to.'

I had no intention of letting him hide in self-pity. 'What about your parents?'

He would not look in their direction and straightened up a little. 'I thought they would take Magda's side.'

I took him back to Maximum.

'What happened at work the next day?'

He thought for a while. 'The Wednesday was the day before the next hanging. They received their last visits.'

'Tell the Court what role you played and how the day went.'

'I was assigned to Wessels. He asked if I could be his escort.'

The Judge looked up sharply at the use of the name but did not say anything. I proceeded as if I had not noticed his reaction.

'Could you please explain the relationship between you and Wessels and how it came about that he asked for you to be his escort?'

He came up with the prepared answer. 'I was on duty in C Section and I got to know him well. He was very quiet. We are not supposed to talk to the prisoners but it gets very lonely there, especially in C Section where there are never more than about six or so prisoners. I started talking to him one day when he was writing letters and he talked to me about his family and about the Bible. We also talked about rugby and what we had done at school. I could not understand how someone like him had come to be in there. We became friends, I think. I was very upset when the State President's letter came. When I was taking him back to his cell after I had taken his measurements and weight he asked me what was going to happen. I said he should not give up hope, he could still ask for a stay of execution, but he said no, he was ready and had made peace with God. He again asked what was to happen. I told him and then he said he would ask the Warrant Officer if I could be his escort because he needed someone to help him to be strong, and to look after him after he was dead. And that is what happened.'

I tried to picture the scene, with the two young men from such similar backgrounds talking about death. 'So how did you look after Wessels during that time?' I asked.

'First I went to read his case record in the archives office. Then I went to speak to him about his case. He wouldn't talk about it, but he said he would die like Jesus. He kept saying, Ek sal gaan soos Jesus. I asked him what he was talking about, but he would not say. He asked me to stay with him for a while. We read the Bible and I prayed with him. He kept saying over and over, As ek gaan soos Jesus sal God my vergewe.'

Labuschagne stopped and then, almost as an afterthought, added, 'I asked him if he was innocent, and he said, Ek sal gaan soos Jesus, vir ander se sondes.'

I had to prompt him again. 'In what other ways were you involved with Wessels before he was hanged?'

Labuschagne had tensed up considerably since the start of the Wessels evidence and his voice had become strained.

'The next day I took him out for exercise and I took him to the shower when it was his turn. He had been notified he could talk as much as he pleased and he spoke to me while I was on duty, telling me how sorry he was. I also sat in during his family visits. His wife and daughter were the last to visit him. I took him to the visitors' room in B Section.'

'How did this visit end?'

Labuschagne was on the verge of tears again. 'I watched as they said goodbye. I became very emotional, so I turned my back on them, which I wasn't supposed to do. His daughter kept looking at me. She reminded me of my own daughter. When their time was up I took Wessels back to his cell and came back to escort his wife and daughter out. I walked with them and showed the little girl a rabbit and the tortoise in the garden near the entrance. The little girl wanted to play with the rabbit but all I could allow was to take her for a walk through the greenery and around the pond. Then I signed them out at the main entrance and took them to the parking lot outside. There was someone waiting for them in a car. The little girl kept looking back at me. Then she waved at me. I stood outside the gate and cried. Then I went back in.'

'What did you do the rest of the day?'

His voice became flat again, devoid of emotion. 'When I came back in I was told to take Scheepers to the visitors' room to see his lawyer. They were making an application for a stay of execution. I sat through that interview too. He signed an affidavit before the Warrant Officer. After that I went off duty. When I came in early the next morning I heard that the Judge had said no and we had to take him up with the others that morning.'

'What were your duties that day, the twenty-sixth?' I looked at the handwritten list in my hand:

> Moatche
> Scheepers
> Wessels
> Mokwena

I had missed Labuschagne's answer and had to ask him to repeat it.

'I had to take care of Wessels.'

'What do you mean, take care of Wessels? Or rather, what did you actually do to take care of him?'

'I did all the things we do at a hanging.'

He was reluctant to speak on this topic, that was obvious. But I had to drag it out of him.

'Please start at the beginning. Tell us what you did and how you experienced this execution.'

The tension was visible in the stiffness of Labuschagne's shoulders and he pursed his lips until they were white. He spoke fast, as he did with most prepared answers.

'Wessels made me promise that I would take care of him, so I stood at his cell and went in when the Warrant Officer unlocked the door. He was already awake and dressed in his day clothes. Then I took him to the fingerprint table and from there to the chapel. I sat next to him during the service and sang and prayed with him. I told him that he had nothing to fear, that it would be over soon, and that he would feel no pain.'

I let Labuschagne talk. The court was very quiet. The rain was drizzling softly on the roof.

'When the service was over I cuffed his hands behind his back. He was shivering. I held him steady, not by the sleeve as we usually do, but by the arm, firmly, and I didn't push and shove him. All the time I spoke softly to him. I walked him up to the gallows. In the room before the gallows room he said goodbye and thank you. He was the last in the line onto the trapdoors, but the first for the rope.' Labuschagne stifled a sob. 'I held his arm tightly and he squeezed my hand between his arm and his body. We stood like that until he went down.'

The usher filled the glass and we watched as Labuschagne drank slowly. He had difficulty keeping the glass steady.

Again I tried to picture the scene, two young men in that room, one on the outside of the rail and the other inside on the trapdoors.

'What then?' I asked. My own voice had become unreliable.

Labuschagne spoke fast. 'I went down to the pit and opened his shirt.

233

I took the handcuffs off and undressed him. They pulled him up and lowered him again and I put him on the trolley. I washed him and I put the death shroud on. We put him in his coffin. Then I screwed the lid down and tied his card with his v-number to the handle of the coffin.'

Judge van Zyl had a question. 'I thought you said earlier that you never used the death shrouds.' He paged back through his bench book, searching for his note on that evidence.

Labuschagne answered before the Judge could find it. 'This was the only prisoner I ever dressed in the shroud.'

'What did you do after placing Wessels in his coffin?' I asked.

'I had to help with the others.'

'How did you treat them in comparison to Wessels?'

'They just threw the other bodies in their coffins and nailed them shut.'

'I thought I heard you mention screws.' I leaned on the lectern.

'The coffins come with screws but we never used a screwdriver because that would take too much time. We used a hammer.' He was leaning heavily on the witness box.

It was time for a reminder of the horrors that had become commonplace to Labuschagne and the other escorts. 'Is there anything in particular that you remember about the bodies after you had taken them down from the ropes?' I asked.

He closed his eyes and opened them just as quickly. 'I remember their eyes when we put them on the trolley. They were popping out and I felt them looking at me. I remember their necks were stretched out, and their tongues sticking out. The ears … the rope almost always tears the ear on the left side. I remember this all the time.'

'What do you mean by remembering this all the time?'

'I see them every time I close my eyes, during the day, at night, everywhere I go, and even when I sleep.'

I watched the Assessors. They were dutifully taking notes.

'Carry on,' I said. 'Tell the Court how the rest of the day went.'

'I attended the funeral service with the family and when it was over I escorted them out. Then I collected the paperwork to register the death. After that I buried them, Wessels and Scheepers.'

'Did anything happen at the cemetery?'

'Nothing.'

'What was your state of mind at the end of that day?'

The bluntness of the question on this topic caused Judge van Zyl to look sharply at me. Labuschagne inclined his head, considering his answer.

'I was tired.'

Labuschagne was not helping and I could not carry his case on my own. I decided to rough him up a bit.

'What did you feel when you were standing next to Wessels, holding on to his arm, feeling him shake just before he went down?'

'I felt nothing.' He was angry, possibly because I had revisited the topic, and his answer could not have been true.

'Did it cross your mind how similar you were, you and Wessels?'

'No, I said I felt nothing.'

'Wessels had a wife, didn't he, and you had a wife, Magda?'

The yes took a long time to come out.

'How old was Wessels again?'

'Nineteen.'

'And how old were you?'

'Nineteen.'

I asked the Judge if I could have a word with Wierda and deliberately wasted time talking to him about nothing of importance. Surreptitiously, I kept an eye on Labuschagne. He was looking at his hands; they were gripping the edge of the witness box in front of him.

'Wessels had a daughter, didn't he?'

'Yes.'

'And you have a daughter.'

This time Labuschagne looked directly at me. 'Yes,' he whispered. 'Esmeralda. But we call her Esmè.'

'Let me see if I have the facts right,' I said, keeping an eye on James Murray who had been remarkably patient with my line of questioning. 'You stood there, next to Wessels, holding his arm, and you felt nothing. Is that right?'

'Yes,' he said defiantly. 'I felt nothing and I thought nothing.'

'You read the Bible with Wessels and you felt nothing?'

'I read the Bible with many of them and I felt nothing.'

Wierda passed me a note and I asked Judge van Zyl to give me a moment: *Wessels killed a woman. And Labuschagne took Roos de Vos up.*

I crumpled the note and put it in my pocket. It would be going too far to ask questions about that. Nevertheless, I decided to hit Labuschagne from another angle.

'Did you seek advice from anyone about your problems with Magda and her father?'

'No.'

'Did you get a lawyer?'

'No.'

'Did you try to communicate with Magda?'

'No, not after they chased me away. What could I do?'

'Did you tell anyone at Maximum that Magda had left you and had taken Esmè with her?'

'No. What could they do?'

I ignored the question. My purpose was to establish a sense of hopelessness on his part, despair even. The answers had given me that. I was ready to move on. As I was turning the page in my notebook I became aware of a change in the atmosphere in the court. For a moment I listened carefully. There was no sound, only the faint hush of the air flowing into the courtroom along the ducts and through the vents in the walls. When I listened more closely I could hear the ambient sounds of the city, cars and buses on the Square, but nothing else. The rain had stopped. The spectators had become silent; there was none of the usual coughing and shifting on the hard benches they sat on.

'Let's deal with the next two weeks,' I suggested. 'What did you do each day?'

'Work was just like before. Every day was the same. I went to work and then I came home to sleep. Then I would go back to work the next day.'

'What did you do at home after work?'

'Nothing.'

'What did you do for dinner and breakfast?'

Labuschagne thought long before answering. 'I must have eaten.'

'Who prepared the food?' I needed detail.

'It must have been me.'

'What else did you do at home?'

'I told you, nothing. There was nothing to do.' Labuschagne would not look at me anymore.

'Well,' I said, sensing hostility from him to the line of questioning, 'let's deal with the matter on a day-to-day basis. What did you do on Friday the twenty-seventh?'

'I went to work.'

'What happened there?'

He thought for a moment. 'We called out the next lot and they went into the Pot.'

'And after work, when you were at home, what did you do?'

'Nothing that I can remember.'

'It was a Friday night. Didn't you go out drinking with your colleagues like you did before?'

James Murray turned to face me with raised eyebrows. I knew it was a leading question, but he did not object and I was able to return my focus to Labuschagne.

'No, I did not feel like going out. I went home.'

I pressed on. 'How did you sleep that night?'

'I had nightmares.'

'Please give the Court some details. What was your nightmare about?'

He wouldn't answer at first. I repeated the question.

'It was about Wessels,' he conceded eventually.

'What about Wessels?'

'They kept putting the rope around my neck instead of his. I struggled and fought and said it was wrong. When I woke up I felt like I was in a coffin. I couldn't see anything.'

I watched as he stood with his shoulders slumped and his head down.

'And Saturday the twenty-eighth? What did you do that day?' I asked.

'I stayed at home during the day. I had the second night shift. I was on the catwalk in C Section. I can remember that clearly.'

'What makes you remember that shift?'

'It was a very quiet shift and I saw the ghosts in c Section again.' Labuschagne kept his eyes down. He must have known that we would be sceptical about the ghosts.

'How did that happen? Could you explain, please?'

'I looked into Wessels' cell, but it was empty. I saw movement above the cells, in the catwalk area. I heard creaking noises. I thought I saw the ghost. It was just a misty, shrouded figure, never straight in front of my eyes, always to the side, but it was definitely there. I sat down and closed my eyes to make it go away. I must have fallen asleep. The next thing the duty officer pushed me over with his foot. He asked what was wrong. I said I was just tired. He told me not to sleep on the job. I decided then to see our pastor after church in the morning.'

'On Sunday the twenty-ninth, did you go to church?'

'Yes.'

'Did you see your pastor?'

'No, he was on leave. There was a young proponent. I couldn't speak to him. He did not even know my wife.'

'What did you want to discuss with your pastor?'

'I wanted him to speak to Magda and her father.'

'Why did you not get an attorney to do that for you?'

'I had no money.' He added, 'It had nothing to do with the law. It was about my family.'

I followed the cue. 'Why didn't you ask your own family to help?'

'I didn't think of that.' Still he could not bring himself to look in the direction of his parents in the well of the court behind the dock. 'I didn't want them to know, I think.'

'Whose fault was it that your marriage broke down? What did *you* think?'

'At the time I thought it was Magda's fault. I know I had got drunk a few times, that I had stayed out late, that I had pushed her around even, and that I had sworn at her father, but that wasn't serious. In the court documents she said it was my fault.'

'What do you think now, whose fault was it?' I asked.

'Now I think it must have been my fault, except I didn't know what was wrong.' He shook his head. 'I just don't know what's gone wrong.'

'But didn't you see that things were going wrong in your marriage and that Magda might leave you? And take Esmè with her?'

'I only saw that when it was too late, when I was in the cells.'

'Let's move on,' I said. 'What happened at work in the week of the thirtieth?'

Labuschagne thought about it for a while before he said, 'We must have called out the ones who were going to go up the next week and put them in the Pot.'

'How many were there?'

'Twenty-one.'

'And that week, did you see your pastor or anyone else about your problems with Magda?'

'No.'

'Why not?'

'I don't know. I didn't think about it.'

'Didn't think about what, your marriage or seeing someone about it?'

'I was thinking of Magda and Esmè all the time. I mean I did not think about seeing someone about it. I couldn't see how anyone could help.'

'So what did you do after work each day?'

'I went home.'

'What did you do during the weekend of the fifth and sixth of December?'

He listed his movements like an alibi witness. 'I was at home the Saturday. I had the second night shift again that night. I went to church on the Sunday but the pastor was still on leave. I got his address. I was going to see him that afternoon but my parents suddenly arrived. They wanted to see Esmè. I told them Magda and Esmè were visiting her parents.'

'The next day, that would be Monday the seventh of December, what did you do?'

'I went to work. I saw the Warrant Officer and said I wanted a transfer. He said, Talk to me in the new year. I need you here. Things are going to get a bit rough this week. You are the only one I can rely on. We can talk about it in January.

'Then he told me to go up and service the gallows. He said the machine was going to work overtime in the next three days and that I should make sure the stopper bags were in tiptop shape.'

'Did you know what he was talking about when he said things were going to get rough?'

'He was talking about those twenty-one.'

'Had you ever had to hang so many in such a short time?'

'No.'

Next, I deviated from the planned questions slightly and it caught him by surprise. 'What was the atmosphere in the Pot like on that day?' I grimaced at the awkwardness of the question.

Labuschagne swayed and I thought he might be about to faint, but he answered, 'The Pot was a mess that whole week and the week before. We had just taken seven up and we immediately put another seven back in.'

'That must have been on the Thursday, then,' I suggested, 'Thursday the third.'

'Yes,' he said.

'Carry on,' I said. 'Describe to the Court the atmosphere in the prison.'

'It was a mess,' he said, shaking his head. 'It was a total mess.'

Just when I thought I was going to have to drag the details out of him he spoke again, slowly, as if recalling distant memories.

'It was bad. They were wailing and singing and praying. The whole place knew.'

He paused and I asked quickly, 'Knew *what*?'

'Everyone knew. They had seen us call them out and they had said goodbye to them as we took them down the passage to see the Sheriff. And everyone could hear the wailing and crying and singing. This went on and on for more than a week, day and night, and we had been tired already at the beginning of that last week. Everyone was tired, finished.'

I stood still, considering what else to explore on this topic when Labuschagne spoke again.

'Sir,' he said with emphasis, 'the whole prison knew, everyone. The whole place went into execution mode, you know? Except this time it was much, much worse. And every day we got more prisoners coming in. So we had the new ones to break in and the old ones to take up.'

They were stretched to the limit, I thought, physically and emotionally. But I saved that point for my closing argument.

'So what did you do the rest of that day, Monday the seventh?' I asked.

The answer came quickly. 'I checked the gallows. I repaired the stopper bags.'

I deliberately delayed my next question. I fussed with my papers, tugged at my robes, turned to whisper to Wierda.

'Did anything unusual happen while you were doing that?' I asked.

Labuschagne nearly ruined it. 'No, sir,' he said promptly.

The answer took me by surprise. We had been through my questions and the answers I expected more than once. I glanced at Wierda. He shrugged his shoulders. I looked down at my notes and weighed another question seeking the same information. 'Did you see anybody or anything while working on those stopper bags?'

'Oh, I see what you mean. No, the ghosts were there, as usual. It didn't bother me that they were there. I just carried on with my work.'

The Judge intervened. 'Would it suit counsel if we took the long adjournment now? I still have to complete my notes on the gallows chamber and the pit room and would like to record those inspection details immediately after the adjournment.'

I headed for the robing room leaving Wierda and Roshnee behind; they could have lunch on their own.

When I got to the front entrance it was raining again, so I went back inside and spent the hour in Cell 6 with Labuschagne.

Hansen faced two charges of attempted murder and two of murder. On 13 December 1986 he had tried to kill Dennis Marthinus and Geraldine Sauls by stabbing them with a knife. On 15 December he managed to kill Geraldine Sauls by stabbing her to death. After his arrest and appearance in court he stabbed Emily Patel to death in the back of the police van taking him to the cells, on 19 December 1986.

Hansen pleaded guilty to all four charges and was quickly convicted. The full picture emerged when evidence was being led on the presence or absence of extenuating circumstances.

In mid-1985 Hansen was released from prison after serving a sentence for theft from a motor vehicle. He moved to Bredasdorp where he met Miss Geraldine Sauls. Her boyfriend was Mr Dennis Marthinus, who was in prison at the time. Hansen and Miss Sauls struck up a relationship after she told him about Marthinus, saying that the affair was over. Hansen warned her that if he ever caught her and Marthinus together he would kill both of them. Hansen moved in with Miss Sauls and her parents and by all accounts their relationship was a fairly steady one until the end of November 1986, shortly after Hansen was convicted of possession of cannabis and given a suspended sentence. Sauls' parents asked Hansen to leave their house just as word arrived that Marthinus had been released from prison and was back in town. Miss Sauls left with Hansen and they moved to another house down the street.

Hansen started hearing rumours that Sauls was seeing Marthinus again. He threatened Marthinus and argued with Sauls about this. On 13 December he sent Sauls to the grocery store, but she did not arrive back home at the time he expected. He took a knife, went in search of her and found her with Marthinus at the side of the road. He tried to stab Marthinus in the heart, but Marthinus turned at the last moment and received a wound in the back and ran off. Hansen could not catch him. Then he turned on Sauls and stabbed her once in the chest and once near the collarbone. After this his senses seem to have returned to him, because he carried Sauls to a doctor's rooms for treatment.

The police arrived at the doctor's with Marthinus. The police sergeant inexplicably told Hansen to close his knife and go home, ordering him to report to the police the next morning. The police took Sauls to the hospital, but her injuries were not serious enough to warrant her admission and she was sent home. She returned to her parents' home.

The next day, Sunday, Hansen went looking for her and, when he saw her at her parents' home, shouted that he was going to kill her. Then he went looking for Marthinus, but could not find him as the police were keeping Marthinus in protective custody. Hansen later told the Court that he had made the decision to kill Sauls so that he could be arrested, reasoning that he would then also have the opportunity to kill Marthinus in the police cells.

On Monday 15 December Hansen hid in a bush across the street from the house where Sauls was staying. He called out to Sauls and she came out of the house, but went back in immediately when her sister Lorna cautioned her. Hansen climbed through a window and went after Sauls, but she had escaped through the back door and had run to a neighbour's house. There Hansen caught up with her and stabbed her several times before dragging her outside where he continued stabbing her. He then picked her up and threw her over a fence into the next property. There he stabbed her yet again. As he was finally walking away from her she called to him. He went back, kicked her and sat down astride her as he stabbed her until she was dead. The police arrived and he handed the knife over to them.

The post-mortem by the District Surgeon of Bredasdorp showed that Sauls, who was one and a half metres tall and weighed only about forty-five kilograms, had died of haemorrhagic shock caused by loss of blood and respiratory failure caused by a collapsed left lung. She had eighteen stab wounds altogether.

On Thursday 18 December Hansen made a full confession to the Bredasdorp Magistrate, admitting guilt on the murder charge and the two charges of attempted murder. In court the next day he gave a detailed explanation. Later in the day he was put in a police van with other prisoners to be taken to the Caledon prison. For some reason the police allowed a female prisoner, the sixteen-year-old Emily Patel, to be transported in the back of the van with the male prisoners. During the journey she asked Hansen to sit next to her. She asked him for money, a paltry twenty rand, to pay her fine for trespassing. He gave her two earrings, but when she asked him if he had really killed Sauls he decided to kill her.

He told her so after asking the other prisoners to close their eyes, but she apparently did not believe him. He stabbed her in the neck with the leg of a broken pair of scissors he had hidden under his clothes. Next he ordered Miss Patel to undress completely and, when she had done so, he stabbed her in the back. He ordered her to dress again, which she did. Then he stabbed her repeatedly until she was dead. The other prisoners in the van did nothing to stop him, to protect Patel or to alert the policeman driving the van.

When the police stopped at Caledon with their load of prisoners they found Emily Patel dead. Hansen immediately admitted that he had killed her and handed over the weapon he had used. Patel died as a result of acute shock caused by a blockage of the heart and loss of blood. She had been stabbed altogether forty-five times.

Hansen repeatedly admitted in open court and also prior to the trial that he had intended to kill each of his victims. Geraldine Sauls' killing had been premeditated and had occurred in plain view of a number of witnesses. He had pursued her over a period of days, had lain in wait for her, and had then stabbed her repeatedly. He killed Emily Patel for no discernible reason at all, and almost defiantly in a police van in the presence of a number of witnesses. It was as if Hansen was thumbing his nose at the law.

A panel of psychiatrists reported to the Court that Hansen was fit to stand trial and that he had the capacity at the time of the offences to appreciate the wrongfulness of his actions and to act accordingly. The Court could see no remorse in Hansen for what he had done and could find no extenuating circumstances. On 8 May 1987 he was sentenced to death on each of the murder charges.

On 1 December 1987 Hansen was called out of his cell and informed that the State President had decided not to grant him mercy. He was hanged on 8 December 1987 after spending seven months in the death cells. He was about thirty years old.

I didn't know what to think of Hansen. He was asking to be arrested and sentenced to death. His behaviour was similar to that of the cell murderers, who killed with a single-mindedness that took no account of the fact that there would be a number of eye witnesses. Did Hansen kill Emily Patel as a substitute for Dennis Marthinus?

The behaviour of the police was astonishing. Instead of locking Hansen up they put his intended victim in protective custody. And, by any reasonable standard, the police were responsible for Emily Patel's cruel death. They put her in the van with male prisoners, and that in the company of a man who had not been searched properly.

Palace of Justice

32

I spent the lunch hour with Labuschagne in Cell 6. I knew we had another heavy session ahead. We both needed a break from the prepared line-up of topics and in any event I could not speak to Labuschagne about the evidence he had already given. The Bar's rules of ethics prohibited that.

I had to make peace first. 'Look,' I said, 'Don't get anxious about my questions. I have to ask them, and we are doing alright. Just don't give up. We are doing alright.'

Labuschagne nodded, but did not make eye contact.

I moved to change the subject altogether. 'Tell me about Tsafendas,' I said. Dimitri Tsafendas had been a mystery to all of South Africa since that day in September many years before when he had stabbed the Prime Minister in the heart in front of a packed House of Parliament. Very little was known about him.

I was sitting on the bench facing Labuschagne.

'There isn't much to tell,' he said.

'Tell me what you know,' I suggested.

He did not speak for a while and appeared to be oblivious to his surroundings. He ignored me even when I looked straight at him. I took the time to study more of the graffiti:

THE FIGHT AGAINST RACISM, EVIL AND OPPRESSION
IS CONTINUING. THIS YEAR 1975 IS NO EXCEPTION

Next I was looking at a crude drawing of a handgun and a penis below it pointing in the same direction. Suddenly he spoke behind me.

'There was nothing wrong with Mr Tsafendas.'

It was unusual to hear anyone refer to Tsafendas as mister.

'That's not what I heard,' I said quickly, to draw him out of his shell.

I was standing in front of another incomplete message trying to decipher the last word, but the damp had obliterated its tail.

'*You* can't know,' he said. I turned around to find Labuschagne studying me. 'How could you know unless you'd met him and spent some time with him?'

It was a good point. I thought of a response as I studied another entry on the wall, one of many on the same theme.

ANC. 2/6/81

SASOL – BOOYSEN

TREASON TRIO

1. —RY TSONTSOBE

2. JOHANNES SHABANGU

3. DAVID MOISE

DISCHARGE OR IMPRISONMENT

LIFE OR DEATH

THE STRUGGLE CONTINUES

VICTORY IS CERTAIN

THERE IS NO MIDDLE ROAD

The message was incomplete. I wished I had the conviction of the anonymous scribe that victory was certain in my young client's case.

'What makes you think there was nothing wrong with him?'

'He was the only sane man there,' he said.

I decided to change the angle slightly.

'Did you get to know him?'

'We were not allowed to speak to him, but he wasn't afraid to speak to us. After Wessels was hanged I stopped paying attention to the Warrant Officer's rules.'

Labuschagne did not say any more, but I had the impression that he was looking for an opportunity to unburden himself.

'What happened between you and Tsafendas?' I could not bring myself to call him Mr Tsafendas yet.

He sighed but did not answer.

'I can't help you if I don't know what happened to you,' I said. 'Talk to me, Leon.'

It was the only time I ever called him by his first name.

He did not answer immediately, but when he did he spoke for a long time:

After we had buried Wessels and Scheepers, we came back to Maximum. The two escorts who had gone off to bury Moatche and Mokwena arrived back at the same time. They were laughing and joking, and I suddenly couldn't stand being in their company any longer. There was no place where I could be alone except in the chapel.

As I was walking towards the chapel, there was a noise behind me. It was Mr Tsafendas. He was making a racket. He called me over. He was very angry. He said someone had taken his newspaper clippings. He was the only prisoner who was allowed to receive newspapers and we all knew that he studied all the political news and took cuttings from the papers. He kept everything in a box under his bunk. I said I would get them later. He said, 'No, I want them now.' I said, 'No, later,' and started walking again. Then he said, 'I know what you are doing there.' He was pointing in the direction of the chapel and the gallows building.

I was surprised, because he was supposed to be mad and he usually didn't talk much. You'd get punished for talking to him, but I asked, 'What do you mean?' and he said, 'You kill people. That's your job.' I shook my head, but he said, 'I know, I can hear the voices in your head. You kill people and they talk to you. And now you are going to the chapel to pray that they should leave you alone.' I said it was nonsense and that he was crazy, but he said that he could see more than other people because he had a special gift.

I decided to walk away, but he then said, 'You don't like killing, that's why you pray and sing with them in the morning and that's why you have come here now, to pray some more.'

I felt like he was seeing right through me when even I did not understand what I was thinking. I also became angry with him because I didn't want to talk about what I was doing. So I told him to shut up and went into the chapel. I tried to pray. I waited for the tension and the guilt, perhaps it was sorrow too, to go away, but it wasn't working. I could feel something building up and building up inside me until I felt as if I was going to burst open. All this time Mr Tsafendas was making such a racket next door that I couldn't concentrate. I told him to keep quiet and went to look for his clippings.

I saw the Warrant Officer in his office and asked him if he knew anything about the clippings. He asked me how I knew and I said Mr Tsafendas had told me. Then he said I had no right to be in that section and that I should have known better than to speak to Mr Tsafendas. He threw a shoebox at me and a heap of newspaper clippings fell out. 'You can take his precious clippings to him!' he shouted, 'and for talking to a prisoner you can do catwalk duty tonight when your shift ends.' While I was on the floor picking up the clippings he stomped around swearing at me, saying that I had betrayed his trust. 'That man killed the Prime Minister,' he shouted, 'and you feel sorry for him.' I then got very angry with him.

I looked at Labuschagne, surprised. He was serious. For a moment I thought I had misunderstood, but then I realised that he was talking about the Warrant Officer, not Tsafendas.

I waited for him to tell me more, but he relapsed into his uncommunicative mode. I felt that he had more to tell and prompted him. 'Did you have catwalk duty that night?'

'Yes.'

'Did you speak to Tsafendas again?'

'Yes, I was locked in his section, up on the catwalk, alone with him all night.'

Again I let him speak without interruption:

The old man didn't sleep well that night and I watched him put his clippings back into order. He kept rearranging them, first in one order and then in another. He asked me why they had been messed up and I told him the Warrant Officer had done it because he was angry. 'What have I done to him?' he asked. 'You killed Dr Verwoerd,' I said. He laughed and said, 'That was before you were born. What do you know?' I said I had read about it in school. He said, 'Make yourself comfortable and I will tell you the whole story.' When I didn't reply, he banged on the wall and said, 'Hey, are you still there?' I said yes. Then he started talking. He talked all night.

'There are two kinds of people,' he said, 'no, make that three. There are those who make history. They are the first and the most important. Then there are those who write history. And last there are those who read history.'

'So what?' I said. 'Who cares?' I was tired and didn't need a lecture from a prisoner. But I was curious at the same time.

He answered immediately, 'Only those who make history know the truth. Those who write it down rely on second-hand information.

And those who read it have no way of knowing whether what they read is the truth or not. They are doomed to be forever uncertain, which is worse than being ignorant.'

I was getting sleepy, so I made myself more comfortable on the catwalk. I sat down with my back against the wall and the rifle across my knees. There is a rule that the rifle may never touch the ground. The rifle just got heavier and heavier.

'My boy,' he said, 'it's a long story, but we have all night, locked in here together for our punishment.' I don't know how he knew I was on punishment shift, but he somehow knew. 'Let me tell you what really happened,' he said, 'and in the morning, if you believe me, maybe you could ask the Medical Officer for some pills for this worm I have inside me before it kills me.'

I said nothing. I had heard the story about the worm before, from my history teacher. He taught us that the Prime Minister had been a very good man, like a prophet who would lead the Afrikaner nation to greatness. Then a madman killed him in Parliament with a knife, a man who believed he was told what to do by a tapeworm inside him. So when the old man spoke of the worm I just let him ramble on.

'You know we Greeks are the world's greatest seamen. We got the biggest shipping companies,' he said. 'I was just an ordinary sailor, a seaman,' he said, 'and I had sailed on many ships and to many places around the world.' He said that was how he learned a few new languages, English and Portuguese and so on. And he said he also got into trouble sometimes.

Then he told me how he came to Cape Town. 'Do you know how difficult it is for an immigrant to get into South Africa?' he asked, but I had no idea. 'It is ten times more difficult for anyone with a record as bad as mine. And for an immigrant who is not white *and* has a record? Almost impossible. You know what they do? They take your fingerprints and they check your previous convictions in every country whose stamp is in your passport. And I had many stamps and many convictions everywhere.' He sounded proud of this.

'So how did you get in then?' I asked. 'Oh, so you are still awake? Well, they came for me.' He said it like this, *They* came for *me*. He also said that they had even given him money to come in and had promised him a job in Cape Town.

'Who's they?' I asked.

'Two men from right here in Pretoria,' he answered. He said they had come to his ship in Lourenço Marques, two men who had recruited him for an important job in Cape Town. 'They said they had been authorised by a man called John Vorster and a man called Rhoodie,' he said.

I had heard of Vorster, but not of Rhoodie. 'That is because I made Vorster the Prime Minister,' he said, 'and Rhoodie was always working behind the scenes.'

I was beginning to see what job it was they had for him, but to make sure I asked, and he answered, 'To kill Verwoerd.'

I told him, 'It doesn't make sense. Why would they get a non-white Greek sailor with a bad record sitting on a ship in Lourenço Marques to come and do something like that in Cape Town? How did they even know that you were there?'

'It was the perfect scheme,' he said. He had applied for a visa to come to South Africa many times before and they had been delaying it for years while they investigated his past. He said, 'I was in Lourenço Marques, waiting for the visa.' They'd refused his application *seven* times before and had even put him on the banned list. Then suddenly they gave him a visa while he was still on the banned list. 'So they found me, a coloured foreign sailor who knew how to handle a knife, who had once taken part in a communist party protest, and who wanted to live in South Africa. Don't you see? It was the perfect scheme. A mad communist non-white foreigner kills the Prime Minister!'

I didn't think it was all that obvious.

'But wait for the whole story,' he said. 'My best point,' he went on, 'is that I was there. I was part of the conspiracy. I made it happen. I made history. No one can take that away from me. I was there.'

'Or made it up,' I said. 'You have had all this time to work out a story.'

'Well, what about this then?' he said. 'Who became the Prime Minister when Verwoerd was dead? It was Vorster, of course. And what did he do? He made Rhoodie, who was just a little whipper-snapper, the Goebbels of the National Party, the propaganda man. So there is the motive, or at least part of it.'

'What's the other part?' I asked.

You know that all of this was long before my time, so I'm telling you what I understood from Mr Tsafendas' story. So he said Vorster thought that Verwoerd was too soft and too much of a professor, and that South Africa needed a man of action, a strong, hard man who did things. Like himself. Vorster said that in 1945 while Verwoerd sat around writing in his newspaper *he* got thrown in an internment camp for his principles. He said that the world was changed by men of big actions, not men with big ideas.

I heard Mr Tsafendas get up from his bed and a short while later he flushed his toilet.

When he sat down again he said, 'So that is what I have here in the box, in all these newspaper clippings. This is the proof that Vorster and Rhoodie killed Verwoerd. All their reasons and their plans.' And he said that he found more of it in the papers every day, so that he could tell the world what had really happened.

'So are you going to write history now?' I asked. I was sorry that I had not taken a closer look at those newspaper clippings when I had the box.

'I can write it because I was there,' he said. We sat like that for a long time into the night. I could hear a man sobbing in c Section, otherwise the place was quiet. It must have been between two and three in the morning when I woke up. I don't know how long I had been asleep and how much I had dreamed, but the old man was still talking.

The duty sergeant arrived and asked if I had been sleeping on the job. I said no and asked him for the time. It was just after three. He looked down into the cell and saw Mr Tsafendas at his table. 'Why aren't you in bed?' he shouted. 'Get into bed immediately!' The old man quickly lay down. Then the sergeant said, 'And stand up when I speak to you!' The old man got up again and then the sergeant walked off.

'Now who's crazy?' the old man said as soon as he was gone. 'He tells me to get into my bed and when I do it he tells me to stand up while he is talking to me.'

I thought he had a point there.

Then he asked, 'If I am crazy, why am I here?'

He had me there. If he was mad he should be in a hospital like Weskoppies. And if he wasn't mad, he should have been hanged.

'I am here because I know why Verwoerd was killed,' he said. 'They are afraid I will tell.'

'Tell what?' I asked.

'Tell everyone that Verwoerd had told me that Nelson Mandela was going to be the first black Prime Minister of the country,' he said.

I thought about that for a while. It had always struck me as odd that he had two cells to himself. One had even been fitted out as a bathroom. His cell had been turned around so that its door opened onto the passage between B and C sections, not into the passage inside B Section like all the other cells there. When I thought about it more it became obvious. That way he would never get into contact with any of the other prisoners and he would also never be able to talk to the visitors who came into the visiting rooms in B Section.

When he spoke up again I could hear that he was getting tired. 'They went for the insanity angle so that no one would ever believe me. So when the Court declared me insane they locked me away in the death cells.'

He kept repeating that he wasn't crazy, but that he thought they were trying to drive him crazy so that no one would believe him.

I tried to work out how many times he must have heard the trap-doors banging against the stopper bags and made a rough calculation; say three hangings every two weeks for fifty-two weeks of the year times fifteen or so years that he had been there equalled about eleven hundred times. And if you counted the six years he had spent in the old prison in Potgieter Street, it was nearer fifteen hundred.

Labuschagne and I sat looking at each other for a while. Wierda was slow in arriving and, when he did, we went up to the robing room and started picking at the next case.

I had only half my mind on the case. The other half was searching for a way to put the Tsafendas prophecy before the Court. I was getting a little desperate. We were halfway through the examination-in-chief with Labuschagne and we still lacked the evidence that would lend credibility to his version of the events at the reservoir. We had expert opinions but expert opinion is no good without a factual foundation.

I looked at my watch. We had ten minutes before the Judge and Assessors would return.

I thought of Marianne Schlebusch, a calm and efficient woman who had a calming effect on me. I had been trying to find out if there was a foolproof way for us to determine whether Labuschagne would be caught out in a lie, that his whole defence was built on falsehood, and that he was really a mass murderer of the worst kind.

'I don't think he is lying,' she had told us, 'but I would have to concede that we can never be sure. My tests have built-in lie detectors and if he had lied to me the tests would have exposed that. But there is a small group of subjects who can defeat those traps, and he fits the profile perfectly. He is way above average intelligence and he can concentrate for a long period without losing focus.'

'And he may be a psychopath,' I ventured.

'No,' she had said, 'but he doesn't have to be to do what he did.'

'So what am I to do with him?' I had asked her.

'You are going to have to make him talk about the events at the reservoir and face up to what he has done. Until he talks about it and admits what he has done, you won't know whether he is telling the truth and I won't be able to begin with a cure.'

Wierda was waiting for me in court. He told me he was ready to give me a summary of the next case.

Prins was a common gangster who killed another gang member on a train in Cape Town. He was a member of the Hard Livings gang and had the gang's initials, HL, tattooed behind his left ear.

The evidence against Prins was short and to the point. On 8 July 1986 the deceased, Joseph Moliefe, boarded a train in Cape Town with a colleague, Bernard Grootboom, and headed home. At Netreg Station they disembarked and re-entered the train at another coach. There was standing room only. Grootboom saw Prins near the door. Prins must have said something to Mr Moliefe because Grootboom heard the latter say no. Whatever he had said to Moliefe, Prins responded to this single-word reply by pulling out a knife and stabbing Moliefe once in the chest. He immediately jumped off the train, which was already in motion. Within a short time Moliefe fainted and died at the scene.

The cause of death was a single stab wound between ribs six and seven into the left ventricle of the heart.

A friend of Prins, Miss Tasneem Julyse, told the Court that she knew Prins well and had on 8 July travelled on the same train with him and two other acquaintances of theirs, Shanien Rich and Ronald Middleway. At Netreg Station they disembarked after Moliefe and another man, probably Bernard Grootboom, had entered the same coach. Just as the train pulled off Prins had jumped back on, quickly stabbed Moliefe and jumped off the moving train again. When Prins rejoined them she asked him why he had stabbed the man on the train and he replied that the man was 'an American' and that they had stabbed his brother. The Americans were a gang operating in the area. Prins also said that he and Moliefe had argued, but Miss Julyse told the Court that she had heard no quarrel between them.

Prins gave a version entirely at odds with that of Grootboom and Julyse. He told the Court that he had boarded the train in Cape Town with Julyse and had drunk enough liquor during the journey to be intoxicated. When the train stopped with a jerk at Netreg Station he fell against Moliefe. He apologised, but Moliefe swore at him. Three other men who could have been friends of Moliefe then came towards him and told him he was full of liquor. They threw him down and kicked and beat him. He jumped up, took out his knife and stabbed blindly in their direction. He knew he had stabbed someone but did not know whom.

The Court rejected this version out of hand. The version Prins gave to the Court differed from the one he had given to a Magistrate when he was arrested. His counsel called Ronald Middleway as a witness to support his version, but Middleway corroborated Miss Julyse's evidence to the degree that when Miss Julyse asked Prins why he had stabbed the man on the train he said that the man was 'an American'.

The Court was unanimous in its finding that Prins had deliberately killed Moliefe because he thought the latter was a member of the gang responsible for the stabbing of his brother. The Court further found that there was an element of cunning in the way Prins had executed his plan. He had waited for the train to start moving, then he jumped on and quickly stabbed Moliefe before jumping off again. The slight effect alcohol might have had on his actions was outweighed by the cunning with which he had achieved his aim and the fact that he had killed a completely innocent man. Although he was relatively young his actions had been related to his gang activities and had been motivated by inherent vice.

He was therefore convicted of murder without any extenuating circumstances and he was sentenced to death on 9 June 1987.

Prins had spent less than six months in the death cells before he was hanged on 8 December 1987. He was twenty-three years old.

Palace of Justice

34

Judge van Zyl started the afternoon's proceedings by reading his final inspection notes into the record. He had to raise his voice against the sound of the rain pelting down on the roof and skylights.

'There is not much to say about the gallows chamber and the pit room, which we have been given to understand will feature in the defence evidence. I do not intend to belabour the issue as the evidence already treats the layout to some extent.'

He looked around the room before he continued. This time I was ready for Wierda, and I handed him a sketch I had made. It was not nearly as good as his sketches and he scoffed at it. He smiled condescendingly when I handed him my second sketch, one of the pit room and autopsy room.

I listened to Judge van Zyl's description with my eyes closed. The image in my mind was that of an abattoir with rows of skinned beasts hanging from hooks and ready for conveyance to the butcheries in the suburbs.

'Are you ready to proceed?' the Judge asked me.

I opened my eyes and the serious work of the afternoon session started.

I rose and addressed the defendant. 'Let's go back to the gallows room, shall we?' I said, and proceeded, 'Was there ever an occasion when you had to use force or violence to get a prisoner onto the trapdoors or to get the noose around his neck?'

Labuschagne stooped to speak into the microphone in front of him. 'Sir, by the time the execution date arrives, the prisoners have been broken in so that they obey orders.' Then he added, 'They did that, most of the time.'

'So my question is,' I said, 'in the time you worked there, did it really always go as smoothly as you have described?'

'There were always things that went wrong.'

'Like what?'

'Like prisoners fainting, and then we had to carry them. Or resisting, and then we had to put them in a straitjacket, and so on.'

I decided to be more direct. 'What is the worst that happened while you were there?'

He took his time trying to recollect. Judge van Zyl said something to the Assessor on his right and Labuschagne used the time to compose his answer.

'It was bad a few times, like when we had to hang four white men on one day – although they didn't resist. It went wrong badly only once.'

I took my reading glasses off and folded my arms before asking, 'How did that happen? Tell us what went wrong and how you dealt with it.'

'The worst was in that last week. We had called them out the week before and put them in the Pot. The mistake we made was to think they had been broken completely so that there would be no resistance. But when we put them into the Pot they suddenly became difficult.'

'Be more specific please. What happened?'

'In the Pot they could talk at any time and to anyone. They must have planned everything then, because they had a plan. I thought we were going to get rid of them quickly, but they had a plan.'

Labuschagne took a sip of water from the glass on the witness box. He was about to put it down again when he changed his mind and put it back to his lips. The usher stepped over and refilled the glass. Labuschagne kept glancing in the direction of the Warrant Officer. The Judge was sitting back. He was not taking notes any longer, either because he had decided to obtain a printed transcript of the evidence or because he was not taking any real interest in this evidence. The third possibility, that he was so absorbed in the evidence that he did not need to take notes, escaped me at the time.

I let Labuschagne tell the story without interruptions or prompts; that way his evidence would probably sound more genuine. He took a deep breath before he started.

'We lined up as usual and the Warrant Officer made his allocations. We waited for the bell. We went in. The prisoners immediately started shouting and screaming abuse at us. The Warrant Officer unlocked their cells and we took up our usual positions, one escort in front of each cell door. We went in and told them to dress and to come out, but they refused. The Warrant Officer ordered us to drag them out. We tried, but it is almost impossible to drag someone out of a two-by-three-metre cell. The door got in the way. They held on to the fittings in the cell, the bunks, the tables, even the toilet bowls. We just could not get a decent hold of them and we were not getting anywhere.

'The Warrant Officer ordered us to withdraw and we regrouped at the end of the corridor, but we were now locked in with the prisoners in A1 Section, and these seven were out of their cells. The Warrant Officer called for gas masks and reinforcements. The seven prisoners stood at their cell doors in their pyjamas. All the other doors were still locked, and the bathroom, the office and the chapel too. The backup arrived with gas masks and riot gear. We put the riot gear and the masks on. Then we drove all of the prisoners back into their cells with our batons and gassed them until they were down and unable to resist.'

I held my hand up to indicate that I intended to interrupt the narrative. Though there could hardly be a South African who did not know how teargas is used to quell riots or to break up demonstrations, the record of the evidence had to be maintained for any possible appeal. 'Could you explain what you mean when you say you gassed them?'

'Just a moment,' said Judge van Zyl. He had his left hand up in Labuschagne's direction and was busy writing a note. We waited for him and when he had finished, he addressed the prosecutors.

'Mr Murray, if the purpose of this evidence is to show that the execution process was traumatic for the defendant, I am sure the State will be prepared to admit that. Would you be prepared to admit that, Mr Murray?' he asked.

'We are prepared to admit that,' Murray said quickly.

'Is there any need for this detail then?' Judge van Zyl was looking at me.

Wierda's pencil went *tap tap tap* between his teeth. 'They are doing damage control,' he whispered. He was right.

Murray was trying to do to our case what we had done to theirs. By admitting the salient facts of the prosecution case, we had denied the prosecutors the opportunity to parade their case through the evidence of a line of emotional witnesses who would have laid the emphasis on the consequences of Labuschagne's actions. We had admitted that Labuschagne's hand had held the gun that had fired the fatal shots. We admitted that the killings had been unlawful. We admitted the identification evidence so that the deceased's relatives did not have to be called as witnesses. We admitted police plans, photographs of the scene and the deceased on the mortuary table, and the post-mortem reports, and by doing that we had robbed their contents of their emotional and persuasive impact.

But we did not want that for the defence case. We wanted everyone to feel the emotion and the pain experienced by Labuschagne in the line of his work, so that they would empathise with him and believe him. We had to make it possible for the Judge and Assessors to believe him. Without that, we were doomed.

I took a deep breath before I made my point. We needed to be gracious and tactful, and I started with an expression of gratitude. 'We are grateful for the concession by the State, but there are two reasons why we are going to have to lead the evidence, unpleasant as it may be.'

Labuschagne watched as I spoke. He appeared as disappointed as the Judge at my persistence, but my job was to make him tell it all. The Judge made his own displeasure known by sitting back and folding his arms across his chest, the classic sign of disengagement.

I had to press on. 'The first reason is that what we, M'Lord and the Learned Assessors and our Learned Friends may imagine, and what the State has conceded was a traumatic experience, does not come anywhere near the true horror of that particular day, and with it, the true effect on someone like the defendant. I can assure the Court that all of us in the defence team are conscious of our duty not to waste time and not to lead unnecessary evidence, but we are equally conscious of our duty to present the defence case fully, so that this essential part of the defence evidence is heard from the mouth of the defendant, speaking his own words, giving the Court an insight into the effect of the events he will describe and giving the Court an opportunity to gauge his credibility.'

I could see that Judge van Zyl had been persuaded, but he still asked, 'What is the second reason?'

Now I had to be even more tactful. It was a question I could not answer in Labuschagne's presence. I chose my words carefully. 'I am afraid I am not able to disclose that to the Court at this time; I can only do so through one of the expert witnesses we intend to call.'

The Judge pondered the issue for a while and then made his decision known with an abrupt 'Carry on.'

I reminded Labuschagne of the question. Murray and Niemand went into a little huddle, their heads close together. 'The question was, could you explain what you mean when you say you gassed them. Please tell the Court.'

Labuschagne had been watching the exchanges and responded immediately.

'We used teargas.'

'How did you remove the seven you were due to hang that morning?'

'We tackled them one by one and trussed them up in straitjackets over their pyjamas.'

Every now and then he slipped into the prison jargon.

I had to keep the record accurate. 'Describe the straitjackets you used, please.'

'The straitjackets are sort of canvass tubes with leather straps. They fit like a jacket that you put on back to front and you fasten the straps at the back. The prisoner's arms are caught against his body so he can still walk, but he can't do anything with his arms or hands. We cuffed their hands in front, under the straitjackets, and we put them in leg irons as well.'

Labuschagne was almost breathless. I noticed that he was sweating, almost as if he was engaged in heavy physical activity again. 'What did you do after removing them from their cells?' I asked.

'Well, we still had to get their fingerprints. We dragged them over to the table at the entrance and put them face down on the floor. The policeman brought his fingerprint pad over and we rolled each prisoner over and lifted his hands up to put the right and left thumb impressions on the form. If anyone wouldn't open his hand we just stomped on his fingers until he opened it and then took the fingerprints. They were kicking and screaming and cursing all the time. They resisted. They fought and tried to bite us; they did everything they could. But we were too many for them and we simply put a boot on their necks while they were on the floor. We still had the gas masks on because the gas was still floating around. We were fighting for breath ourselves.'

'And after you had finished the fingerprinting process, what did you do then?' I asked, standing with folded arms.

'We dragged them up and hanged them.'

'You mentioned earlier a last church service in the chapel before prisoners are taken up to the gallows. Did you have a church service for them?'

'No, sir. The Warrant Officer told us to take them up straightaway. So we dragged them up the stairs and onto the gallows. We threw our gas masks down at the top of the stairs. We didn't stop for last requests or the hoods; we just lined them up in the right order and went straight in. We put them on the trapdoors. There were two of us for each of them, one on each side. Then the Hangman came and put the ropes on. We held them fast. Then the Warrant Officer shouted to let go and they went down.'

'How did that execution end?'

'One of the prisoners did not die immediately, but we were too tired to pull him up again and the Warrant Officer said to leave him. It took about fifteen minutes before he was dead. Then we were told to report to the Medical Officer after we had taken the bodies down and we were given the rest of the day off.'

'How did this incident affect you?' I had to ask.

Labuschagne closed his eyes and pulled his head back until he looked almost straight up at the ceiling. He exhaled noisily through pursed lips.

'We all got very sick. I was nauseous and my eyes were burning. I could taste the gas in the back of my throat for days. I also had a tick in my one eye and I had a rash.'

'How did you feel inside?' I insisted as he had not answered my question fully.

'I felt nothing,' he said. He was not helping, or perhaps he was.

'Did you feel regret?'

'No.'

'Guilt?'

'No,' after a pause.

'Were you proud of what you had done?'

He did not hesitate. 'I did my job.'

We stood looking at each other, neither willing to back down.

'Did you receive any treatment or counselling after this event?' I asked.

'Some eye drops and some Valoid.'

'Were you offered any counselling?'

'No, sir.'

'None at all?' I wanted there to be no doubt about this.

'No.'

'Didn't anyone say anything?' I asked.

Labuschagne pulled at his ear as he thought about it. 'We got a lecture from the Warrant Officer. He reminded us that we were not allowed to discuss the incident with anyone. He did say that we were entitled to psychiatric treatment, as he put it, and said that our medical aid scheme covered the cost. But he said that we should not tell the psychiatrist what work we did. And he said it would go on your record and could affect your promotion.' The incongruity did not appear to strike him, seeing a psychiatrist but concealing the true causes of your problems from him.

I checked the time on the clock. We had a lot of time left.

'Was there ever an occasion when something went wrong during the execution process itself?' I asked.

'Yes, sir,' the answer came on cue, 'but that did not happen often.'

'Could you give us some examples, without going into too much detail?' I suggested. 'Please leave out the names of the prisoners or warders concerned and deal with the matter in broad outline only.'

Labuschagne nodded and answered methodically, raising a finger to count off each example. 'Yes. When a prisoner fainted or was unable to walk to the gallows or stand on the trapdoors. Or when a warder fainted or was sick. Or when the prisoner did not die immediately.'

I interrupted quickly. 'Please don't go into the detail. Just tell the Court briefly how you dealt with those situations.'

'Well, we had special aluminium chairs, like a barstool, for the prisoners who could not stand up. So we would sit them in the chair and put the chair where they had to stand. The chair would then drop down with them. One prisoner was in a wheelchair. The calculations were made with the distance he had to fall from wheelchair height and the wheelchair fell down into the pit with him. If a prisoner resisted violently we would tie him in a straitjacket onto a lightweight aluminium stretcher. Then we would stand the stretcher upright with the prisoner strapped to it on the trapdoors.'

There was still too much detail, but the Judge and Assessors were listening intently, so I allowed Labuschagne to proceed at his own pace.

'If a prisoner did not die when he dropped down, we had to pull him up again and drop him from the right height. We were not allowed to touch him while doing that. The Warrant Officer said the law required the man to be hanged by the neck until he was dead, and that it was the Hangman's job to kill the prisoner. We were there to help only so far as putting the prisoner in the right spot. Then we had to let go. After letting go of their sleeves we did not touch the prisoners until later, when they had been certified dead. So what we did, was to …'

This time I had had enough and I interrupted him without any apology. 'We have dealt with what you had to do and how you did it, haven't we?' Then I added, 'When you told the Court a few minutes ago about the seven prisoners who fought all the way from the cells of the Pot to the trapdoors.'

'Yes,' Labuschagne agreed readily, 'I have told all that.'

It was my turn to look for the water jug. I took a sip of water and turned to the next page in my trial notebook. It was heavy going and I was feeling Labuschagne's anguish. The thought crossed my mind that I was matching him sip for sip.

'Did anything ever go wrong at the service you had to attend?' I asked.

'Yes, the members of the family sometimes threatened us, said we had killed the prisoner, that we were as guilty as the Judge and the State President and the Hangman.'

'Did anything ever go wrong at the burial sites?'

'Many times.'

I nodded for him to continue.

'Sometimes the graves were half full of water and then we had to drain them first. Sometimes we just lowered the coffins into the water and filled them in. Locals threw stones at us. We had to take police protection with us. We were attacked by bees. Sometimes we found that the graves were not ready and then we had to wait for the municipality to send a digger. It could take all day, and then we had to face the Warrant Officer when we arrived back at the prison late. Sometimes there were not enough graves and we just put two or even three coffins in one grave.'

'Wouldn't that make a mess of the record-keeping, putting two or three in one grave?' I asked.

'Sir, no one ever called for the grave numbers. And what else could I do?'

I was about to change the subject when the door next to me opened and the Chief Registrar came in after bowing to the bench. Judge van Zyl held up his hand and I had to wait. The Chief Registrar spoke hastily with the court registrar and she turned to the Judge. They had a whispered conversation.

'I have been called to the Judge President's chambers for an urgent meeting,' explained Judge van Zyl. 'We'll have to adjourn for a few minutes.'

'Tell me about your next case,' I said to Wierda as soon as the Judge and Assessors had departed. 'But make it short.'

v3769 Sizwe Goodchild Leve   35

Lungile Tandamisa, Sizwe Leve and Vuyani Pikashe robbed and murdered Mrs Anita Webber.

Mrs Anita Webber was a forty-one-year-old housewife who lived with her husband and two children, twelve and fifteen years old respectively, in a suburban house in Paarl. On Thursday 19 June 1986 Mr Webber went to work and the children went to school. Mrs Webber had previously invited a neighbour, Mrs Aletta Ferreira, to come over for tea at ten-fifteen that morning. Mrs Ferreira told the Court that she had seen three men working in Mrs Webber's garden and when the agreed time approached she went across to the Webbers' house. She pressed the doorbell after hearing something in the Webbers' bedroom. She called to Mrs Webber when there was no response. Then she saw three men coming out of the garage. One of them said, 'Madam is in the kitchen. She just paid us.' She went in but could not find Mrs Webber in the house. She left and called her husband. They returned to the Webbers' house and eventually found Mrs Webber's body in the garage. There was a wire ligature around Mrs Webber's neck which Mr Ferreira untied. They called the police, who arrived promptly. When a detective picked up a blue tracksuit top next to the body, the handle of a knife fell out of it.

The Senior District Surgeon was called to the scene and he certified that Mrs Webber was dead. He also performed the post-mortem examination on her body the next day and found four groups of serious injuries. In his opinion any one of these on its own could have caused Mrs Webber's death. The first of these injuries consisted of an eight-centimetre-deep stab wound on the chest, on the right side, which had penetrated the right lung and caused it to collapse. Secondly, there was a five-centimetre-deep stab wound on the left side of the neck, the blade of the knife impacting on one of the vertebrae and cutting into it. The blade of the knife was still in the wound; it had the inscription SABLE and the cutting edge was seven point one centimetres long. Although the blade had missed the carotid artery, there was some bleeding in the sheath of the carotid. Thirdly, ribs six, seven, eight and nine on the left and one, two and three on the right side of the chest were fractured. In the fourth place, there were internal bruises on the neck associated with a central depression around the neck caused by the wire ligature. The bruising was deep enough into the structures of the neck to affect the trachea and bony elements of the neck. The hyoid and thyroid cartilage bones were fractured. All of these injuries were suffered while the deceased still had a heartbeat.

These were but the main injuries. Mrs Webber had been struck so hard on the left eye with some blunt object that she would have lost her sight in that eye had she survived. There were fourteen stab wounds altogether, including a further one to the neck and eleven to the chest. According to the pathologist the most brutal force would have had to be used to inflict the injuries he had found, but after the ligature had been tied around Mrs Webber's neck she would have expired from lack of oxygen within minutes.

The three accused were arrested soon after the discovery of the body. Each was linked to the scene by forensic evidence and by admissions made to the police, to the Magistrate before whom they first appeared, and at the trial. Tandamisa's palm print was found on the left rear side-window of the car at the house. Hairs matching Leve's were found on a blue tracksuit top next to the deceased's body. He later admitted to having left that tracksuit top at the scene. The handle that had fallen out of the tracksuit top when the body was discovered matched the blade found embedded in the deceased's neck. A fingerprint matching that of Pikashe's left ring finger was found on a transistor radio that had been discarded in the shrubbery next to the house.

Leve took a senior police officer to the scene and explained what had happened:

When we were opposite the gate a white woman on the cement block (pointed out) called us. We went to her. We entered the yard and met her halfway. She asked if we were looking for work. We said yes. She went to fetch weeding implements. We weeded here (pointed out). She went into the house. She came out again. She asked my friend to work under the tree. She took a bucket and rinsed it under the tap. My other friend who has not yet been arrested then said we should grab the woman. We all agreed to grab her. She was back from the tap and went in through the garage door. We followed her.

Inside the garage I grabbed her by the arm. The man who has not yet been arrested stabbed her with a knife. I took the knife from my friend and stabbed her again with the knife. The knife fell and my other friend who has been arrested picked it up and stabbed her again. The knife broke. I held her again while the one who has not been arrested went to fetch a wire while I was holding her by the neck. My friends tied her up with the wire.

We entered the house through the window. We searched the room. Each searched a different room. My friend who is not here told us he had found twenty-four rand. My other friend who is now at the police station peeped out the window and said someone was coming. We climbed through the same window and found another white woman in front of the house. She asked us where the madam was. We said she was in the back yard. She went into the house and we ran away.

Pikashe gave more information about Leve and Tandamisa's actions. He told the police that Leve had grabbed the deceased from behind after following her into the garage. Leve then threw her down on the garage floor and sat on top of her with his knees on her chest and throttled her with his hands while Tandamisa was hitting her in the face with his fists. Tandamisa told Pikashe to look for some wire and he found a piece in the garage and tied it around the deceased's neck. Tandamisa then stabbed the deceased next to the heart with the knife. When Tandamisa stabbed her again, the knife broke. Pikashe's version explained the broken ribs and the severe injury to the deceased's left eye.

Tandamisa also admitted involvement, but implicated Pikashe in the stabbing too. At his first appearance in court Tandamisa told the Magistrate that all three of them had stabbed the deceased with the same knife. He admitted that he was the one handling the knife when its blade broke off in the deceased's neck.

The Court convicted each of them on both counts – murder and armed robbery – as charged in the indictment. This meant that the death sentence was available on the robbery charge, if the Court in its discretion deemed it appropriate. On the murder charge, however, the Court would be obliged to pass the death sentence unless there were extenuating circumstances present or a particular accused had been under the age of eighteen at the time of the murder.

The District Surgeon had earlier conceded under cross-examination that he had examined both Pikashe and Tandamisa to determine their respective ages, and that both of them could have been under the age of eighteen years at the time of the crimes concerned. The Court sentenced them to twenty years' imprisonment on the murder charge and to ten years' imprisonment on the robbery charge. The sentences were to run concurrently.

According to Leve's own evidence the plan to break in somewhere had already been hatched the night before they killed Mrs Webber. The Court held that there were no extenuating circumstances in respect of Leve and sentenced him to death on 26 May 1987. He received a further sentence of ten years' imprisonment on the robbery charge.

He was twenty-three years old when he was hanged on 8 December 1987 and had spent six months under sentence of death.

'Why do you think they killed her,' I asked Wierda, 'when there were three of them and they could so easily have held her down and taken what they wanted?' I had asked a similar question about Mr Marx.

'I'm fucked if I know,' he said with unexpected vehemence. Then he added, 'And I don't care either. We are wasting our time and energy with these cases. We should find out why our client killed those guys at the reservoir instead. We still don't know.'

Wierda looked at me with his head cocked to one side. 'We know nothing at all. We are running headlong into a dark tunnel with no idea what is going to come out of his evidence, and here we are, reading and discussing cases that happened in Cape Town.'

I ignored his outburst. 'No, there must be a reason. It might not be a good one, but it should at least be comprehensible.'

'Well,' he said, 'I think they were scared. They were just scared and the thing escalated as the events unfolded.'

'Isn't that what happened at the reservoir, that panic set in, and that the thing was not planned?' I suggested.

Wierda did not answer, but he had given me an idea about an alternative argument, one that would help us to establish extenuating circumstances if our client were convicted. But there were flaws in Wierda's premise.

'I don't buy that,' I said immediately. 'They had planned to tie her up before they followed her into the garage. That means it was premeditated, doesn't it?'

'No,' said Wierda, sticking to his guns. 'There was a fair degree of overkill here. They held her down, strangled her and stabbed her until the knife broke off in her body. They even took turns. It is as if they were caught up in an event beyond their control.'

'There has to be some rational explanation for this kind of behaviour.'

Wierda was not to be put off so easily. 'They are animals, not in control of their actions like you and me. They hunt in packs. They don't give a damn about anybody's life, their own included.

'Isn't that what happened with the others?' he asked and then answered his own question, 'Let's start with Scheepers, and Wessels, and Moatche. A gang behaves differently to the way one would expect of its individual members. That much I have learnt from my previous cases. As soon as there is a gang all reason goes out the window. And what about those three in the Free State? What were their names again, Marotholi and the other two? Didn't they behave in exactly the same way? And what about those guys in Leeuwkop?'

I did not have an answer. Perhaps Wierda had a point and, instead of debating the motives of the killers they had hanged during those last two weeks, we should have been searching for a motive for our client's actions. Wierda had spoken with vehemence, and I had listened in silence. Roshnee, as usual, did not participate. Even if Wierda's theory of mob psychology were able to account for the ease with which our client had become part of the execution team at Maximum, it still did not provide a rational and cogent account for his actions at the reservoir.

At the reservoir Labuschagne had been alone, and finding a coherent reason for his actions was not easy.

36

Judge van Zyl and his Assessors returned after the short break.

'There is half an hour left. Please proceed,' said the Judge. James Murray looked bored. Niemand was ready to take notes, but the Judge and Assessors looked like they had had enough for the day. I decided to lead the evidence of the events of the tenth of December the next morning. Labuschagne also needed the rest. We would all be refreshed. I also did not want James Murray to have the whole evening to prepare their cross-examination on the events at the reservoir.

'Tell the Court about Mr Tsafendas,' I suggested.

James Murray was still halfway out of his seat when the Judge took up the cause.

'What is the relevance of this?' he demanded. He did not wait for an answer. 'I have given the defence a lot of leeway, far more than I ever imagined I would in a case like this, but this is going too far. What could Tsafendas possibly have to do with the charges the defendant faces?'

I had to make my point in one hit. If it became a debate, or if Murray also entered the fray, I would lose.

'M'Lord,' I argued, 'they locked this young man up with the worst murderers and the vilest criminals for eighteen months. Every day of those eighteen months he was locked up just like them, with the doors being secured behind him wherever he went, all day long. During the day he cared for the prisoners, saw to it that they were fed, that they had a wash and a haircut. They sent him to buy them stuff at the tuck shop. He watched over them and helped them read their Bibles and he heard them pray. Then he was told to call them out and to help kill them, to pray with their families and to bury them. Why are we so surprised at the events at the reservoir? He came to Maximum Security quite well adjusted, by all accounts. Then he killed seven men. We need to explore the reasons for the changes within him. And his encounter with Mr Tsafendas played a role in that.'

'Get to the point,' said Judge van Zyl, 'what is the relevance of the evidence you propose to lead?'

Wierda was in sympathy with the Judge, apparently. 'What's this about?' he hissed through clenched teeth, his pencil still for once.

'It is relevant to the defendant's state of mind,' I said simply, partly to Wierda and partly to Judge van Zyl.

Wierda did not respond, but the Judge threw his pen down. It bounced off the bench and landed on the registrar's desk three feet below. 'And I told you to keep names out of it, didn't I?' he said. Then he covered his eyes with his hand, but I knew what he really meant. I have had enough of this, is what his body language told me.

I waited for a formal ruling, but the Judge did not speak again all afternoon.

'Tell the Court, please,' I said to Labuschagne, 'of your encounter with Mr Tsafendas and how it affected you.' I spoke quietly, as if the altercation with the Judge had not happened at all.

There was not a sound except that of scribbling pens and rustling pages for the rest of the afternoon. The Judge eventually came out from behind his hand, to listen and to watch, like the rest of us, in silence and amazement.

When Labuschagne had completed his story the entire court remained silent for a while. The evidence of his interaction with Tsafendas and the Tsafendas prophecy had turned our comfortable world upside down. Then whispers started in the spectator seats, until there was a buzz in every part, except for the bench. The Judge and his Assessors still sat in stony silence.

Tsafendas had long been our bogeyman, but here he was, scrambling about in a shoebox, hunting for stale newspaper clippings like a hobo in a rubbish bin and speaking in riddles. Vorster had been our champion, our Prime Minister, but here *he* was, scheming and conniving, doing things we could not have imagined.

Outside it was still raining. The light inside the courtroom had taken on the grey of the sky outside, with mist attaching to the inside of the windows. It lent an eerie aspect to a courtroom which, until that day, had basked in direct sunlight through the skylights overhead.

In the well of the court where the Officers of the Court sat and I stood everyone was dressed in the same drab dark or charcoal grey, the advocates and the registrar in black robes and white shirts and bands. The Judge, on the other hand, stood out like the leading lady in a Hollywood film, his scarlet robes the only item of colour in the room.

When we came out of the building the cameras were waiting for us on the steps. After the evening news on television the first death threats arrived at the hotel where Roshnee and I were staying. It was agreed that Roshnee would return to Durban for the time being; there was nothing left for her to do anyway. Pierre de Villiers came to pick me up and I moved to my sister's for the night.

'No self-respecting killer would give you a warning before he came over to kill you,' he said.

I agreed with him and planned to return the next morning.

The work did not stand still. I had to read the next case, and I finished the summary before dinner. The case was just another of the many that made one despair of the human race and its total lack of empathy for others.

v3770 Stanley Smit

37

Smit broke into Miss Catherina Hanekom's house and indecently assaulted and killed her. He was charged with housebreaking, rape and murder.

The deceased was an unmarried woman in her forties. She lived alone at 26 Park Street, Moorreesburg. She was feeble-minded and physically deformed with what was described as a pigeon chest. She was small, weighing about fifty kilograms and was about one point six metres tall. Although she was able to perform some of the rudimentary daily chores of her household and personal care she needed the assistance of a social worker and a neighbour, Mrs Wahl, for more demanding tasks. Miss Hanekom received a monthly disability grant from the State. She received help with her financial affairs as she was incapable of handling those responsibilities herself.

Mrs Wahl was away for the weekend of 30 August 1986. When she returned on 3 September she went to the deceased's house. She found the front door open and, upon entering, found Miss Hanekom's body under some blankets in the bedroom next to the bed. She went to the neighbours and they called the police.

The police found a trail of blood from the telephone in the passage to the body. It was plain that the deceased had been dragged from the telephone to her bedroom. There was blood on the sheets of the deceased's bed and spattered blood on the headboard of the bed and the wall above the bed. There was a pool of blood on the linoleum floor at the feet of the body and smeared blood on the walls of the passage. Some fingerprints were found on the frame of the front door and on the inside of the door itself. The rest of the house was fairly neat and tidy, with no obvious signs of a struggle or ransacking.

When the blanket was removed from the body it was noted that Miss Hanekom had been partly undressed. Her panties had been removed and were found on the floor near the door. Several injuries to her frail body were visible to the naked eye. These were more fully explained by the pathologist who performed the post-mortem examination.

He described the injuries as follows:

In the back of the chest was a two-centimetre oblique incised wound, eleven centimetres from the posterior midline and nine centimetres below the prominent spine of the seventh cervical vertebra. The track of the wound could be followed forwards and medially and slightly upwards passing through the third left inter-costal space, through the upper lobe of the left lung, through the edge of the aorta and onto the back of the sternum at the front. The total length of this wound was eighteen centimetres. On the left side of the neck just below the left ear was a three point five centimetre stab wound through the carotid and internal jugular. Miss Hanekom had also suffered a broken nose. There were abrasions of the back of the head. The left lung had collapsed and there was some bleeding on the right side of the brain. Blood was found in the airways.

Miss Hanekom had died of the stab wounds of the chest and neck. She had been subjected to a systematic and cruel beating before she died.

The fingerprints taken at the scene were those of the accused. Smit gave evidence at his trial. He blamed his conduct on drugs and liquor – the usual scapegoats of a desperate defence.

The Court rejected this version for a number of reasons. It was inconsistent and self-contradictory. It didn't match Smit's actions in the house; they were the actions of a calculating mind. Smit also told the Court that he had spent some time with a certain Jakob Afrika, but the latter was actually in police custody at the time given by Smit. Smit kept changing his evidence to match the known objective facts and it was soon apparent that his evidence on the effects of alcohol and drugs on his state of mind was also a pack of lies.

The Court found that on all the acceptable evidence it was clear that Smit had entered the house with the intention of committing a crime. When he encountered the frail Miss Hanekom he first beat her mercilessly with some blunt object, breaking her nose and causing bleeding of the one side of the brain. Then he stabbed her in the back with a knife and dragged her, feet first, to the bedroom. There he removed her panties and indecently assaulted her. Then he stabbed her on the side of the neck. When blood from this last stab wound spurted onto his clothes, he pulled some blankets over the body and, after taking some precautions to ensure that no one would notice anything untoward at Miss Hanekom's house for a while, he left.

The Court convicted him of housebreaking, indecent assault and murder. The inquiry into extenuating circumstances revealed none. Smit had been nineteen and a half years old at the time he murdered Miss

Hanekom. His relative youth did not in itself constitute an extenuating circumstance. The Court found that he had killed in order to avoid detection, which was an aggravating factor.

On 5 June 1987 Smit was sentenced to three years' imprisonment on the housebreaking charge and a further twelve months' imprisonment for the indecent assault he had committed. He was sentenced to death on the murder charge.

Six months after being sentenced Smit was hanged, on 8 December 1987.

He was not yet twenty-one.

De Villiers Residence, Pretoria

38

Smit's case was of no use to me in attempting to understand why Leon Labuschagne had killed seven men at the reservoir. I put the file away and went to look for my sister. Annelise was in the kitchen preparing dinner. The innocence of the scene reminded me of the cases where the men whose death warrants I had seen had crept into a house to kill the woman inside. I offered to open a bottle of wine. After the dishes had been cleared from the table, Annelise left to supervise her children's homework. Pierre and I retreated to his lapa. He carried a bottle of very old French cognac.

We sat down and I accepted a cognac from him. I sniffed at the rim of the bulbous glass. 'What's the difference between brandy and cognac?' I asked.

He smiled. 'If you have to ask you won't understand.'

We sat staring into the night. Although the sky was clear you could not see the stars; the city lights created a haze. I pondered a conundrum that has intrigued me from the time I first moved to the city: why do I feel unsafe in the city at night when I never feel unsafe in the dark nights in the bush?

'Listen, Pierre,' I said, 'I really need to talk some more about killing.'

'What exactly is it that you want to know?'

'I want to know if it is possible to kill someone in cold blood because you are angry with him or hate him.'

He sighed and shook his head and asked, 'Is this a rhetorical question?'

'No,' I said, 'it isn't. Let me rephrase the question. What I want to know is this: could you kill *seven* people in cold blood because you are angry with them, or because you hate them for their race?'

'Yes, you can,' he said, nodding. 'But what I can't understand is how such a man could think that he is a Christian.'

The conversation was going in the wrong direction for me, although he had partly answered my question. 'Christians have killed a lot of people in the name of the faith,' I reminded him. 'But that is not what I have trouble understanding. What I am trying to grasp is how a man feels while he is killing. What does he think? How does he feel? How does the killer's body react to the thing he is doing – killing?'

'God knows,' Pierre said very softly, 'I know about that.'

'Are you willing to tell me?' I suggested gently. 'I cannot get through to Labuschagne and I am trying desperately to understand what was going on in his mind.'

'Not now,' was all he said.

Knowing well that he wouldn't be moved, I was on the point of giving up. But then he said, 'Maybe later, after I have put the children to bed.'

I realised that he meant *after I have had a few more cognacs* and I assisted him in getting greased up quickly. By the time he started opening up my head was spinning.

'I think we have a physical aversion to killing, which has nothing to do with religion or morality,' he said. 'It's incredibly difficult to kill someone. I found it difficult even when they were shooting at me and it was him or me.'

'How do you mean, it was physically difficult?' I asked.

'I mean that you go to custard. You shake, you stiffen up, there is a roar of blood or whatever in your ears, and all your training goes out the window. Worst of all, time stands still. And in that void all your senses become hyper sharp and all your sensations are magnified tenfold. So you feel dangers greater than they really are, threats more serious, while at the same time your capacity to think is compromised and your reactions are slowed down.'

'So what happens then?'

'You make mistakes, and plenty of them. Big ones, too.'

He sipped at the cognac. I had given up trying to match him drink for drink. I had to go to court the next day with a clear head.

'And you relive those mistakes every day after that; you experience the whole event exactly as it happened, with all the physical sensations you experienced at the time. You go back there but you can't turn the clock back. When you wake up the consequences are still there for you to deal with.'

I brought the discussion back to the point. 'But how do you force yourself to do it, even in those cases where you have to kill, I mean when your whole being resists, as you've explained?'

He stood up abruptly and went into the house without looking back. I thought he had gone to sleep, when I heard a toilet flush. He returned to the dark of the lapa.

'I know exactly how they felt,' he said as he sat down.

'Well,' I said, 'he doesn't talk about it and on this topic I have so far had to beat every word out of him.'

'I am not talking about Labuschagne,' Pierre said gruffly. 'I am talking about the thirty-two men they hanged.'

This threw me somewhat off balance. I played with the glass in my hand, swirling the cognac higher and higher towards the rim. How could he know what those men felt? He was so unlike them. He answered without hearing the question.

'I read all those cases, remember,' he said. 'I know what every one of them went through. You become someone else in the pack. Your own identity and values are absent somehow, they get submerged in a morass of other personalities and value systems. For a time each killing is easier than the previous one, and then they start getting more difficult than the prior ones. Eventually you have this thing inside you that you can't talk about and you can't bear thinking about. And you end up where it is easier to be awake than to be asleep. You pick up a momentum.'

We sat staring at our glasses for a while. I thought of Wierda's words. *They hunt in packs.*

'Yes, it is a momentum. You start slowly and pick up speed until you feel comfortable. Then you pick up more speed until you reach the extreme limits of your self-control, the point just before you know you are going to lose it.'

He did not say what *it* was. I assumed he was referring to his self-control or his sanity, perhaps both.

I asked him about Mrs Webber's killers. There were three of them and they could so easily have overpowered her and taken what they wanted. Why did they have to stab her, and beat her, and strangle her with a wire tied around her neck? Why?

'They were in a panic. You can only kill if you go into a state of panic. You can't do it otherwise,' Pierre said. It was not a complete explanation.

We drank some more and talked about what had happened to him in Angola deep into the night. I got the impression that I was the first one to hear it from him and that not even my sister knew.

'Let me tell you something else,' he said, changing the topic. He was slurring his words. 'When someone you know well dies, the awfulness of the death is offset by the weight of the memories you have of that person's life, and of your shared experiences. But when you kill a stranger all you have are the act of killing and the process of dying. Together, the killing and the dying constitute your sole memory of that person, and your shared encounter. It is a memory of their agony and your hand in it.

'The only thing worse than killing a stranger would have to be to kill someone you know well, with whom you have shared memories and shared experiences. Because then the memory of the act of killing and the process of dying would make nonsense of all those prior memories and shared experiences; it would mock them and piss on them.'

Pierre was not given to swearing, and when I looked up sharply I saw he was oblivious of my presence.

'We killed strangers, and that was difficult enough,' he said as we staggered from the lapa, long after midnight. 'I just can't see how you can kill someone you know.'

The way he said it gave me an idea. 'When you shot at those people, did you think of them as people, you know, like you and me? Or how did you see them?' The question wasn't very coherent. We were at the gate and I was ready to drive back to the hotel.

'No, no,' said Pierre. 'You don't shoot at people. You shoot at uniforms. All you see is the uniform.'

'What about the ones who don't wear a uniform?'

'If they don't wear your uniform, whatever they're wearing, that is the enemy's uniform,' he said.

The war in Angola was not very clearly defined in my mind. We saw very little on television. I had no picture of the enemy's uniform. What we were allowed to know was that there were Russians and Cubans assisting the local forces.

'So you shoot at uniforms. Does that help you not to think of them as people?' I asked.

'We have our uniforms and they have theirs. I told you, soldiers don't shoot at people; you shoot at uniforms. You don't think of them as people while the fighting is going on.'

There was a qualification in Pierre's response, unintended perhaps, but it was enough of an opening to allow another question.

'Do you think of them as people after the fighting has stopped?'

It was a question too many. Pierre turned on his heel and walked back to the house, his reaction an answer more eloquent than words.

I drove back to the hotel carefully. I should not have been driving, but the streets were deserted. I thought of the events in the gallows chamber and at the reservoir. Maybe there was something in Pierre's reaction to my last question. Men in uniform see the enemy as a human being only when he is dead. And their job, of course, is to kill them.

But I was more interested in the warders and prisoners in Maximum, where warder and prisoner alike were dressed in prison green.

DAY FOUR

Defence: 7 October 1988
Execution: 9 December 1987

v3625 William Harris
v3626 Brian Meiring
v3627 Christoffel Michaels
v3628 Herold Japhta
v3629 Jan Swartbooi
v3630 Pieter Botha
v3631 Anthony Morgan

39

The warders stood waiting in the passage. The Sheriff was late and the new arrivals could not be taken to their allocated cells before the Sheriff had taken their fingerprints and compared them with the prints on the death warrants.

The initial briefing by the Warrant Officer had been completed. The five prisoners stood in front of the Warrant Officer. They were dressed in the prison uniforms of the men who had been hanged less than a week earlier, the drab garb giving no hint of the agony of the desperate last moments of those who had last worn them, or of the many before them.

But first, the new prisoners had to be taught the rules of Maximum Security Prison.

'Obey orders at all times. Understand?'

Smack, smack.

'Say, yes sir, when a warder speaks to you.'

Smack, smack.

'Don't look at me! Look at the floor. Keep your eyes on the floor at all times.'

Smack, smack.

'Didn't I tell you to say yes sir?'

Smack, smack.

'Don't ever talk, not to another prisoner, and not to a warder unless it is to say, yes sir. Understand?'

'Yes, boss.'

Smack, smack.

'Don't call me boss. I told you to say, yes sir, didn't I?'

'Yes, sir.'

By the time the Sheriff came in, the prisoners knew their place in the system. They were quickly fingerprinted and placed in their cells. They were brutal men, but they had never seen such brutality before.

It was going to be a very long day; the make-or-break day for the defence. I went to court early and entered as soon as they opened the doors to the public. I counted the steps as I walked up; there were thirteen. I wasn't superstitious, but I had been up and down those steps four or five times a day for two weeks; why had I not noticed it before? I hoped it was not an omen for the day.

I stood aside as the usher unlocked Court C. I took my seat at the defence table and started going through my notes. There was only one topic of substance left. After three days of wrangling and manoeuvring we had finally got to the point where Labuschagne was going to have to explain what had happened at the reservoir. Nothing else really mattered, neither the brutality of the execution process nor the unfairness of making these young men participate in it. It didn't matter whether one was for or against the death penalty. The only thing that mattered was this: what was the explanation for what had happened at the reservoir? No one else could give that explanation; it had to come from Leon Labuschagne. His fate would be determined by what happened on this day of the trial. He would have to talk, and he would be cross-examined.

When the cell sergeant came in I asked him to bring Labuschagne up early. He said that he could not leave him unattended in the dock and that he had other work to do, so I was obliged to go down to Cell 6 again. The sergeant locked me in and left. Labuschagne sat with his eyes downcast as I spoke. He looked tired.

'The rules of ethics don't allow me to talk to you about the evidence you have already given,' I said, 'but you know where we are heading. We are going to have to cover the events of that last day, from beginning to end.'

He nodded without looking up. There was reluctance in the slump of his shoulders. I thought I saw a slight shake of his head.

'We have no choice. You and I have been there before. You told me and you are going to have to tell the Court. We get only one opportunity to tell your story and this is it. It will be you and me, just the two of us. But you are going to have to do the important talking.'

Labuschagne fiddled with his tie. His facial expression was impenetrable. I could not see whether he was afraid or tired, whether he had given up hope or was, like me, hanging in there at the very limits of his emotional reach.

'I will be there with you every step of the way. I will talk you through every part of your story. But I need to know that you will do your best, that you won't give up and that you will help me too. I can't do it on my own.'

He did not react, so I asked him directly, 'Will you help me?'

Labuschagne took his time before he looked up and nodded.

'Good,' I said. 'Now please take the notes Wierda has prepared for you and run through them one last time before we start.'

He nodded again. Fatigue and resignation were apparent in his eyes. I was also tired, but I wasn't ready to give up.

I spent the next half hour watching as he went through the events as summarised in Wierda's briefing notes. I turned page by page with him, keeping an eye on him to ensure that he did not skip pages.

When the cell sergeant came for us, I went up into the dock behind Labuschagne and sat down on the bench in the dock next to him. The sergeant kept watch from his table behind the witness box.

James Murray came in, followed by Sanet Niemand. 'How long are you going to be?' Murray wanted to know. He was referring to the examination-in-chief.

'Maybe an hour,' I said. There was no reason to keep them guessing any longer.

'Are we going to finish by the end of next week, Johann?' he asked. 'I have another difficult case starting in Johannesburg the week after that.'

I was a little surprised at the implication that he regarded the case as a difficult one.

'I sincerely hope so,' I replied, making a joke of it. 'I like your city, but it's time to go home.'

Studiously avoiding Labuschagne's gaze, he joined in the small talk. 'Yes, I can understand that.'

The court filled up quickly. I recognised a few lawyers among the spectators. They must have come for the cross-examination.

We bowed as usual when Judge van Zyl and his Assessors came in. When everyone had settled down and Labuschagne had taken his place in the witness box, I started with an open question. There would be more specific questions later, many of them.

'What happened on the eighth of December?'

The answer was given without any hint of emotion. 'We hanged seven.'

I looked at the list I had. In alphabetical order: *Busakwe, Hansen, Kodisang, Leve, Marotholi, Prins, Smit.*

'What happened on the ninth?'

'We hanged another seven.'

Botha, Harris, Japhta, Meiring, Michaels, Morgan, Swartbooi.

'And on the tenth?'

'We hanged the last seven.'

Gcaba, Gcabashe, Maarman, Mbambani, Mjuza, Mkumbeni, Njele.

It was time to get more specific. 'Did anything unusual happen on the eighth?'

He thought for a while. 'Not as far as I can remember.'

'And on the ninth?'

'That was the day of the teargas,' he said, and then added, 'I think.'

'You think?' I asked.

'Yes, it was a Tuesday.'

I corrected him. 'No, the ninth was a Wednesday.'

'It must have been the eighth then.'

Judge van Zyl intervened. 'How certain are you of the day? Or the date?' he added.

Labuschagne looked towards me, but I could not help him. Indeed, I did not want to help him either. His uncertainty was good for his case even if he did not realise it.

'I can't remember, sir,' he said.

'Try to think back,' suggested the Judge. 'Cast your mind back to that week and tell me on which day was the teargas incident.'

Labuschagne shook his head before he answered. 'I think it was the Tuesday.'

'How sure are you it was that week and not another week?' asked the Judge.

Labuschagne did not answer.

Eventually the Judge looked at me and said, 'See if you can get an answer.'

I waited for Labuschagne to make eye contact before I asked, 'Are you able to answer His Lordship's question?'

He took a deep breath before he answered. 'I am sure it was that week, but I don't know what day.'

I glanced at the Judge and when he nodded, I continued. 'Let's deal with the tenth. Did anything unusual happen that morning during the executions?'

This time he did not hesitate. 'Yes, sir, that's the day when we had to pull one back up and drop him down again.'

'What part did you play in that incident?' I asked.

'It was my prisoner.'

It was time for me to be cruel. 'How did you feel, what went through your mind during and after that incident?'

'I don't know what you mean,' he said.

I had not primed him for the question because I wanted a spontaneous response.

'There was no time for thinking.'

I hurried the next question. 'I would like you to tell the Court how you felt after pulling the man up and dropping him and hearing his neck break.'

'I felt nothing. I was just tired.'

'How did you feel inside?' I insisted.

He resisted. 'What do you mean inside?'

'What emotions did you experience, that's what I mean,' I explained, manoeuvring him to the position I wanted.

But Labuschagne wasn't giving in. 'I can't remember.'

Judge van Zyl had been watching this exchange with his head cocked to one side. Now he intervened again. 'Are you telling us that you felt nothing at all inside while you were doing that and after the man was dead too, that all you felt was a physical sensation of fatigue?'

It was a troublesome question, but the Judge had the right to ask whatever he wanted.

'Sir, all I can remember was that I was so tired. I was finished.' Labuschagne was not looking up; his eyes were fixed on the floor a few feet in front of the witness box. 'That's all I can remember, how tired I was, how tired I was of everything.' He leaned heavily on the witness box.

That was the answer I had been looking for. I gauged that his emotional state was ripe for what I had in mind and started dealing with the day's events in detail.

'You had to report for duty before six o'clock that morning?' It was a leading question but Murray did not object.

'Yes.'

'And you lined up behind the Warrant Officer and went into the Pot to call out the ones who were going up that morning?'

'Yes.'

'Their fingerprints were taken and you took them to the chapel for the service?'

'Yes.'

'You sang and prayed with them?'

'Yes.' The answer was almost inaudible.

'You then handcuffed them?'

'Yes.' It was now hardly more than a nod of the head.

'Please speak up, and speak towards me,' the Judge ordered.

I didn't wait for Labuschagne to acknowledge the caution.

'And you took them up to the top floor?' I suggested.

'Yes.'

I decided to make him tell it himself again. 'Did you have any difficulty getting them all the way up the steps to the top?'

He answered automatically. 'Not more than usual.'

This gave me the opening I needed. 'Well, what amount of trouble is usual?'

'They drag their feet. They plead and beg. Some faint and some fight. I can't remember anything specific about that day. We got them to the top, that's all I know.'

I kept up the pace of the questions. I did not want to lose momentum now that he was talking. 'And you put the white hoods on their heads after the Sheriff had asked them if they had any last words?'

'Yes.'

'And you took them into the gallows chamber and made them stand on the painted feet on the trapdoors.'

'Yes.'

Gcaba, Gcabashe, Maarman, Mbambani, Mjuza, Mkumbeni, Njele.

'And, you have said, your prisoner was difficult?'

'Yes.'

I had asked a whole series of leading questions deliberately. I was trying to get Labuschagne into the habit of dealing with the hanging step by step, without leaving out any important detail.

James Murray had not objected, but I could not carry on leading indefinitely.

'Tell the Court what happened then.'

He began haltingly, then slowly picked up the pace. As he spoke, his voice became stronger. I let him do the talking, but he left out some crucial details, so I had to take him back to clarify some of these. The way he had described it, it was just another hanging.

'Did anything unusual happen during the execution process?'

'Yes,' he said. He did not look at me any longer when I asked the questions.

'What happened?' I kept the questions short.

'As I said, my prisoner did not die when the trapdoors opened.' His voice sounded reproachful. I ignored it.

'How did you deal with that?' I pressed for the detail.

He explained the whole process again.

'How did you feel at the end of that?' I asked.

'I was tired.' He became defensive. 'It is very difficult to pull a man up by the rope, and there were only two of us, it was hard, hard work.

We had to hold him steady. He was kicking and gasping. I just didn't have the strength.'

'Carry on,' I said. 'Please tell the Court what happened from then on.'

When Labuschagne had finished with the events in the pit room, step by step, I led him through the funeral service with the relatives and the registration of deaths at the various departments.

'And when you returned from the offices where you had to register the deaths, you still had to bury the bodies?' I asked.

'Yes.'

'And on that occasion you had six black men and one coloured to bury,' I suggested.

'Yes, I think so.'

'Where did you have to take the bodies?' I could have told him, but I needed him to say more than yes or no.

He obliged. 'The coloured had to go to Eersterus Cemetery. I had to take the blacks to the Mamelodi Cemetery.'

'Where is Mamelodi in relation to Maximum?' I asked. The Judge looked at me and shook his head. He must have remembered that I was from a distant jurisdiction.

'It is on the other side of the city.'

Judge van Zyl helped out. 'I think I can take judicial notice of the geography of the city where the Court sits. Mamelodi is on the north-eastern outskirts of the city, approximately twenty kilometres from the prison complex. Is that about right?' he asked Labuschagne.

'Yes, sir.'

'And from the prison you would have to travel through the centre of the city to get to Mamelodi, wouldn't you?' The Judge had also fallen into the habit of asking leading questions.

'No, sir, we went along Jacob Mare Street, then Rissik and Walker, then left into University Street, and from there we took Lynwood Road until we got to the Wilgers Hospital. We turned left there, but I don't know the name of the road, and carried on until we were in Denneboom Road. The cemetery is not far from there.'

The Judge nodded. 'I know exactly what you mean. It is much quicker that way, isn't it?'

'Yes, sir.'

When I didn't take over, Judge van Zyl looked at me and said, 'Carry on.'

'How did you transport the bodies to the cemetery?' I asked immediately.

'We used a minibus that belonged to a funeral undertaker.'

'How many people went along?'

'It was just me and the driver, Isaiah.'

'Was he a warder?'

'No, he works for the undertakers.'

'How many coffins did you have in the minibus?'

'Six.'

'Did anything unusual happen on the way to the cemetery?' I asked, holding my breath for the inevitable objection, but no one stirred.

'We had an accident.'

'Can you tell His Lordship what happened and what you did?'

'Yes.' For a moment I thought he was going to make me ask another question. A long ten seconds passed before he spoke again. 'When we were going along Lynwood Road we came to a shopping centre on the other side. A car coming from the right did not stop and came right across. Isaiah braked and swerved and went up on the pavement on the other side and we went down a bank into the parking area. The minibus jumped and nearly rolled. I hit my head on something and I fell under the dashboard. Then everything went black.'

Labuschagne stopped speaking and looked at me. I nodded for him to continue.

'When I woke up there was one of the bodies on top of me. The coffins were open and the bodies were out. I crawled out and got out of the minibus. I saw Isaiah running away. There was a lot of blood in the minibus. I had to put the bodies back in the coffins, but I didn't know which body went with which coffin. The name tags were on the coffins. I kept the doors shut so that people could not see inside. After that I had to get a hammer and nails. I locked the minibus and went to a hardware store. They gave me a hammer and nails. Then I went to Mamelodi and buried them.'

'What did you do at the cemetery, with six bodies to bury on your own?' I asked.

'I must have buried them.'

'Tell His Lordship how you did it.'

'I don't remember,' he said.

'Do you have any memory of what happened at the cemetery?'

'No. I can't remember anything after fixing the coffins with the hammer.'

I stood for a while, contemplating whether I needed to ask the next question. I could not make a decision and asked it anyway.

'Why were you alone at the cemetery when there were six bodies to bury? Shouldn't there have been some of the other escorts?'

Labuschagne pursed his lips. 'The minibus was full. We should have had another one, but it was the Warrant Officer.' He glanced in the direction of the seat behind the prosecutors. 'He was angry with me because I wanted to leave.'

I was tired and was beginning to make mistakes. There was no need to antagonise the Warrant Officer.

'What is the next thing that you remember, after the cemetery?' I asked, not looking at the Warrant Officer. I saw Sanet Niemand turning in her seat to talk to him. The Warrant Officer sat with folded arms, his face expressionless.

Labuschagne spoke very slowly. 'I remember being in the shower.'

'What was the time then?'

'It was three o'clock.'

'What duties did you still have to perform that afternoon?'

'We had new arrivals.'

'How many were there?'

'Five, I think. Yes, there were five.'

'How did you handle them?'

'As usual.'

'What part did you play in the initiation of the new arrivals?'

He did not answer the question directly. 'I was sick. I wanted to throw up, but my stomach was empty. I think I fainted. They took me to the medic.'

The court had become very quiet again. There was always some ambient noise in the courtroom. People shifted in their seats, coughed and sneezed and made the ordinary noises people make when they are at ease or bored – but on this occasion the court was absolutely quiet. I knew that we had everyone's attention.

'Did you suffer any injuries in the accident in Lynwood Road?' I asked. The question might have sounded mundane but I was trying to lay one of the cornerstones of the defence case without drawing too much attention to it just yet.

'I had a bump on the left side of my head and I was bleeding from my ear.'

'Did you receive any treatment for your injuries?' I asked. I looked towards the Warrant Officer. Arms folded high across his chest, he sat motionless and gave no hint whether he agreed or disagreed with the evidence.

'No, the medic just cleaned my ear and gave me some headache tablets.'

'How did you feel at that time?' This was another innocuous question laying an important stone for us.

'My head was sore and I was tired.'

We had come to the final phase.

'At what time did you come off duty that day?'

'The day shift came off at four.'

'Where did you go from there?' I asked.

'I went to my bakkie.' I waited, but he did not give the additional detail I had anticipated.

I prompted him. 'What did you intend to do when you left?'

'I was going to see my pastor in Lyttleton.' He saw that I wasn't going to prompt him about this and added, 'I wanted to ask him to speak to my wife and her father.'

'Did you see the pastor?'

'No, he wasn't at his home. The maid said he would only be back on the Sunday.'

'So what did you do next?'

'I went home.'

'What route did you take?'

'I came down the Old Johannesburg Road.'

'What was the weather like?'

'It was raining hard and the wind was blowing. There was hail too, I remember.'

'How were you feeling at the time?'

He did not expect the question and just looked at me.

'How were you feeling at the time?' I asked again, in the same tone of voice.

'I was tired. My head was sore. I couldn't see. I just wanted to get home. There was a lot of noise and thunder and lighting. I could not see anything.'

'Why couldn't you see?'

'It was the rain.'

'What is the next thing that happened, as you were driving along?'

'I was in another accident.'

'How did that happen?'

'A minibus came from the left and nearly sideswiped me.'

'And then? How did you experience the events from that point onwards?'

Labuschagne did not answer at first. I pressed ahead.

'Let me remind you of the evidence of the prosecution witnesses. Then you can tell the Court whether they described the events correctly,' I suggested.

Before I could continue Labuschagne spoke up. 'They are right. It happened like that.'

I had to make sure. 'You have heard the prosecution witnesses describe to the Court how you and the other man were driving and you agree with that evidence.'

'Yes,' he said softly. 'That's how it happened.'

But there were no eye witnesses to what had happened at the reservoir, so I had to lead him to that point.

'Let's pick up the events when you were on the track between the signal station and the reservoir on Magazine Hill. You were still driving?'

'Yes.'

'Was it still raining?'

'Yes, very hard.'

'Where was the minibus?'

'I don't know.'

'What do you mean, you don't know? Either it was in front of you or behind you.'

He hesitated. 'I don't know if it was in front or behind.'

'What happened next?' I wasn't going to give him any more help; he had to tell it in his own words.

'We stopped.'

'Where?'

'At the reservoir.'

'What were your relative positions?' I looked at the prosecution's photo album. One of the photographs showed the precise positions in which the vehicles were found later. Labuschagne watched me as I paged through the album.

'We were as the photographs show, sort of side by side.'

'The photographs show your bakkie to be slightly behind and to the left of the minibus.'

'Yes.' The answer was ambiguous and I had to try again.

'Well, were they like that?'

'I can't remember,' he said.

I went for broke. 'Tell the Court in your own words what happened next.'

The answer was as confusing as it had been when he told me the first time months earlier, even if the words were different and his emotions had got the better of him.

'I heard the trapdoors open and …'

The Judge interrupted before he could continue. 'Could you say that again?'

'Sir, I heard the noise of the trapdoors opening.'

The Judge raised an eyebrow. I stood perfectly still. The answer had to come out exactly right.

'Proceed,' I said. 'Take your time and tell it slowly.'

Labuschagne took a step back in the witness box until his back was against the wood panelling behind him.

'I know you won't believe me, but I heard the trapdoors opening.' He smacked his fist into his palm. 'And then I saw the bodies falling down with their white hoods flapping, and then I heard the Warrant Officer shouting, Trek hom op! Maak gou! Maak gou! I knew I had to hurry to help and I stepped over and the place was lit up by the lightning and then everything went dark again and I couldn't see anything for a while and I heard thunder and thunder and thunder. I just felt the water on my face.' The words had come out in a flood, like the rain pelting down on the roof of the court.

I stood still and watched in silence as he breathed in and out, as we had instructed him. I gave him some time to recover. He was as pale as a sheet. I didn't want to make him tell it twice, but I was going to have to, I thought. I decided to return to the reservoir later. I checked if Judge van Zyl had another question, but he didn't.

In the witness box Labuschagne shivered and squirmed like a prisoner on the trapdoors. All we needed to complete the picture was the white hood and the rope. I found that I was breathing quite heavily myself. I heard a *tap tap tap* and something snapped between my fingers, and when I looked down, I saw that I had Wierda's pencil in my left hand. It was in two pieces.

'What did you do when you felt the water on your face?' I asked.

'I ran. I just ran and ran.'

I decided to cut it short. 'Well, we know from the prosecution evidence that you were nearly run over by a car in the valley below the hill and that another motorist found you lying in the grass near the Voortrekker Monument. An ambulance was summoned and you were taken to hospital. Can you remember those events?'

'I remember them shining a light in my eyes and I remember being put on a stretcher and being on a stretcher at the hospital.'

'I have to ask you,' I said, 'I have to ask, do you remember what you did at the reservoir?'

'I don't remember.' The answer sounded earnest.

I pressed him a little. 'Have you tried to remember?'

Labuschagne didn't answer. I asked another question.

'The police came and arrested you while you were still in hospital, is that right?'

'Yes.'

'What happened there?'

'The policeman said he was arresting me and said that I had the right to remain silent. Then he asked me why I did it.'

'What did you say?'

'I didn't know what to say.'

'Did you know what he was talking about?'

'No, not then.'

'Well, let's deal with the situation as matters stand now. How do you see your position now?'

'I don't know,' he said. 'I don't know what you mean.'

I was about to ask him something else when he said, 'I'm not feeling too well. I think I'm going to …'

Judge van Zyl stepped in. 'Are you feeling faint?'

'Ja.'

'Do you want to sit down?' Then, not waiting for an answer, he said, 'I'll just adjourn for a few minutes. Send word through the usher when you're ready.'

I asked Wierda to take Labuschagne a glass of water. I sat contemplating the affair. Marianne Schlebusch had told me that we had to make Labuschagne say it in his own words, to own up to the killing. It would be the beginning of his cure; he had to say it himself, she had said. I knew I had to make him say it, but for a different reason altogether. I wasn't there to cure him; my job was to save him from the gallows and in order to achieve that I had to get him to tell as much as he knew, and he had to do it in open court. I sat on my own while they fussed about him. We sent the usher for the Judge and

Assessors as soon as Labuschagne had regained some of his colour.

Judge van Zyl turned to me as soon as he had taken his seat. 'Is he ready to continue?'

'I'll ask him if M'Lord pleases.' I turned to Labuschagne. 'Are you feeling better?'

'Yes, a little bit.' He sounded weak.

'Would you like more time?' asked the Judge. I thought at first he was addressing Labuschagne but found that he was looking at me.

'M'Lord, I would like to press ahead.' I was trying to give effect to Marianne's advice. I had to make Labuschagne talk, make him say that he had killed the men at the reservoir.

'Very well,' the Judge said, 'you may carry on then.'

I took a deep breath. I didn't like what I was going to do and decided to get it out of the way as quickly as possible.

'You killed them,' I said. 'You killed them. Everyone here knows that.' I waved my arm in an arc which included everyone from the jury box to my left to the spectators behind me. 'Everyone knows,' I concluded, with only the faintest note of a question in my tone.

Labuschagne started crying, softly at first, but then his sobs increased until his weeping was a torrent. I didn't get to ask a question. He tried to speak through his tears. 'I know too,' he said. 'I know, I know,' he said between sobs. 'I don't know how I did it but I know I did. How could I have done it?' he wailed. 'How could I have done it? God help me, how could I have done that?' He was bent over at the waist and shook his head as he asked, faintly this time, 'How could I have done that?'

'That's enough,' said the Judge and walked out of the courtroom. The usher rushed after him, but the Judge was through the door behind his chair before the usher could get to the bench. Nobody moved or made a sound as Labuschagne stood in the witness box and sobbed and sobbed.

Eventually I said to Wierda, 'Take care of him. I'll be back later,' and walked out.

The robing room was deserted. I sat with my head in my hands. I had rammed a question deep into my client's heart without warning, without preparing him for it. I had done so deliberately. And I was going to have to traverse the events at the reservoir once more.

It was half an hour before Wierda came to the robing room to fetch me. We walked back to court in silence. When we got there, the room was anything but silent.

'Mr Labuschagne, I have to ask you again about the events at the reservoir,' I said as soon as the court had settled down. Labuschagne nodded. He had a deathly grey pallor to his face. I ran the back of my hand over my brow. It came away sticky. I stopped just short of bringing my wrist up to my lips to taste the salt I knew must have accumulated there. Marianne Schlebusch had said that we would not get the truth out of him unless we could cause him to break down.

Make him cry, and you will get the truth, she'd said. However, I had no way of knowing if the truth would help his case.

'But before I deal with that, I need you to clear up something for me.' I waited for Labuschagne to show that he had heard before I set out to do what Marianne had advised.

The truth will help him. That was her opinion.

'You told us the Warrant Officer had said that you could see the prison psychiatrist if you needed help. Why didn't you seek help? A psychiatrist could perhaps have helped you,' I suggested.

He had broken down in tears again. His voice rose as he spoke, until the words came out in an anguished roar. 'Why didn't you tell me that before I started beating up my wife, before I lost my child, before I drove other people off the road and got into fights in pubs I did not want to go to? Why didn't you tell me that before I lost my child? Why didn't you tell me that before I killed seven people?'

He emitted a primeval, guttural animal cry, like a tortured beast under the branding iron. Every hair on my body stood upright and my skin felt too tight. The shapes around me lost their definition. I think I heard Wierda asking, 'Are you alright?'

Judge van Zyl left with his Assessors and I again escaped to the robing room, leaving Wierda to mop up behind me. I sat down in the robing room to compose myself. Labuschagne's outburst had shaken me. I had tried to present a case based on a solid foundation of fact with a touch of emotion to it, but now the emotion was starting to run away with us.

I made my way back to Court c and found Labuschagne sitting in my chair. His sister Antoinette and Marianne Schlebusch were fussing over him. I went and stood at the back of the court until they had propped him up in the witness box again.

When the Judge and Assessors had taken their seats, I started gently and adopted a more personal tone.

'Mr Labuschagne, I want you to try and remember as much as you can. Please tell the Court what you remember from the moment the bakkie and the minibus came to a stop at the reservoir.' I leaned heavily on the lectern. God knows, I was tired.

At first Labuschagne stood mute, rocking forwards and backwards slowly.

I had to help. 'Let's start with the weather conditions,' I suggested. 'Was it still raining?'

'Yes.' He spoke softly.

'Was it light or dark?'

'Dark.'

I had to draw him out more. 'How hard was it raining?'

'Very hard, I think.'

'What is the first thing you saw after you had stopped the bakkie?'

'The reservoir.'

'And the next thing you saw, what was that?'

'The minibus.'

'Where was the minibus?'

He looked at me. We had been over this ground before. There was a question in his eyes as he answered. 'It was in front of me, to the left.' He immediately corrected himself. 'No, I mean right.'

'What was your next sensation?' There was no easy way to ask the question. I did not want to just ask what happened next, because I wanted him to deal with his sensations and perceptions. 'What did you see or hear or feel?' I added.

'I saw lightning and I heard thunder and at the same time I smelt the hanging ropes. I could taste the smell in the back of my throat.'

This was more than I had hoped for and much more than he had previously told me.

'What is the very next thing that you became aware of?'

'I told you,' he said, with resignation in his voice. 'I heard the trap-doors opening.'

I could see that he was fully aware of the incongruity of his answer.

'Are you able to describe the sounds you heard?' I asked.

He stood for a while. 'No,' he said eventually.

'What did you see at that moment?' I was venturing deeper than I had gone before.

'I saw the bodies falling towards me.'

'What is the next sensation you remember?'

'I heard the Warrant Officer's voice,' he said looking down at his feet. He was still rocking, holding on to the sides of the witness box, but rocking slowly, forwards and backwards, as if to a beat only he could hear.

'What was the Warrant Officer saying?' I had to play along. We could explain later, in the closing argument.

'Trek hom op! Maak gou! Maak gou!'

I didn't know whether my next question was going to help his case but if I didn't ask it, James Murray or the Judge would. 'And what did you do when you heard the Warrant Officer say that?'

He paused for a long time, rocking, looking at his feet. 'I must have killed them. I think I killed them,' he said eventually, very softly.

I was quick to confirm his answer before the Judge could ask him to repeat it. 'You said, I must have killed them. I think I killed them. Is that what you said?'

'Yes.'

'Please remember to speak up so that His Lordship can hear you,' I said. 'What makes you think you killed them?' I asked, again taking the risk of an unhelpful answer.

'When I was running I did not understand, but later, I just knew I must have killed them.'

'How sure are you now that you killed them?'

'I am sure, but sometimes … I am not sure.'

'Can you explain that, please? How can you be sure and then not be sure?'

I watched Judge van Zyl as we waited for the answer. I tried to encourage Labuschagne by nodding when he made eye contact.

'There was one part of my mind that said, You have killed them, but I wasn't sure. I could not remember doing it. All I could remember was the bodies afterwards, lying in a row, with blood and water over them. And I was the only one there, so it must have been me. And now I know it must have been me.'

It wasn't as complete an answer as I had wanted, but the best I was going to get.

I gave him no warning as I changed the topic.

'Have you been able to make up with Magda?'

He started to speak but was overcome by tears again. The Judge cast a strong look of disapproval in my direction. He was ready to adjourn again, but I did not want him to.

I ignored the snivelling. 'Have you seen Esmè since your arrest?'

Labuschagne looked at me through his tears and shook his head. 'No.'

I feigned ignorance. 'Have they, Magda and Esmè, not come to visit you in the cells?'

'No.' He blew his nose. He did not know that we had asked Magda to give evidence, but that her father had intervened and had sent Wierda packing. But we had a subpoena ready and the Sheriff was going to serve it later in the day.

'They have not attended court at any time, have they?' I asked, even though that had been widely reported in the media to be the case.

'No,' he said looking towards the back of the court as if he expected to find them there.

I changed the subject again without warning. 'Mr Labuschagne, how did you feel while you were in hospital, and afterwards, after you had been arrested and charged?'

'I just wanted to be dead.'

'Do you still feel like that?'

His silence was the answer. He stood crying with his face in his hands. The Judge was about to speak, offering another break so that Labuschagne could recover, but I spoke first. 'I would like to carry on, M'Lord.'

'Why?' I asked Labuschagne.

'I am so ashamed of myself.'

'Why are you ashamed?' The answer was obvious, but I had to ask.

He tried to control the sobbing and spoke with a heaving chest. 'I can't believe I did that. How could I have done that?' he asked me. I noted that he referred to the incident as *that*, indicating that he was still not able to associate himself with it.

That gave me the opening I needed for my last question. 'Could you tell His Lordship how you see yourself now? Two years ago you were a school prefect and active in the church, and now you are here in court, on trial for murder.'

'I don't know. I don't understand. I just don't understand.'

I did not wait for Judge van Zyl to offer a further adjournment. 'I have no further questions, thank you,' I said and I sat down.

The Judge suggested that we take the tea adjournment early and we agreed. Wierda and Antoinette went over to the witness box, each with a glass of water.

Labuschagne was still crying, but softly now, as the cell sergeant escorted him down the steps to the cells. I stayed in court because I wanted to be alone.

I was about to sit down when Antoinette Labuschagne suddenly spoke behind me. 'How could you be so cruel?' she demanded.

Caught by surprise I turned around, but wasn't given a chance to answer.

'How could you do that to him?' She stood with her hands on her hips. Her eyes were red and puffy and it crossed my mind that she must have been crying. 'It is your job to protect him and instead you hurt him,' she said. In her anguish Antoinette looked a little like her brother. They had the same eyes.

The court had emptied quickly and Antoinette's parents were the only ones left with us. I looked at the elderly couple behind the dock. They were watching their daughter remonstrating with me.

'My job is to defend him,' I said to Antoinette, 'and that is what I am trying to do.' I spoke so that her parents could hear.

Antoinette wasn't having any of that. 'You don't have to hurt him to defend him.'

I didn't agree with her, but there was no point in getting into an argument about it.

She wasn't done yet. 'You don't believe him either, do you?' she said, wagging a finger under my nose. 'You think he is guilty.'

I waited for her to leave, but she stood her ground. 'It is not for me to believe,' I ventured. 'All I have to do is to defend him.' It is a lawyer's gambit, but it never works with the public.

Antoinette turned to her parents in triumph. 'You see,' she said, 'I told you he doesn't believe Leon. We should have got him a Pretoria advocate.'

I wished they had, but didn't respond. There was no arguing with Antoinette when she was on the verge of tears. My silence just aggravated her more.

'What kind of lawyer are you?' she said. 'What kind of lawyer doesn't even believe his own client?' She shook her head. I noticed that her shoulders were shaking.

I didn't know what to say, so I started walking away, but she grabbed me by my robes and pulled me around to face her again. 'Don't you dare turn your back on me,' she said. 'Why don't you answer me?'

She was extremely annoying and I felt like smacking her out of her hysteria. She reminded me of my own sister as a child, nagging, mocking, teasing and pushing – well within range for a smack but at the same time totally out of range because she was a girl. When I spoke I did so very softly, so that only she could hear. 'Antoinette, I am doing my best for your brother, but it is not an easy matter defending him. The case is difficult enough without my having to deal with distractions like this. Please leave me be.'

She too dropped her voice. 'But how can you not believe him?' she asked again.

I shook my head. How could I tell her that the worst thing I could do to her brother was to believe him?

When I took too long to come up with a response she turned abruptly and left with her parents. By the time she got to the door she was bent over and in tears. Her father put his arm around her and led her into the foyer.

When I turned to sit down I realised that she had followed me all the way across the floor to the foot of the registrar's dais. Only then did I find the answer I should have given.

'I can't believe him and defend him at the same time,' I said to the empty courtroom.

Palace of Justice

41

After Antoinette and her parents had left the courtroom I stepped up to the registrar's dais and sat down in her chair. I tried not to think about the case. I was bone weary, tired to the depths of my soul. I sat back and wished I had never laid eyes on Court C. I was looking up at the skylights when reality slowly returned. It was a truly magnificent courtroom. I closed my eyes and searched for an escape, anything to take my mind off the trial, but there was none. I looked at the room from the front, taking in the registrar's view of the proceedings. I had been working with my back towards two-thirds of the room. I took in the features of the room. I was in awe of the quality. Even though the whole building was badly in need of a facelift, the underlying class was there in every fitting, in every decorative feature and in the roof lights and glasswork. I was a little surprised that I had noticed only the decay earlier.

I looked down from the registrar's chair. The registrar's dais was two steps up from the floor, but not as high as the ornate bench behind it, and had the second best view of the courtroom. Below the registrar's desk was a smaller desk where the court stenographer sat with her machine. We had microphones at every position, including the dock. Sound wires crisscrossed the floor.

The jury box was to my right, against the wall. It was also on a raised dais, and enclosed. There were two rows of wooden benches in the jury box, with seats of red leather. To my left, hard up against the registrar's throne, was the witness box. There was no comfort there; it had no seats and imprisoned the witness in a space no more than one square metre. Behind the witness box were the old press boxes, now occupied by the usher and the investigating officer.

The room was empty and I thought I would be able to just sit there in peace. I tried hard not to think about the case, about what I had done, about what the Judge was going to do, but there was no escape. I imagined the Judge's view of the courtroom. What did he see from above?

Immediately in front of the registrar's dais there were six curved tables, arranged in three rows of two. These were for the lawyers. The furniture was of heavy, solid hardwood with turned legs and beautiful carved patterns. The tables had working areas inlaid in maroon leather and the seats of the chairs were similarly covered.

Underfoot the carpet was pale pink; it had once been maroon or dark red.

The Warrant Officer had been sitting in the same position every day in the row immediately behind the prosecutors, but there were no papers on his table. He was a man of sparse habits, I thought, a man of secrets. I wondered how many young men he had broken in for duty as gallows escorts and how many of those had been broken as a result. I noted that the defence table, the witness box and the Judge's chair formed a perfect triangle, each leg about five paces.

The dock was situated behind the rows of lawyers' tables and effectively divided the room in two as it ran virtually the full width of the room. A steep and narrow staircase connected the courtroom to the cells below. That would be the route Labuschagne would take, if we lost.

Take the prisoner down, Judge van Zyl would say.

Antoinette Labuschagne kept superimposing herself on my random thoughts. She had reaffirmed what every woman in my family had taught me over the years.

Men are scared of other people's pain, but women rush in to help, to cradle and to comfort.

I shook my head to banish Antoinette from my thoughts and shifted my attention deeper into the room. Behind the dock was a waist-high wooden barrier extending across the room, with small gates where it abutted the walls on either side. The public had hard benches arranged in rows with an aisle down the middle. There was more seating in a balcony at the back of the room.

There were distinct shadows under the tables and benches. As I looked up to find the source of light I saw a row of lights along each of the side walls. Then I counted ten large lead glass windows on either side above the light fittings. These had intricate patterns and let in copious amounts of natural light through their ivory, green and turquoise panels. The higher I looked, the more light there was. Beautiful though these windows were, they were outshone by the large copper chandelier and the two skylights overhead.

The glass in the windows was dirty and needed cleaning.

Wierda was the first to return to court. He came in, saw me in the registrar's seat and without a word went to our table and sat down. He didn't make eye contact with me. I joined him when the cell sergeant brought Labuschagne up from the cells; I was annoyed that the sergeant also avoided my eyes.

The court quickly filled up in anticipation of the cross-examination. There was excitement in the spectator benches.

I had been on my feet for nearly three days and would have the opportunity to take the weight off my feet and to rest the tired muscles of my lower back. But I would have to keep up the concentration.

This was where our case would be subjected to the scrutiny of cross-examination, where its improbabilities and inconsistencies would be exposed.

Cross-examination is the greatest tool to discover the truth, someone had said once. It might have been something of an overstatement, but in many cases it was true.

Palace of Justice

42

Judge van Zyl started by inviting James Murray to begin. 'Yes, Mr Murray.'

Murray rose to cross-examine. Sanet Niemand sat next to him, keeping her back stiff, a neatly tabulated notebook on the table in front of her. The book was open, her neat writing on display. The spotlight was back on the prosecutors for the first time in a week. The registrar reminded Labuschagne that he was still under oath.

At the defence table our heads were turned to the right. We were keen to see what style of cross-examiner Murray was. While he too held the rank of senior counsel I had not previously encountered him in practice. But then, I dwelt almost exclusively in the civil courts; the prosecutors were criminal law specialists attached to the Attorney-General's office. Murray's reputation was a concern. According to robing room talk, he was a deadly mix of tenacity and competence. We call him the Angel of Death, a local junior had said, because he always gets the death sentence.

When the Judge nodded Murray put his notes on the lectern in front of him and started with the standard acknowledgement. 'As the Court pleases,' he said and continued, 'So you say that the execution process and the work in the pit room upset you greatly? Is that what you're saying?' No introductions, no niceties, and no warm-up. He went for the jugular. I could see immediately that the cross-examination was going to be short, brutal, and to the point. This man was not going to take any prisoners.

Labuschagne nodded.

'You'll have to speak up,' said Murray. 'The evidence has to be recorded and a nod or a shake of your head will not be recorded.' He gave no sign that he had been affected in any way by the displays of emotion that had preceded the tea break.

Labuschagne nodded again, surprised by the bluntness of the attack and the proximity of his antagonist. Murray was less than eight feet from the witness box, directly in line with Labuschagne's left shoulder.

'You have to speak and when you speak you have to speak up, understand?' Murray said a second time. He was making sure that Labuschagne knew who was in charge.

Labuschagne turned to face him. 'Yes, I understand, sir.'

The Judge wasn't having any of that either and entered the fray. With a glance in Murray's direction, he said, 'Please turn back towards the bench so that you face us. Mr Murray is right. You must please speak up, but you must direct your answers to us.' He indicated himself and the two Assessors. 'You may look at Mr Murray when he asks a question, but you must direct your answers to me. Can you do that?'

'Yes, sir.'

'Go ahead,' said the Judge. Murray repeated the original question, word for word. It was obviously a prepared question. 'So you say that the execution process and the work in the pit room upset you greatly. Is that what you're saying?'

'Yes,' said Labuschagne.

'But haven't you been playing the fool in all the sections of the prison, including the gallows room, the pit room and even in the chapel?'

'No. Not me.'

I could see that the Judge had caught the subtle qualification of the answer. I turned to Wierda and whispered, 'We are in for a torrid time. This is going to be a bloodbath.' Wierda passed a hastily scribbled note to me. *Yes, but whose blood?* I don't know how he could have had any doubt about that.

Murray stared at Labuschagne for a while, his attitude exuding disbelief. 'Well, let me see if I can give your memory a jolt. Can you recall an occasion when you gave a new warder a fright by putting white chalk on your face and hiding in one of the freezers in the autopsy room?'

The slightest flicker of recognition appeared in Labuschagne's eyes, an answer in itself.

'And then that warder was sent over by one of your friends to open that freezer and you sat up and pretended to rise from the dead? Do you remember the incident now?' Murray insisted.

'It wasn't me,' said Labuschagne, but there was no conviction in his voice. He appeared surprised by the angle of attack.

Murray ignored the answer. 'You were even dressed in one of the death shrouds and you stuck your tongue out of the side of your mouth.'

'No. I told you it wasn't me. It wasn't me,' Labuschagne repeated.

'So it was one of the other warders, was it?' Murray could not lose on this tack. It did not matter whether Labuschagne had participated in the tomfoolery. What mattered was that the atmosphere of the place was not as serious or sombre as he had described in his evidence-in-chief.

'Yes, it was,' Labuschagne agreed.

'But you smiled when I reminded you of the incident. Why?'

'I don't know that I smiled.'

Judge van Zyl had been watching the exchange intently. 'Yes, you did,' he said. 'I saw it too.'

Labuschagne shifted his weight to his left and looked towards the defence table, but we could not help him, of course, and had to feign indifference. Wierda had told him more than once that he would be on his own once cross-examination started. 'When you're under cross-examination you will be on your own. We can't help you. So keep your answers short. Don't volunteer information. If we want an explanation, we'll ask you about it later.'

'So what is your answer?' asked Murray. 'You remember the incident now, don't you?'

'Yes, I heard about it.' Labuschagne had had time to think. He was quick on the uptake.

Murray changed topics immediately. He had made a small gain and was not going to ruin everything by inviting an explanation.

'Didn't you personally incarcerate two prisoners in those cells next to the gallows after you had caught them fighting? And didn't you show

310

them the gallows and tell them they were to be hanged the next day because they had been giving you too much trouble?'

'No, I did not,' said Labuschagne. 'I could not possibly have done that. Do you know how many different doors there are from the general cell sections to those cells?' He answered his own question. 'Six at least. Every door has its own key. No one has more than one key. The Warrant Officer kept the keys to the gallows in his safe. I could never have got in there.'

'That's how I know what happened. All those other warders played along,' suggested Murray. If he could goad Labuschagne into losing his temper he could immediately exploit that.

'The Warrant Officer would have fired the lot of us for breaking his rules. He is fanatical about security.'

Labuschagne was holding his own during the exchange, but I was concerned that he was getting too expansive in his answers.

Murray sealed his point with a question that Labuschagne could not answer. 'Yes, but you told us you were the only one who went up there to work on the stopper bags, didn't you?'

There was no answer.

'You used to smoke, didn't you?' Murray then asked without bothering to look towards the witness box.

'I started smoking the day of my first hanging.'

'And you were allowed to smoke in the prison, even when on duty?'

'Yes, everyone was allowed to smoke.'

I wondered where this was leading.

'You once put a lit cigarette in the mouth of an executed prisoner before you closed the coffin and took his body down to the chapel, didn't you?' There was a faint smile on Murray's lips.

'No.' The answer was blunt.

'And then, during the funeral service, and with the man's family in attendance, smoke came from the coffin, didn't it?'

Labuschagne shot a worried look at the Warrant Officer who was still sitting in the row of seats behind Murray. Their eyes met and stayed fixed for a moment. Labuschagne shook his head almost imperceptibly before he turned towards the Judge to answer.

'No,' he said. I had been watching Labuschagne and did not notice whether Judge van Zyl or the Assessors had seen the interaction between Labuschagne and the Warrant Officer.

'And you were the hero of the day when you quickly went and turned on the ventilator fans, weren't you?'

'No,' said Labuschagne, this time with an emphatic shake of the head.

'You did a number of things like that, didn't you? You played the fool in many ways.'

'No.'

'Let me give you some further examples,' said Murray. He picked up his notes and read from them.

'You crept up on the catwalk and scared the prisoners in C Section by making strange shuffling and groaning noises.'

'No, that's just not true. We heard those noises too and we even investigated them.'

'And you sprayed each other with the hose when you were cleaning the pit room?'

'No.' Labuschagne shook his head. He was getting animated. 'Some of us did get wet while cleaning up the pit, but it was not a joke. If you sprayed any of the warders with the hose in that room they would have beaten you to a pulp right there, and the Warrant Officer would have put you on the catwalk or the guard towers.'

Murray decided to re-establish his authority. 'Please listen very carefully to my questions. All you have to do is to say yes or no. If any explanations are required, I will ask you for an explanation. Otherwise you can leave your explanations for later when your advocate re-examines you. Understand?'

'Yes.'

I looked at Judge van Zyl. How would he respond to Murray's admonishment of the witness? This was the Judge's domain. The Judge did not stir.

I decided to watch him more closely. I didn't know how well he knew James Murray and wanted to check whether he would treat Murray differently from the way he had treated me.

Murray had not finished the topic. 'You made fun of the dead prisoners' bodies by making jokes about their anatomy?' he suggested.

'No.'

There was a seamless change of direction. 'I suggest to you that your evidence that you were upset by the execution process and by what you had to do in the pit room is just a facade, and that in truth you really enjoyed the work.'

'No.'

'You, like others who were working there, saw yourselves as the Executioner's assistants and you were eager to be on his team.'

'No,' he said with a note of indignation.

'Being a gallows escort was preferred to walking the catwalks or sitting on your own for hours in the guard towers, wasn't it?'

There was a long pause before the answer came. 'We didn't like working in the towers, and the Warrant Officer allocated catwalk duty as punishment to warders who had done something wrong or displeased him somehow. But escort duty was worse than any other job in there.'

'My point is that you volunteered for escort duty rather than taking catwalk or tower duty.'

'I did not volunteer for it.'

Murray pounced immediately. 'But you did not like catwalk or tower duty, did you?'

'No one did.'

'I am not interested in the others. I am asking you. You did not like catwalk or tower duty, did you?'

Labuschagne was provoked into ignoring Wierda's instructions to keep the answers short. 'The catwalks are like a cage,' he said. 'Like a separate prison inside the prison. They lock you in for the shift, with your rifle and ten rounds, just below the steel roof. Even in winter it is hot up there. You're up there alone, hot, uncomfortable, thirsty and you have to walk around and look at the prisoners through the windows into their cells. It would be more comfortable in the cells below than up there.'

Labuschagne was about to start again when Murray suggested an answer. 'So that is why you volunteered for escort duty, is it not?'

There was no answer. Labuschagne stood with his head down, staring at the microphone in front of him. All his talking had allowed Murray to score a direct hit.

Murray decided to press the advantage.

'You called the prisoner whose eyes bulged the most after an execution Pop-Eye.'

Labuschagne looked directly at Murray, then at the Warrant Officer.

'No,' he said at last. It was not clear whether he was denying Murray's suggestion or whether he was reprimanding the Warrant Officer.

Murray again changed tack to keep Labuschagne off balance.

'The warders on the catwalk and in the towers were armed with R1 semi-automatic rifles and ten rounds of ammunition, you said?'

'Yes.'

'But you never used those rifles, did you?'

The answer came very promptly. 'No, that is not right. They have shot some prisoners and some warders have shot themselves.'

Murray appeared surprised by the answer and turned to look at the Warrant Officer. When the Warrant Officer shook his head, Murray turned back to Labuschagne.

'I put it to you,' he said in a stern voice, 'that there has not been any occasion when a prisoner was shot by a warder.'

Labuschagne picked up one of the registers on the edge of the witness box. He answered as he was paging through it.

'That is not true. We shot four dead.'

The answer was not what Murray had expected. He turned to look at the Warrant Officer again and raised his eyebrows in an unspoken question. The Warrant Officer shook his head again. Murray measured his next question carefully.

'When did that happen?'

'On the thirtieth of September 1962.' Labuschagne picked up one of the registers and started reading from a flagged page. 'Here,' he said, pointing with his finger at the page, 'we shot four who were trying to escape on the thirtieth of September 1962. Philemon Mhlungu, Titos Malinga, and,' he turned over a few pages, 'Sam Ndhlovu and Robert Shangase.'

I thought Judge van Zyl would object to the use of the names, but he didn't. He was watching the contest with keen interest.

Murray sneered at the answer. 'You weren't even born then. And Maximum Security Prison had not been built yet, had it? And you were not personally involved, were you?' The questions came out in a cluster.

'But you said that we've never shot a prisoner. That's not true,' said Labuschagne.

'*You* never did.'

'But you said we never shot anybody.' Labuschagne had turned to face Murray.

'Don't speak to Mr Murray. Direct your answers to me,' said the Judge.

'Yes, sir.' Labuschagne turned back to face the bench.

'What register were you reading from there?' asked Murray.

Labuschagne opened the register at the first page and slowly turned all the pages over until he got to the last page. 'It is the register of death sentences from November 1956 to April 1965.'

I was anticipating another salvo of questions from Murray when the Judge intervened. 'How did you know about that incident?' he asked.

'The Warrant Officer told us about it, sir,' said Labuschagne. 'He reminded us of it constantly. He said our job was to keep them in custody until the Hangman had to take over and if we had to do it by shooting them when they tried to escape or caused a riot, then that was what we had to do.

'And I saw it in the registers while I was waiting in the cells,' he added.

James Murray tried to salvage what he could from the situation. If Labuschagne had ever had to use his rifle he would surely have mentioned it by now. 'But you personally have never shot a prisoner, have you?'

'No.' He paused and added, 'But I nearly shot a lawyer once.'

Everyone burst out laughing, except Labuschagne. I watched as Judge van Zyl whispered something behind his hand. I could work it out for myself. *There have been many a day when I felt like shooting a lawyer myself!*

Murray waited for the titter to settle down. 'Yes, I know,' he said. 'That was when he strayed from the warder escorting him to the gate and you were on the tower with orders to shoot, wasn't it?' Murray showed that he knew more about Labuschagne than we might have thought.

Labuschagne nodded and Murray asked his next question, the moment of levity forgotten already. 'But how could a prisoner escape with all those gates and locks and with all that re-enforced concrete and toughened steel bars and high walls? And with the keys being kept by different people?'

'They couldn't get out, but if they threatened a warder or tried to set fire to the place I would have to shoot them. There wouldn't be anything else I could do from the catwalk. And we were told to do that.'

'And no warder ever shot themselves on the premises?'

'No, but they shot themselves when they were off duty.'

Murray reined him in again. 'Please answer only what I ask you. If I want you to explain or elaborate I will ask you, understand?' He stared at Labuschagne until he heard the answer.

'Yes.'

The round went to Labuschagne, I thought, but I was secretly pleased that Murray had pulled him up short. I did not want Labuschagne to get too cocky or clever with his answers.

The next line of cross-examination had me baffled.

'Are you suggesting that Mbele was not a suicide, that the warders had killed him?'

Labuschagne blinked. 'Mbele? I did not say that.'

'You suggested in your evidence-in-chief that his case was not a genuine suicide, didn't you?'

'No, I said the District Surgeon found injuries and things that did not agree with suicide, and that we were blamed for his death, that's what I said.'

'But by doing that you are suggesting that he did not commit suicide but was killed in the prison, by prison staff.'

'I just told what I know. It happened exactly as I said.'

'Well, let's look at the matter from another angle. There was an open inquest at the Magistrates' Court and you were one of the witnesses, right?'

'Yes.'

'And the Magistrate, after hearing all the evidence, including your own, returned a finding of suicide, didn't he?'

'Yes.'

'And you have told us of the danger the prisoners in Maximum constituted not only to the warders but to each other. You said they were brutal, evil men who would kill you as soon as look at you.'

'Yes.'

Murray half turned and conferred briefly with the Warrant Officer. 'Mbele was a troublemaker, wasn't he?'

'Yes.'

'Well, I suggest that the abdominal injury that the doctor found had probably been inflicted by one of the other prisoners; you cannot dispute that, can you?'

'No, but I know we also gave him a hiding.'

Murray was on the verge of losing his temper. 'Don't speculate. You are to tell us only what you know.'

There was no answer.

Sanet Niemand handed Murray a note. 'What do you say about Muller then, was that a genuine suicide?' Murray asked. He pocketed the note.

'Yes, I think so.'

'He made it obvious, didn't he, and even left you a note?'

'Yes, in his shoe.'

Murray turned the pages of his notebook. 'M'Lord, may I ask your indulgence to take a moment to speak to my Junior?'

'Yes,' said Judge van Zyl, 'take your time.'

The courtroom was quiet for a while, then the Judge asked, out of the blue, 'What do you do with prisoners like Muller, who want to commit suicide and at the same time appear to mock you?'

'We play along, sir. There are many of them, especially the gangsters from Cape Town who play the fool all the time, even in there.'

'What do they do, and how do you play along?'

'They tease us and they mock us. They pretend to be very obedient but they say things behind their hands. For example, they would say, Ja, my Kroon, but add softly behind their hand, My Kroon se gat! And

317

when you ask, Wat sê jy? they say, Niks nie, my Kroon. Others mock us by saying that the Hangman will never get them, like Muller, and they exercise their neck muscles and say, My nek is te taai vir die tou!'

'You said you played along,' said Judge van Zyl. 'How did you play along?'

'We hit them, but not hard, sir. And with the ones we saw exercising their neck muscles we added three inches to the drop, just to be sure.'

Murray and Niemand came out of a huddle with the Warrant Officer and the Judge called them to order. 'Carry on when you're ready,' he said.

Palace of Justice

43

There was three-quarters of an hour still to go before the lunch break. James Murray stood up to face Labuschagne in the witness box a few feet away.

'No one briefed the prisoners in the Pot about what was to happen to them during the hour between six and seven o'clock on the day of their execution, is that correct?' I noticed that Murray had avoided calling Labuschagne by his name.

Labuschagne looked perplexed. 'I don't understand what you mean by briefed.'

Murray sighed. 'What it means is that no one explained beforehand to the prisoners exactly what was going to happen during that hour. They were simply woken up, told what to do, how to dress, where to go, where to stand and so on. They were told what to do only at every step, right up to when they were on the trapdoors, but not before.'

Labuschagne nodded his agreement to every fact that Murray listed, and then added, 'No, not really.'

'What do you mean, not really?'

'Well, they *were* told there would be a service for them before, and a service after.'

'But they weren't told that they were going to have to put on their day wear without shoes, socks and underwear?'

'No. They were told in the morning.'

'Nor that they would be fingerprinted to make sure that the right person was going to be hanged?'

'No.'

Murray held his hand up with his fist closed. 'Nor that their hands were going to be cuffed behind their backs.' He raised one finger and Labuschagne nodded as he did so. 'Nor that a white hood would be placed over their heads.' He raised another finger. Labuschagne nodded again. 'Nor that they would have to stand on the painted footmarks on the trapdoors.' He straightened his middle finger. 'Nor that the rope would be put around their necks and that the lever would be pulled without another word.' The ring finger and little finger joined the others.

'No,' said Labuschagne. 'What would be the point of telling them?'

Murray ignored the question but provided an answer of sorts in any event. 'You rushed them from one place to the next until they were on the trapdoors, and then the lever was pulled?'

'Yes.'

'None of the black warders was involved in the execution process, is that right?'

Judge van Zyl looked up in surprise. Then he looked at the defence table. There was no denial from our quarter. I simply didn't know the answer since the topic had never come up during our preparation. I wondered where Murray was going with it. I didn't have long to wait.

'No,' said Labuschagne. 'They refused.' It was an unnecessary elaboration, and it could be used against him.

Murray saw that and quickly exploited the opportunity. 'So they refused to take part in the execution process, did they?'

'Yes.'

'But you did not?'

'No.'

The court fell silent while the ramifications of this disclosure were considered around the room. Labuschagne was the first to find words, but he came across as spiteful and cocky.

'The real reason why black warders were not involved,' he said, 'is that the Warrant Officer didn't trust them.'

'And the reason you didn't refuse is that you were in favour of the death penalty, not so?' The question was superfluous, but Murray had asked it. Now he had to accept the consequences of trying to argue his case in cross-examination.

'I was in favour of it in the beginning, but I started to have doubts about it in the second year, and now I don't know anymore.'

Murray pressed on. 'And while you were in favour of it, you thought you were doing important work for the government?'

'Yes,' Labuschagne said defensively, and then with emphasis, 'but it *was* important work. The Warrant Officer said so.' He looked directly at the Warrant Officer, but the Warrant Officer wasn't looking at anybody.

'And you became a willing and active member of the team of warders, the special team chosen by the Warrant Officer to do the execution shifts, didn't you?'

Labuschagne swallowed before he answered. He must have seen where the cross-examination was going. 'Yes.'

'And you felt special because you were entrusted with this special job?' 'Yes.'

'You were part of the whole execution process, weren't you? Without your help they couldn't do it?' James Murray again invited an argument, a dangerous ploy, but the rewards could be high.

'They could.'

'Well,' suggested Murray, 'they would have had to get someone else to do your job, wouldn't they?'

'Yes.'

'That means your part was indispensable. Without you, or someone like you, the Executioner couldn't carry out his own job, could he?'

'Yes.'

'That is what I meant earlier,' Murray said while glancing at his notes.

He didn't wait for an answer. 'You got used to this special work very quickly, didn't you?'

'I got used to it.'

'This special work of killing,' Murray added, glancing at the defence table, 'you got used to it.' It was a statement, not a question, the way he put it.

There was a very long pause before Labuschagne answered. Our briefing sessions had not prepared him for this line of cross-examination. 'Yes.'

'You thought those people deserved to die, didn't you? Otherwise you wouldn't have participated in the process of killing them, would you?'

It was a trick question and Labuschagne could see it. He hesitated. 'I thought if the Court had sentenced them to die, then they deserved to die.'

'So you thought you were helping the Executioner to administer to these people what they deserved, and that was death?'

'Yes.'

'And that must have made you feel important and powerful?'

When the answer came after a long pause, it did not deal with the crux of the question. 'No one except us knew about the work we were doing. Only we knew, so how could we feel important and powerful?'

'Don't ask me questions,' said Murray. 'You felt so special that you and your fellow escorts looked down on the new warders who fainted or became sick or ran away during the hanging, didn't you?'

'No.'

'And you must have thought the same about the warders who worked in other sections of the prison and even those in other prisons.'

'No.' Labuschagne had reverted to monosyllabic answers.

Murray had not finished with him. 'You knew that you were immune to prosecution. You were killing with the blessing of the law, weren't you?'

'Yes.' The answer hung in the air.

Murray came back to his earlier point. 'That must have given you a tremendous feeling of power, that knowledge that you could kill and not be prosecuted for it.'

'*We* didn't do the killing. The Hangman did.'

'But you agreed you were an indispensable part of the process, just a

minute ago you admitted that. Do you want to change your evidence?'
Murray was taking a risk with this style of cross-examination, but the
rewards could be high too.

'No,' said Labuschagne.

'So you were part of the killing process, weren't you? And you
were immune from prosecution because you were the State's killers.'
Murray did not seem to realise that he had asked two questions.
When Labuschagne hesitated, he insisted on an answer. 'Well, what
is your answer?'

'I wouldn't put it like that,' said Labuschagne after another pause. 'We
all knew that nothing could happen to us if we did our job properly.
The Warrant Officer told us that. He also said that we must not touch a
prisoner during the hanging process and we were not even allowed to
touch the prisoner in the pit room until the doctor had certified him
dead. He said we could be prosecuted for murder or culpable homicide
if we touched the prisoner. He said that only the Hangman had the
right to kill the prisoners. He said that no matter what we did to get
the prisoners up onto the trapdoors, it was the Hangman who did the
killing. It was his hand that did the killing.'

That long answer opened up another line of cross-examination and
Murray explored it without hesitation.

'Yet you have told the Court that on more than one occasion you
and other escorts had to pull a prisoner up by the rope and drop him
again, haven't you?'

'Yes, but we did not touch them. We only touched the rope. That's
what the Warrant Officer told us to do.'

'You hauled them up by the rope, is that what you say?'

'Yes.'

'That must have been very hard work, physically challenging even
for strong young men like you.'

Labuschagne fell for the flattery, not seeing the point behind the question. 'It was very tough. You try to lift something that heavy with your
arms away from your body, up to the level of your shoulders; someone
that squirms and kicks and jumps. You try it and see.'

'But you were able to do it, and did it, more than once,' Murray suggested innocently.

'Yes.'

'And then you dropped them again, so that their necks would break cleanly, didn't you?'

'Yes.'

'And one, you said, you had to haul up twice before his neck would break cleanly, is that right?'

It was a mistake on Murray's part. Labuschagne had not said anything about pulling any prisoner up twice. But he didn't notice the mistake in the question either. 'Yes, but there were a few like that. We had to pull them up twice.'

Wierda groaned beside me, but I thought that Murray's error had made our case better.

'So in those cases the hands that did the killing were not the Executioner's, were they? They were yours.' Murray had answered his own question.

'We didn't see it that way.'

'Well. Let's look at the facts, at what you yourself have told the Court. The Executioner pulled the lever …'

'Pushed,' said Labuschagne. 'He did not pull the lever, he pushed it.'

Murray was nonplussed. 'It doesn't matter whether he pushed or pulled the lever, but his hand did not cause the prisoner's neck to break. Your hands did, didn't they?'

I rose to object and Murray sat down quickly. 'M'Lord, with respect, the question is actually an argument, not a question the witness can answer.'

Judge van Zyl didn't wait for Murray's response. 'Well, you've told us on more than one occasion that the defendant's state of mind was relevant, and that every piece of evidence, every event that had a bearing on his state of mind is relevant and admissible. And I have allowed the defence a lot of leeway on this. It seems to me that this evidence is relevant to the defendant's state of mind. I would like to hear the answer.'

Murray nodded enthusiastically as the Judge quoted my own words back at me. I muttered, 'As M'Lord pleases,' and sat down. I was not being sarcastic, but I was sure the Judge had been. I had given him the opportunity to overrule an objection, and he had grabbed it with both hands. I decided not to intervene again. Labuschagne would have to sink or swim on his own.

Murray reminded Labuschagne of the point, but with a slightly different emphasis so that the answer would suit his case either way. 'Surely you can see that it was your hands that did the killing in those cases where you hauled the prisoner up and dropped him down again until he was dead?'

'We didn't see it that way. We didn't touch them,' Labuschagne added. The distinction was important to him.

'You didn't ask the Warrant Officer why *you* had to haul the prisoner up and drop him again, why the Executioner couldn't finish the job himself?'

'Sir, Oom Doepie is an old man. He could never do it himself.'

Neither the Judge nor Murray reacted to the use of the name.

'You could have left the prisoner hanging on the rope until he was dead, couldn't you?' Murray suggested.

'We had other work to do. We could not hang around there waiting for him to die. It could take a long time. The whole idea was to make them die quickly.'

The Judge was about to say something when Labuschagne added, 'Anyway, the Warrant Officer said we had to do it because the sentence of the Court was death by hanging, not death by strangling.'

'It's not quite as simple as that, is it? You physically raised the prisoner to the right height and then dropped him again?'

'Yes.'

'And your purpose was to cause his neck to break, wasn't it?'

'Yes.'

'So that he would die, yes?'

'Yes, so that he would die quickly and painlessly.'

'And that is exactly what then happened, isn't it? They died quickly and, you assume, painlessly?'

'Yes.'

'Exactly as if the Executioner had broken their necks when he pulled …' Murray had to correct himself, 'or rather, when he pushed the lever?'

'Yes.'

The Judge intervened. 'Mr Murray, where is this going? You've made your point, surely?'

I also thought Murray had made his point, but he had not yet succeeded in his secondary purpose with this line of questioning, which was to unsettle Labuschagne, to soften him up for the cross-examination that was still to follow.

Murray was diplomatic. 'I've nearly finished with this topic, M'Lord.'

'Continue,' said Judge van Zyl and Murray wasted no time.

'When the prisoner's neck broke after the trapdoors had opened, you saw the Executioner's hand as the one that had done the killing, didn't you?'

'Yes. It was his hand.'

'And by the same token, when you hauled the prisoner up, dropped him down and his neck broke, it was not the Executioner's hand that did the killing, was it?'

'I see what you mean,' Labuschagne conceded, looking at the floor.

'So it was your hand that did the killing.' Murray turned to his left towards Sanet Niemand and let the statement hang in the air. The answer did not matter. Labuschagne's own evidence now showed him to be capable of killing, with his own hands.

Labuschagne didn't have to answer.

It was time for lunch, but Murray was keen to strike another blow.

'And it was your hand that did the killing at the reservoir, wasn't it?'

Again Labuschagne did not have to answer.

Labuschagne was taken back to Cell 6 and Wierda and I at first headed for the Square, but changed our minds to walk around the building. Wierda hadn't spoken to me since before the tea break.

'What's up?' I asked him when we got to the first corner. 'Are you cross with me?'

Wierda sighed heavily. He didn't look at me. 'I don't know how you could have done that to him. Why didn't you give him some warning that you were going to do that?'

It was one thing getting this from Antoinette, but quite a different matter coming from my own Junior. Wierda was supposed to be above the emotion of the moment. Still, with him I could argue the point, and I did.

'It would have been less effective if he knew what was coming. He would have been unconvincing. He would have sounded prepared, artificial, unemotional, and unpersuasive.' I ran out of words to describe Labuschagne's emotional flatness when he had to deal with matters involving his emotions.

'Maybe, but it would have been less traumatic for him, and for his parents too.'

It was my turn to sigh. I saw that I couldn't win this argument so I just changed the subject. 'What's the next case about? Is there anything we can use?'

'No,' he said, 'it's just another cell murder.'

We strolled along in the sunshine. I took in more of the features of the Palace of Justice.

'So tell me about the cell murder,' I said. 'Anything special about the case?'

'Nah,' he said, 'it's a common Cape Town prison case.'

We walked slowly as Wierda briefed me on the events that had taken place in the Allandale prison near Cape Town and gave rise to seven men from that cell being hanged in Pretoria on 9 December 1987.

I interrupted him when we were behind the building. 'Why is the dome so low? I thought the whole idea of a dome was that it should dominate, but this one is almost obscured and the towers at the corners are inconspicuous too.'

Wierda's response was immediate. 'They added an extra floor after the architect had completed the design, but they wouldn't allow the expense of raising the dome and towers to compensate and to get the proportions right. That nearly broke the old man, my grandfather said.

'And look at this monstrosity here,' Wierda said, 'just look at this building here.' He pointed to a building in the back courtyard of the Palace. 'That should be open space, a park, but they allowed the police to build a seven-storey building there. It looks crap, doesn't it?'

I had to agree with him. We returned to our discussion of the cell murder case.

v3625 William Harris
v3626 Brian Meiring
v3627 Christoffel Michaels
v2628 Herold Japhta
v3629 Jan Swartbooi
v3630 Pieter Botha
v3631 Anthony Morgan

44

Eight prisoners were charged with the murder of one of their cellmates and with two counts of assault with intent to do grievous bodily harm to two others. Seven of them were convicted and sentenced to death. Pieter Pienaar was found not guilty.

Cell 6 in the Allandale Prison near Cape Town was about ten by five metres and its regular occupants were the eight accused and at least seventeen other Category A prisoners. In the corner of the cell were a toilet and a shower; neither had a door. The cell was so overcrowded that when the prisoners rolled out their sleeping mats there was no more than a hand's width between them. When an additional prisoner was allocated to Cell 6, there was no space for another sleeping mat and arrangements had to be made so that three prisoners were to occupy two sleeping mats. There were members of at least two prison gangs in Cell 6, the 26s and the 28s, who were mortal enemies.

The scene was set for murder.

About two days before his death the deceased Sharief Hendry was sent to Cell 6. For a night or two the existing sleeping arrangements were kept in place: the 26s slept in a row against one wall and the 28s against the other. There were a few independents in the cell, prisoners who had not joined either gang, but even they had formed a loose alliance with the one gang or the other in order to secure some protection. The prisoners were all classified as Category A prisoners, which meant that they were still thought to be relatively manageable and capable of being rehabilitated, notwithstanding that every one of them had many previous convictions and that all were serving medium to long sentences.

Hendry decided to rearrange the sleeping positions on the evening of 5 January 1985. This was achieved by moving three men out of the right-hand side where the 26s had their territory to the opposite side, traditionally the 28s' side, and moving two men from that side over to the right. The result was that space in the 28s' territory became more cramped than before. Two of the accused, Meiring and Botha, were directly affected by this move. Although they were independents, it was known that their sympathies lay with the 28s.

The 28s decided to do something about the newcomer's cheek. Earlier in the day there had been an altercation between Harris and Swartbooi on one side and Hendry and another prisoner on the other. The two sides exchanged threats. The consequence was that the 28s held a formal gang meeting in the early evening, wearing their full prison uniform, with caps on their heads, as was the custom of their court. They did this in full view of the other inhabitants of the cell and everyone knew that trouble was on the horizon. Their decision was evident from their subsequent conduct.

First they put on their pyjamas and went to bed. Some time after the rest of them had fallen asleep, Japhta came around to wake them up. They got dressed. Then, with Harris at the front, armed with a home-made knife, the eight accused went to Hendry's bed at the opposite end of the cell. Harris pulled the blanket from Hendry who was lying face down. Harris then stabbed him in the lower back, just above the cleft of the buttocks. Hendry turned over and Harris stabbed him twice in quick succession in the upper chest below the left nipple. Hendry started squirming and Harris stabbed him a fourth time, at the top of the left shoulder blade. Hendry was in distress immediately because both stab wounds of the chest had penetrated his heart.

Then the gang turned their attention to other inmates. They beat up Leon Jacobs with a belt reinforced with a padlock. Michael Erasmus fled to the toilet. Harris stabbed him in the back as he went past. In the toilet Meiring, Michaels, Botha and Pienaar set upon Erasmus with their belts. Each belt had a padlock tied to the end. Erasmus shouted for help and the prison warders came to the window to see what was going on. Japhta told the others, 'You haven't finished your work,' and pointed towards Leon Jacobs. The warders outside the cell heard this and sounded the siren for the officers to bring the key they needed to open the cell.

By the time the cell was eventually opened, Hendry was dead. The eight prisoners who were later to be charged with murder were standing to one side, dressed in their day uniforms, with their bedrolls neatly tied up and stacked. They had anticipated their removal from the cell.

After a messy trial in which no two witnesses other than the prison officials told the same story, the Court convicted seven of the accused of murder. The Court entertained a reasonable doubt whether accused number seven, Pieter Pienaar, had taken part in the killing or had committed any act in pursuance of a common purpose with the others, and acquitted him. Harris, Meiring and Swartbooi were further convicted of assault with intent to cause grievous bodily harm to Michael Erasmus. Swartbooi and Harris were convicted on a similar charge in respect of the assault on Leon Jacobs.

Cell murderers always get the death sentence. Over the years the Supreme Court in Cape Town had sent many of them to the gallows. The Judge could see no extenuating circumstances in respect of any of the accused. She imposed the death sentence on all seven. She also imposed prison sentences for the assaults, but they were soon to become of academic value only.

On 9 December 1987 the seven men went to the gallows together. They had spent a year and two months in the death cells.

When I came into the courtroom, James Murray was already on his feet at his lectern. Labuschagne was in the witness box with the sergeant sitting behind him. We waited for the Judge to enter. Murray and Labuschagne ignored each other. When the usher left to call the Judge, Murray leaned down to speak to Sanet Niemand. After a whispered conference she handed him a folder. He put it on the lectern without opening it. What would the theme of the next series of questions be? I didn't have long to wait to find out; it was ingenious.

Judge van Zyl and his Assessors came in and Murray went straight on the attack again.

'So you say you can't remember what happened at the reservoir?'

Labuschagne did not respond.

'What's the question?' I whispered.

Murray obliged. 'You can't remember what happened at the reservoir. Is that what you say?'

Labuschagne shrugged. 'I've told you what I can remember.' He looked uneasy, but the puffiness around his eyes had gone.

'Well,' said Murray, 'let's retrace your steps as the events developed. You were driving your bakkie, right?'

'Yes.'

'And you were very tired, you have told the Court, right?'

'Yes.'

'Your bakkie has a manual gearbox, hasn't it?'

'Yes.'

I was beginning to see where this line of questioning was going.

'It was raining very heavily and the roads were awash with water and debris from the storm, right?'

'Yes.'

'And you were travelling at speed up Magazine Hill and down to the reservoir, weren't you?'

'Yes.'

'And the road was narrow and winding going up the hill, and going down to the reservoir it was even worse, wasn't it?'

'Yes.'

'You had managed to avoid a collision with the minibus earlier, at Saxby Road, when it was a near thing, hadn't you?'

'Yes.' The answer came reluctantly. Labuschagne could sense a trap, I thought. He was right, but it was well hidden.

'And the road from the signal station to the reservoir is just a dirt track, isn't it?' suggested Murray.

After our own inspection I could visualise the track on the ridge of the koppie. It was undulating, narrow and wound its way through the trees.

'Yes,' said Labuschagne, a puzzled frown on his face.

'Please look at these two photographs.' Murray produced a stack of photographs mounted on A4 paper from the folder on his lectern and handed them to the usher. Sanet Niemand slid two sets across to me. When the Judge and Assessors had received their copies, Murray continued, 'These two photographs show the rising and falling topography of the track in the last fifty metres or so to the reservoir, don't they?'

'I don't know.'

'The route you had taken that afternoon?' Murray had not listened to the answer.

'I haven't been back there.'

Murray ignored the answer – deliberately, I thought.

'The light was fading?'

'Yes.'

'You were driving in the fading light, in pouring rain, at speed?'

'Yes.'

'At the same time you were duelling with the minibus, weren't you? That's how I understood your evidence,' he added.

'Yes.' The answer was tentative.

'And there were trees on either side of the track, very close to the track, weren't there?'

Labuschagne studied the photograph as if he had never been to the scene. He looked up and said, 'Yes, I can see them.'

'And you managed, despite the difficult terrain and all the obstacles, to steer your bakkie safely all the way down to the reservoir, didn't you?'

'Yes.'

At this point I might have stopped if I had been the cross-examiner, but Murray was not content with having made his point with such subtlety that the lawyers in court could admire his skill. He wanted to make it brutally clear to Labuschagne and to the spectators.

The Judge tapped with his pen on the edge of the bench above the registrar's head and she immediately stood up and faced the Judge. 'What is the number of that exhibit?' he asked her. She turned to pick up her notes and whispered an answer before she sat down again.

Murray scribbled down something and was ready with his next question. 'And once you had stopped, you sat in your bakkie for a while, taking in the surroundings, didn't you?'

Labuschagne thought about the matter for some time before he answered. 'For a moment,' he said.

'And you knew exactly where you were and how you had got there, didn't you?'

'I didn't know where I was. I had never been there before.'

Murray thought about the answer. 'Well,' he suggested, 'you might not have been there before, but you would have been able to find your way back home from there, wouldn't you?'

'Yes, I think so.'

'So we have you at the reservoir in your bakkie, the bakkie you had driven there, and the minibus was slightly ahead of you and to your right. Do I have the scene correct so far?' Murray was setting Labuschagne up for something, I could see it coming.

'Yes.'

'And you had the pistol to hand, on the seat between your legs?'

'Yes. There is no other place for it in the bakkie.'

'And it was ready to fire, wasn't it?'

'Yes, it always is.'

I could see that the riders Labuschagne was adding to the answers were beginning to rile Murray, but he resisted the temptation to deviate from his path.

'Then, in the words of your advocate, you killed them?' he said.

It was a foul blow, but there was nothing I could do about it. Labuschagne looked at me for a long time before he answered. 'Sir, I know that now.' It was no more than a whisper.

I thought again that I would have stopped at this point and moved on to something else, but Murray followed a different approach.

'You used a gun, a pistol?' he suggested. He was holding the pistol in his hand. It was Exhibit 1.

'Yes.'

'It held thirteen bullets, one in the chamber and twelve in the magazine, right?' Murray pointed at the relevant parts of the pistol.

'Yes.'

'And you fired thirteen shots, didn't you?' He had his finger on the trigger, but he did not pull it. I fully expected him to.

'Yes, I accept that.' The answer came from Wierda's briefing. 'What should I say if they ask me whether I shot them? I don't remember it,' Labuschagne had asked early on in our preparation. Wierda dealt with it well. 'You have to accept that you did shoot them, even if you have no memory of it. So I think you should make that clear.'

Murray was relentless. 'And every shot you fired struck one of the deceased; every shot struck someone in a vital place, the upper torso or neck, didn't it?'

The answer was a faint yes.

'But you claim that you have no memory of the shooting, this very accurate shooting that you did; is that how we are to understand your evidence?'

Labuschagne seemed lost for an answer for a while. 'But I don't remember it,' he said eventually.

'So,' said Murray, 'your defence is not that you didn't shoot them, but that you can't remember shooting them? Is that how we are to understand your defence?'

I had to object.

'M'Lord, it is not for the defendant to answer questions of law. He is entitled to give evidence of the facts and the events that occurred; I alone answer questions such as the one posed by my Learned Friend. And I answered that question in the plea explanation and in my opening address.'

'I'll move on to something else,' said Murray, who hadn't even bothered to sit down when I objected.

'Yes,' said the Judge, 'carry on.'

Murray stood for a moment, then said, 'On second thought, I do have a few more questions about what happened at the reservoir.'

Labuschagne immediately tensed up again. James Murray watched him intently, like a cat about to pounce on an insect.

'You must have some memory of what happened at the reservoir. Surely you must remember pulling the trigger and seeing them fall over, and their blood staining their karate uniforms.'

'I remember crashes of thunder all around me, and flashes of lightning, bright lights, and then everything was very still and white, and then there was some red too.' Labuschagne's head was sagging almost to his chest. He suddenly seemed at the end of his endurance again.

'So you remember red? Why didn't you tell us about that before?' Murray demanded. 'Are you making things up as we go?'

Labuschagne was rocking forwards and backwards in a slow metronomic beat. His answer came in a voice devoid of tone or emotion. 'I saw it now, as you were talking about blood, I saw the red too. It was there, among the flashes of white and the noise.'

Judge van Zyl then did a strange thing. I had seen judges doing it in the past, but it didn't happen often: when the cross-examiner got the better of a witness the Judge started protecting the witness. Like a referee in a boxing match he stepped in to protect the man who had taken too much punishment.

'Let's take a fifteen-minute adjournment. The defendant has been on his feet all day.' We stood up as the Judge and Assessors rose and returned their bow. Then, almost as an afterthought, Judge van Zyl said, 'Let him sit down and give him a glass of water.'

I was looking over my notes, thinking about topics for re-examination, when I became aware of a figure behind me. I looked up. It was Antoinette. She put her hand on the back of my chair.

'I am sorry,' she said softly.

I stood up and put my hand over hers. 'It's all right,' I said. 'We're all having a rough time here.'

She nodded and returned to her seat behind the barrier. Antoinette and I were the only ones left in the courtroom; everyone else had left to stretch their legs or smoke a cigarette.

Palace of Justice

46

James Murray had more surprises for us when we resumed.

'You collected beads?' he said. He was looking at his notes and was still not making eye contact with Labuschagne.

Labuschagne hesitated. 'No,' he said, but it was a rather tentative no.

'One of your special tasks was to order the coffins required for each execution.'

'Yes.'

'And you said that you had attended every execution last year, is that so?'

'Yes.'

'You didn't volunteer for the job as escort, you did it because the Warrant Officer allocated you to that duty, you said?'

'Yes.'

Murray immediately followed with a short jab. 'And you were the only escort who was present at every execution last year, weren't you?'

Labuschagne took his time answering. 'Yes, I think so.'

The delay in answering only lent emphasis to Murray's point.

'Come on,' he said. 'Don't play games with me. We know this from your own evidence. You had to be, because there were occasions when you had only one prisoner to hang, and you said you were present at every hanging.'

Labuschagne did not answer. The Judge scribbled in his notebook. I feigned indifference. Wierda muttered, 'What a fucking bully.' I didn't see it like that. James Murray was being efficient.

After a while Murray turned a page. 'The coffins came with screws for the lids, with pre-drilled holes and with the screws lightly set in them, is that right?'

Light was beginning to dawn in Labuschagne's eyes. He looked hard at the Warrant Officer, but the Warrant Officer was putting on a show of looking at his fingernails. There might have been just the slightest hint of a smirk on his ruddy face.

'Yes,' said Labuschagne. He was still looking at the Warrant Officer.

Murray opened the folder on his lectern and took out a photograph. He pretended to study it as he asked, 'And the screws came with little plastic beads.' He squinted as he leaned forward to study the photograph from close up. 'Yellow ones and green ones and white ones.' He looked up. Then he looked at the photograph again. 'Oh, and little pink ones too.'

For a moment Labuschagne stood with his eyes closed. Then he started rocking again, slowly. 'No, they were washers,' he said, his eyes still closed.

'They were washers, you say?'

'Yes, washers.'

'That's what I mean,' said Murray. 'You collected those washers. You kept one washer for every prisoner you escorted to the gallows, didn't you?'

'It wasn't like that.' The answer came late and half-heartedly. The Judge and both Assessors were looking at Labuschagne. He didn't make eye contact with them.

'Well, how was it then?' asked Murray. 'You tell us how it was then.'

Labuschagne stared at the floor. There was no answer. Murray moved on. No answer was as good as an affirmative answer.

'You kept one washer from each coffin; they were like notches on a gunslinger's six-shooter!'

'I said it wasn't like that.'

Murray repeated a question he had asked a few minutes earlier. 'You were the only warder who attended every execution last year, weren't you?'

'And the six months before that,' said Labuschagne. He was not making his case any better by volunteering the additional information.

'I stand corrected,' said Murray, feigning sincerity. 'You did so because there was a competition between the warders to see who could collect the most beads – washers, I mean – didn't you?'

'No, I was ordered to do that work.' Labuschagne sighed heavily.

'Take a sip of water,' the Judge said, then watched as Labuschagne drained the glass. The usher filled it immediately from the carafe on the prosecutors' table.

'Carry on,' said Judge van Zyl, and Murray was at it again like a terrier.

'Please look at this photograph.' He handed a batch of photographs to the usher and waited for the usual distribution process to be completed. I studied mine. It showed a necklace of sorts with coloured beads. Labuschagne glanced at his copy and put it down on the front edge of the witness box. He had paled significantly in the last few minutes.

'These are the washers you collected over the eighteen months before you were arrested, right?' The implication was that there would have been more but for Labuschagne's arrest.

'Yes.'

'The photograph was taken at your house when the police searched your house for the murder weapon. You kept the washers in your drawer.'

I stood up to object but the Judge pre-empted my effort. 'Refer to it as the pistol or as Exhibit 1. We'll decide if it is a murder weapon.'

'As M'Lord pleases,' said Murray, but he had made his point.

'You were paid extra for every execution you attended, weren't you?' he said. The Warrant Officer had obviously been a mine of information.

'Yes.'

Niemand became agitated and pulled at Murray's gown. He leaned down to listen to her and when he straightened up, said, 'M'Lord, I am sorry, I need to clear up one more thing before I proceed along this line.' When the Judge didn't react he returned his focus to Labuschagne. 'And when you were arrested, you had one of those washers in your pocket, didn't you, from the tenth?'

Labuschagne nodded. I spoke to Wierda from the corner of my mouth. 'Did you know this?' He shook his head.

'You had already placed the washers from the executions on the eighth and ninth on the string, hadn't you?' said Murray.

Labuschagne nodded again, signalling defeat on this issue. He could no longer bring himself to speak. The record would reflect that there had been no answer.

Then Murray came at him from a different direction. 'You were keen to receive the extra money, weren't you? That's another reason why you volunteered for this work.'

Labuschagne came to life again. 'It was only five rand.'

Murray left the topic as abruptly as he had introduced it.

'I suggest that you've exaggerated the resistance shown by prisoners during the execution process.'

Labuschagne squinted at the change of direction. 'They resisted.'

'I am not suggesting no one ever resisted. I am suggesting that you have exaggerated the frequency with which that happened and the extent of the resistance.'

'No, that is not true. They often resisted. It didn't happen every time, but it happened often. Why do you think we had four or five warders on standby each time? To watch?' he asked.

'You are not to ask questions,' said Murray. 'That is my job.'

Labuschagne looked up at Judge van Zyl. 'Sir, do you really think they would go quietly? That's why we didn't tell them what was going to happen; they would be on the trapdoors with the ropes around their necks before they knew what was happening. Does anyone really believe they would go up without resisting?' He looked around the court, but no one answered.

Judge van Zyl listened patiently to this outburst. 'The prosecutor is right; you should not ask him questions. Please confine your answers to what is being asked, no more,' he said, but his voice was kind. 'Can you do that?'

'I'll try, sir.'

Murray was not going to let go. 'I suggest that the prisoners may have been slow to follow orders, but generally they went along calmly.'

'That is just not true. They were not calm. They were taut as wire. They were shaking and shivering. They cried. They prayed aloud. They wet themselves, and … many fainted. They had to be pushed and prodded every step of the way.' Murray held his hand up, but Labuschagne paid him no heed. 'We had to drag some of them every single step from the chapel to the top floor, up fifty-four steps, and some we had to carry up because they had fainted. We took up some of them tied to those aluminium chairs we used, and we put them on the trapdoors in their unconscious state and dropped them, chair and all.' He paused for air. 'It is just not true.'

'May I have a moment, M'Lord?' said Murray and the Judge nodded. Murray conferred briefly with the Warrant Officer and turned back to the witness box.

'I am instructed that in the eighteen months you were there, there was never an incident of extraordinary resistance.'

'No, that is not true. There was a lot of resistance,' said Labuschagne. 'We hanged about two hundred people in that time and there was a lot of resistance.'

The Judge intervened. 'Mr Murray, are you saying that all those prisoners went to their deaths quietly and without causing any trouble?' Murray had overplayed his hand.

'Generally yes, M'Lord,' he said after a pause.

'And what do you mean by extraordinary resistance?' asked the Judge. 'I would have thought that it implies that a certain amount of resistance is taken for granted. Are you and the defendant not perhaps sparring with words?'

'May I take instructions, M'Lord?' said Murray.

'Yes, go ahead.'

Murray again conferred with the Warrant Officer. When he turned back to face the bench he abandoned that line of cross-examination with a curt, 'I won't pursue that line any further, M'Lord.' He closed his trial notebook and I quickly gathered my notes for re-examination, but it seemed he hadn't yet finished. 'Let me put my case to you step by step,' he said without reference to notes.

'You got involved in an argument on the road with the deceased in the minibus. Am I correct so far?'

'Yes.'

'You drove to the reservoir, as we discussed earlier, in terrible conditions, but you got there safely. Correct?'

'Yes.'

'Then you got out of your bakkie and you emptied your pistol into the seven deceased.'

'Yes.'

'Then you ran away when you found that you couldn't start your bakkie.'

Labuschagne looked up sharply. 'No, I never tried to start the bakkie. I just ran.'

'You killed them because you were angry.'

'No.'

'You knew very well what you were doing, and that is why you refused to speak to the police or to anyone after the event.'

The question was argumentative but I let it go. 'No,' said Labuschagne, 'I was just so ashamed and I didn't know what to say. What could I tell them?' he asked. 'What could I tell them? I still don't know what I can say.'

It struck me that he could speak of the events in the prison, but couldn't face what had happened at the reservoir.

'You didn't tell anyone what had happened because you knew all too well that you had killed those young men in a fit of anger and you had no excuse for what you had done.' Murray stood with his arms folded across his chest.

There was no reply.

Murray stood for a while, paging through his notes; then he placed them face down on the lectern and looked up at Labuschagne. 'Let me tell you what I'm going to argue really happened that afternoon.'

I picked up my pen to take notes. I saw Judge van Zyl doing the same. Murray was about to put his case to Labuschagne and we would have a preview of his argument. I put my notebook on the arm of my chair and leaned back. I wrote down every question and answer verbatim.

Murray was looking at a spot above and behind the witness box. He held his left arm low across his waist and his right elbow resting in his left palm. He spun a pen between his fingers like a conjurer's coin, around and around. He spoke slowly, at dictation pace, knowing that the Judge would take detailed notes.

'After the skirmishes on the road, the two vehicles ended up at the reservoir, correct?'

'Yes.'

'You were angry?'

'Yes,' but after a pause.

'You took your gun, the pistol, didn't you?'

'Yes.'

'The seven deceased, the men who are now dead because you shot them dead, came out of the minibus, correct?'

'Yes.'

'And you shot them all dead, all seven of them?'

There was a much longer pause this time. 'Yes.'

'One by one, you shot them, some more than once, correct?'

'Yes,' in a very low voice.

'One by one you shot them, and you shot them all dead, didn't you?'

There was no answer at first. Murray waited until the silence became obvious and then asked the same question in exactly the same tone of voice. When the answer came it was hardly above a whisper.

'Speak up, please,' said Judge van Zyl. Labuschagne did not acknowledge the admonition and Murray took the opportunity to make his point a third time.

'You shot them all, one after the other, and you shot them dead.'

'Yes.'

'They were unarmed, weren't they?'

'Yes.'

Labuschagne looked at me as if to say, 'What is this about?' I knew what it was about but I couldn't come to his assistance.

'Then you arranged the bodies neatly in a row next to the minibus, didn't you?'

'I don't remember that,' said Labuschagne.

'I am not asking about your memory,' Murray admonished. 'I am asking about your actions.'

'I don't remember shooting them.'

That was not what Murray wanted, but he carried on as if the answer did not matter.

'Then you fled from the scene.'

'Yes, I can remember running.'

'Across the road that goes up the side of the hill, on the side where the monument is, am I right?'

'Yes.'

'Then you ran further down the hill until you got to the highway?'

'Yes.'

'And you made your way across six lanes of traffic, didn't you?'

'Yes, I must have.'

'Then you got to a fence and you climbed over it?'

'Yes.'

'And you went into hiding?'

'I wasn't hiding. I fell asleep.' After a pause, noted by the Judge I am sure, Labuschagne added, 'Or passed out, I don't know.'

'But you ran away as soon as the security patrol from the monument found you there the next morning, didn't you?'

There was no response and Murray did not press for an answer. He had made his point. There was a faint twitch at the corner of Labuschagne's mouth, but Murray was not watching him and the moment passed.

'I have no further questions,' Murray said suddenly and sat down. He leaned back in his chair and flung his arm over the backrest. His attitude said: Is this the best witness you have?

I wondered why he hadn't asked more questions about the monument.

I had told Wierda earlier that he would have to do the re-examination, but it turned out too delicate a task to leave to him. It could go wrong very easily and then he would bear the blame for it. I stood up and waited for the Judge's signal.

'May it please M'Lord,' I said when he nodded.

I thought long and hard before I faced the witness box. Re-examination is an important phase of the evidence, but it is somehow paradoxical. If your witness has been demolished in cross-examination there would be no purpose in re-examining. *All the King's horses and all the King's men couldn't put Humpty-Dumpty together again.* If the cross-examiner has done no harm to your case, you don't need to re-examine either. But if the cross-examiner has done some harm that could be repaired, re-examination is essential. I had some work to do.

'Mr Labuschagne, Mr Murray has asked you about your silence afterwards. I need to clear up some aspects of that period,' I said.

Labuschagne stood with his head bowed and gave no indication that he was listening. I did not want him to appear furtive, so I admonished him gently. 'Please look at me when I speak to you.'

He looked up. There were tears in his eyes and his face was puffy.

'Let's take it one step at a time,' I suggested. 'Let's start with the ambulance. You were taken to hospital in an ambulance. Did you speak to anyone in the ambulance about what had happened?'

'No.'

'Why not?'

'I wasn't sure what was going on.'

'Did you know at that time what you had done?' I asked.

'I suspected.'

I took a chance with the next question. 'What did you actually remember of the incident at that time?' I held my breath.

'I remembered the trapdoors and the thunder and lightning, and the colours, and then later seeing the bodies.'

I let my breath out slowly. 'Let's go to the next stage. You were in hospital for three days. Did you tell anyone in hospital what had happened?'

'No.'

'Why not?'

'No one asked, except the policeman who came to arrest me.'

'Did you tell the policeman?'

'No.'

'Why not?'

'He said I had the right to remain silent, and I didn't know how to explain to him what I could remember. I thought he would think I was mad, and that they would lock me away until I was old and confused like Mr Tsafendas. I thought he wouldn't believe me if I said I didn't remember.'

'Then you appeared in the Magistrates' Court for a number of remands. Did you tell anyone at or in court what had happened at the reservoir?'

'No.'

'Why not?' I asked for the umpteenth time.

'I also felt ashamed. I didn't know what to do, so I just kept quiet.'

'Then Mr Wierda came to see you.' I put my hand on Wierda's shoulder. 'He told you he had been appointed as pro Deo counsel for you. Did you tell him what had happened?'

'No.'

'Why not?'

'I didn't want to speak to anyone.'

'Did you ever tell your parents what you could remember of the incident at the reservoir?'

'No.'

'Why not?'

'I just couldn't speak to them.'

'Who is the first person you told?' I asked.

'You,' he said. I felt all eyes in court turning to me, even Murray and Niemand were paying attention for the moment and dropped their pose of disinterest in the re-examination.

I had asked enough 'why' questions. 'When did you tell me?' I asked.

'It was in July, as far as I can remember.'

'Have you told anyone else, other than here in court?' I asked.

'I told the doctors who came to see me.'

It was time to introduce our expert witnesses.

'Are you talking of Dr Schlebusch and Dr Shapiro, the two persons sitting here behind me?' I half turned and pointed at them.

'Yes,' he said.

That was enough on this topic.

I asked Sanet Niemand to pass me the pistol. It sat on their table. She brought it over to me; she wasn't going to slide it along the desk like she had done with the documentary exhibits. I thanked her with exaggerated politeness and put the pistol on the lectern in front of me.

'This pistol, Exhibit 1, belongs to you, doesn't it?'

'Yes.'

'How long have you had it?'

'It was a birthday present when I turned eighteen.'

'Had you fired it before the night at the reservoir?' I asked innocently. I knew full well what he was going to say.

'Yes.'

'How many times?'

'Many times.'

'How did that come about?'

He explained, 'I was in the shooting club and we practised.'

Murray objected. 'M'Lord, this evidence does not appear to arise from my questions.'

I was ready for it. 'M'Lord, I'll get to the point in a moment, but I should perhaps mention that my Learned Friend asked some detailed questions about the shooting. The evidence I intend to elicit is relevant to the points my Learned Friend was making, or was trying to make.'

Judge van Zyl quickly made up his mind. 'Carry on, but see if you can speed things up a bit. We've had a long week.'

I couldn't agree more.

'As M'Lord pleases.' I turned to Labuschagne. The next piece of evidence was crucial to the defence's case, and if Labuschagne didn't give it we would have to call the instructors at the pistol club to give evidence after the weekend.

'Can you take this pistol apart and put it back together?'

'Apart in less than a minute, and I can put it back together again in two minutes. I know it well.'

I picked the pistol up and weighed it in my hand. It was a 9-milli-metre Heckler & Koch P7M13. The prosecution ballistics expert who had given evidence earlier had explained its characteristics. The pistol didn't have an external hammer. You cocked the pistol by squeezing the grip; for that there was a sliding mechanism on the front edge of the grip. It was known as a squeeze cocker, the expert had said, and when you squeezed it, it disappeared into the grip and the pistol would be ready to fire. What is more, you could empty the whole magazine in seconds as long as you kept the pressure on the squeeze cocker and the trigger. It is a unique type of pistol, the ballistics expert had said, one of the very best, and one not many people would have seen before.

'Have you ever timed how long it takes to empty the magazine in one burst?' I asked.

'Yes, it takes less than three seconds.'

I took another risk. 'Do you have any memory of the three seconds or so it must have taken to empty the magazine at the reservoir?'

He answered before James Murray could object. 'No.'

Of course, there was no evidence to suggest that the shooting at the reservoir had been over in three seconds. For all I knew Labuschagne could have lined them up against the minibus and shot them one by one.

I had to clear up another matter, but there was some risk attached to it. I needed to ask the question in such a way that I could get the right answer without telling Labuschagne what the answer was. So I did it in a roundabout way.

'You said the Warrant Officer had you do the drop calculations for him?'

'Yes,' he said.

'Did you do that for every execution last year?' I asked.

'Yes.'

'You also said you were present at every execution last year. Why was that, do you think?'

He got the message. 'I think it was because I had done the calculations.'

That would answer at least one of the prosecution's points.

'I have no further questions, thank you,' I said, 'but please remain where you are in case His Lordship or the Learned Assessors have some questions for you.'

I sat down and watched the Judge. He appeared lost in thought as he paged through his notes. Then he turned to each of the Assessors. Both shook their heads. The Judge turned to Labuschagne. He had just begun to tell him he could return to the dock when Murray stood up.

'M'Lord, I have a few questions arising from an answer given by the defendant in re-examination.'

Judge van Zyl held up his hand and indicated to Labuschagne to wait. He was still in the witness box. Then the Judge turned to me and asked, 'Do you have any objection?'

I took a neutral position. 'We leave it in M'Lord's hands.'

The Judge was too clever for that.

'Since there is no objection I will allow it. But keep it short,' he said to Murray.

When Murray turned to face the witness box, I saw disbelief on Labuschagne's face and his shoulders slumped. His fists were clenched by his sides.

Murray got to the point immediately.

'You said you did the drop calculations for every execution last year.'

'Yes.' The answer was given hesitantly.

'You also did them on that day when you had to pull the prisoner up, didn't you?'

'Yes.'

'So it was your fault that he didn't die immediately, and that you had to pull him back up.'

Labuschagne looked at Murray in disbelief. 'It was not my job to do those things. It was the Hangman's job.' He raised his voice. 'Why did I have to do it? Why did I have to do it?'

The Judge had had enough. 'If I had known what you were going to ask, I would not have allowed any further questioning,' he said to Murray.

Murray sat down abruptly.

'You may step down,' said the Judge and Labuschagne made his way past Murray and Niemand and squeezed behind the Warrant Officer's chair on his way back to the dock. They didn't look at him as he passed within arm's reach of them.

The Judge adjourned the proceedings for the long weekend. Monday, 10 October, was Oom Paul's birthday and consequently a national holiday.

I asked Wierda to drive me to the airport so that we could discuss tactics on the way. I asked him why he thought the Judge had asked no questions.

'We either did a very good job or he has decided the case already,' he said.

We had four witnesses left to call. We agreed that Wierda would lead the two lay witnesses and I would lead the two experts.

I needed a break and the weekend had come just in time. I was going home.

DAY FIVE

Defence: 11 October 1988
Execution: 10 December 1987

v3541 Khuselo Selby Mbambani
v3663 Joseph Gcabashe
v3664 Mnuxa Jerome Gcaba
v3721 Siphiwo Mjuza
v3752 Andries Njele
v3753 David Mkumbeni
v3771 Willem Maarman

After the tremor of the trapdoors slamming against the stopper bags at seven that morning had subsided, the prison fell back into the regular programme for the day. The prisoners were let out of their cells to wash. Breakfast was served. For the prisoners the dull routine of life on Death Row had resumed. By late afternoon a relative calm had settled over the prison.

For the gallows escorts a different routine was followed. The subsidiary tasks and formalities of the execution process had been completed, from the removal of the bodies from the ropes to the death registrations and the burials. Their day had been a long one, but they came off duty at four o'clock and with the exception of one of their number, who had left in his bakkie to see his parson, they were relaxing in their common room. They were debating their options for the evening when the Warrant Officer walked in. The mood in the room changed immediately.

The escorts did not have to stand up for the Warrant Officer – he was not a commissioned officer – but they struck more upright poses wherever they sat. The Warrant Officer stepped over the first pair of legs and, when the second warder didn't remove his feet from the coffee table fast enough, the Warrant Officer kicked them off the table and took the chair next to the bemused man.

'I have good news for you and I have bad news,' he announced.

The warders knew him well enough to know that he would tell them whatever he wanted to say at his own pace; any prompting would only delay the communication of the news.

True to form he kept them waiting before he broke the news. He looked them in the eye, one after the other, until he was sure he had their undivided attention. He noted the old eyes in youthful bodies, the fatigue in their slumping shoulders, but neither concern nor guilt crossed his mind. He was, as always, focused on the job, the immediate task at hand. If he were to take a step back to analyse himself, the Warrant Officer would have been proud of what he saw, a man who got the job done, a problem solver. He was not a people's person. His job was to cut through the emotional stuff that came with attachments and relationships and the like. He liked the order and control of schedules, duty rosters and the table of drops; he liked to give orders and to see them followed. He was a man who got the job done, no matter what the cost.

'The good news is that we are done for the year. The Minister has gone on holiday and there is no one else who can sign the documents. That means we have had the last hanging for the year.'

One of the warders risked a rebuke. 'So what is the good news then?'

The Warrant Officer fixed him with a contemptuous stare and held it until the warder averted his eyes.

'Only married staff will get leave over Christmas. I want every man at his post on every shift. We'll also have a number of fire drills, and some architects are coming in to add another wing. We need another section above A3.' He gestured with his thumb in the direction of Magazine Hill.

There was no response. They knew better than to argue with him.

The Warrant Officer stood up to leave. 'Oh, I forgot to tell you,' he said from the door. 'We have broken the record. One hundred and sixty-four for the year. Congratulations. Well done.'

The warders exchanged looks. 'Really?' ventured the one. 'We hanged twenty-one in the last three days. Isn't that a record too?'

'It is,' said the Warrant Officer, 'but don't tell anyone. You know the rules.'

When no one said anything he left the room.

Any elation the escorts may have felt as a result of the news that there would be no further executions until the New Year was offset by the certain knowledge that there would continue to be new arrivals. And indeed, as the warders sat contemplating the Warrant Officer's news, the fingerprints of Bakiri Nelson who had been sentenced to death in Grahamstown that very afternoon were being placed on a death warrant in preparation for his journey to Maximum. There would be another dozen prisoners arriving before Christmas, and the New Year would start exactly as the one before it.

The escorts waited until they were sure the Warrant Officer was out of earshot.

'There goes my holiday,' said the warder whose feet had been on the coffee table.

'Why didn't you object?' asked one of the others.

'I don't feel like doing catwalk or towers for the rest of my life, that's why, stupid.'

'You can always get married this weekend,' suggested one. 'Then you would qualify for leave, wouldn't you?'

'Fok daai liefde!' *Fuck that.*

The meaningless obscenity caused great mirth among them.

'Where are we drinking tonight?'

'Anywhere we can have a good fight,' said a brawny warder with cauliflower ears. 'Those soldiers last week were a bunch of pussies!'

More exaggerated tales of brave feats in bar room brawls were exchanged.

'You know what?' said the brawny one. 'If we hanged them faster we wouldn't need another wing.'

'Yes, but who will tell the Warrant Officer?'

They collapsed in laughter again.

Eventually they left to look for trouble.

Evening Flight to Durban   48

I read one of the cases on the flight to Durban. I had not intended to do so; I was too tired and thought I wouldn't be able to concentrate. The aircraft was packed, mostly with businessmen returning home after a day's business in Johannesburg. They looked as ragged as I must have. In the relative luxury of business class I had a gin and tonic in my hand before the Boeing started to bank to starboard and headed for the coast. I leaned my seat back as far as it could go without landing in the lap of the passenger behind me and closed my eyes. I tried to relax but Antoinette Labuschagne haunted me.

A sister's loyalty knows no bounds.

I worried about her brother. He had not spoken to his parents since the events at the reservoir; he claimed he was too ashamed to face them. But at some point he was going to have to, I thought. Labuschagne's attitude to the case was also a concern. There were times when I got the distinct impression that he would have been quite satisfied if he were to be found guilty and sentenced to death. He was not positively courting the death sentence, but his attitude came close to it. His demeanour in the witness box had been a contradictory mix of arrogance and indifference, of self-blame and blame-shift, and of hope and despair. I struggled with the image of him being dragged away to the trapdoors. Would he behave differently from the regular condemned, or would he be resigned to his fate? Would he have to be dragged or would he walk on his own? It nagged at me that I still could not see a clear answer. The outcome of a trial ought to be obvious or at least fairly clear long before the last witness enters the witness box.

Labuschagne hadn't been as helpful as he could have been as a witness either, and on several occasions there had been surprises for us in the answers he had given under cross-examination. His words and his actions didn't quite match. He said he did not care, that he wanted to be dead, but then he put up quite a fight when he was under cross-examination. There was also the atmosphere of the place. Did the escorts really play puerile pranks on each other? What if all those suggestions were true? How would that affect our case? I realised that we were going to have to argue the case on the evidence Labuschagne had given, but how could we ask the Court to reject part of his evidence but accept the useful bits? I would have to ask the expert witnesses for explanations.

Apart from the day he broke down, Labuschagne's appearance was in sharp contrast to his sister's. Concern was apparent in every feature in Antoinette's face, the tearful, downcast eyes, the white around the lips and the dark rings below her eyes. But Leon Labuschagne's face showed a lack of concern, his was sullen, withdrawn, with his jaw set. I thought of my sons, carefree boys running and laughing, always at play, never still. Why did some boys grow up to become angry young men? What about all those young men who made up the majority of the prisoners on Death Row? How did it come to that for them?

That was one thing I had learned from all those cases I had read: that playful boys could grow up to become murdering fiends in one fatal moment. Look at all these young men who had thrown their lives away and in the process had ruined so many other lives.

It struck me that Labuschagne's life was ruined whether he was found guilty or not guilty. How could he have a normal life after what he had been through?

I must have dozed off and was awoken by a passenger bumping into my seat from behind. The stewardess rushed over to offer me another drink. I sat up and took the next case out of my briefcase. It took me to Cape Town.

I sorted the contents of the file Pierre de Villiers had prepared for me. There were two death warrants, but they had been issued by different judges. After scratching around some more I found the reason: the one accused had already been sentenced to death before the second had even been caught by the police. For once, there had been some intrepid work by the Cape police.

And it was another case of young men throwing their lives away.

v3541 Khuselo Selby Mbambani
v3721 Siphiwo Mjuza

49

Mbambani and Mjuza were charged with the robbery and murder of Mr Abner Monakali. Mbambani's trial was heard first, long before Mjuza had even been arrested.

The events occurred at about seven in the evening of 20 April 1985 in Langa, a sprawling, overcrowded township outside Cape Town, inhabited mostly by African people who work in the city – or those lucky enough to be employed. It is a depressing place where the levels of poverty are such that even those who manage to scrape a few possessions together immediately become the target of criminals. Mr Abner Monakali was on his way home to his house in Sigcau Lane at about seven o'clock. He was fifty-eight years old and walked with some difficulty, relying on a walking stick. He was returning from church where he was a lay preacher and was carrying his Bible. He was not in good health and every now and then he had to stop his already slow progress to use his asthma ventilator.

Mrs Vuyiswa Yoyo was at home at her house in Jungle Walk. She heard Mr Monakali's sister Nobuhle shouting that someone was being robbed outside. She went outside and saw three men crouched over a fourth. She recognised Mbambani and Mjuza and also Mr Monakali. Mjuza had something shiny in his hand. When some other women shouted at Mjuza he swore at them. She saw Mr Monakali trying to protect his pockets as he pleaded, 'Don't kill me!' The third attacker ran away. Then the police arrived and Mbambani and Mjuza also ran away. A young neighbour by the name of Tamsanqa and a policeman ran after Mbambani. Mrs Yoyo later found Mr Monakali's torn Bible and broken walking stick at the scene.

Constable Koli and Constable van der Westhuizen were on patrol in Langa when they came across the scene in Jungle Walk while the crime was in progress. In the headlights of their van they saw two men robbing a third, who was lying on the ground. Van der Westhuizen attended to the injured Mr Monakali while Koli and Tamsanqa gave chase after Mbambani. They caught him at a house in Sandile Street. Koli pulled Mbambani from the house by his arm. As they came out of the house Mbambani threw away a seventeen-centimetre-long sharpened iron rod with a makeshift wooden handle.

The police took Mbambani to the police station and subjected him to a thorough search. Constable Koli found a number of Mr Monakali's possessions in Mbambani's pockets: an identity document, the cover of a United Building Society savings book containing papers belonging to Mr Monakali, his wristwatch, ten rand and two cents in cash, and his dentures. There were no injuries on Mbambani and no signs of intoxication.

Mr Monakali died on the way to the police station.

Mr Monakali had been of slight build, about one point seven five metres tall and weighing only fifty-three kilograms. The evidence of the specialist pathologist was to the effect that the cause of death was a stab wound to the chest on the right side. The wound entered the chest between the fifth and sixth ribs and passed backwards, downwards and medially through the right lateral border of the heart, transfixing the right ventricle. From the heart the path of this wound continued through the lower back surface of the pericardium, through the diaphragm, and through the liver to end on the front of the spinal column. The length of the wound was measured at sixteen centimetres. It was of uniform width throughout.

Mbambani admitted he had inflicted this wound. Moreover, the dimensions of the wound matched the weapon recovered from him.

The pathologist found a further thirteen wounds on Mr Monakali's body. All of them could have been caused by a weapon similar to the one recovered from Mbambani.

The Court found Mbambani guilty as charged and could not find any extenuating circumstances on the murder charge. Hence, on 3 June 1986, Mbambani was sentenced to death. He received eight years' imprisonment on the robbery charge.

Mjuza was arrested a month later, in July 1986, when Mbambani was already in the death cells. Mjuza denied being present when Mr Monakali was killed and robbed. He said that he had been at work that day, that he had taken a train and a taxi home after eight o'clock in the evening and therefore could not have been at the scene of the crime. He pleaded not guilty on the basis of an alibi supported by his employer.

Three witnesses identified Mjuza as one of Mr Monakali's killers. The first was Mr Monakali's sister Nobuhle. She had recognised Mjuza, whom she knew well. They had attended the same school from a young age and she had often seen him in Langa. In fact she had seen him earlier in the day and had spoken to him. When she heard the man on the ground shouting, 'Don't kill me. Take what you want,' she ran to her friend's house and told her that Mjuza was robbing someone in the street outside. At the time Nobuhle had no idea that the victim was her brother.

Two further witnesses identified Mjuza as one of the attackers. They also knew him well. 'Voetsek!' he'd told them when they'd tried to intervene to save Mr Monakali, as if they were dogs.

Mjuza's advocate called his client's former employer to support Mjuza's alibi that he had been at work at the time Mr Monakali was being robbed and killed in Langa. The employer's evidence was rejected as a pack of lies. Mjuza's own evidence was rejected. The version he gave in court contradicted what he had told the investigating officer. The defence version was no match for the evidence of the three eye witnesses.

Mjuza was found guilty as charged, with no extenuating circumstances. He was sentenced to death on the murder charge on 6 March 1987, and ten years' imprisonment on the robbery charge.

Mbambani and Mjuza were hanged together on 10 December 1987. They were the same age: twenty-five.

Durban

50

I took the boys for a run on the beach. It was our Saturday morning ritual.

They irritated me from the first step. They were either running too fast or too slow and they kept getting under my feet. I had to check my stride more than once and they were joking and chattering away like monkeys, as usual. After enduring this for some time I snapped at them.

'Cut it out!'

They ran on in single file from then on, but cast reproachful glances over their shoulders at me.

Afterwards we had a shower at the municipal swimming pool and went to the shopping centre for breakfast. I felt removed from the conversation around the breakfast table and stood frustrated in the queue at the bank.

I moped around the house the rest of the day until my wife had had enough.

'Why don't you go and play tennis with your friends?' Liesl suggested.

'I don't know where we're supposed to be playing,' I said.

Liesl picked up the phone and said, 'I'll find out.'

The game was at Colin Steyn's. Months earlier when the game had been at my house, he had said, 'He is as good as dead.' That day felt a lifetime removed. I did not want to field a thousand questions about how the case was going and fell asleep in front of the television instead. The boys tiptoed in and out of the room from time to time to see if they could interest me in some game in the backyard, but I pretended to be asleep. Eventually I had to get out of the house. I was depressing everybody.

I found them still on the court at Colin's house. They were playing with their usual gusto, rugby players who had come to tennis late, hitting the ball with more power than finesse. I sat under the shade of the pergola and waited for the tea to arrive. Colin's teenage sons were wrestling with their dogs. It was a happy scene, the sounds of birds mixing with the drone of suburban traffic in the background. The shouts of the boys and the heavy breathing of the bull mastiffs were punctuated by the thuds of the tennis balls on the racquets.

I had to get up a few times to fetch balls that had gone over the fence and once I was called upon to settle an argument over a line call. I called the play, as I had seen it, against Colin and his partner. They appealed as soon as I announced my ruling, but I ruled that the appeal was out of time. Play resumed.

My sweaty mates came up from the court as I poured the tea.

'My, but you look miserable,' said Colin.

'I saw you on television,' said Mark. 'And you were looking miserable then too.'

I told them about the week's events in Pretoria.

'How old did you say your client was?' Colin asked, keeping an eye on his sons. They were now wrestling each other while the dogs tried playfully to get a bite of a leg or an arm.

'Eighteen when he first escorted a prisoner, and just over twenty now,' I answered.

'It is a disgrace,' said Colin. 'They are making normal people do things for which they are not suited or qualified. It is a disgrace, making boys do their dirty work for them.'

'But haven't you sentenced some people to death yourself?' asked Mark.

Colin was quick to admit that. He finished his tea before he launched into a monologue.

'There is a process of denial involved here, I think. Everyone passes the buck to someone else. I sentence them to death, and say I do it in the name of the law. The Sheriff says he just stands and watches; it is the Hangman who does the killing. Even the State President absolves himself of blame. He simply says the law must take its course; he will not intervene. I bet you the Hangman will also have an excuse.'

He looked at me. 'Isn't that so, Johann? What does he say?'

I thought about it for a while. The Hangman had not featured prominently in the trial. 'I think he would say that it is gravity that kills, not the pushing of the lever.'

'Well, he may say that or something else like orders from higher up,' said Colin. 'But you see, there is a collective denial of responsibility by everyone. The worst part of it is that the public bay for the death penalty but they have no idea of the extensive legal and administrative processes involved. And, of course, there is so much secrecy surrounding the execution process itself that their opinion on the death penalty is the opinion of the uninformed.'

'I say hang the buggers,' said Paul, an industrialist who had been suffering regular burglaries and labour problems.

Colin ignored him. The conversation had turned too serious for a tennis afternoon. 'You are in denial too,' he said pointing at me with a biscuit.

I didn't know what he meant. However, he lost no time elaborating on his theory.

'The legal profession is part of the collective denial surrounding the death penalty. You, me, everyone. We stand mute as the bulk of the death sentence cases are being handled by the most junior advocates, ostensibly at the request of the Court, but in reality because no one else cares enough to ensure that there is a competent defence available to every person accused of a capital crime. And those junior advocates appear without any support system. There is no instructing attorney or an investigator to assist them.'

I opened my mouth to argue that a poor defence is better than no defence at all, but he cut me short. 'Didn't you do your share of those cases in your first six years? I know I did. And I can tell you with the benefit of hindsight, I was ignorant, unskilled and a poor excuse for a defence lawyer.'

He was at full speed now. 'Look,' he continued, 'they hanged at least a hundred each year in those years and we just stood and watched. We acquiesced. We'll be condemned for that one day, mark my words.'

What could I say? He was right, and everyone in the profession knew it. The profession as a whole, as a collective, would carry the shame forever. We were damned both ways. If you participated in a capital trial you were an unmistakable part of the machinery, as much a part of the killing process as the Hangman's rope. And if you didn't step forward to defend the hapless soul on trial for his life your decision could equally result in his finding himself on the trapdoors with his feet on the marks and a white hood on his head.

The discussion did nothing to lighten my mood and we eventually turned to our usual chatter about the tennis and where we would play next week. They nominated my court. 'Then you can tell us all about the outcome of the case,' they said.

They went back on court and I left after watching for a while. The next Saturday was a long way off.

I went for another run the next morning. A heavy mist had settled over the area, giving it an eerie *Wuthering Heights* feel. Tall trees became mere stumps as the mist obscured their higher reaches. There was no traffic – it was too early on a long-weekend Sunday for that – and none of the usual birdsong and animal noises associated with a spring morning in the leafy suburb. My running shoes made squelching noises on the oily surface of the road and the humidity quickly wet my hair and glued my running singlet to my back.

As I ran my thoughts wandered in and out of the case in much the same way that I entered and left foggy patches. Various images sprang up in my mind, the gallows chamber in a fog of its own, a car backfiring in the distance sounded like a gunshot. One after the other the crime scenes played in the theatre of my mind like those half-hour serials before the main feature in the matinee shows of my schooldays, except there was no Green Archer, no Zorro to rout the criminal and save the distressed victims. One by one I revisited the cases Wierda and I had been studying.

Halfway across a pedestrian bridge over a railway line – I don't know why I took the bridge, because the trains were no longer running – a revelation stopped me in my tracks. Wierda and I had been pressing Labuschagne repeatedly to tell us what was so unusual about the men they had hanged during those last two weeks, but on each occasion he had denied any insight. Yet my subconscious now suggested there was something in it after all. I leaned on the bridge railing to catch my breath and to allow my thoughts to settle. What if these men did have something in common that our client had discovered? What if that discovery had driven him to despair, or violence, even murder? What if what these killers had in common was not the fact that they killed in gangs or packs, or their stupidity, or lack of rational motive? What if the only thing they had in common, apart from their utter evil and the complete lack of empathy they had shown for their victims was the way they treated women? I thought of Moatche and his two companions repeatedly stabbing their defenceless victim on another pedestrian bridge over a railway line, in full view of their female friend. They acted as if she was not there. Scheepers and Wessels had killed the women they and their companions had abducted and raped, and turned a deaf ear to their victims' pleas for mercy. Mokwena raped and killed an old woman, then buried her in a shallow grave before he treated himself to a meal of chicken prepared in her kitchen. Delport savaged a young girl and threw her into the river to drown. And so it goes on, one after the other. There was Klassop, killing an old lady who could have been his mother, Mbele, Rabutla and Phaswa, abducting and raping Sarah Ngobeni. Hansen, Leve, Smit, Maarman, they were all the same in this respect. I had just finished reading Mbambani and Mjuza's cases and could recall clearly what they had said to the three women who were protesting as they robbed and stabbed Mr Monakali. 'Voetsek,' they had shouted at the women. These men had treated women worse than dogs.

And when it came to crying for these men after their execution, the ones who came to the funeral service and cried over the coffins were the women. I thought of Liesl. Had I neglected her in the two weeks I had been in Pretoria? I had. I had hardly called.

I walked home slowly as the sun started clearing the mist. How could I not have seen this earlier? Was this perhaps what Labuschagne had realised, looking at his own circumstances, and why he was so desperate to seek help from his pastor? Had he treated Magda worse than had been exposed thus far? Maybe that would explain her father's refusal to let her have anything further to do with Labuschagne. And it would explain the interdict.

Was there any relevance in this at all? Perhaps there was nothing in it, but I couldn't help wondering why Labuschagne had not allowed his mother and his sister to comfort him. Was that not a form of abuse, and why was he continuing with it?

I spent most of the Monday in my chambers, reading up on the law. I had avoided criminal law for almost a decade and had some catching up to do.

When I got home in the late afternoon, it was time to pack my bags for the next morning's flight. I have hated Sunday afternoons all my life, ever since my boarding school days when Sunday afternoon meant packing your bags and getting ready to say goodbye. This Monday, the last day of the long weekend, was much worse. I would have given anything not to have to return to Pretoria.

Liesl came in and watched me pack in silence until I sat down on the edge of the bed.

'You have to get out of this case,' she said.

'I know,' I said, 'but it's just another week and then it will be over.'

'A week is a long time when you're away from home.'

She had caught me by surprise. I looked at her more closely. There was a double meaning there, but was it deliberate? Liesl was looking out over the garden. The boys were playing tennis and there were squeals of delight and grunts and laughter and the usual arguments.

'For the boys,' Liesl added, but she couldn't fool me. There was just the faintest hint of a smile.

She took my hand and we sat there until the boys came trooping back to the house for dinner.

I was in that deepest part of sleep that sailors call the ghost watch when I was woken by our pair of geese. They were the most reliable watchdogs and they guarded the front section of my property between the house and the tennis court, always announcing the slightest encroachment into their domain with loud and indignant fanfare. The goose had been sitting on a clutch of four eggs for some weeks, slowly losing her feathers and condition. This time there was distress in their protests and I could hear the flapping of their wings in the otherwise quiet night. I heard some panting and beasts running around.

Liesl slept on peacefully; I had always marvelled at her ability to sleep through any amount of noise but to wake up at the slightest squeak from one of our sons. I slipped out of bed quietly and grabbed a pair of jeans. I dressed in the passage and took my pistol from the safe. I tucked it in the waistband at the back of my jeans. Torch in hand I slowly opened the sliding door onto the veranda and stepped out into the night.

The geese were quiet now, which was unusual. They usually took some time to settle down after a disturbance. I ducked behind some azaleas on the terrace and snuck up on the goose's nest. When I turned the light on, I saw them. They were dead or in the throes of dying; that much was obvious from their grotesquely splayed wings and broken necks. Their blood-stained wings fluttered in the night air, but they were dead.

I swung the torch around, looking for the killer and two dogs rushed past me towards the corner of the yard. The first jumped up and was able to drag itself over the wall, but the second hit the wall three-quarters of the way up and fell back towards me. I found to my surprise that I had run after them and had the gun in my hand. I aimed the light and the gun at the dog and followed it as it tried a second time to clear the wall, but it hit the wall somewhat lower than at its first attempt and again landed at my feet. After a third attempt it surrendered and cowered in the corner, heaving and panting.

The light shone on the dog; it was a bitch, heavily pregnant. I took careful aim. She turned and squirmed in the light. I squeezed the trigger but nothing happened. I shook the gun and squeezed the trigger a second time but still nothing happened. The safety catch was on. I released it and took careful aim again. She looked at me with fearful, guilty eyes. I pulled the trigger, but there was no power in my shaking hand.

I slipped the safety catch back on and waited for the rush of adrenalin to pass and my ragged breathing to return to normal. The bitch lay down after a while, panting, feathers stuck to the side of her jaw. I stood there for a long time before I walked away and opened the gate and watched as she slunk off into the night. Then I fetched some plastic bags and picked up the bodies and the bloodied feathers. The dead geese were limp and warm to the touch. It was not going to be easy to tell the boys their pets were dead, killed by a neighbour's dogs.

I was sitting at the kitchen table trying to work out how to tell the boys when Liesl walked in; I had not heard her bare feet on the stone tiles. The gun lay on the table in front of me. She stood at the door with her hand at her throat. Her eyes went from the weapon on the table to me. I told her about the geese. She sat down with me. We had a cup of tea.

'You are going to have to dispose of the geese and tell the boys,' I said. 'I just don't have the strength for it right now.'

Liesl nodded. 'They'll be sleeping when you leave,' she reminded me. I should have remembered.

'Take a shower and come back to bed. You have a hard week ahead,' she said.

I looked down and saw that my feet were dirty and my hands sticky with blood and feathers.

They came for me too at six o'clock, James Murray and the Judge.

'Put on your day clothes, no shoes and no underwear,' they said.

'It's not my turn,' I pleaded.

'Everyone gets a turn. Today it is yours,' they said.

When I didn't move they dragged me out of my warm bed. I looked down and saw that I was dressed already, exactly as they wanted, in my day clothes. I couldn't see my shoes. Where were my shoes?

They tried to take my fingerprints at the table in the passage but I fought them off. I clamped my hands firmly under my armpits and twisted from side to side, shouting at them, 'Leave me alone, it's not my turn!' But they held on and tried to drag me away. They couldn't hang me without taking my fingerprints, could they? They forced me to the floor and I landed on my side, my knees drawn up into my abdomen and my hands still clamped under my armpits. I tensed up for their next assault.

I felt a cool hand on my cheek. 'It's okay, it's okay,' Liesl said and held me. She pushed her fingers through my hair until I fell asleep again.

I woke up aching all over. Liesl's face was only inches away, her big questioning eyes staring at me.

'You have to get out of this case,' she said again, this time at the airport, and kissed me goodbye. I was ready to board my flight.

'I have to get the case out of me,' I said. I tried to make a joke of it, but she knew me too well to let me get away with it.

My wife smiled knowingly and walked away.

Guilt followed me through the gates to the departure lounge. I had been home for three days, a long weekend at that, and couldn't remember any meaningful interaction with my sons.

I caught the six-thirty flight from Durban and Wierda picked me up at the other end at seven-thirty. We made small talk until we got to the outskirts of Pretoria. I was desperately tired. We were driving past the old prison in Potgieter Street.

'What have you decided?' Wierda wanted to know. 'What are we going to do today?'

I thought about it as we passed the prison complex. I looked for the sign that had been there when my father and I had come into the city from Johannesburg many years earlier.

PRETORIA SENTRAAL GEVANGENIS
PRETORIA CENTRAL PRISON

I turned to look back as we passed the last few buildings of the complex, but the sign was no longer there. I felt a strange disappointment.

We had four witnesses to call: Magda Labuschagne, who in all likelihood was going to be an unwilling witness; the principal of Labuschagne's high school, who had volunteered to give evidence; and two experts, Marianne Schlebusch and Dr Shapiro.

'I think we should call the wife and the principal first, and then the two experts. That way the experts can use the facts established by the wife and the principal to support their opinions,' I suggested. 'What do you think?'

Wierda agreed. 'Yes, I could go along with that. We need to finish with a strong witness.' He caught my eye. 'I think we are going to need to finish strongly if we are to stand any chance of winning.' This perfectly echoed my own view.

We drove in silence until Wierda parked his car in the basement of his chambers. 'Shall we have some breakfast?' he asked.

'Good idea,' I said, 'and you can talk me through the next case.'

The case took me right back to where I had started earlier that morning, in the province of Natal, to a remote place an hour or so south of Durban.

v3663 Joseph Gcabashe
v3664 Mnuxa Jerome Gcaba

51

Four men, all in their early twenties, broke into the home of Mr and Mrs Jeffreys and robbed the elderly couple. In the process they injured Mrs Jeffreys and killed Mr Jeffreys.

Mr and Mrs Jeffreys owned and ran the Oribi Gorge Hotel about twenty-four kilometres inland from Port Shepstone. Mr Jeffreys was eighty-one years old and suffered from emphysema. During the night of 4–5 June 1986 the couple went to bed at about midnight after Mrs Jeffreys had unlocked one of the external doors to enable an employee of the hotel to come in early the next morning to light the fire in the kitchen.

At about two o'clock in the morning four men wearing balaclava masks burst into the bedroom and attacked the old couple in their beds. One of the intruders stabbed Mr Jeffreys in the back and Mrs Jeffreys suffered a cut on the ring and little fingers that severed the tendons and rendered those fingers permanently useless. Mr Jeffreys had a revolver, which he raised towards the attackers but did not fire. He was overwhelmed and disarmed. The intruders then ransacked the room. One took Mrs Jeffreys' purse, which had two hundred or three hundred rand in it. They removed the safe keys, the kitchen keys and another set of safe keys from the purse.

Mrs Jeffreys asked what they wanted and one of the intruders replied, 'We want money and firearms.' She offered to show them where the money was. One of them held a knife to her back and threatened to kill her if she made any noise. She led them towards the veranda and pushed Mr Jeffreys ahead of her. Once the intruders were outside she slammed the door shut and they ran off into the night. Mrs Jeffreys telephoned her son Kenneth who lived about a hundred metres away. He, in turn, called the police. The police put Mr Jeffreys in their car and drove at speed to the Port Shepstone Provincial Hospital. By the time they arrived Mr Jeffreys was dead.

He had died of a stab wound high up on his back between the right shoulder blade and the spine, penetrating his right lung and causing it to collapse. The progressive accumulation of blood in his chest cavity had led to an inability to breathe. In effect he had died of a lack of oxygen. There was a small wound on his left shoulder, probably inflicted with a screwdriver. He had defensive wounds on his forearms consistent with a struggle and with being held by the arms.

The four accused were rounded up quickly. Their campaign had not been well planned. They had made their intentions clear to local workers and they had left vital clues at the scene. The way they fled when Mrs Jeffreys slammed the veranda door in their faces also testified to a bumbling approach to robbery. They wore balaclavas to avoid recognition, but one of them left a clear palm print on the doorframe at the hotel.

At the trial they all recanted, saying they had been tortured by the police and told what to say. They gave most improbable, inconsistent versions of what had happened. There was insufficient evidence against Skofu Dlamini and he was found not guilty. Joseph Gcabashe was linked to the scene by his palm print and possession of the keys they had taken from the scene. He had also admitted to the Magistrate that he had participated in the robbery. The Court convicted him of murder, housebreaking with intent to rob and robbery, with aggravating circumstances. Jerome Gcaba and Bhekisisa Dlamini were similarly convicted on the strength of their admissions to the Magistrate. Gcabashe and Gcaba were also convicted of assault with intent to do grievous bodily harm to Mrs Jeffreys.

The Court found that there were no extenuating circumstances as far as Gcabashe and Gcaba's conviction on the murder count was concerned and, by a majority decision, held that there were extenuating circumstances as far as Bhekisisa Dlamini was concerned. He appeared to have taken a lesser role and may have acted under the influence of the other accused.

On 12 December 1986 the Court sentenced Gcabashe and Gcaba to death on the murder count. Then, almost in the same breath, the Judge sentenced them to death on the housebreaking charge also. The Judge sentenced Gcabashe to eighteen months' imprisonment for the assault upon Mrs Jeffreys, and Gcaba to two years. Bhekisisa Dlamini received ten years' imprisonment on the murder charge, eighteen months' imprisonment for the assault and eight years' imprisonment on the housebreaking charge.

The Appeal Court confirmed the death sentences on the murder count but determined that the death sentences on the housebreaking charge could not stand because the Judge had made an elementary error. The Appeal Court therefore set aside the death sentences on the housebreaking charge and substituted in their place fifteen years' imprisonment.

Gcabashe and Gcaba were hanged on 10 December 1987. Gcabashe was twenty-three years old. Gcaba was twenty-four.

Pretoria Zoo

52

We were in court, robed and ready, waiting for Judge van Zyl and the Assessors to enter. Wierda was ready to lead the first witness of the day. We were hoping to finish the evidence during the course of the day and to start the closing addresses the next day.

I turned in my seat and studied Labuschagne. He was sitting head down in the dock. He must have felt my eyes on him and looked up. He did not blink. I tried to read in his eyes the state of his mind. Sullen, bored, withdrawn, uncommunicative, listless, are the words that sprang to mind. He looked at me with what I saw as insolent indifference. I was suddenly sick of him.

Wierda stirred next to me. 'Where are your car keys?' I asked him on an impulse. I had to get out of there. I needed to sit down on my own somewhere and think.

He absentmindedly reached into his pocket without taking his eyes off the notes he was studying. 'Here,' he said, holding them up.

'Thanks,' I said. 'I'll see you at the lunch break.'

'Where are you going?' he asked, suddenly alarmed.

'I need to take a long walk,' I said. I relented a little when I saw the consternation on his face. 'Don't worry, I'll be back by lunch and you'll still be busy with the first two witnesses.'

Wierda nodded.

'Where can I go to get away from the noise?' I asked him.

'The zoo is your best bet, at this time of the day, I think,' he said after a pause.

I left the car in the zoo's parking lot in the care of a self-appointed car guard, a young man with a toothy white smile on his face and township dust in his hair. I gave him fifty cents and promised him another fifty if the car was still in the same place on my return. He offered to wash it for an extra two rand fifty, payable on my return. I said I would be some time and paid him in advance.

There was a high wall around the zoo to shield it from the world outside.

At the main entrance I paid and picked up a brochure. After studying the map on the wall I turned hard right and immediately encountered some desultory looking vultures sitting on dead tree stumps in front of an artificial rock face made of cement and river sand. A huge Defence Force helicopter thundered overhead, but the birds in the cages didn't stir.

I walked fast and tried not to think of the case. I passed two chimpanzees in a large cage. They sat as far apart as the cage would allow, facing opposite directions like a couple in dispute over some domestic arrangement. The male sat hands on knees, the female with folded arms. With lifeless, unblinking eyes they watched the few visitors passing by.

I walked faster, past the camels and the llamas, towards the flamingos. The camels had taken all the shade under the tree in their enclosure and the llamas were forced to lie in the sun. It was getting hot and I flung my jacket over my shoulder. The flamingos were separated by colour, the white and the pink. They were exercising, marching up and down, sifting through the silt in their ponds with their beaks, silently, with exaggerated movements of their skinny legs. They lifted their feet high as they stepped over imaginary hurdles under the surface of the pond. I saw small, numbered rings on their legs.

I took a wrong turn and arrived at a water fountain. I was watching the birds frolicking in the water when I became aware of a presence behind me. A row of cages held a variety of exotic birds. A scarlet ibis whose colours matched the Judge's robes exactly stared at me with accusing eyes. It was flanked by two grey females, as colourless as he was garish.

I walked away; there was no escape for me in the detail of the fauna and flora of the zoo. There was so much birdsong but not a sound from the ones behind bars. It was as if they had been forbidden to talk. It was a mistake to come here, I thought.

On the way up I came across a gorilla in a large enclosure with a cement-lined moat. The large silverback sat on the cool cement of the moat with his back against the wall, with folded arms and protruding lower lip, sulking, staring at nothingness, like a petulant child. I stood directly in his line of sight but he didn't acknowledge my presence.

The big cats had the pride of place, at the highest slope of the koppie overlooking the Apies River. I was sweating profusely by now. The sun was in my eyes and there was just a hint of a breeze behind me. Above their moats the big cats had cages of brick and mortar with heavy steel bars. A catwalk, enclosed on all sides by inch-thick steel bars, allowed their keepers to study them from all angles and to dart them with anaesthetics when necessary. A group of American tourists came along with a warden in a prison-green uniform. 'This is where we keep the most dangerous predators,' said the warden.

The nine-metre-high stone turrets at the top of the walls matched the guard towers of Maximum exactly in style and purpose and, most of all, in their menacing overseeing presence. I could not see into the dark interior of the warden's enclosure at the top of the nearest turret, but I felt the presence of men with guns in the shadows inside. There was no corner of the cats' enclosure where their keepers could not keep them under constant surveillance.

It was a long walk back to the car, although downhill. The path under my feet was smooth, but the earth on either side was dry and scuffed. Inside the pens it was worse. The animals had trampled the earth to a powdery dust and I saw that in every enclosure their hooves had beaten a single track along the inner perimeter, their pen an exercise yard of sorts. The only greenery was high up, near the tops of the few surviving trees, above the reach of the rhino and the antelope. In the elephant enclosure the bark had been stripped from the trees. Now and then an animal looked wearily at me, following my progress with grudging acceptance, stomping a hoof on the hard ground, scratching in vain for something to eat, but the place was barren. I felt shame and embarrassment.

Why did I come here? I asked myself. I should have gone to a bar and had a beer instead. The truth is that I was still seeking answers. There had to be a good reason for Leon Labuschagne to have killed those men at the reservoir.

The gorilla was still sitting in exactly the same place and the same pose as when I first passed his enclosure. He was utterly disconsolate.

I decided to hurry back to court.

Guilt overcame me, thinking of Labuschagne. Had I misjudged his attitude by so wide a margin? Wouldn't I be disconsolate if I were in his position? Had I mistaken despair or shame or the absence of hope as sullenness, indifference, insolence even?

At the main entrance the attendant thrust a pack of forms into my hands. 'Please fill this out and provide your name and address.' For a moment I thought I was required to sign out and would have to wait for him to unlock the door, but it was only a form asking me for my comments on my visit to the zoo. I wrote a sarcastic comment: *Now I get it. It's like a prison for animals.*

I regretted it as soon as I had handed the form back. The man was just doing his job.

I flipped the car guard another coin where he stood with a broad smile next to the car. His eyes followed me as I walked around the car to check if all the hubcaps were still there. The car was spotless, cleaner than it had been for a long time. Wierda should be pleased, I thought. I looked around; the sights and sounds of the city were reassuring.

A minibus packed with schoolchildren squeezed into the parking bay next to me as I fiddled with the unfamiliar key in the lock. The sliding door opening behind me startled me.

Kellunck! Shoosh! Wham!

I stopped fiddling with the key and turned. A teacher had come around the minibus and was herding the children into some sort of order, not quite a row. When she had succeeded in lining them up properly, she closed the door again.

Kellunck! Shoosh! Wham!

The teacher looked at me with her head askance. I realised I was staring.

There was something nagging at the back of my mind as I drove back to court, but it kept eluding me. It was like the ghosts in Maximum, which could only be seen in peripheral vision. The harder I concentrated, the more elusive the thought became.

In the end I tried not to think about it, and then it slipped my mind.

Palace of Justice

53

Back at court I peeked through the double doors at the back and saw that Wierda was on his feet. It was just before one o'clock and the school principal was still in the witness box. He was a rotund little man wearing a very short tie. I went to the robing room and waited for Wierda. I looked for Magda but she must have left.

Wierda came in behind James Murray and Sanet Niemand. We nodded a greeting.

'How far did you get?' I asked as Wierda started removing his bands and wing collar.

He was facing the ceiling, struggling with the stud at his throat holding the wing collar in place. 'We finished both of them,' he grunted.
'They didn't cross-examine either of them, so we were able to finish
them quickly.'

'I could see no reason to cross-examine,' said Murray.

I didn't think the two and a half hour morning session was short for
two witnesses, not when there had been no cross-examination. Magda
Labuschagne must have been difficult. I decided to ask Wierda about it
out of earshot of the prosecutors.

As we were leaving James Murray spoke behind me. 'How long will
your experts be, do you think?' he asked.

'With a bit of luck we could finish their evidence this afternoon,' I said.

'Good,' he said.

I didn't know what he meant by that.

On the way to the Square I asked Wierda, 'Why did it take so long if
there was no cross-examination?'

'You won't believe it,' he said shaking his head. 'Van Zyl went on for
ages. It was almost as if he had waited for you to leave before he decided
to come to life.'

'Did he cross-examine her?' I asked. I was concerned.

'No,' said Wierda, 'I wouldn't call it cross-examination. He just had
lots of questions.'

'What sort of questions?' I was concerned that the Judge might have
manipulated the evidence to suit his own views. Judges can do that,
and they often do.

'Oh,' said Wierda, 'he went over the same ground I had covered
mostly, but in far more detail. He kept asking about what sort of
person Labuschagne was before he started working at Maximum,
how he had related to other people, whether he had ever mistreated
Magda, and so on.'

'Hmm,' I said. Trying to guess what a judge is thinking is an unprofit-
able pursuit at the best of times; you can only know for sure when the
judgment is handed down.

'And Murray, why do you think he had no questions?' I went on.

Wierda walked next to me in silence as we hurried across the street to the Square.

'I think they have decided not to take any risks.' He bumped into a pedestrian and made a show of apologising before he continued. 'They probably think their case is strong enough without having to attack Magda and the headmaster.' He threw his hands in the air. 'How the fuck would I know? Maybe they are happy with the Assessor's questions.'

I was even more alarmed. 'What questions? Which Assessor?' Assessors do not usually ask questions, and when they do have a question they have to put it through the Judge.

'The one on the left asked some questions about Labuschagne's political affiliation and his father's political activities.'

It was all we needed, an Assessor with a political agenda.

'How did Magda do?' I was keen to know. She had been unwilling to come to court and we had to send the Sheriff with a subpoena, but maybe it was her father who had stood in her way.

'Kind, understanding, loving, worried, I would say,' said Wierda. 'But she had van Zyl in the palm of her hand. You wouldn't know it but he has a reputation for being a bit of a ladies' man around here.'

Another angle to an already untidy case, I thought. 'And the head-master?'

Wierda smiled. 'He was trying very hard but came across as too keen and too protective. I'm not sure that he did any good, but he didn't do any harm either.'

I never thought we would win the case on the evidence of these two witnesses and decided to leave it there.

'What's the next case about?' I asked. 'But be quick, please. I need to have a word with our experts before we resume.'

My muscles were still stiff and tense, especially across the shoulders. It was difficult to concentrate. The events in the car park at the zoo swilled around in my mind.

Wierda tried to give a detailed account as I kept walking around Oom Paul's statue, causing him to have to follow me around. I stopped every now and then to look at one of the plaques set in the stonework.

v3752 Andries Njele
v3753 David Mkumbeni

54

Three young men robbed and killed Mr Pieter Grobler and cremated his body on a pyre of wood and car tyres. One was shot dead by the police and the other two stood trial together.

Mr Pieter Grobler was an employee of Checkers. In his mid-forties, he still lived with his mother. On Sunday 15 June 1986 he left for work just after eight o'clock in the morning. He stayed only for a short while and left work again at about twenty to nine. His mother and his co-workers never saw him again. He did not return home that afternoon and he did not turn up for work the next day. His remains were found more than two months later, on 18 August. They consisted of a few bones. His body had been incinerated.

An eye witness described Mr Grobler's last movements. Miss Miriam Booysen was walking along the road to Zuurbekom on the afternoon of 15 June when Mr Grobler stopped next to her in his Audi. He offered her a lift, which she accepted. They drove towards Westonaria. Along the way Mr Grobler offered to pay Miss Booysen for sex. She agreed. Mr Grobler drove the car into a wooded area near Zuurbekom and stopped in a secluded place in the bush. They got into the back seat of the car and started having sexual intercourse.

Three young men suddenly appeared next to the car. They were the two accused, Andries Njele and David Mkumbeni, and Mkumbeni's brother Eddie.

According to Njele, David and Eddie had recruited him to do some extra work that Sunday and they had met at the appointed place. He had been told that he was going to work as a mechanic, but when they met David Mkumbeni told him that what he and his brother really did in their spare time was to rob people. They persuaded him to go along with them for the day and Eddie gave him a spare knife to use.

As they were walking through the bush they saw Mr Grobler's car approaching. Eddie told Njele that he was to wait in the bush with David until Eddie gave them the signal. They were then to come forward and help rob the victims.

Njele and the Mkumbeni brothers lay in wait in the bush and watched as Mr Grobler and Miss Booysen parked the car and made their preparations in the back seat. After a while Eddie gave the signal and Njele and David Mkumbeni ran over to the car, one on either side. They tried the door, which was locked. The three men shouted at Mr Grobler to open the doors, but he did not comply. Instead he tried to get into the front seat. One of the men broke the driver's side window and they dragged Mr Grobler out of the car. He emerged with a whip in his hand. He struck out at the attackers with it. All three of them stabbed at him with knives and they overpowered him quickly. They threw him to the ground and tied his hands and feet together. Then they put him in the boot of the car. Miss Booysen had also alighted from the car by then, but the three men told her to get back in. They then drove the car deeper into the bush.

When they opened the boot, Mr Grobler had somehow managed to untie the rope around his wrists and he sat up as soon as the boot was opened. He asked for water. They tied his wrists again. He asked them to let him go, offering them money, but they refused. Eddie told Njele and David Mkumbeni not to hurt the deceased. Njele asked Mr Grobler if he could remember what the next day was. Njele was alluding to the fact that 16 June was the remembrance day of the Soweto uprising of 1976.

Njele was standing behind Mr Grobler. He licked the blood from the knife. Eddie again told his brother and Njele not to kill Mr Grobler; he did not want to see that. Njele had a hammer. He asked Miss Booysen where he should hit the deceased. She said she didn't know. Eventually she said anywhere. Njele then hit Mr Grobler with the hammer behind the right ear. Mr Grobler fell into the boot of the car. While he was prone in the boot Njele hit him twice more on the head with the hammer. Njele then placed a nylon rope around Mr Grobler's neck and he and Eddie pulled at the ends to strangle him. When Mr Grobler's head protruded from the boot of the car, Njele slammed the lid on his neck. Miss Booysen couldn't stand what was going on any longer. She said,

'That's enough. He's dead.' They closed the boot and drove off with her.

Later, the three men let Miss Booysen out and gave her some of Mr Grobler's possessions, two blankets, three T-shirts and a set of jumper cables. They told her that if she went to the police they would kill her. She went home. The three men went off to buy some beer first and then drove to Eddie's place of employment where they picked up some audio cassette tapes to play in the car. They waited until dark before they drove the car back into the bush.

Eddie organised a search for combustible material. He sent Njele to look for wood and David to look for old car tyres. They built a pyre of dry wood, placed the body on it and then placed car tyres on top. They found a can of motor oil in the boot of the car and poured its contents over the body. Then they lit the pyre.

They left the scene once they saw that the fire was burning fiercely. They fetched Meisie Njele from her home and picked up Njele's girlfriend and a mutual friend. Meisie was David Mkumbeni's girlfriend. There were six of them in the car. They took turns driving. While Meisie was driving, Constable Lefakane of the South African Police stopped the car. Eddie and the friend ran away. The other four were taken to the police station at Westonaria. They told Constable Lefakane that they had been to a festival in Pretoria. When the police searched the men they found them in possession of knives. The police tried to establish whether the car had been stolen, but there had been no report to that effect. So the police let them go. The police actually gave them a lift to Eddie's house. But they kept the car because none of the occupants could produce a driver's licence. They were told that they could fetch the car later, provided they brought someone with a valid licence to drive it.

When Mr Grobler did not arrive home on 15 June and did not turn up for work the next day his mother and co-workers started making inquiries and eventually reported to the police that he was missing. They gave the police details of his car. For the next two months there were no leads. Then Captain F J la Grange took over the investigation on 13 August. He traced Mr Grobler's car – it was still in police custody – on 15 August. The Westonaria police had placed it in the pound and had forgotten about it.

When Captain la Grange found the car he started picking up the threads of available evidence. He traced Constable Lefakane who gave him the details of the driver, Meisie Njele. She, in turn, led the police to Eddie. Captain la Grange arrested Eddie on 17 August. A search of Eddie's room led to the discovery of Mr Grobler's gold pen, his watch and a cassette tape, *Sing the Gospel*. A yellow Checkers T-shirt was found at the same time. These items constituted sufficient links to the disappearance of the deceased to warrant Eddie's arrest.

Eddie took the police to the bush on 18 August and pointed out the spot where Mr Grobler's body had been disposed of. Some small bones were visible in the ashes of what must have been a large fire. Two pathologists attended. Under their supervision the ashes were sifted and a number of small items came to light. The police took possession of some metallic remnants while the pathologists took the few bones they had found. The metal items included a bunch of keys, a small buckle and some small rings.

Eddie escaped from police custody, but was re-arrested on 22 August. He tried to escape again and the police shot him dead. However, while he had been alive Eddie had given the police sufficient information to enable them to identify Njele and David Mkumbeni. In September the police arrested them. Both admitted their involvement in the scheme to rob Mr Grobler and that they had jointly killed him and disposed of the body by incinerating it.

The Court found both of them guilty on both counts. No extenuating circumstances were present on the murder count. The robbery had been accompanied by violence, serious injuries and exceptional cruelty. Those were aggravating circumstances, and on 20 May 1987 the Judge gave Njele and Mkumbeni double death sentences.

They were hanged on 10 December 1987. They were both still in their mid-twenties.

Oom Paul, in stone two and a half times his size in life, stands facing north, easily six metres above ground level on a blue granite pedestal set on top of an octagon of Transvaal sandstone. He is guarded by four burghers in commando uniform at the foot of the octagon, each facing outwards at ninety degrees from his neighbours. They hold their German Mauser rifles at the ready. There are four copper relief panels depicting important events in Oom Paul's personal part in the history of the Transvaal Republic; the relief panes are set in alternating facets of the octagon, the burghers with their rifles occupying the facets between the panels.

I allowed my subconscious mind to find solutions while I busied myself with trifles, but the answers were slow in coming.

Wierda and I had to wait for a white minibus taxi to pass before we could cross the road. It stopped in front of us, on the pedestrian crossing, and we had to wait while the driver's assistant jumped out and opened the sliding door for a clutch of passengers to alight. The young man slammed the door shut and the taxi drove off. I stood looking after it for a long time.

Wierda interrupted my thoughts. 'Come on, we're going to be late. What's wrong with you?'

I was trying to think, but that was the problem. Thinking only made it worse.

Palace of Justice

55

We had just crossed the street in front of the Palace of Justice when it finally struck me.

'I need to show you something,' I said to Wierda. We were on the steps.

'We need to find a minibus taxi quickly,' I said as I turned back towards the street. 'Come with me.'

Wierda looked at me with uncomprehending eyes. 'We're going to be late,' he insisted, but I didn't have time to explain.

We stepped back into the street. I tried to flag a taxi down, but the driver and his assistant drove past, craning their necks to look at these strange white people in suits wanting to ride in their township taxi. We could have been the police.

We gave up and had to rush back into court.

Wierda and I made it just in time before Judge van Zyl and his Assessors took their seats.

Dr Shapiro slowly gathered his papers when I called him to the witness box. He was dressed like the professor he was, in brown rubber-soled shoes, chino pants, white shirt and a light tweed jacket. Roshnee had gone to great lengths to find him and to persuade him to give evidence for us. His credentials were impeccable and the fact that we had called an expert witness all the way from America would make headlines that evening and the next morning. A registered medical practitioner and psychiatrist of many years' standing, he was also on the psychiatric evaluation panels of the United States District Court of the Central District of California and the Los Angeles County Superior Court. He owned and ran a psychiatric medical centre and held numerous fellowships and consultancies. The court was hushed when he spoke; reporters followed the example of the Judge and both prosecutors in writing down every word he said.

We needed Dr Shapiro to explain why Labuschagne had killed the seven men at the reservoir and how he could have done so in circumstances that meant that he could not be held criminally responsible for his actions. The evidence was technical and it took a while to lay the proper foundation for the opinions on which our case depended.

Dr Shapiro kept his main opinions simple.

We humans were descended from the apes, he said, and a large part of our behaviour was still being directed by inherited instincts. Those instincts, he explained, were present in us and found expression in emotion-driven acts. Certain stimuli produced anger, others feelings of love, and so on. But, he added, we had evolved beyond the realm of the apes, since God had also given us an intellect, the capacity to think, to work new things out from what we knew already, to plan future activities, and even to ignore or override most of our emotional responses. That was what elevated us above all other animals: our ability to think, to reason, to remember, to learn. Thus, Dr Shapiro advised the Court, everyday human conduct was driven by a mind that in the normal person was controlled in more or less equal measure by emotion and intellect.

He called it the equilibrium of instinct and intelligence.

I checked that the Judge and Assessors were following the evidence. They had the written report we had handed in as the basis of Dr Shapiro's evidence and were alternating their attention between listening to the evidence and taking notes. We went on very slowly.

For a person to behave according to the norms of contemporary society, said Dr Shapiro, the emotional and intellectual sides of the mind need to be more or less in equilibrium. When the emotions overshadow the intellect, we get irrational actions. When the intellect overrides the emotions, we get unduly flat, distant, unsympathetic behaviour.

I took a deep breath because I knew that the most crucial piece of evidence was to follow.

'What in your opinion happened here?' I asked Dr Shapiro when the foundation had been laid.

What happened, he said, is such a build-up of external stimuli over an extended period of time that the patient – and I noticed how he referred to Labuschagne – entered a state where his intellect was completely drowned by his emotions. In that state the emotional load on him was so great that he would not have had a conscious awareness of his physical acts. Yet the eyes would see, the motor functions would remain, like they do in a sleepwalker. Thus he could shoot accurately while having neither intellectual control nor any memory of the shooting. His acts were neither conscious nor voluntary, he concluded.

Judge van Zyl intervened with a question. 'What would cause a situation where the intellect would be submerged by the emotions in an ordinary law-abiding member of society?'

'Oh, Your Honour,' he said, addressing the Judge as if we were in California, 'there could be any number of causes, for example, extreme intoxication, drugs, emotional entanglements such as love or hatred, and there have been cases where severe and chronic spousal or child abuse has led to such a breakdown of the mind.'

'But is such a condition not insanity?' asked the Judge before I could pick up the strings again. 'Surely that is insanity as defined by law.'

Dr Shapiro must have met the question before and was able to answer immediately. 'Your Honour would be correct if the condition was permanent or even of lengthy duration; where it is chronic, to use the medical term. But if it is acute, meaning that it happens on one discrete occasion, and before and after that occasion the patient functioned normally, then that person is not insane within the definition of insanity adopted by medicine. At best it could be said that he or she is temporarily insane, and then only for the duration of the moment when the intellect is submerged completely.'

It was, for the defence, the perfect answer. It was even better that it had been elicited by a question from the Judge.

I had two prepared questions left.

'Dr Shapiro, in your professional opinion, and taking into account all the facts of the case and the evidence you have heard during this trial, what was the defendant's state of mind during the incident at the reservoir when he shot the deceased?'

Dr Shapiro measured his answer. 'In my professional opinion, to such a degree of medical certainty as I require, the defendant was in a state of automatism. As a result of prior events and trauma he had suffered, his mental processes were not functioning normally and his intellectual mind had been swamped so completely by emotions that he did not act voluntarily or consciously.'

'Dr Shapiro, my last question is this,' I said. 'If his intellectual mind was not functioning, how could he have fired those thirteen shots with such deadly accuracy?' I had to deal with the point before James Murray could cross-examine on it.

'That is not unusual, Your Honour,' said Dr Shapiro, 'in fact, it is quite common. When the intellect no longer functions, the emotional or instinctive mind is still functioning. Learnt or instinctive conduct would still be possible. The sleepwalker walks without bumping into anything. The drunk drives the car with a manual gearbox for miles without incident, even though he has no memory of it afterwards. There are many examples of such instinctive behaviour. Rote activities, especially, can be performed with a fair to complete degree of accuracy. And in this case the patient has always been a good shot with the very same pistol he used at the reservoir. He would be able to shoot with the same degree of accuracy he had acquired as learnt behaviour on the shooting range. And he would do that while unconscious of it; his eye would see, his hand would take aim, his finger would pull the trigger, and he would not have any intellectual control over the physical acts of his own body.'

'We have no further questions, thank you, M'Lord,' I said. 'Thank you, Dr Shapiro. Would you please wait where you are in case my Learned Friends have questions for you?'

Of course they were going to have questions.

The cross-examination was predictable in most respects, but James Murray started with a question we had not anticipated. Murray was able to see angles that Wierda and I could not.

'Does California have the death penalty?' he asked.

'Yes,' said Dr Shapiro.

'When did you last have an execution?' asked Murray. It was not clear from the way he intoned the question whether he actually knew the answer.

'It must have been in 1973 or even before that, I can't remember.' Dr Shapiro looked as baffled as we must have. 'We had regular executions, by our standards, until the Supreme Court declared the death penalty as it was then applied unconstitutional in 1973. The State Legislature reinstated the death penalty in 1977, but even though a number of persons have been sentenced to death since then, none have been executed.'

Murray made his point. 'Do you have any personal experience of the effect of participation in the execution process on the warders who attend executions, here or in California?'

Dr Shapiro had to concede. 'No, I do not.'

'What method of execution is used in California?' asked Murray. For a second time I could not quite see where he was heading.

'The law prescribes lethal injection.'

'Don't you use gas?' asked Murray.

'We started with hanging, then we went to the electric chair, and then we went to gas.'

'Electricity and gas are far more dramatic methods of execution than hanging, aren't they?' Murray suggested. He stood with one hand behind his back, toying with his pen, with the other hand resting lightly on the lectern in front of him, the picture of calm and control. The thought crossed my mind that he was, like me, comfortable when he was on his feet in court while nervous and restless when not. I wondered if surgeons were like that, nervous wrecks until they make the first incision, returning to their former state only when they have closed the patient up.

I had missed the answer and asked Wierda to read it back to me: 'I think those three methods are equally dramatic, to adopt your description. They burn, break, distort and disfigure the body, and that is why we have moved on to lethal injection.'

'I would suggest that hanging is far less traumatic for everyone involved than the electric chair or the gas chamber.'

'Sir,' said Dr Shapiro, 'I cannot think of anything more traumatic, of any torture more cruel, of any practice more certain to cause a total breakdown of a perfectly sane and well-balanced young man than exposing him to a hanging, to multiple hangings that is, week in and week out, to the tune of a hundred and sixty-four people in a year.' He shook his head. 'Do you realise that you made him attend the killing of twenty-one men in three days? Why do you act surprised that he has broken down, that he has departed from normal behaviour to such an extreme extent that he is standing here facing the death penalty himself?'

When Murray didn't immediately respond to the outburst, Dr Shapiro's voice rose in both volume and tone. 'Do you realise that you made him kill and then you made him clean the bodies? You made him responsible for them in life and in death. You made him kill, and then you made him feel guilty.'

Murray held his ground. 'My suggestion is that the electric chair and the gas chamber are worse methods of execution than hanging. What is your answer to that?'

'My answer to that is that you don't seem to see the point. It does not matter whether the electric chair or the gas chamber is worse or better than the gallows; the point is that making a man do this kind of work is bound to cause him to break down. He would have broken down if you had used the electric chair and he would have broken down if you had used the gas chamber. It is not the method that matters; it is the fact of killing a human being you have known for a long time, or watching him being killed.'

'Have you finished?' asked Murray with exaggerated politeness.

'Actually, I haven't,' said Dr Shapiro. 'The British hanged no more than thirteen or fourteen people a year this century.'

'What does that have to do with this case or, for that matter, my question?' asked Murray, but I could see that Judge van Zyl was interested in the evidence. He was lapping up every word the witness spoke.

'It has this to do with this case,' said the American, visibly upset. 'The British always used a professional executioner who only ever met the prisoner on the morning of the execution and was assisted by a man, sometimes two, who were not warders who had looked after the prisoner during his stay in the death cells. And they never hanged more than one person at a time, even if two or more had to be hanged on the same day.'

'They hanged more than that at Nuremberg,' Murray said tartly, but Dr Shapiro was no fool.

'They hanged them one at a time, and the Hangman was an American soldier.'

'And he made a mess of it, from what I have read,' said the Judge unexpectedly.

'Exactly,' said Dr Shapiro. 'That is exactly my point, Your Honour. Executions are for professional executioners, and that soldier was not a professional executioner. And prison warders are not soldiers or executioners.'

Murray ignored the bait. 'In California you don't have to contend with racist murderers who go around killing black people in order to make a political point, do you?' he asked.

'No, thank God we don't!'

'Well, we do. And you don't have any experience in dealing with such killers, do you?'

'No, I don't.'

'Well, we do. And I suggest to you that you have no way of knowing whether this defendant isn't just such a killer.'

At first Dr Shapiro didn't answer. I watched the Judge and his Assessors. They were watching Labuschagne. I turned to see what had caught their attention and saw Labuschagne sitting bolt upright, with his eyes closed, rocking slowly, forwards and backwards. He showed no interest in the evidence. He looked like someone who did not want to hear.

'Is that a question I have to answer?' asked Dr Shapiro.

'Yes, Dr Shapiro,' said Murray, 'and what is your answer, please?'

'I'm not aware of any evidence that he is a racist or a killer.'

This gave Murray the opening he had been waiting for.

'Well, let's examine that,' he said. 'Let's recount the facts one by one.'

'Take a note,' I whispered to Wierda. It was quite unnecessary; he was studiously recording every word of the exchange.

James Murray started with apparently innocent facts. 'The defendant participated in every execution in 1987, according to his own evidence; we know that for a fact.'

'Yes, it appears so.'

'When he could have refused or asked for a transfer. We know from his evidence that other warders refused or asked for transfers.'

'Yes.'

'And he cleaned and serviced the equipment when others refused to work in that room, is that not so?'

'Yes,' the American sighed.

'And he took the measurements and calculated the drops when that was not his job to do, am I right so far?'

'Yes.'

'And we know from his own evidence that he pulled a prisoner up by the rope and dropped him a second time to ensure that his neck was broken, don't we?'

Dr Shapiro was again forced to say yes. He had become a little subdued after the heat of the earlier exchange with Murray.

'That must have taken considerable physical and emotional effort, for sure. Do you agree?'

'Yes.'

'No one who was physically or emotionally weak could have done that, could they?'

'I should think not,' Dr Shapiro conceded.

Murray pressed on. 'And we know from the records for that year that almost every prisoner who was hanged was either black or coloured, don't we?'

'There were some whites too, I've been told,' said Dr Shapiro. Wierda had taken him through the registers.

'No more than three all year,' said Murray. 'Scheepers, Wessels and Delport.'

'I don't know, but I'm not disputing that.'

'And he killed the seven men at the reservoir, didn't he?'

'Yes.'

'And they were black too, weren't they?'

'Yes.'

'Forgive me, Dr Shapiro, if I express some incredulity at your opinion that the defendant is not a racist and is not a killer. I would suggest that his actions demonstrate that he is both.'

'Am I to comment on that?' asked the witness.

'Yes, I am afraid so, Doctor,' said Judge van Zyl.

'Thank you, Your Honour,' said the witness. 'I disagree with the prosecutor's suggestion. What I meant when I said he was not a racist or a killer is that he is not a racist or a killer in the sense implied by the charges against him. He acted without control over his actions, without volition, and in that state they might as well have been from Mars; he would still have shot them.'

Murray decided to call it a day and sat down. His questions had cut our case open to the bone, but the witness hadn't let us down. I conferred briefly with Wierda and announced that we had no re-examination, but the Judge had some questions of his own.

'Doctor,' he said, playing with the cap of his pen, 'Mr Murray has asked you to compare different methods of execution. I have been wondering. Is there anything significant about the method of execution we use here, that is, hanging?'

Dr Shapiro stood head up, looking at the ornate canopy over the bench as he contemplated the issue. We had not covered this in his briefing. Then he squared up to the Judge. 'I think there may be, Your Honour, but I have not really thought this through.'

When Judge van Zyl did not respond he continued. 'I think there is something obscene in the fact that in a hanging you use gravity to kill the prisoner. You use the weight and momentum of the prisoner's own body to sever his spinal cord.'

The Judge intervened. 'No, I meant as far as the defendant's involvement in the process was concerned.'

'Oh,' said Dr Shapiro, 'I am sorry. I misunderstood.' He paused for a moment. 'Yes, there is something significant, I think. It is this: An execution is traumatic at the best of times. A multiple hanging must be worse than any other process of execution practised anywhere, with the exception perhaps of a public beheading. And to have to participate in the execution of a person you have known intimately, as these warders must have known the prisoners after such a long period of taking care of them, must be doubly so. I should think that the two factors combined, that is the trauma of a multiple execution together with the close relationship that must have developed between the prisoners and the warders, would make your execution process uniquely disturbing.'

'Thank you,' said the Judge with a nod and then addressed me and James Murray. 'Do you have any questions arising from the question I have put to the witness?'

To my surprise Murray decided to ask more questions. 'I do, M'Lord,' he said.

'Carry on then,' said the Judge as he picked up his pen.

'Doctor,' said Murray in a solemn and formal tone, 'are you saying that our method of execution is cruel?'

'I don't think I have been asked to comment on that.'

'But that is the impression you want to give, isn't it?' Murray insisted.

'No, I don't want to give any impression. If I want to give an impression, I will say exactly what I want to convey.'

'You are against capital punishment and that is the point behind your evidence, isn't it?'

The American would have none of that. 'My own views on capital punishment are not up for debate and I have refrained from expressing any view.'

'Then what is it that you are really saying?'

That was a mistake on Murray's part. The question allowed Dr Shapiro to give free rein to his views.

'I am saying that hanging is, to the onlooker and participant, an offensive, grotesque manner of execution. It is bound to overwhelm the senses. The physicality of it is intense. The noise made by the machine coupled with the cries and groans of the prisoners being executed must be severely disturbing. It is the very stuff that our worst nightmares are made of. It is bound, in my opinion, to break the participants just as it breaks the necks of the prisoners being executed. It inflicts physical injuries on the prisoners beyond the mere breaking of their necks and is bound to inflict incalculable psychological damage on the escorts. That is what I am saying.'

The answer left Murray little choice but to become argumentative. 'You make it plain that you are against capital punishment, and I suggest to you that your views in that regard have coloured the opinions you have expressed here today.'

Dr Shapiro was an experienced psychiatrist who had been cross-examined many times in the courts of his home state. He knew how to handle hostile and argumentative cross-examination.

'It is for His Honour to decide that,' he said, 'I cannot comment on my own evidence.'

Murray left it at that and when the Judge asked me if I had any re-examination, I declined the invitation.

'You may step down,' Judge van Zyl said to the witness, 'and thank you for coming all this way to give us the benefit of your experience.' The tone was friendly, but I wasn't altogether sure that there wasn't a hint of sarcasm in it.

Palace of Justice

56

Our second expert was Marianne Schlebusch, a psychologist who looked younger than her years, a smallish brunette with closely cropped hair. She gave detailed evidence of all the tests and evaluations she had performed before we turned to the topic of automatism.

'Dr Schlebusch, could you please explain the phenomenon of automatism to the Court? We are interested in its medical and psychological aspects, please.'

Marianne Schlebusch closed her report and gave us a lecture.

'Automatism is related to conditioned responses,' she said. 'You can condition a person to behave in a particular way in any given set of circumstances. At the same time,' she cautioned, 'you cannot do something in a state of automatism that you cannot do in a normal, functioning state, such as riding a bicycle, playing the guitar or driving a car.'

They must have wondered where we were going when she got closer to the point.

'Killing can become a conditioned response, even killing on a grand scale,' she said. 'That is what we do with soldiers not far from here, just on the other side of the hill where the reservoir stands,' she pointed out. 'We train soldiers so that they will instinctively behave in a desired way when they are on the battlefield. The problem,' she said, 'is not so much in the training; almost all men can be conditioned to that extent. The problem lies in the unlearning. The problem reposes in the inability of the returning soldiers to adjust to civilian conditions when they come home after lengthy periods of combat.'

I asked her to give some examples and she said she would mention three.

'After the First World War,' she told the Court, 'a disproportionate number of returning soldiers were hanged in Britain for crimes they had committed shortly after their return. At the time their condition was not understood and they were treated as ordinary criminals and some of them were executed. The second example has its roots in the Vietnam War. Returning American soldiers exhibited such varied and severe psychological disorders that the War Veterans Administration was still struggling to cope with their treatment nearly twenty years later. These men could suffer consequences for a very long time, from an inability to sleep or to concentrate or to maintain a conversation. They have violent mood swings, and react to the slightest provocation with excessive violence. They relive their experiences in the jungles of South-East Asia in the form of flashbacks day and night, at the most unpredictable times. Many resort to drugs and large numbers have committed suicide.

'The same problems became apparent here in South Africa as soon as the first of our soldiers started returning from the war in Angola,' she said. 'That was in 1975, but we only started taking notice in about 1980.'

I didn't have to prompt her and took the opportunity to watch Judge van Zyl and the Assessors closely. The journalists on my left were scribbling furiously.

'It is now more than thirteen years since we got involved in that war,' she said, 'and at 1 Military Hospital we have whole wards dedicated to the treatment of the psychological scars of those soldiers. Do you want me to explain?' she asked.

I wasn't sure whether she was asking me or the Judge, but Judge van Zyl nodded and she continued.

'Let me explain in more detail what happened to them,' she said.

I looked behind me to see how Pierre de Villiers would react to this evidence. He sat entranced, his eyes on the witness box. I saw the man next to him digging an elbow into his ribs and Pierre frowning, irritated at the interruption. I had to turn my own attention back to the witness box.

Marianne Schlebusch spoke evenly, in a soothing tone, sure of her way and confident in her knowledge. 'First we train them to handle their weapons expertly, in all conditions,' she emphasised. 'We drill them night and day until they can literally fire their weapons with deadly accuracy under any circumstances. We make them practise in wet and dry conditions, in sunlight and in the dark, to fire slowly and also quickly, at visible and also at hidden targets. We make them practise shooting at static targets, and then we teach them how to shoot accurately at moving targets and targets that appear suddenly, by surprise. They learn to live, eat, sleep and even to go to the toilet with their weapons always at the ready.'

I was concerned that she was taking too long to get to the point, but when I looked at the Judge and his Assessors they were watching her intently. I let her give her evidence free of interruptions from me.

'In the second phase,' she said, 'we train our soldiers to react in a particular way to the circumstances they would encounter in the field. Every man in the platoon is given a specific role and not only must he perform under all conditions, the rest of his platoon must know that they can rely on him to do his job while they do theirs. For example, they are taught that if they are on patrol at dusk, they must set up a perimeter and arrange their sleeping bags so that they form the spokes of a wheel with every soldier facing outwards. And then we train …' She corrected herself, 'No, we *order* them to shoot everyone and everything that moves outside their circle. In the field at night they lie in that situation of heightened tension and anticipation of danger and we have found that they do shoot anything that moves outside their circle, whether it is a genuine threat or not. The training pays off, but now and then it has unintended consequences. Soldiers conditioned in this way have shot members of their own platoon who had slipped out for a cigarette and they have shot many innocent civilians who just happened to be in the wrong place at the wrong time.'

The Judge was beginning to fidget. Marianne was taking a bit longer than I had planned and I asked her to deal more specifically with Leon Labuschagne's case.

'What I think happened here is very similar,' she said. 'Over the last eighteen months before the events at the reservoir Labuschagne was invested with a conditioned response. He had already become expert at handling and firing his pistol, but the prison also conditioned him to kill. It doesn't matter that the killing was lawful; he still had to overcome the natural inhibition we all have to killing a human being.' She slowed down as she spoke with emphasis. 'His active and very physical participation in the killing process, coupled with the tasks he had to perform in preparation for the killing, such as taking the measurements and calculating the drops to the nearest inch, cleaning and servicing the gallows equipment, turned him, in his subconscious mind, into a killer. In his own mind he sees himself as a killer.'

I stole a glance at Labuschagne to see how he was reacting to the evidence. He sat with his head up and eyes closed, but I could not help noticing that he was on the edge of the wooden seat in the dock. He might have feigned disinterest, but he wasn't fooling me. He had stopped rocking.

Marianne took a sip of water before she continued. I had to lead her evidence by asking the appropriate questions, but she needed very few cues from me.

'How did you say he sees himself? And could you explain, please?'

'He sees himself as a killer,' she said, 'but he is at war with himself over that. And then we have the disintegration of his psyche in the weeks before the incident at the reservoir. This escalated dramatically in the last two weeks before the tenth of December. His wife left him together with their child and all his efforts to see them were thwarted. His emotional attachment to Wessels made matters worse when he was required to assist with that execution. The sheer number of executions and the other things that went wrong in that last week brought him closer and closer to the point of breakdown. His emotions were running amok and, to top it all, he had suffered a head injury that was severe enough for him to lose consciousness. He was dehydrated after all that physical exertion in the sun at the cemetery, then there was the drive in the rainstorm, the aggressive response from the other driver and their reckless game of tag all the way to the reservoir. All of these contributed to bring him to the point where he was on the verge of a mental breakdown. He was,' she said, 'at the end of his reach and on the verge of the disintegration of his psyche.'

She paused again and took another sip of water.

The spectators craned their necks to hear better as Marianne explained that something must have happened at the reservoir to push Labuschagne over the edge into an abyss of such depth and blackness that even psychologists and psychiatrists could not predict with any degree of accuracy how he would respond to any new stimuli.

'Some event must have occurred that triggered a violent, conditioned response,' she said. 'The fact that the dead bodies were arranged in a neat line next to each other shows that in his subconscious mind he was at work in the gallows chamber. The trigger event does not have to be an important or otherwise significant event. It could be something ordinary, an everyday occurrence, entirely innocent on its own.'

I waited for Judge van Zyl to finish his note taking and then asked Marianne for her concluding opinions.

She started by expressing the opinion that Labuschagne had acted in a state akin to an acute catathymic crisis. She explained that as a condition where the person in the grip of the crisis acted in accordance with the overwhelming dictates of his emotions and lost intellectual control over his actions.

'Such a person would have no memory of the events because the memory function of the mind is an intellectual function,' she explained, 'and when the intellect is turned off, the memory is also turned off. That is why he cannot remember what happened at the reservoir, his mind was literally absent,' she said.

'Were there any other indications of a loss of memory?' I asked.

'He also has no memory of the newsworthy events of that week,' she added. 'We had three significant events and during our psychometric testing he has demonstrated no memory of any of them. But that loss of memory is of a different nature. It had been caused by Labuschagne's progressive loss of grip on reality. His mind was too preoccupied with other things to concern itself with the world outside.'

Judge van Zyl asked what the events were. She mentioned President Reagan's historic meeting with Mr Gorbachev in Reykjavik; the South African Airways 747, the *Helderberg*, crashing into the sea near Mauritius; and a female spy who had been caught and tortured by the Zimbabwean police. These events had made the news worldwide, but when she ran her tests Labuschagne had no memory of them.

'This shows,' she said, 'that he was no longer in touch with reality during that last week; he was disengaging from the reality with which he could not cope. His memory of events that week is fragmented.'

I thanked her and sat down in anticipation of the cross-examination, but Judge van Zyl asked a question I had not considered.

'What do you say about his interaction with Tsafendas? How did that affect his state of mind, in your opinion?'

'M'Lord,' she said, 'the fact that he believes what Tsafendas told him, and that Tsafendas appears to him to be sane, shows that what the rest of us know to be insane nonsense, he experienced as logical and truthful. His mind was beginning to play tricks on him, a very sure symptom of the beginning of dissociation, the breakdown of the psyche that led him to complete psychological disintegration at the reservoir.'

After a long and pensive pause the Judge told James Murray that he could start his cross-examination.

It was war, but not one fought with anger and aggression. No, James Murray was too good for that. He employed subtlety and guile. We were in for a torrid afternoon and would have to wait and see if our expert witness could defend her opinion.

'There had to be a trigger event, you said, a final trigger event that set in train this cascade of killings, right?' Murray looked at Marianne Schlebusch for confirmation.

'Yes,' she said calmly. 'Although the stress had built up over time and through a number of different events and circumstances, there still had to be a final event or stimulus that caused his psyche to break down completely. It doesn't have to be a big event, but it has to be significant in the sense of being in consonance with the cause or causes of the disintegration of his psyche.'

'And he says,' Murray paused and pointed with his arm in the direction of the dock, but without looking, 'he claims that he does not remember what happened at the reservoir to cause him to act as he did.' It was a statement of fact rather than a question, and we could all still remember the defendant's evidence vividly.

'Yes,' she confirmed.

'So you can't say with any degree of certainty what the trigger event was, can you?'

'No, I can't,' Marianne conceded. 'I have said so from the beginning. It's in my written report too.'

'And it follows,' said Murray, the terrier in action, 'that if you can't say what the trigger event was, you can't be sure there was a trigger event, doesn't it?'

'No,' she said, 'there must have been a trigger event. Something must have happened that in his mind was linked to his work in the prison.'

'Even though you can't tell the Court what that trigger event was?' said Murray. Sarcasm and incredulity dripped from his words.

Marianne Schlebusch whispered the answer but stood her ground. 'Yes.'

'Your opinion depends to a large extent on the credibility of the defendant, doesn't it?' Murray suggested.

'Yes.'

'And he could easily fake a lack of memory, couldn't he?'

'He could fake it, but not easily,' she said, responding to the challenge. 'All of our tests have built-in lie detection processes.'

Murray leaned down to speak to Sanet Niemand. She handed him a slip of paper and he studied it carefully before he read the question she had given him.

'And if he has successfully misled you, as you have just conceded was possible, then the meticulous arrangement of the bodies at the reservoir after he had killed them would take on a very sinister aspect, wouldn't it?

It would mean that he was sending a message to the world, wouldn't it?'

Marianne considered the question carefully before she responded. 'Only if he has successfully misled me and had beaten all the subtle traps in our tests,' she said. 'But the prospects of that happening are remote.'

Murray shrugged – I don't think he meant anyone to notice – and tried another approach.

'There is also the accuracy of the shooting to explain,' he said. 'You've not explained that. How could anyone fire with that degree of accuracy while acting in a state of automatism?'

She had watched him intently as he framed the question. 'M'Lord,' she said slowly, 'in a situation like this, when mental functions are disintegrated, the accuracy of his actions would depend on the mental explosion and the force of the explosion and the ingrained or learnt behaviour. Once the explosion has occurred, the learnt behaviour takes over. The accuracy of the shooting is learnt behaviour, which is a conditioned response, and the fact that the shooting was so accurate actually demonstrates that there had been such an explosion.'

Murray could not believe his ears. 'Are you saying that the accuracy of the shooting actually supports your theory that he didn't know what he was doing?'

'Yes, M'Lord,' she said. 'Who would be able to shoot so accurately in the circumstances that must have prevailed at the reservoir, unless the shooting was a conditioned response?'

Murray tried to retrieve the situation. 'But you would still have to have a trigger event that sets the conditioned response in motion, don't you?'

'Yes, I've said so.'

'And you have said that you don't know what the trigger event was.' He was rubbing it in.

'Yes.'

Murray started a new line of cross-examination quietly and without fanfare. 'You only have his word for what happened at the reservoir, don't you?'

Marianne Schlebusch took her time before she replied. 'I don't know that anyone else can tell us what happened there,' she said.

'What I'm getting at,' said Murray, 'is that if his version is found to be untrue or unreliable your opinion will have been based on an incorrect set of facts.' It was a statement, not a question, but it invited an answer.

'I haven't caught him in a lie.' She shook her head and wiped a hand across her brow. 'Everything I have heard during the trial is consistent with what he has told me.' She gave Murray a small concession, 'But what you say is true in principle.'

Murray turned a page in his notes. Marianne Schlebusch watched him with the eye of a trained observer. I wondered what she thought of him and, for that matter, of me. She stood watching Murray and her eyes drifted down to the notes on his lectern. Her attitude said, How many more questions do I have to answer? We were all exhausted; I wasn't the only one.

Murray took his time before he embarked on his next topic. 'The defendant collected a washer from the coffin of each prisoner he had escorted to the gallows. That we know from his own evidence. My first question is this: did he tell you about that?'

'No.'

'So you heard about that here in court for the first time?'

'Yes.'

'The defendant withheld that information from you.'

'He didn't tell me and I didn't know to ask.'

'His collection of those washers is inconsistent with your evidence that he was traumatised by the hanging process, isn't it?' It was a good point, I thought, but not unanswerable. What if collecting the washers was entirely consistent with his steady descent into inappropriate behaviour? And for that we could blame his work.

I watched Marianne closely. She scratched the side of her nose and turned towards Murray to engage him in the debate, but the Judge intervened to remind her to face the bench.

She obeyed immediately. 'I disagree, M'Lord. Obsessive-compulsive behaviour of that kind is entirely compatible with the trauma that he suffered. In the beginning he might have collected the washers because his peers were doing it, but later he would have been unable to stop himself. The culture of the prison had become part of him.'

Murray was entitled to be displeased. This was the last thing he would have anticipated. He had to change the topic of his questions or sit down on an unfavourable answer. He did the former.

'There are parallels between this case and the cases of the two soldiers in the Eastern Cape and the two Johannesburg policemen who went about killing black people, aren't there?'

It was a question that had preyed on my mind from the first day when Roshnee had come to my chambers to ask me to undertake the defence. Our witness had to concede.

'Yes,' she said.

Murray wrapped the point up quickly. 'And if what the defendant told you is untrue, then we would have every reason to think that he's no more than a racist murderer, wouldn't we?'

'That is for the Court to decide,' she had the grace to concede.

'I have no further questions for this witness, thank you, M'Lord.' Murray sat down after the favourable answer.

I was about to say that I had no re-examination when the Judge spoke. 'I wonder if I could ask you to elaborate on a few matters that are still unclear to me.'

'Certainly, M'Lord,' said Marianne. I sat down and watched.

Judge van Zyl started with an observation. 'I watched the defendant very closely when he gave evidence and I don't know whether he was acting or not when he said that he couldn't believe that he could have done what he did at the reservoir. He said it more than once. How would that fit in with your theory, if that reaction is not faked?'

'M'Lord, this is a known phenomenon in psychiatry and very typical of a catathymic crisis. We say that the patient experienced events as unreal, ego dystonic. In other words, the patient cannot understand how he could have done something like that. The event clashes with his own perception of himself.' She looked at the Judge. 'I hope I've made it clearer rather than confusing the issue.'

'Thank you, I think I followed that,' said the Judge. 'My next question relates to the defendant's behaviour after his arrest. We learned here that he wouldn't speak to anyone, not even his parents, for months. Why would he do that?'

'It is not uncommon in this kind of crisis that for a long period the patient is devoid of emotion and withdraws into a cocoon of silence. We have to treat that, of course, because the patient cannot hope to be able to deal with the reality of the current, post-crisis situation unless he learns to accept what he has done and to live with the consequences.'

Judge van Zyl looked up at the spectators in the balcony at the back of the court, but his eyes were not focused on them. Something was troubling him, it appeared.

'How certain are you that the defendant has told you the truth about his work?' he asked at last.

There was an even longer pause. Marianne bit her lip and I saw just the slightest shake of her head.

'You don't appear to be certain,' said the Judge, but his tone was not unkind.

She sighed and a small crack opened in the facade of our case. The Judge opened it wider. 'Please tell us what doubts you have.'

'I think his work gave him satisfaction,' she said. The answer was as enigmatic as it was vague.

'He did his job willingly and it made him feel good, is that what you think?'

'Yes.'

Wierda whispered under his breath, close to my ear, 'Fuck!'

Judge van Zyl had not finished either. His next series of questions had nothing to do with guilt or innocence.

'I'd like to hear your comments on another aspect, Dr Schlebusch,' he said.

Marianne was an attractive woman and Judge van Zyl had turned his charming side to the witness box.

'It appears from the evidence that the gallows escorts are all young men in their early twenties. How is the work they have to do going to affect them in the long run, in your opinion?'

It was a question Wierda and I had been afraid to ask. The answer could so easily go against our client. What if the other warders coped perfectly well with their situation?

'M'Lord,' she said, 'how this type of work would affect an individual escort would depend on a number of circumstances, of which two factors are perhaps more significant than the others. The first is that they may develop a dependency on the adrenalin rush the process induces. The other is whether they receive appropriate counselling on a regular basis.'

The Judge watched her as she added, 'I could elaborate if you want me to.'

'Thank you,' he said. 'Perhaps you could tell us what you mean by developing a dependency? Are you saying that a person could become addicted to killing in this way?'

The question had come out in a particularly menacing way, for the defence, but the Judge's tone was inquisitive, not suggestive, and I didn't quite know what to make of his line of questioning. Wierda and I knew very well that Labuschagne had confessed to us that he had become addicted to escort duty.

Marianne Schlebusch gave another lecture. 'M'Lord, you can develop a dependency on killing just as you can become dependent on alcohol, or drugs, or tobacco, or even sex.' There was a semi smile on her lips when she continued, 'A dependency can be created deliberately or accidentally. It is created accidentally when repeated use of the substance or participation in the event leads to an addiction to the effects that the substance or activity produce. It is deliberately created if the subject is manipulated in such a way that the dependency is created in a controlled fashion. I could give two examples. The first is a medical example. Some orthopaedic surgeons deliberately create a dependency on opium-based painkillers in patients who have suffered severe injuries that produce chronic pain of such severity that the patient is in danger of suffering psychological damage. The opiate dependency is not in itself the desired end result but a means to treating the patient. The philosophy behind it is that it is easier to cure the patient of the opiate dependency later than to cope with the psychological fallout from chronic, unbearable pain.'

The court had again become very quiet. Marianne did not speak very loudly and her voice could not have carried beyond the first few rows in the public gallery. Everyone was straining to hear. She waited for a hint from the Judge and when he lifted his pen, she continued, 'The second example is in the training we give our soldiers, especially the men in the Special Forces such as the Parabats, the Navy divers and the Recces. We train them for special activities that produce large amounts of adrenalin in their bodies and they become addicted to those activities or, should I say, they become addicted to the adrenalin and in order to obtain it they initiate the activities concerned. They want to jump out of the aircraft when every sane person – I should not use that word, because they are all sane soldiers – when every ordinary person would baulk at the thought of jumping out. The same goes for the divers, they want to go down into those cold, murky and dark waters when the rest of us are too scared to go anywhere near.'

She wanted to say more but the Judge stopped her. 'We get the point,' he said. 'What these specially trained men do is to participate in extraordinary and dangerous activities and they look forward to it. Is that what you are saying?'

'Indeed, M'Lord.'

Judge van Zyl received a nudge from the Assessor on his left. 'What was the other factor you mentioned?' he asked.

'It is whether counselling is available, M'Lord,' she said.

'Tell us about that, please.'

Wierda had stopped taking notes. I pretended to write down every word but was more concerned about the direction of the Judge's questions. I did not like the idea that control over the evidence was slipping away from me.

'The escorts should have received regular counselling and should not have been threatened with dismissal or punitive duties or any form of disciplinary action if they availed themselves of counselling.' Marianne turned her head to look directly at the Warrant Officer, but he avoided her eyes and sat staring at James Murray's back.

'How would counselling help them? I mean, can a counsellor really do anything for someone with this kind of job?' asked the Judge.

'They can indeed, M'Lord. They can help by encouraging the subject to speak, to talk about his experience and by talking about it to start processing it and coming to terms with his fears and anxieties and feelings of guilt or even inadequacy. You must remember, M'Lord, that what is expected of these escorts in the prison is an attitude and behaviour that would not be acceptable outside the prison gates. Inside they are expected to be controlling, harsh, even cruel, and then, as soon as they are outside the gates, they have to turn into sympathetic husbands and dutiful fathers, or into obedient sons. To make that change is not easy to manage without counselling. In fact, I think it's impossible and this case is proof of that.'

At last she had come up with a fact clearly in our favour.

The Judge had no more questions and invited us to ask any questions we might have arising from the exchanges between him and our psychologist.

I had one question. 'How is the evidence you have given about counselling to be applied to the defendant from this time forward?'

'Oh,' she said, 'M'Lord, I think he's the lucky one, the one who has escaped from the oppression of the code of silence they have in the prison. He has escaped by talking, first to his lawyers, then to me, and now to the Court. He has by the force of his circumstances been compelled to confront his own actions in open court, here in front of his parents and the public, and in front of the relatives of his victims. He has progressively told more and more, disclosing the most intimate details of his actions and his life. He has been castigated in cross-examination.'

Marianne stood silent for a good ten seconds before she added, 'I would never have thought of cross-examination as therapy, but I think the court process may have been as good a psycho-therapeutic session as my profession could ever hope to achieve. He has been forced to talk about his worst experiences and to do so in public. It doesn't matter that he had no choice; what matters is that he has talked about it.'

I sat down immediately.

James Murray had only one question. 'He told his lawyers more than he told you, and he told the Court more than he told his lawyers.

It would appear that there is probably a lot more that he could tell, but hasn't. Do you agree?'

She did not have to think long about the answer. 'Yes, of course,' she said, driving another nail into our case.

Judge van Zyl conferred briefly with his Assessors before he told Marianne that she was released from further attendance.

When she walked past me I held up my hand and whispered for her to wait. It was just as well, because James Murray asked for permission to recall Dr Shapiro for further cross-examination and the Judge granted it.

I took notes as the battle of wits continued.

Murray wasted no time after Dr Shapiro had been reminded that he was still under oath. 'You were in court while the previous witness gave her evidence?'

'Yes.'

'You heard her opinion that the defendant enjoyed participating in the killing process and that it was addictive.'

Dr Shapiro nodded his answer.

Murray didn't wait for an audible answer. 'It follows that the defendant's evidence here was not true when he said that he did not and only took part because he had no choice, doesn't it?'

Dr Shapiro was stoic in his response. 'Yes.'

'You must have noticed too that Miss Schlebusch changed her own evidence. She first said that she had not detected any untruthful answers and that her tests did not reveal any. Yet she admitted to having some doubts and that she formed the view that the defendant probably enjoyed participating in the hanging process.'

'What is the question?' asked Dr Shapiro. He stood upright but very still in the witness box, his eyes on James Murray, his hands held together in front of him. 'What is the question you want me to answer?' he insisted.

Murray obliged. 'I would like to suggest to you that you cannot form a reliable expert psychiatric opinion in this matter when the defendant has been untruthful in some respects and has not taken the Court completely into his confidence.'

Dr Shapiro turned very slowly towards the bench and when he spoke it was in even, professorial tones as if he was lecturing a class of undergraduate students.

'Your Honour, there is something I should perhaps explain before I answer.'

Murray shifted and was about to interrupt, but the Judge stopped him with a raised hand and a shake of the head. When Dr Shapiro spoke again I wrote down every word.

I was glad to see that the Judge and both Assessors were doing the same.

'You see, Your Honour, when you have to report to the Court on the mental state of a person the process you adopt is at once scientific and intimate. Where it is scientific it is objective, but where it is intimate it is subjective. Indeed, one has to form an intimate relationship, for want of a better word, with the patient in order to gain a complete understanding of his psyche. When one does that, I mean the psychiatrist or psychologist who conducts the investigation, one cannot help but become subjectively involved with the patient's dilemma. No one, except perhaps a psychopath, a person without feelings for others, a person without the ability to connect with others on an emotional level, can avoid being affected by the crisis that the patient faces.'

Dr Shapiro's eyes swept the room from corner to corner. 'What happened here is that in Miss Schlebusch's initial opinion the objectivity to which we strive may have given way to that subjective element I've tried to explain. But we are trained to resist and overcome that kind of personal involvement – call it taking sides, if you will. And it appears to me that she did just that when the prosecutor's questions steered her in the direction where she made the concession that the defendant in her opinion probably enjoyed his work in the gallows chamber.'

'So the truth eventually came out?' said Murray.

Dr Shapiro had been cross-examined before, and by lawyers in a far more sophisticated system where capital cases were handled by only a select few, the most gifted and skilled, the most experienced members of the legal fraternity. He had the perfect answer.

'Yes,' he said, 'our systems are designed to achieve exactly that, for the truth to be revealed.'

The thought crossed my mind that the legal process was designed to do much the same, to uncover the truth, but we had the same weaknesses, having to work with unreliable evidence and with our own loss of objectivity. We are particularly vulnerable when we have to decide who or what to believe, and we are so easily misled. I looked up at Judge van Zyl to determine whether he might have noticed the parallels between his job and that of the psychiatrist, but he gave no indication either way.

James Murray wrapped up quickly.

'So the defendant enjoyed participating in the hangings, and he was untruthful in his evidence on that score. Would that be a correct summary of your opinion?'

Dr Shapiro was slow and deliberate in his answer. 'I prefer to say that he gained some satisfaction from his participation in the execution process, that he probably did his job very well and received recognition for that, which satisfied his Calvinistic sense of duty. But he did not enjoy it in the sense that a sadist enjoys inflicting pain. And that is why in his own mind he cannot admit that he has participated willingly in all those executions. His mind looks for an excuse and he finds it in the idea that he was forced to do it, or had no choice.'

Murray left his final point unspoken, and was later to use it in his closing address. If Labuschagne could be untruthful about his willingness to participate when the killing was lawful and sanctioned by a death warrant issued by a Court of Law, how much greater the motive to lie about the killings at the reservoir, which were not sanctioned by the law and did not occur in circumstances of self-defence?

Nevertheless, the American had served our cause well and I nodded my appreciation as he came past.

It had been a long session, and I had been operating at the extreme limits of my concentration and stamina. Although we had reached the end of the defence case as we had prepared it, we had one more task to take care of before we could move on to argument. It would be the last roll of the dice for us, but I was confident that no matter how the dice came to rest, our case couldn't get any worse.

I asked the Judge if we could see him in chambers.

Wierda and I walked through the back passages to the Judge's chambers with the prosecutors, the usher leading the way.

Judge van Zyl's chambers were furnished with the same heavy wooden furniture as the courtroom. The wall behind his desk was covered from the floor to the ceiling with solid bookshelves filled with *Law Reports*, textbooks and journals.

'What's the problem?' he asked. He was undoing the cummerbund of his elaborate scarlet robes. When he'd finished at last he sat down.

'I would have thought you'd close your case now.' He was looking at me.

'I need another inspection, Judge,' I said. 'At the reservoir this time.'

'Won't the police plan and photographs do?' he inquired.

'No, I am afraid not,' I said. I did not explain.

He turned to James Murray. 'What do you say, James?'

'It's their case,' Murray said.

Judge van Zyl smiled at me. 'You heard that – it's your case,' he said. Then, as an afterthought, 'You know, I grew up in the southern parts of the city, but I've never been up there. Maybe it's time for me to see the place.' He spoke softly, in his chambers voice. There was none of the formality of the courtroom and no need for his voice to carry to the last row of spectators.

'May we make transport arrangements for you and the Assessors then?' I asked, but the Judge said that they would make their own arrangements.

Murray then cleared his throat. 'Judge, we would like to call an expert witness in rebuttal, but he can only attend in the morning, so I was hoping that we could take his evidence before we go on another inspection.'

'How long will he be?' asked the Judge.

'No more than an hour, I think.'

'And the inspection, how long do we need for that?' The Judge looked at me.

'We'll finish by lunchtime,' I answered immediately.

I was keen to get agreement without having to explain why I wanted to go to the reservoir, but I saw Murray shaking his head. The Judge must have seen the slight shake of the head too and he asked, 'You don't agree?'

'It is not that I don't agree, Judge, it is that I have a second witness to call in rebuttal and I think he will be a while.'

'Oh, who do you intend to call?' Judge van Zyl appeared as surprised as I was.

'We want to call the Warrant Officer.'

For a moment I did not know what to say. Wierda and I had toyed with the idea that the prosecution might call the Warrant Officer at some stage, but we had dismissed the thought because the Warrant Officer's name did not appear on the list of prosecution witnesses and no mention had been made of his evidence during the prosecution's opening statement or cross-examination of our witnesses. It must have been an afterthought.

'I would object to that,' I said, thinking on my feet as I was speaking. 'You can't call witnesses in rebuttal except where the defence bears the burden of proof on a special defence, or where the evidence is of a technical nature or involves expert opinion in response to defence expert evidence.'

'I'm going to call him on the facts underpinning the expert opinions, yours and mine.' Murray sounded confident and addressed me directly.

Before I could respond Judge van Zyl intervened. 'I'm going to allow that.' He looked down at his hands. They were palm down on his desk with his fingers spread wide. 'I am going to allow it unless you convince me otherwise tomorrow when we start. And then you had better have good authority that says I can't do this. I would like to hear what the Warrant Officer has to say.'

I wanted to continue arguing the point, but there was something in his eye that made me stop. I could address him on the point in open court in the morning; it would not be so easy to silence me then. But it would not be easy to persuade him to change his mind either.

'We'll resume as usual in the morning then, and take it from there,' he said. 'We'll hear the rebuttal expert James wants to call, and then go on the inspection. We can hear what the Warrant Officer has to say when we get back.'

We walked back in silence to the robing room. Murray and Niemand must have been wondering what we were plotting as much as we were with regard to them.

Wierda and I had been working on the closing argument from our first meeting months before. Up to now all we needed to do was to finalise a few details, but now we would have to think of the different angles that might be introduced by the further evidence.

We left Murray and Niemand in the robing room.

Wierda walked me back to my hotel and told me about our last case as we strolled among the workers and shoppers on their way home. We had had a relatively good day and the city was serene in the late afternoon, but we still had a lot of work to do and the forthcoming evidence of the prosecution expert and the Warrant Officer added an element of uncertainty I could have done without.

v3771 Willem Maarman

57

Willem Maarman was twenty and Gert Engelbrecht seventeen when they broke into Mrs Sophia Schoch's house and robbed, raped and killed her.

Mrs Schoch was a seventy-three-year-old widow who lived alone in her house at Halmanshof near Piketberg. She was last seen alive on the morning of Saturday 4 October 1986, at about seven o'clock. Her car was found the next morning in a damaged condition a short distance from her home. When enquiries were made, Mrs Schoch was found dead in her home.

Mrs Schoch had numerous injuries suggesting that she had been subjected to a prolonged and sustained attack. Her skull had been driven into her brain by at least three heavy blows delivered with a large stone she had kept in her house as a doorstop. She had bruises and abrasions of the mouth, internally and externally, and a cut on the chin. There were bruises of the neck. She had been beaten so savagely about the head that the conjunctiva of the left eye had become detached. There were numerous bruises and abrasions of both arms – classic defensive injuries usually suffered when fending off an attack by raising one's forearms in front of one's face or above one's head. There were similar injuries to Mrs Schoch's legs. Her liver, stomach, left kidney and spleen had been bruised. There were also injuries to her genital organs consistent with rape.

Maarman and Engelbrecht were arrested shortly after Mrs Schoch's body had been discovered. They gave slightly different versions of the events at different times. At a preliminary hearing in the Magistrates' Court they gave explanations.

The Magistrate questioned Maarman first:

Q. Did you break into Mrs Schoch's house at Halmanshof on 4 October 1986?
A. Yes, the door was not locked. I opened the door and walked in.
Q. What did you do then?
A. Mrs Schoch wanted to get out, but we prevented her.
Q. Why did you go into the house?
A. I wanted to take things in the house.
Q. What did you do when you were in the house?
A. When Mrs Schoch tried to leave we prevented her and wrestled with her. When I saw that she had lost her spirit I took a knife in the house and stabbed her one blow behind her neck with the knife. She wanted to wash off the blood and I took her to the bathroom where she washed herself. I then took her to the bedroom and told her to take off her clothes or I would cut her throat. She took her panties off. I lay on top of her and had sexual intercourse with her. She said I should not, she was too old for that type of thing.
Q. What happened after you had had intercourse with her?

A. I was afraid she would tell other people of me and I then took a stone that was lying near the television and hit her three times on the head with it.

Q. Did you want to kill her?

A. Yes.

Q. Did she die as a result of the blows you had struck her?

A. Yes.

Q. What did you do then?

A. We took things in the house and put them in the car.

Q. Was it those items the prosecutor read out?

A. Yes.

Engelbrecht gave a far more detailed version. He had known Mrs Schoch as he had previously done some work for her. He said they were collecting wood in the bush near Mrs Schoch's house when Maarman asked him if Mrs Schoch had a firearm:

I said I did not know. He said we should go and look […] We walked around to old lady Sophie's house […] When we got to the back door [Willem] and I took our shoes off. [Willem] opened the back door. He walked in front and I followed him […] [Willem] opened his pocket knife.

The old lady came out of the lounge to the kitchen. Just as the old lady put her foot in the kitchen, [Willem] grabbed her. He pinned her down on the floor and asked her where her money was and if she wanted to live. [Willem] said I should go to the bedroom and search it in the meantime. When I came out of the room again, I saw blood running down the old lady's face. I went to another room and searched for money because [Willem] said I had to look for money and a revolver. I found nothing there. When I came out of the room I found [Willem] and the old lady in another room. [Willem] was pressing the old lady on the ground. [Willem] asked me if I had finished searching the house. I said no. I went to the kitchen […] In the door of the fridge there was a bottle of wine […]

413

I went to tell [Willem] that I had found a bottle of wine. When I came into the room, I saw that he was having intercourse with the old lady. The old lady asked me to speak to [Willem]. But I went to the kitchen again [...] I saw that there was a lot of tinned food in the cupboards. I stacked some of the tinned food on the table [...] I then went back to the bedroom and [Willem] and the old lady came and lay on the bed [...]

I packed the groceries I had put on the table in the kitchen in a sack. While I was busy packing the things in the sack, [Willem] and the old lady came out of the bedroom. When they got to the passage, [Willem] hit the old lady against her head with a type of a rock thing. The old lady collapsed on the floor. When she groaned, he hit her two more blows on her head. [Willem] helped her get up and took her to the bathroom. I went along. The old lady washed the blood from her face [...]

[Willem] asked the old lady if there was more wine. The old lady then walked to the dining room and said I must open the cabinet [...] I found a bottle of KWV brandy in the cabinet. I took the bottle to the kitchen. After that all three of us went to the room where [Willem] and the old lady had been lying down. [Willem] opened the wooden chest there and he found a new shirt, still in its packaging, and a pair of used socks. We walked out of the room again. When we got to the passage the old lady collapsed. [Willem] left the old lady in the passage and he and I went into the lounge. I found the car keys in a basket there and showed them to [Willem] [...] Behind the radiogram was a big tape recorder and [Willem] took that out [...]

I took the tape recorder to the kitchen. While I was there I heard the old lady groan, and saw [Willem] just hitting her repeatedly. He and I went into the bedroom again. I found a shiny wristwatch and gave that too to [Willem]. We went out. Each of us carried a sack with the goods. When we got outside we put our shoes on. [Willem] threw the rock with which he had hit the old lady across the ditch. He and I went to the garage and I opened the doors. [Willem] got in behind the steering wheel and I got into the passenger's side. He pulled the car out and drove nearer to the house and we then loaded the things we had packed in the car.

The Court found Maarman and Engelbrecht guilty of murder on 3 June 1987. The robbery and housebreaking charges overlapped and the Court substituted a single crime for the two, housebreaking with intent to rob and robbery.

Since Engelbrecht had been under the age of eighteen years at the time of the murder the death penalty was not obligatory in his case. There were no extenuating circumstances in Maarman's case. On 4 June 1987 the Judge sentenced Maarman to death for the murder. He also sentenced him to three years' imprisonment on the housebreaking and robbery charge and to eight years on the rape charge. There was no appeal.

Maarman was one of those hanged on 10 December 1987. He was twenty-two years old.

There was nothing new to learn from Maarman's case. We had seen too many killers just like him killing old women in their homes. Rape and pillage was their way of life. I didn't have the energy to argue against Wierda's proposition that no one would shed a tear for Maarman.

Wierda and I had by now read and analysed the cases of all of the thirty-two men hanged during those last two weeks before the events at the reservoir. I couldn't say that the lessons we had learnt were consistent, and I still couldn't see a clear picture behind the matter-of-factness of the killers' own account of their deeds.

We spent the night preparing themes for the cross-examination of the Warrant Officer. We had quickly given up on the idea of objecting to his evidence being given at such a late stage. The authorities were against us. The Judge is not a referee; his function is to ensure that justice is done according to the law, and to that end he was entitled to allow witnesses to be called out of turn and even to call witnesses himself.

We divided the work. Wierda worked on the expert witness while I prepared for the Warrant Officer's evidence. We called Pierre de Villiers in, but he could offer nothing that could be used in cross-examination. There was nothing on the Warrant Officer in the official records.

I made a list of the themes I would explore with the Warrant Officer:

Lack of selection criteria
Lack of training
Lack of support – counselling
Prison culture of violence
Unrelenting pressure on warders to act as escorts

Wierda interrupted my train of thought with a question about the prosecution expert. In the early hours of the morning it struck me that the Warrant Officer might be called to say that Labuschagne had been a willing, perhaps even a keen participant in the execution process.

I added themes on a different tack to my list:

Suicides (of prisoners)
Suicides, alcoholism and violence / fighting behaviour (by warders)
Levity, pranks and jokes as defence mechanisms

The Warrant Officer would be a fifty-fifty witness. His evidence would no doubt hurt our case, but there would also be opportunities for us to elicit favourable evidence from him.

We went to bed tired but pleased with the results of the work we had done.

CLOSING

Prosecution & Defence: 12–14 October 1988

58

When James Murray called their expert to the witness stand, I half turned in my seat to see who it was. A tallish, bespectacled man in his mid-forties was shuffling past the knees in the second row of the public gallery behind the dock. All eyes were on him, except Leon Labuschagne's. He had reverted to his zombie state.

The man made his way towards the witness box carrying a red folder. As he passed me he looked down and surreptitiously winked at me. For a moment I didn't know whether I had imagined it, but when I saw a little smile on his lips as he turned in the witness box to face the Judge I knew I had not been mistaken. I was intrigued. Did he know me? Did I know him?

I turned to Wierda. 'Do you know this guy?'

'No,' he said emphatically, 'never seen him before.'

But I had. The man had been sitting in court every day of the trial so far, always in the same seat two rows behind the dock, on the left side of the court behind me, a perfect position from which to observe Labuschagne without being detected. I had to admire the prosecutors for their tactics; they must have planned this well in advance. I had not once seen the man with them. They had hidden him well, in plain sight. They must have conferred with him in their offices in the mornings, or after hours.

What was worse was that the man had been sitting next to Pierre de Villiers most of the time and that I had seen them talk to each other. I looked at Pierre but could not catch his eye. He was watching the witness intently.

The registrar stood up and faced the witness box. 'What is your full name, please?'

'Gerhardus Petrus Nienaber.'

There is something odd here, I thought, as the witness took the oath. He spoke in a deep baritone.

When Murray led his evidence he addressed him as Professor

Nienaber. There was an easy familiarity between them that suggested a prior relationship.

We listened to his evidence with a sense of foreboding. James Murray would not call a witness unless the witness was going to make the prosecution case better. But Wierda and I were not entirely unprepared. During many hours of preparation we had taken turns to play devil's advocate, asking 'what-if' questions of ourselves. 'If we were prosecuting this case,' I had asked Wierda, 'how would we respond to the expert evidence of Doctor Shapiro and Marianne Schlebusch?'

We had agreed on the answer. If we were in Murray's shoes we would call a State psychiatrist or a lecturer in psychology in rebuttal and we would attack the defence expert's opinions at their weakest link, the facts on which the opinions might be based. The litigation textbooks made it plain: an expert opinion is only as good as the facts upon which it is based.

Since no State psychiatrist had examined Labuschagne before the trial – it could only be done with our consent or if we had raised insanity as a defence – we knew that Professor Nienaber's evidence would have to be restricted to general observations and such conclusions as could be drawn from the evidence given in court.

Nienaber spoke with the confidence of a man of superior academic qualifications in familiar surroundings. Murray addressed him with deference throughout. There was an instant rapport between Professor Nienaber and Judge van Zyl. Pretoria was not a very large city and the power of the executive government seated there was held in relatively few, albeit very powerful, hands. Murray was Deputy Attorney-General and his witness was Professor and Head of the Department of Psychiatry at the medical school of the University of Pretoria. I wondered if they were both members of the ultra-secret Afrikaner Broederbond, the organisation that held ultimate sway in all political matters. The thought crossed my mind that the Judge might be a member too, but after thinking about it for a while I dismissed the idea. No self-respecting judge would compromise his independence and objectivity – perceived as well as real – in such an obvious, even crass, fashion. Maybe, but maybe not, a sceptical little voice whispered in my paranoid ear. I watched Judge van Zyl very closely after that, but he treated the witness exactly as he had all the others, with courtesy and with experienced even-handedness. The Judge gave nothing away. No witness would know whether the Judge believed him or not; not before the judgment was delivered anyway.

The witness, however, worried me a little. Why had he winked at me? That was a bit cheeky of him. What did he know that I didn't?

When Murray neared the end of the examination-in-chief I whispered in Wierda's ear that he would have to cross-examine Professor Nienaber.

We listened to the rest of the evidence. The attack on our case was based on a few factors, each explained in laborious detail and with reference to scientific papers, most of them written by the good professor or one of his many protégés, but it all boiled down to this: First, he asked rhetorically, why, if the work was so stressful, other escorts did not break down and go out and murder people. I noticed that he had used the word *murder*, not kill. Second, he said that we had only the defendant's word for what had happened at the reservoir. Road rage was a common phenomenon worldwide and the facts fit that scenario perfectly. Third, he cautioned that the defendant's claimed amnesia could be feigned, but even if it was real it probably was retrograde amnesia. The mind wiped out unpleasant memories after the event, he explained. And the minds of highly principled people were more efficient in wiping out such memories. So that was not necessarily a case of such a total breakdown of the mind that the defendant had acted in a state of automatism. Last, he said, the accuracy with which the defendant had fired the thirteen shots gave the lie to the defence experts' opinions; no man could shoot with that degree of accuracy while acting as an automaton.

When Murray sat down I stood up immediately.

'May it please M'Lord, my Learned Friend Mr Wierda will cross-examine this witness.'

'Very well,' said Judge van Zyl.

Wierda and I had spent hours working out lines of cross-examination, taking turns in the roles of counsel and witness. You could attack an expert witness on limited grounds, their expertise, their methodology, the facts upon which their conclusions were based, or their reasoning. The last one was a tough row to hoe because experts always knew more than the cross-examiner and could easily make a fool of you. We had decided to stick to the methodology and some isolated facts. Now it was up to Wierda to implement our plan.

I moved over for him to get to the microphone and sat down in his chair. I caught the professor looking at me, a slight frown on his face. It was the perfect opportunity to return his wink. I opened my notebook to keep track of the cross-examination. This is going to be fun, I thought to myself.

'Professor,' said Wierda without further ado, 'you did not at any time conduct a clinical interview with the defendant, did you?'

Professor Nienaber looked at the Judge. 'I was not given an opportunity to examine him.'

'You did not ask for one either, did you?' Wierda said tartly.

'Correct,' said the professor as if he were marking a student's script.

Wierda was tougher than I had thought. 'But you would have liked to, wouldn't you?'

It was a beautiful question. If the professor said yes, Wierda would have him on the ropes and we would be able to undermine his opinions in our closing argument. And if the professor said no, we could argue convincingly that his methods were unscientific.

But Professor Nienaber was also tougher than I had anticipated. 'I would have liked an opportunity to examine the defendant but assumed that I would not be given access to him. I therefore did the best I could with the material at my disposal. You know, M'Lord,' he said as if they were old friends, 'in psychiatry we often have to make diagnoses without being able to interview or examine the subject.'

'And that's what you did here, isn't it?' suggested Wierda. 'You assumed you would not be given access to the defendant, and you therefore based your opinions on the evidence you heard and the observations you made here in court, is that right?'

'Correct.'

'Because you did not have access to the defendant you did not have an opportunity to conduct the usual tests you would otherwise have done, is that right?'

'Correct.'

'You did not conduct a neurological examination of the defendant to test his brain function?'

'No, and I would not have done so either. That can only be done by a neurologist.'

'Indeed,' said Wierda, 'and you did not conduct an IQ test, did you?'

'Correct.'

'You did not conduct the usual battery of psychometric tests, nor have you seen the results of the battery of tests conducted by Miss Schlebusch, I assume?'

'Correct.'

'You did not conduct the Minnesota Multi-phasic Personality Inventory?' Wierda read the words carefully from his notes. 'Did you?'

'No.'

'Nor the Millon Clinical Multi-axial Inventory Test?'

'No.'

'Nor did you complete the 16 Personality Factor Questionnaire?'

'M'Lord, I have already said that I did not have access to the defendant. How could I have conducted these tests?'

But Judge van Zyl didn't come to the professor's assistance. Wierda was undeterred.

'Nor the Thematic Apperception Test or the South African Wechsler Adult Intelligence Scale?' he asked.

'Correct,' said the professor. 'And, M'Lord,' he added with a trace of sarcasm in his tone, 'the Wechsler is the IQ test Mr Wierda referred to earlier. It is not a second intelligence test.'

Wierda didn't bat an eyelid. 'These are the tests you would have preferred to conduct for a proper evaluation of the defendant if he had been assigned to you as a patient, are they not?'

'Correct.' The professor returned to marking scripts.

'The result is that you could not arrive at any positive diagnosis of your own, am I right? You were reduced to making the best you could with the evidence you heard here and your own observations in court? And in the process the only option open to you was to fault the opinions of Dr Shapiro and Miss Schlebusch, was it not?'

Wierda had put the question in such a way that it was argumentative, but James Murray didn't object. I glanced in his direction. He and Niemand were both taking notes.

'Well, I question the correctness of their conclusions. I don't think they are correct,' said Professor Nienaber. 'I am here to help the Court understand their evidence.'

It was time to get something positive from the witness and Wierda did it superbly.

'Professor Nienaber, you do not deny the existence of the condition described as a catathymic crisis, do you?' he asked.

'No, but I would prefer to call it a dissociated state.' He looked up at the Judge. 'May I add something, please?'

'Yes,' said Judge van Zyl.

'I would like to add that I disagree with the defence categorisation of the condition as a catathymic crisis. We use that term only when a personal relationship is involved, and when events within that relationship give rise to the complete breakdown of the psyche. I would agree that such a condition is similar to a dissociated state, but the mechanisms giving rise to them are different.'

'Fair enough,' said Wierda, 'we don't have to debate those issues here. But it means that there is a separation of intellect and emotion to the extent that an individual's mental equilibrium is overwhelmed and his or her logical thinking is so disrupted that the individual does not act consciously.'

'May be disrupted,' the professor corrected. 'The individual who experiences a catathymic crisis or who is in a dissociated state may not do anything at all. So it is not correct to assume that such a person will do something wrong.'

'Professor Nienaber,' said Wierda, 'you don't deny the existence of the phenomenon of a catathymic crisis as a condition known to medical science and you don't dispute Miss Schlebusch's evidence that it has the eight known features she explained in the course of her evidence, do you?'

'No, M'Lord, but I do dispute her conclusion that it was present in the current case.'

This was exactly what I didn't want to happen. The additional question had given the professor an opportunity to strike a blow against us.

When Wierda didn't immediately respond to the last answer, the Judge intervened. 'Mr Wierda, if you are going to another topic, perhaps we could take the short adjournment now?'

'As M'Lord pleases,' said Wierda. The Court adjourned for tea.

I went to speak to Pierre de Villiers. He had a batch of papers for us, but I cut him short.

'What was that about?' I asked.

'What do you mean?' he said.

'I mean you sitting next to the other side's expert witness all the time and talking to him like you are old friends.'

Pierre shook his head and smiled. 'So who's paranoid now?' He pointed at me. 'It's you, buddy.'

Wierda, who had joined us now, intervened. 'What have the two of you been talking about?'

Pierre played hard to get, a trace of mirth still present in his voice. 'You mean the professor and I?' he asked.

'Yes, the fucking two of you,' said Wierda, the stress evident in his voice.

Pierre pressed a batch of papers against Wierda's chest. 'I have nothing to say to you,' he said to Wierda.

Then he took me by my arm and pulled me aside. We went into the atrium under the cupola. 'He's the psychiatrist who treated me at 1 Mil,' he said.

I sighed. 'I hope the two of you haven't been discussing the case.'

Pierre looked disappointed. 'As a matter of fact we have.'

'What did you tell him?' I asked.

'It's not what I told him. It's what he told me.'

'Fuck off, Pierre,' I said, suddenly tired of his game. I was beginning to sound like Wierda. 'Get to the point. What did he have to say?'

'He said he thought we were going to win.'

I looked at my brother-in-law long and hard.

'I'm not joking,' he said.

We returned to Wierda, who had been studying the documents Pierre had so unceremoniously handed to him. They gave us another line of cross-examination. We were too busy for the usual stroll to the Square and worked at the defence table. Every now and then we would ask Pierre a question and he would produce more information.

By the time the Court resumed Wierda was ready to question Professor Nienaber on his work at 1 Military Hospital and his treatment of soldiers who had returned from the war in Angola, but I vetoed the idea. Our case was not going to get any better with more cross-examination. We needed to finish on a high note, however, so I allowed Wierda to parade one of our themes.

'I have only a few more questions, M'Lord,' said Wierda. Judge van Zyl gave him the nod. The professor, buoyant from his little victory just before the break, smiled and leaned with his elbow on the side of the witness box.

'I take it, Professor Nienaber,' said Wierda, 'that you would agree that the execution process is by its nature traumatic for all its participants?'

'Yes,' said the professor, then checked himself and added with a little smile, 'to a greater or lesser degree, depending on your role in it and, obviously, most of all for the condemned man.'

Wierda seized on the unexpected opportunity. 'Jokes aside,' he said acidly, 'a multiple execution must be even more traumatic.' He looked at his notes. 'And so it must be also for the condemned men, not so?'

'Correct.'

'The more people you execute at once, the more traumatic it must be for everyone?'

'Yes, I said so.' Professor Nienaber was beginning to see where we were heading.

'And the amount of psychological trauma any individual would suffer in that situation would be specific to the make-up of that particular individual, would it not?'

'Correct.'

'Repeated exposure to executions would exacerbate the trauma, correct?'

'Correct.'

'And it would be much, much worse with multiple hangings on consecutive days, wouldn't it?'

'I'm sure it would be,' said the professor, minimising the effect of his concession with a bland answer.

Wierda's next question came from left field. 'Professor Nienaber,' he said with a smile, 'is it true that psychiatrists submit themselves to psychoanalysis every second year or so because they know that exposure over an extended period to other people's phobias and anguish may rub off on them?'

'Yes, that is so,' said the professor. 'May I explain?'

Before Wierda could answer, the Judge said, 'Yes, please do.'

'Thank you, M'Lord,' said the professor with exaggerated politeness and a slight bow in the direction of the bench. 'Psychiatrists have submitted themselves to analysis for a long time, but in recent years they have put a name to the phenomenon that causes such analysis to be desirable. It is called compassion fatigue. It is a known psychological condition suffered most commonly by health professionals like doctors, nurses, psychologists and, yes, psychiatrists.' He nodded an acknowledgement in Wierda's direction. 'It is common where the carers become victims of secondary traumatic stress disorder, another name for compassion fatigue, as a result of helping or wanting to help a traumatised patient. You could also call it vicarious traumatisation; you suffer because you watch someone else suffer.

'M'Lord,' he concluded, 'that's why we go through a cleansing process of analysis and counselling and do so regularly to get rid of the accumulated trauma of our patients' suffering.'

'And prison warders are in a similar position, aren't they, to suffer vicarious trauma as a result of their close relationship with the condemned prisoners and their daily exposure to their prisoners' suffering?'

It was a question we hadn't scripted, but there could only be one answer.

'Yes.'

'Does it surprise you then to hear that the defendant and the other prison warders, who by nature of their duties had to participate in executions, received no advance counselling, and received neither analysis nor treatment after the event?'

Professor Nienaber thought for a while. Wierda had him in a corner again, and again there could be only one answer. 'Yes, I'm a bit surprised at that, because the prisons usually make extensive use of analysis and counselling for prisoners.'

Wierda was ready to play one of our trumps. 'I suppose, Professor, that it would serve no purpose if I were to ask you if anyone has done scientific research to determine the effect of participating in multiple executions, day in and day out, on a young man of previously good character and exemplary behaviour.'

'M'Lord, I don't expect that anyone could do research of that nature; it would simply be impossible to reproduce the conditions prevailing at the prison.'

Wierda had established one of the fundamental points of our closing argument and he had done it with a witness called by the prosecution.

I distracted him with a meaningless note to allow the implications of the answer to sink in.

'Professor,' said Wierda after reading the note, 'I have a series of propositions to put to you in conclusion. Could you please tell me each time whether you agree or disagree with my proposition and add any explanations or elaborations you think fit?'

Then, without waiting for an answer, he put the first proposition.

'The warders chosen for duty as gallows escorts should have been profiled for their psychological suitability for the work they were required to do, do you agree?'

'I do.'

'And they should have been given counselling on a regular basis, do you agree?'

'Yes, I do.'

Wierda continued in the same vein. 'Even so, it is not a good idea that

428

the warders, who had to guard the condemned prisoners for months or years, should be involved in the execution process.'

'I agree.'

'The roles should be separated so that those who guard the prisoners are not involved in the execution process, do you agree?'

'I do, M'Lord, you cannot be a shepherd and a butcher at the same time.'

I tugged at Wierda's robes to get his attention.

'M'Lord,' he asked, 'may I confer with my Leader before I sit down?'

Judge van Zyl nodded absently, scribbling a note without looking up.

Wierda leaned down so that I could speak in his ear, but I made a show of handing him a note. He played along and held it up, reading it slowly. All eyes were on us.

'Sit down,' I whispered to Wierda.

'No further questions, thank you,' Wierda said with exaggerated courtesy and sat down.

When James Murray had completed a perfunctory re-examination we immediately departed for the reservoir, ostensibly for Labuschagne to point out the various positions as far as he could remember them, but in reality for me to test a theory that had been growing in my mind. I made sure all three expert witnesses came along.

'I know why you did it,' said Wierda as we were going down the steps at the front entrance on the way to his car.

'Did what?' I asked.

'Let me cross-examine Nienaber. You wanted to minimise the impact of his evidence by pretending that it was unimportant. Then, for the same reason you pretended not to listen to my cross-examination, to undermine his opinions.'

'Nah,' I said, 'I just thought it was time for you to do some work in the case.'

The cross-examination had gone well, and we were in reasonably good spirits.

'Fuck!' Wierda exclaimed. A woman going up the steps gave him an angry look. 'I haven't done any other work the last six weeks. I have had to pass one good brief after another on to my colleagues. And you say I haven't been working on this case. I've been doing nothing else!'

I elbowed him on his upper arm. 'I know,' I said, 'my own practice is no more than a distant memory now.' I thought of Liesl again, and our sons. I wanted to go home very badly.

Wierda drove us to the reservoir. 'Thanks for having my car washed,' he said. 'Now it's bound to fall apart.' I looked at him, and he added, 'It was held together by good old Pretoria dirt and grime, and you've washed it all away.'

I myself had a lot of Pretoria dirt and grime on me by now, but not the kind you can wash away. I thought about what the professor had said about accumulated trauma and the need for cleansing, and wondered if lawyers were also at risk of suffering from compassion fatigue.

Magazine Hill & Maximum Security Prison 59

When we arrived at the reservoir, the minibus and the bakkie we had arranged for the experiment were already in position and the Warrant Officer was standing next to his car in the shade of a tree. Judge van Zyl drove up in his Mercedes with his Assessors. He negotiated the last stretch carefully and parked off the track behind Wierda's car. James Murray and Sanet Niemand turned up and next the handcuffed Leon Labuschagne arrived in the back of a police van. The cell sergeant was there to look after him. To my surprise Professor Nienaber arrived with Dr Shapiro and Marianne Schlebusch; they were chatting amicably. Birds of a feather, I thought.

It was hot and cicadas were screeching mercilessly in the trees on both sides of the track. Gnats swarmed around us and got trapped in sweaty folds. Still, everyone looked glad to be out in the open in the spring sunshine, the brooding atmosphere of Court C some distance away down the hill. We huddled around Judge van Zyl, but I noticed the Warrant

Officer standing on his own in the shade of a tree, his eyes hidden by military-style reflective sunglasses. His arms were folded across his chest. He was close enough to observe but too far to be a party to the immediate events.

'Right,' said the Judge. He must have been hot in his suit. 'Who's going to begin?'

We might not have been in the courtroom but the events at the inspection were as much part of the evidence as the evidence given from the witness box.

I stepped forward and stood directly in front of Judge van Zyl. He was flanked by the two Assessors. 'Judge, I'll take the lead, if you don't mind. I would like the defendant to stand next to the door of his bakkie so that we can measure the exact distance from there to the left side, to the sliding door of the minibus.'

We turned to watch as Labuschagne was brought out of the police van. He walked over to the bakkie. The handcuffs had been removed, but the cell sergeant stayed at his side.

'And now I would like the defendant to point at the sliding door of the minibus,' I said.

Labuschagne raised his right hand and pointed, not as you would do with a pistol in your hand, but sufficiently close to it for our purposes. I had not told him the purpose of the inspection and he looked sheepish. I had not seen him in natural light before. His skin was pallid from lack of exposure to the sun.

'Can we agree that the distance from the defendant's hand to the side of the minibus is no more than four or five paces?' I asked. Then I stepped over and dramatically paced out the distance. 'Three and a half to four and a half meters, I would say,' said the Judge. His Assessors nodded. 'Did anyone bring a tape measure?'

No one had, but the Judge's estimate was accurate enough for my purposes.

'Anything else?' asked the Judge.

I stood right next to the sliding door of the minibus. Then, without warning, I gripped the door handle firmly and opened the sliding door.

Kellunck! Shoosh! Whabam!

Labuschagne groaned and fell over backwards instantly as if he had been shot, his legs pulled up into his chest and his hands clamped over his eyes.

He calmed down as suddenly as he had fallen over. The atmosphere at the reservoir was electric. Marianne Schlebusch rushed over and put her arm around Labuschagne's shoulders. She and the cell sergeant led him back to the police van. He was crying. I had a lump in my throat. I was glad his sister wasn't there to see what I had done.

I heard a car start up behind me, and the next moment the Warrant Officer sped away from the reservoir in a cloud of dust, his jaw clenched in a deathly white face. We stared after him until he disappeared around the first bend of the winding track. No one spoke until Labuschagne had also been taken away, handcuffed as before, in the police van. This time they put him in the front, where he sat squashed between the driver and the cell sergeant.

Another car started up and then stood there idling. It was Professor Nienaber's and he had Dr Shapiro and Marianne Schlebusch with him in the car.

'Why did you bring us here?' Judge van Zyl was angry. I felt Wierda's eyes on me. When he had brought me to the reservoir months earlier he had been the one taking risks. I owed him an explanation.

'There is something to these doors, Judge,' I said.

I demonstrated by opening and closing the sliding door three times. The sound it made when it closed was the same as when it opened.

Kellunck! Shoosh! Whabam!

We stood in a row staring into the interior of the empty minibus, the sun behind us and our shadows on the ground in the exact positions in which the police had found the bodies of the seven young men of the Diepsloot Karate Club.

I counted the shadows. There were seven, of different heights and textures on the uneven ground, devoid of class or distinction, reduced to dark outlines in the dirt; the Judge and two Assessors, the two prosecutors and Wierda and I.

Calm slowly settled over the scene at the reservoir.

'Fine,' said the Judge. 'James, is there anything you want to point out now that we are here?'

Murray's shadow moved out of the line and said, 'Yes, we would like the Court to take particular note of the winding and undulating nature of the track leading to the reservoir.'

'And the rocks lying in the roadway too,' said Niemand.

The dust of the Warrant Officer's hasty departure still hung in the air.

Judge van Zyl made a note. 'Yes, we were just talking about that in the car coming down.'

When no one said anything further, he added, 'Shall we reassemble at court then?'

I told him that I had one further request, to return to the gallows room, but that it would have to be done in the absence of our client. After explaining what I wanted to do, we got back into our cars and headed down the hill.

Five minutes later we were at the front entrance of Maximum. We insisted that the warder on duty in the guardhouse call the Major.

'We need to see the gallows again,' explained the Judge.

The Major looked at the women, but before he could voice his objection Judge van Zyl cut him short. 'The women are coming with us.'

The Major led us through.

This time we had caught them by surprise and the prison was in its normal daily routine, not the inspection mode in which it had been when we had come for our first inspection a week earlier.

There were prisoners in the corridors with rags tied to their feet, shuffling to and fro and polishing the floors in the process. They stood heads down with their backs to the wall and did not make eye contact as we filed past, but I sensed that they were glancing at us under their eyebrows and in their peripheral vision. Their anguish was palpable, their eyes perhaps searching for the Sheriff with his folders of letters from the State President.

The Major led us straight to the door leading to the staircase with its fifty-four steps and briefly stood aside for the warder with the keys to let us through. I watched the others disappearing ahead of me into the stairwell. Only the warder with the keys and I remained at the foot of the steps. Then the door behind me slammed shut and I heard the key turn with the rattle of the tumblers in the heavy lock. I felt alone and suddenly very afraid.

I reluctantly put my foot on the first step. My foot felt heavy, sticking to the floor. I put my hand on the inner guardrail. It was cold and I jerked my hand away when I remembered its purpose, to serve as a handhold for the warders when they had to drag reluctant prisoners up to the gallows. The staircase was narrow and the wall on my left and the steel mesh on my right pressed inwards; the only escape was upwards. I looked up. The shuffling sounds of the others' footsteps drifted down towards me. Vertigo and claustrophobia overwhelmed me and I froze on the spot.

If Wierda hadn't come down for me I would have stayed there.

'What's wrong?' he asked. 'They are waiting for you.'

When I looked up there was light at the top. I held out my arm and Wierda took my elbow and led me all the way up. It felt like an eternity before we reached the ante room before the gallows. I saw that the door to the gallows chamber was open. I took a deep breath and went and stood against the wall under the window.

The gallows machine was primed but there were no ropes attached to the beam overhead. I could smell fresh machine oil. There were six hanging ropes, coiled and ready, on the table next to me. A sheet with names and measurements lay on the table next to the ropes. It was as Labuschagne had said: I could smell the blood on them. I moved a few paces away from the ropes.

'What do you want to show us?' asked Judge van Zyl without ceremony.

I stood with the flat of my hand against the wall behind my back. I asked the Major to push the lever forward. My voice was shaky. The Major pulled out the safety pin and moved slowly to the front of the trapdoors. He put his hand on the handle of the lever and engaged the clutch gingerly as he looked over his shoulder at the Judge. When there was no countermand from Judge van Zyl he slowly pushed the lever until the trapdoors suddenly disappeared in a thunderous *Kellunck! Shoosh! Whabam!*

The wall shuddered under my hand.

We stood in silence for a long time, looking into the darkness of the pit.

'I think we should get back to court,' the Judge said pensively.

We followed the Major down. On the way out we could hear singing behind the walls.

When we got to the guardhouse at the front the Major called me aside. He was angry.

'We have six men to hang tomorrow; they are in the Pot. You can hear them singing, and you've come to muck about with the gallows. Now the whole prison is tense. No one is going to sleep tonight because they think we are doing secret and unscheduled executions.'

I apologised and explained why I had done it.

The Major nodded, but did not say anything.

'I am defending a man's life,' I added, 'and I'll go as far as I have to in order to save him from the killing machine you've just shown us.'

We stood facing each other on the hard concrete next to the summer garden. The walls of the prison towered above us, the sun against a clear blue sky beating down on us so that we had to squint. Cicadas were screaming in the hillock overlooking the complex and in the jacarandas in the parking area in front of the main gate, drowning out the singing from A Section. There was birdsong in the summer garden, but the heat had forced the animals into the shade.

'I understand,' he said eventually, 'and I hope you win. He was one of my best men.'

He used the past tense and I felt a cold drop of sweat run down my spine into the waistband of my trousers. What did it mean to be a good man in a place like this?

The guard at the main gate was humming the same tune as the prisoners while he signed me out.

I caught up with Wierda in the parking lot outside. The hair on my arms and the back of my neck were still standing on end, but we had found our trigger event.

The Warrant Officer was still nowhere to be seen.

When we entered Court c I could sense that something was wrong. James Murray was speaking in a hushed voice to a uniformed policeman. He would not meet my eyes. The Judge and Assessors walked in and took their seats. The policeman bowed and left.

'Yes, Mr Murray,' said Judge van Zyl.

Murray fidgeted with his papers. I noticed that his hands were shaking. The usual composure with which he had handled all the incidents of the case thus far was gone.

'I have no further witnesses. I am not calling the Warrant Officer,' he announced.

The Judge interrupted before Murray could explain his change of plan. 'Why not? I thought I had made it clear that I was going to allow his evidence to be given in rebuttal, and even that I was keen to hear it.'

I looked over at the Warrant Officer's seat. There was no one there.

Murray resolved the mystery quickly and without emotion. 'He's dead, M'Lord,' he said. 'He died while we were at the inspection in the prison.'

No one spoke and there was no movement. I suppose we had all been caught unawares. We had spoken about death and killing and of the dead for days now, as if death were a foreigner, but it had come to visit us in the most obvious way by taking one of the principal actors in our own play of life and death. There was a perceptible increase in the tension in the courtroom.

'How did it happen?' asked the Judge. 'He was with us just an hour or so ago. I remember seeing him at the reservoir.' He turned to his Assessors for confirmation.

Murray's answer was terse. 'His car collided with a bridge, M'Lord.'

When no one responded he added, 'The police came to inform me a few minutes ago. There were no other cars involved. They showed me his identity document and told me that he was killed instantly.'

'Where did it happen?' asked the Judge.

'It was on the highway to Johannesburg, M'Lord.'

We would learn later that the Warrant Officer's car had collided at high speed with the stanchions of a bridge over the highway. According to witnesses there was no apparent reason for his car to have left the road and no sign of avoiding action on his part. There were no brake marks and no signs of physical breakdown that could have caused his car to veer off the road as it had.

'I'm very sorry to hear that,' said the Judge at last.

There was another lengthy silence before he spoke again. 'Please convey my and my Assessors' condolences to his family.'

Murray nodded dutifully. 'We shall do so, M'Lord.'

'Shall we adjourn to tomorrow for closing argument then?' suggested the Judge.

Murray shook his head. 'If it pleases M'Lord, we are ready to argue now.'

Judge van Zyl turned to the defence table. 'Are you ready to proceed?'

'We are, M'Lord.' I remained standing. 'But we need to recall one of the expert witnesses to explain the significance of the events at the reservoir and at the prison during this morning's inspection. That should not take more than a few minutes,' I added.

'Call your witness,' he said and picked up his pen.

I called Marianne Schlebusch to the witness box and, as soon as she was ready, I asked the one question that remained.

'Miss Schlebusch, could you please explain the significance of the events at the reservoir and in the gallows room?'

'Yes,' she said. 'We have found the trigger event, M'Lord.'

'Please go slowly,' said Judge van Zyl. 'I want to take notes.'

'Yes, M'Lord.' She measured her words in small bundles, at dictation pace. 'The trigger event had three components, each consisting of a separate stimulus. Each was significant enough on its own, but cumulatively their weight or influence was far greater. The first was the sound of the sliding door of the minibus, reminding the defendant of the opening of the trapdoors. The second was the men rushing out of the minibus, resembling the falling of the bodies after the trapdoors have opened. The third was the white headbands or bandannas they wore. In those conditions they would have resembled the white hoods used during the execution process.'

The image was stronger than the words I have to describe it.

'It was staged, a setup,' Sanet Niemand hissed, but James Murray did not cross-examine.

Marianne Schlebusch took her seat behind me.

When I sat down Wierda handed me a note. It was from Pierre de Villiers: *Why was he driving away from the court? And why was he going so fast?*

Palace of Justice

60

James Murray kept his argument simple – almost certainly in keeping with the adage that if you have a good case you must keep it simple. It was a solid, technical argument with no obvious flaws.

The defendant fired thirteen shots, he said, and every single one of them was fired with such deadly accuracy that it hit the target in the vital spot, the upper chest or neck.

He asked the Judge and Assessors to look again at the autopsy photographs and pointed out, one photograph at a time, where the bullets had struck. One bullet had gone through a raised forearm first; its victim must have been in a defensive pose, he demonstrated with care.

The shell-casings were distributed over a wide area, he pointed out. He waited for the Court to find the markings on the scene plan and rattled some of the shell-casings in his palm. The defendant must have moved around between shots, Murray said, while he poured the shell-casings from one hand to the other. Murray held up the ballistics report and reminded the Court that the defence had not disputed its contents.

Thus, he concluded, the accuracy of the shooting and that fact that the defendant had moved around from target to target proved beyond reasonable doubt that his mind was fully functional, that he could not have been in a state of automatism.

It was murder, said Murray, it was murder seven times over. The Court should declare it to be such, he said, so that the scales could be brought back into equilibrium again.

The argument was, of course, not quite as simple or as short as that. Murray and Niemand had prepared a lengthy written argument dealing comprehensively with salient points of law and the anticipated defence argument. They discussed the facts and the evidence, the experts' opinions and their reasoning, the usual legal technicalities.

The Judge didn't ask a single question during Murray's argument and I saw more than one member of the media nodding in agreement every time he made a telling point:

Road rage
Time to reconsider actions
Familiarity with firearm
Expert marksman
Herded victims to a secluded area
No provocation at reservoir
Careful arrangement of bodies a message or statement
Fled when engine would not start
Went into hiding
Gave no explanation when confronted by police
Defence a concocted self-serving pack of lies
Willingly participated in escort duties
Physically participated in the act of killing, pulling prisoners up, some twice
Not a good witness, evasive, unresponsive
Uncaring attitude, no genuine remorse
Reaction to minibus sliding door staged
A far-fetched unconvincing effort to save his life

Wierda and I had considered all of these points during our preparation. Individually they didn't amount to much, but cumulatively they came down on our client's neck with the weight of lead.

It had been a mistake not to eat anything at lunch. My blood sugar levels were getting low and I wasn't sure that I would be able to sustain a lengthy argument. The events at the prison earlier in the day also preyed on my mind. I tried not to think of the six men waiting in the Pot as their time ran out.

Wierda and I had decided long before the trial started that we would keep our argument simple; in fact, that had been the cornerstone of our trial tactics. Murray had to keep his argument simple because he had a good case; we had to keep ours simple because we had a bad one.

We had two main difficulties: we had to make a difficult case look easy, and we had to have an answer for each of the prosecution's most telling points. An argument that does not answer the opponent's best points is worthless because an argument is never judged on its own; it is always measured against the opposing argument. It may be different in mathematics, but that's how it is in law.

So we started by dealing with the main points. The evidence of Dr Shapiro and Miss Schlebusch proved, I argued, that the degree of accuracy could be achieved by a person acting in a state of sane automatism where the action concerned is in the nature of a conditioned response. And we had good evidence from the school principal, backed up by the school's yearbook, that the defendant had been a crack shot, even at competition level. We also know that he had received combat training with the very same pistol he had in his lap during the drive down the Old Johannesburg Road.

Secondly, I said that the argument about the positions of the shell-casings could not withstand any serious scrutiny. There was no scientific support for the prosecutors' contention.

Judge van Zyl interrupted me. 'But the ballistics report is undisputed.'

That was true, but I had to point out that it reflected where the shell-casings were found after the event, not how they had got there.

'You've lost me,' said the Judge.

I offered to demonstrate. I called for the scene plan and asked Sanet

Niemand for the shell-casings. I rattled a handful of them like dice in my hand, just as James Murray had done. I waited until all eyes in the room were trained on my hand; then I casually leaned over my lectern, held my arm out at shoulder level and opened my fist. The shell-casings dropped onto the threadbare carpet and bounced away in different directions.

I watched the Judge and Assessors closely. They were too experienced to show what they thought, but the members of the media could not hide their excitement. It was the usher's job to recover the shell-casings, but he found all seven of them, some up to three metres apart.

So much for the theory proposed by the prosecution, I said, wiping the sweat from my brow. I stole a glance at Labuschagne; he was taking no interest in the argument. I took a good swig from the water glass before I was ready to continue.

We still had to deal with our best points.

I started with a question, a dangerous gambit, but very effective when it works. The technique is to answer your question quickly before someone can come up with a clever answer.

What explanation did the prosecution theory offer for Labuschagne's actions at the reservoir? It didn't make sense when you took into account his exemplary past. The prosecutors contended that they didn't have to prove a motive, and they were correct in law, but what explanation could there be that was supported by real evidence before the Court? It didn't make sense, and we were looking for an answer that made sense, I argued. The law did not require a motive, but logic did.

I didn't point out to the Judge that I had just read the cases of thirty-two murderers and that their actions didn't make any sense to me either.

Conversely, I said, the defence's theory was backed up by the evidence of the defendant and the opinions of eminent experts; even the prosecution's rebuttal witness had supported the defence's case to some extent.

I felt strangely energetic during the argument, as if I could go on forever. But we had to keep it simple.

An acquittal might be unpopular and might even be uncomfortable to lawyers; after all, we liked to think that what we practised in a courtroom was science, not voodoo, and that we could achieve results that, when they are measured objectively, were accurate and just, I said to the Judge. It was the Court's job to separate the science of the law and of medicine from populist beliefs and emotions. Where would Tsafendas have been, I asked, if the Court had acceded to the public demand for his blood? Decide the case on the evidence, I challenged them; the defence has no fear of a verdict derived from the evidence before the Court.

During the argument the Judge peppered me with questions that were getting progressively more difficult to answer. Who carried the burden of proof when you had a special defence like this? Wasn't it for the defence to prove the defence on a balance of probability? What if we didn't believe him? What if we found his evidence unreliable in important respects?

I watched the Assessors carefully to gauge their reactions to my submissions, but they gave nothing away.

I decided to try another approach.

'M'Lord and gentlemen Assessors,' I began, 'there is a question that remains unanswered. How did this young man go from a good Christian home and a good school in *your* town to the dock in *your* court?'

The Judge avoided my eye and would not, perhaps could not, answer my question. His silence emboldened me.

'What does it take,' I asked, 'to pull a man up by the rope and to drop him down and to hear his neck break? How does it feel when you have to pull him up a second time, to ensure that he dies quickly? What goes through your mind when you stand there struggling with the weight of the squirming prisoner, someone to whom you have read Bible texts, waiting for the Warrant Officer to count to three so that you can drop him to his death?'

I took a deep breath and spoke very softly. 'What compelled a young man from a Christian home in your city to participate in something as macabre as that? How did it get to that for Leon Labuschagne?'

I didn't wait for answers. I found the document I was looking for and asked them to look at Exhibit G. At first neither the Judge nor his Assessors could find it, but the registrar recovered their copies from under several files and papers on the bench.

'What's the purpose of this?' asked Judge van Zyl. His tone was un-sympathetic and sceptical.

'I'll elaborate in a minute, if it pleases M'Lord.' The legal niceties required him to give me a chance to present my argument. To his credit he allowed me to speak without further interruptions but I saw him put the exhibit face down on the bench before he sat back and folded his arms.

As a counterpoint I held my own copy of Exhibit G higher and kept it there, right in front of my face and between me and the bench, the top of the sheet a centimetre or two below my line of vision.

'This extract from the Death Sentence Register might look to us like just another list of names and dates and numbers, but to Leon Labuschagne the names on this list were real people.'

I turned the exhibit around so that the writing faced the bench. 'The names on this list were people who entered the defendant's life. Their lives became intimately and irreversibly linked to his.'

Judge van Zyl must have misunderstood the direction I was taking and said, 'This is not the time or the place for a debate on the death penalty.'

I agreed with him and said so, disavowing any intention to make submissions on that issue.

'The list is incomplete,' I said abruptly. 'There is a name short.'

I turned the list over again. 'Oh, we know what happened to the names on the list,' I said. 'But let me remind the Court in any case.'

I had to be quick, because I didn't know how much longer the Judge's patience would last. I followed James Murray's example. The Judge could hardly let him list his best points but deny me the same opportunity.

They came in and were processed by admin – Labuschagne was part of their initiation

They were placed in cells – he was put at the door

He woke them up and saw that they were fed

They were taken to the showers – he was put at the door

They were taken out to the exercise yard – he stood in the sun watching them

They received visits from their family and lawyers – he stood and
   watched and listened

They moved from place to place – he had to search them, and touched
   them

He read their letters

He did Bible study with the ones who could not read, these men
   whose names are on the list

When I stopped I realised that I had raised the list above my head.
I put it down on the lectern. It had served its purpose. I had their
attention.

Wierda passed me the glass. I drank slowly, trying to regain my
strength.

'Then, when he had got to know them really well, he had to walk
with the Sheriff and tell them to *Pak!*

'And after that, he had to take some out to their families in the parking area, out into the sunlight, while the rest he had to take into the Pot,
and from there to the chapel, and to the gallows, and back to the chapel,
but this time in coffins marked only with a number.'

I waited for effect. None of the men on the bench was looking at
me. Even Wierda had become motionless, his incessant *tap tap tapping*
silenced for once.

'To us, to you and me,' I said, including the press and the prosecu-
tors in the sweep of my arm, 'to us the names on this list mean nothing.
They are like sheep, anonymous in the flock, devoid of identity. To Leon
Labuschagne they were real people.

'And some we made him kill with his own hands,' I concluded.

I took the list and read the names of the thirty-two men who had
been hanged in those last two weeks. I read them out fast, trying to do
it in one breath, in the order they appeared on the list:

Moatche Scheepers Klassop Marotholi Kodisang Busakwe
Mbambani Mpipi Mohapi Delport Wessels Harris Meiring Michaels
Japhta Swartbooi Botha Morgan Gcabashe Gcaba Mbele Rabutla

Phaswa Mokwena Mjuza Hansen Njele Mkumbeni Prins Leve Smit Maarman

I was out of breath. The Assessor on the right stirred and spoke quietly to Judge van Zyl. I took the opportunity to take another sip of water. My mouth was dry and my voice had become hoarse.

The Judge turned to me and asked the Assessor's question. 'You said there was a name missing from the list?'

'Yes,' I said. 'Leon Albert Labuschagne.'

It took them a moment to realise I was referring to the defendant.

The Judge exploded. 'That's ridiculous.'

'Ridiculous, M'Lord?' I responded, my voice rising. 'Ridiculous, when he spent his days locked in with them, when he was made to share every living moment of their last days with them, and then made to share even their dying with them?

'His name should be on the list because we have sentenced him to death as surely as we did the others. They were sent there after a trial and for capital offences. He was sent there for a minor disciplinary infraction!'

'That is a ridiculous submission,' Judge van Zyl said a second time. He was angry, but so was I.

'No,' I said, 'it is not ridiculous. What is ridiculous is the denial of what we have done to this man.' I pointed at Labuschagne. He, for once, was watching me.

'I need M'Lord and the gentlemen Assessors to pick up Exhibit G and to look at it. I need M'Lord to give it serious attention,' I added when the Judge didn't move.

He picked it up, reluctance in every gesture, but I was pleased to see that his Assessors had obeyed.

'Now let's give this document the attention it deserves,' I suggested. I counted the number of names on the schedule. 'There are fifty-one names on the list. Let me remind the Court what happened.'

'You don't need to remind me,' said Judge van Zyl. 'I can see from the list what happened to them.'

'Yes, I know we all know what happened to *them*, but it seems to me that we have forgotten what happened to Leon Albert Labuschagne.' I dragged the names out, Leon – Albert – Labuschagne.

The Judge was still antagonistic and I decided to make my submission to his Assessors. 'M'Lord, gentlemen, imagine the scene every time they called these men out. The defendant would stand next to them at the admin office, and he would stand there with them when they heard their fate. You go up, you go out. Your appeal succeeded, you go up.

'We made him stand next to these names, these men on the list, as the selection process was completed. We made him stand and watch as we selected the men for hanging from his flock.'

The Judge had given up trying to stop my rant.

'Tshuma, you go out. Moatche, you go into the Pot. Burger, you go with Tshuma. Scheepers, you go into the Pot. And you too, Wessels. And you, Labuschagne, you take Moatche to the Pot and come back quickly so that you can take Scheepers and Wessels to c Section. But let's take their measurements first.'

I didn't realise that I had sat down until I heard James Murray speak in reply. I didn't hear what he had to say either, I was too tired. Exhaustion overcame me.

In the rush of my heartbeat in my ears I thought I was hearing African voices, rising and falling in a plaintive, insistent cry for salvation.

When Murray had completed his reply to our argument, the Judge conferred very briefly with each of his Assessors and announced that the Court's judgment would be handed down at ten a.m. the next day.

I stayed in my seat, too exhausted to leave. I looked across and saw James Murray also sitting down while Sanet Niemand was packing up around him. James looked as tired as I was; he was spent.

The case was now a spider web of strands, each with its own tension and direction, but all apparently connected to the same centre. But where that centre was and how the spider controlled its domain was unclear. They say that the truth is revealed by the litigation process, but I was no longer able to see it. Was the spider at the centre of the web perhaps the truth that all lawyers fear, the objective truth, what really happened, and not the truth as revealed by the evidence?

I felt a hand on my shoulder. It was Antoinette Labuschagne. 'Thank you,' she said. She had tears in her eyes.

I was too tired to cry with her.

That evening the Wierdas entertained Dr Shapiro to dinner. It was a social engagement I couldn't avoid. He had flown halfway across the globe and had sacrificed a week of his time to give us the benefit of his expert insights and experience. We owed him a great debt of gratitude and entertaining him when we were tired was a small price to pay. Marianne Schlebusch had a prior engagement at her university and her seat was empty.

Wierda and his wife were impeccable hosts and served a variety of traditional dishes matched to local wines. The red was a Rust en Vrede. Rest and Peace. I had too much of the wine.

The talk around the table turned to the history of Pretoria. The American said that he wanted to visit the Voortrekker Monument before he caught his flight back to Los Angeles; he had read about the monument and its place in the Afrikaner psyche in James Michener's *The Covenant*.

'I would like to pay it a visit,' he said. 'I've always wondered what those Afrikaners are really like.'

'Oh,' said Wierda, 'I think you might bump into one but never know.' There was just the faintest of smiles on his lips. His wife looked down at the tablecloth. I drank more of their wine.

Dr Shapiro wanted to know about the men who had been hanged between 26 November and 10 December 1987. He and Wierda revisited them all, looking for common patterns and explanations. Wierda, on the other hand, wanted to know more about Los Angeles and the death penalty debate in the States. Would those men have been sentenced to death in California? Wierda asked finally. You bet, said Dr Shapiro, but they would have died of old age before their appeals had been exhausted.

I was poor company at dinner. I tried to keep up with the conversation, but I found that I had lost interest; perhaps I was just too tired to take part in the debate. I had depleted my allocation of physical and emotional energy.

In the midst of the debate I heard Dr Shapiro say, 'One hundred and sixty-four in twelve months, and of those, twenty-one in three days. That must be a record.'

Wierda became defensive. 'What's wrong with that?' He argued from behind the rim of his glass.

'Look,' said Wierda, 'you just don't understand. I know you are against the death penalty, but there is no way that we can function without it here. Even the African population want it, not only here but in every other African country.'

'But that's my point,' said the American. 'That is an outdated and primitive attitude.'

Wierda was speechless for a while. I saw his face turn white. When he spoke again there was a hiss in his tone.

'You think of grand theories and he,' Wierda pointed at me, 'he makes lists of the prisoners we hanged and he studies the names in the execution registers, but who makes lists of the victims of these men? Eh? And who keeps a register of the victims?'

Dr Shapiro appeared startled at Wierda's vehemence. I decided to keep out of their argument.

'Come on,' said Wierda, 'let's look at the facts of a few cases and you can then tell me whether the victim was treated any better than the prisoner we hanged.'

Wierda didn't forget his manners and refilled our glasses. 'Take Moatche. He and his accomplices chased, then caught and stabbed their victim, many times. Do we remember that the poor man running for his life, struggling in vain as the knives cut into him, was William Matatule, an ordinary workaday man on his way home? We don't even know if he had a family, a wife and children. The case records don't even record that most basic information.'

Wierda's voice was shrill. 'My question is this: who remembers *his* suffering? Who holds a candle for Mr Matatule? Who organises a protest or writes a book about the victims?'

He answered his own question. 'No one. We don't care for the victims.'

When we didn't respond, Wierda went further, 'Do you want to talk about the suffering of Ginny Goitseone, spending an hour in the boot of the car as the killers drove from one place to the next in the middle of the night? Does anyone think of her despair, feeling the heat as the car burned, slowly suffocating as the oxygen ran out? Or any one of those women in the Cape being raped and strangled or having their heads bashed in with a stone? What about Mrs Webber, throttled, stabbed and beaten? And what about Mr Jeffreys, drowning in his own blood in the arms of his wife and son?'

I intervened when Wierda's wife came back from the kitchen with the dessert. 'I think that's enough on this morbid topic.'

After that I faded in and out of the conversation; I couldn't care less about concentration camps or the politicians of Pretoria. The words at the table washed over me without touching me, like the wine, and eventually I found comfort in the TV room with Wierda's children and their world of innocence and trust. I wrestled with a small boy for a place on the couch and before I knew it I was asleep with the boy lying partly over me. Wierda woke me gently and lifted his child off me. Then he took me back to my hotel. I was in no state to drive.

Back at the hotel I found that I couldn't sleep. The nap on Wierda's couch had taken the sleep out of me. I tried, but the sleep wouldn't come, so I ordered a bottle of L'Ormarins cabernet sauvignon from room service and packed my bags. I organised all of the files and documents I had in the hotel room into neat piles and put them in the stackers; everything was ready for collection by Roshnee's clerk the next morning.

I finished packing too quickly; I still could not sleep, and the bottle was far from empty. After lying in the dark with wide open eyes for a while I got up again and sat down at the small desk. The stackers with the files Pierre de Villiers had brought me stood in the corner; I eyed them while pouring another glass of wine.

Wierda's comment about my lists of the executed prisoners had hurt me, even though I had not said anything while a guest in his house. I looked at the files for a long time before I could work up the energy to pull out the first file. I started a new list and wrote their names out in full, as a penance.

William Matatule Ginny Goitseone Elizabeth Mokoena Wynand Dercksen Elizabeth Dercksen Girley Ndzube Johannes Modise Charmaine Opperman Joseph Mashiloane Sarah Ngobeni Johannes Bekker Geraldine Sauls Emily Patel Joseph Moliefe Anita Webber Catherina Hanekom Sharief Hendry Abner Monakali Timothy Jeffreys Pieter Grobler Sophia Shoch

I fell into a dreamless sleep after that. We had run our case. The Court was going to find Labuschagne guilty or not guilty. Nothing we could do now could affect the outcome. The process of washing the facts of the case from my memory banks had already started. I no longer cared about the case or the client; my job was done. I wanted the troublesome facts and details washed out of my memory.

The tension was still in every fibre of my body.

I was desperate to go home, but we still had to live through one more day of the trial.

Roshnee's clerk, a young man with a ponytail and an earring, arrived while I was still having breakfast and collected all the files and my luggage. I found his fawning ways quite irritating, his addressing me as advocate, as if it was a title or mode of address. But at least he was being polite and efficient.

The Judge kept us in Pretoria for another day. When Wierda and I arrived at court we found Roshnee on the steps. The usher was waiting for us in the foyer.

'The Judge wants to see you as soon as possible,' he said.

'Let's put our robes on first,' I said to Wierda, but the usher intervened. 'No, sir, you must come immediately.'

Roshnee carried our bags with our robes into court and Wierda and I followed the usher.

When we arrived at the Judge's chambers, James Murray and Sanet

Niemand were waiting at the door. Murray caught my eye and shrugged his shoulders, as if to say that he was as much in the dark as I was. We followed the usher in. The Judge had his Assessors with him.

'Morning,' said the Judge. 'I am sorry, but as you can see, I don't have enough seats.'

He had cleared his desk of other papers and the files and papers of our case now occupied every square centimetre of it. There were three piles, one in front of each of the men who were going to decide Leon Labuschagne's fate. The registrar sat at a small table next to the Judge, with a shorthand pad and a typewriter on the table in front of her. She was already dressed for court, but the Judge was still in his suit. The Assessors had half turned to face us, but apart from nodding to acknowledge our arrival, took no part in the discussion.

'It won't take long, anyway,' said the Judge. 'There is a slight complication. We won't be able to give judgment until tomorrow.'

My heart sank to my knees. I had hoped to be home that evening. Now we were going to have to stay another night.

James Murray had the presence of mind to ask if the Judge and his Assessors required further argument from us on any particular point, but the Judge waved the question aside.

'I'll come into court to remand the case to tomorrow.'

We nodded and turned to leave.

'There is no need for senior counsel to robe,' he said. 'Wierda and Niemand can appear.'

While Wierda and Niemand did the honours in court, James Murray and I stood outside in the atrium. We stood in silence, watching the other lawyers milling about with their files and briefcases and clients in tow. After a while the silence became embarrassing. Murray was not a talkative man. I looked up at the boy with the scales in the glasswork in the windows high up. His scales were even. The girl's pen was in the air. What verdict would she record?

'What do you think is going on?' I asked Murray.

He coughed behind his hand before he answered, his eyes on a clerk rushing past us on the way to the Chief Registrar's office. 'I think one of the Assessors may not agree with the proposed verdict. Or maybe the Judge doesn't agree with what they want to do.'

I nodded in agreement. 'Did you see the set of his jaw when he said that they were not ready? There is definitely something going on there. But you know him better than I do, what do you think?'

He smiled wanly. 'He's definitely not in a good mood. Maybe it is just as well that we don't have to appear before him today. He can be quite irascible when he's in a bad mood.'

I wasn't sure that I agreed with this assessment. If Judge van Zyl was not in a good mood he would not have called us in or extended us the courtesy of not having to robe to go into court. He could simply have entered the court and announced there that they weren't ready.

'Maybe they're just being careful, taking their time to write an appeal-proof judgment,' I finally suggested.

'Yes,' said Murray, 'but that should be bad news for you. They would have to take more time with a conviction than an acquittal.' He was alluding to the fact that a conviction could be taken on appeal but an acquittal was final.

We stood together, the battle fought and the outcome in the hands of others. It was, in a way, a release from further responsibility. We just had to see out the remaining time. I looked at my colleague. We had both won and lost many cases. It is difficult to work out why anyone would choose this profession where every case is a contest. We fight in someone else's cause, and when we win or lose it is the client who enjoys the benefit or feels the pain.

So we stood and waited, two old workhorses of the legal profession, so comfortable in our environment that we didn't need to fight with each other. Yet one of us was going to lose when the verdict was announced. To the outsider it might have appeared as if we didn't care about the outcome, but that impression would have been false. One of us was going to lose, and the trial would live with us forever.

When the others came out of the courtroom Wierda suggested that we fetch Dr Shapiro from his hotel and take him to the Voortrekker

Monument. It was better than sitting around in a hotel room and easier on the nerves.

But first I needed to see Labuschagne to brief him on the continuation of the trial. We had to be ready for every possibility. Wierda and I went through the courtroom and down the steps to Cell 6 to speak to him. We found him in tears, and he became hysterical when he saw us. The more we tried the less sense we could get out of him. The stress must have taken its toll and the delay in the announcement of the verdict must have been the last straw; he was inconsolable and I couldn't discuss what I had wanted to with him while he was in that condition. The cell sergeant offered to take him to the District Surgeon for medication. We offered to accompany Labuschagne, but the cell sergeant said that he couldn't allow that; the prisoner was his responsibility and his alone.

We waited in Cell 6 until they came for Labuschagne and we watched him being led down the narrow passage to a police van in the courtyard.

Roshnee and her clerk had no interest in the monument, so only Wierda and I went to the hotel to collect Dr Shapiro.

Voortrekker Monument   61

Dr Shapiro resumed his conversation about the death penalty with Wierda in the car on the way to the monument.

'We didn't talk much last night about the other variable in capital cases, the judges who impose the death sentence, did we?' said Dr Shapiro from the passenger's seat as we passed the prison complex in Potgieter Street.

'There are other variables too,' said Wierda, one eye on the traffic. 'Such as the fallibility of witnesses.'

I studied the American from the relative privacy of the back seat and wondered whether he would see Wierda's remark as a dig at him.

'Or the police,' I said quickly, to divert the point in an innocent direction.

'No,' said Dr Shapiro, 'I'm referring to the personalities and value systems of individual judges. Do they play a role here like the composition of a jury makes a difference in California?'

We drove in a long and steady curve around Magazine Hill. I craned my neck to follow the narrow road going uphill where the bakkie and the minibus had jostled and duelled their way to their fateful meeting at the reservoir. From the highway one would not suspect that there was a road up there; it was well shielded from view by the side of the hill and the vegetation. I was content to let the other two run the conversation.

Wierda took up the argument. 'There are at least three ways I can see in which a judge could affect the outcome of a capital case here: firstly, by making a mistake on the facts or the law; secondly, by having a predisposition in favour or against the death penalty; and thirdly, by not recommending clemency afterwards.'

'Are there any examples of those in the cases of these thirty-two?' asked our guest.

'Mistakes of law or fact are fixed by the Appeal Court,' said Wierda, 'and clemency is really the State President's domain.'

We reached the gate to Schanskop, the hill on which the Voortrekker Monument stands. I passed the money for the entry of one car and three adults to Wierda.

'You would have to be a fool to think that the disposition of a particular judge towards capital punishment does not play a role,' Wierda said once we were picking up speed again.

This was my first visit to the monument. It dominated the landscape for miles around and turned out to be far larger than I had imagined. The parking area at the foot of the koppie was relatively deserted and we made our way towards the entrance. A laager of sixty-four ox wagons carved from local granite encircles and protects the monument. We entered the laager through a black wrought-iron gate with an assegai motif symbolising the black enemy. We approached the bronze sculpture of a Voortrekker woman and her two children at the foot of the monument. On either side of her, black wildebeest representing the dangers of Africa were chiselled into the walls.

We entered through the solid teak doors at the main entrance and I took in the features of the massive hall. The floor was local marble, shiny and cold. The internal walls at ground level were covered by a frieze consisting of twenty-seven two-and-a-half-metre-high panels of Italian marble. Each frieze depicted a scene from the Great Trek. Four large arched windows of yellow Belgian glass filtered copious amounts of natural light into an eerie glaze that lent a sepulchral atmosphere to the main hall.

We moved around the hall slowly and stopped in front of each panel. No one spoke anywhere in the hall; the only sound was that of shuffling feet. My eyes may have been on the frieze, but my mind was trapped in the next day's activities in court. I separated myself from Wierda and Dr Shapiro and searched out the lesser halls and rooms of the monument, my thoughts wandering as my feet moved from room to room and from one display to the next.

Poisoners and stranglers and multiple killers are always hanged; there never is a legal reprieve for them – their killings are deliberate and takes a concerted effort to complete. The poisoner has to obtain the poison and then administer it. Death comes slowly to the victim and the killers usually watch with false concern as the victims gag and gasp while they are dying. The strangler has to get his hands around the victim's neck and squeeze for as long as it takes for the victim to stop struggling and to go limp. The multiple killer has to regroup after the rush of blood associated with the first killing has receded. Then he has to kill again and again.

There were men on Death Row for having murdered multiple victims, some as many as three or four, but none for as many as seven. My assessment was that beyond three there was no hope of a reprieve, and even then, hadn't Hansen been one of those hanged in that last week, for killing two women? If two was too many, seven was as good as dead, as my friend Colin had said.

What could I say in favour of our client? Labuschagne's actions seemed deliberate and callous. Shooting seven people dead after engaging them in a game of cat and mouse over many kilometres in the traffic did not sound like an impulsive act, committed in anger on the spur of the moment. Multiple killers always got the death sentence.

We had argued the opposite, but my mind was playing games with me.

I thought of Scheepers and Wessels. Would Scheepers have killed Ginny Goitseone if she had been white, like Scheepers and his companions? Would Burger and the others have allowed him to kill her if she had not been black? Surely Wessels would never have treated a white woman like he had Elizabeth Mokoena. Scheepers and Wessels had killed black women, displaying in every act an inhuman disregard for their victims as people.

If Scheepers and Wessels were hanged for killing across the racial divide, then Leon Labuschagne would in all likelihood follow them onto the trapdoors. A multiple killer who picks his victims for their race is as good as dead, I thought. Labuschagne was as good as dead.

In the windowless and dimly lit museum in the basement of the monument I stooped in front of an extract from a contemporary article in a newspaper stating the intention of the Voortrekkers. They had complained about the way they were being treated by their own government. They wanted self-determination and freedom from oppression. They promised to treat all races they were to encounter on their trek fairly, to negotiate with unknown chiefs for peaceful coexistence.

I rejoined Wierda and his guest at the cenotaph in the middle of the main hall. Wierda was giving Dr Shapiro a history lesson. They walked off again and I decided to shun the lift and instead to take the stairs to the top. I had hardly started when I was struck by vertigo for the second time that week, in addition to a far worse attack of claustrophobia. I wanted to turn around but a grossly overweight German couple had followed me into the stairwell. I was forced to go higher. I looked for a way out of the stairwell but there was none. The space between the concrete walls got narrower the higher I went up the spiralling stairwell, which I knew to be an illusion, a trick played on me by my own mind. I tested it by stretching out my arms and touching the walls every now and then. The distance remained constant even as my mind told me otherwise. Not wanting to be alone in there, I had to wait for the Germans every few steps to catch up with me. I was bent on beating the demons and fought my way up and up, the drumming in my ears getting louder with each leaden step, all the while stubbornly refusing to look down. But I needed someone near to take care of me should I be overcome by fear.

Halfway up I stopped, but there was no way out. Above the rush of the river in my ears, there were African voices again. I shook my head and they faded away. I looked out of a small window in the wall on my left; the ground below was a long way down. I felt a strong pull towards the window. Leaning towards the inside of the stairwell, I turned my head to face the grey wall to the right, away from the outside world. My heart was hammering against my ribs and my throat felt constricted.

I forced myself to go higher and higher. The rough plaster of the central pillar provided some comfort but no handhold. The stairway eventually opened into a large open space under the cupola; a suspension bridge spanning crevasses on either side was the only pathway to the top. I had to drag myself along hand over hand, step by step, gripping the handrails, pulling hard on them as my legs refused to co-operate.

Two hundred and eight steps after I had left the museum in the basement I reached the very top. I had come all the way to look out over the parapet of the circular balcony. Much as I did not want to approach the waist-high wall, I was compelled to do so. I went down on hands and knees just as the Germans reached the top. They stood looking down at me. I lost all shame and asked them for help. They held me by my upper arms, one on either side, and escorted me to the edge. I pushed against the parapet with my hands as I peered over the wall down to the cenotaph below. By a trick of the light it appeared as a square pit the size of the one underneath the trapdoors, and that shocking image combined with the demons of vertigo to force me back to my knees, and then to all fours again. I struggled against the efforts of the Germans to keep me upright and begged them to take me to the stairwell at the opposite corner. My breathing came in wheezes and then great gulps for air that arched my back as I crawled around the low wall to the stairwell at the opposite corner.

The German couple helped me to my feet at the top of the stairs. On the way down I found an exit and stepped out into the sunshine.

The moment I was outside the vertigo dissipated. I slowly regained my strength and walked around to the other side. I stood looking over the city of Pretoria. My eyes found the reservoir in the distance, directly between the monument and the city. I traced the path of the minibus and Labuschagne's bakkie. They had come off the Old Johannesburg Road, on my left, and took the freeway in the valley between the monument and the reservoir almost directly below me. Then they'd slewed around the reservoir. That road was hidden from view. Near Maximum they had turned around and come back, but took the turn up the hill and through a sharp turn down to the reservoir. I traced their route a second time with my finger. They had had so much time to reconsider, to concede defeat, to call off their stupid game.

I took a deep breath before I went back inside to find the staircase, and it felt like an impossibly long time before I was back at the front entrance, waiting for Wierda and Dr Shapiro. I was glad they hadn't seen me. My hands were cold and clammy. I sat down on a rock with my eyes closed, my face turned to the sun.

When they didn't come out I went back inside. I walked slowly from display to display, taking my time to study the past. Did I have ancestors in the events depicted here? I couldn't be sure. It struck me that Cell 6 and this edifice were both monuments to freedom fighters. The battle scenes in the friezes of the monument had their counterpart in literary form on the walls of Cell 6, yet the inscriptions on the walls of Cell 6 told me that the oppressed who had built this monument had become oppressors in turn.

The photographs in the exhibits I saw in court flashed before my eyes, the seven black men, hardly out of their boyhood, lying in the debris of the storm, and again, naked on the mortuary slab. And superimposed on that was the image of Leon Labuschagne being taken away from court to be hanged by the neck until he was dead.

I went outside again to wait for Wierda and the American.

'I've never experienced an atmosphere like that, except maybe once,' said Dr Shapiro. 'Have you ever been to Masada?' he asked back at the car.

'I have,' I said when Wierda didn't respond.

'Well,' he said, 'then you will know what I mean. You can't walk on Masada without feeling a presence. There is a higher presence there, and I think it's partly the presence of the dead and the presence of God.'

'I felt like that when I visited Jerusalem,' said Wierda, 'at the Wailing Wall, at the Dome of the Rock and at the Greek Orthodox Church on Golgotha. It was exactly like the monument, at all three of those places.'

I had been to Jerusalem too and had experienced the same sensations, but I kept it to myself. I also didn't mention that I had felt the same presence at the Taj Mahal and the Great Pyramid of Giza. What if all that those edifices had in common was human suffering that could be felt across generations?

What if what I had thought was vertigo or claustrophobia was something completely different, the fear of death, or the presence of the dead, or of God?

'Did you see that manifesto in the newspaper in the museum?' Dr Shapiro asked me. 'They promised to treat everyone they met on their trek north fairly and equally. And then almost every frieze shows them subjugating the African tribes they encountered by force of arms, most brutally, without mercy. And ultimately you ended up with apartheid.'

I didn't answer. What could I say? I remembered reading somewhere that Verwoerd had made an announcement shortly after he had been appointed Minister of Native Affairs. His party, he'd said, had developed a policy that granted to other races what it claimed for whites and was calculated to provide the same opportunities to everyone within his own race group. This was the policy of apartheid, which had discrimination on the ground of race at its core, and was enforced with a single-minded viciousness that would destroy the fabric of the nation.

I didn't hear much of the heated debate between Wierda and Dr Shapiro, and I don't know why I asked Wierda to stop at the reservoir on the way back. We walked across the rough terrain to a spot due south above Maximum. The three legs of A Section glistened in the sun. The gallows building towered over the other buildings. There was no sign of life.

Behind us the monument looked down on the reservoir.

Wierda dropped me off at my sister's. Annelise looked at me askance where I stood at her door with my suitcase in my hand. I had forgotten to phone her to ask if I could stay the night.

'Come in,' she said. 'Where is Pierre?'

I wiped my feet and followed her into the house. 'I thought he would be here.'

'I haven't seen him since early in the morning. He said he was going to court.'

I didn't know what to say. I could not recall seeing Pierre at court. When I thought back to the events of the morning I remembered that I had not gone into the courtroom at all. I had stood outside talking to James Murray while they went through the formalities of remanding the case.

'You are just in time for dinner,' Annelise said. 'I think you might like what I have prepared.'

The smell was familiar and harkened back to earlier times when we were little, but I could not quite place it. It turned out to be oxtail prepared according to my mother's recipe. We were about to sit down when we heard a car at the gate and doors slamming. Pierre stepped onto the porch with heavy feet and I could hear him cursing as he tried to find the keyhole. I went to the door and opened it for him. He was drunk and fell against me.

I sat him down at the table and Annelise dished up for him. He looked at us from under belligerent eyebrows.

He stared at the food on his plate.

Annelise would not meet my eyes. We sat in silence for a time. Eventually I stood up and took Pierre by the arm.

'Let's go for a walk,' I suggested.

Pierre jerked his arm away but stood up anyway and led the way to the door. I glanced over my shoulder at Annelise; she had her hands over her eyes.

We walked for miles and miles through the suburbs. If it wasn't for the fact that Pretoria was laid out in a square grid I would have been lost very quickly. The further we walked, the less agitated Pierre became. In due course he started talking, at first rambling on about perceived slights and persecution, but ultimately about death and killing.

'You wanted to know about killing and dying and death,' he said. 'Well, let me tell you a few things about that.' I said nothing and let him speak.

'Where do you think I have been all day?' he asked.

He did not wait for an answer. 'We did a job in Maputo today. We killed some people today. We bombed their house. They were bad people, and we killed them.'

'What are you talking about?' I said. 'You are on sick leave.'

My brother-in-law stopped and put his hand on my chest when I turned to face him. He drunkenly waved a finger under my nose.

'That is just a ruse,' he said. 'I'm on a special assignment. I take the killers to the people who need to be killed, and then I bring them home again. That's what I do.'

'If it is your job to do it, why are you crying?' I asked.

At first he did not answer. A couple of blocks later he mumbled. 'I think we bombed the wrong house.' He was sobbing now. 'I think we bombed the wrong house. I heard women and children inside.'

He was inconsolable. I put my arm around his shoulders and we walked and walked and walked.

He jabbered on and on until we arrived back at the house hours later. Our food was in the oven and Annelise had gone to bed.

I didn't sleep well that night and was wide awake at four o'clock. An argument on extenuating circumstances played over and over in my mind without ever reaching completion. I kept running into unpersuasive, hollow-sounding submissions and then abandoned the line of argument to start from the beginning.

I went for a run at five o'clock. The city was only beginning to stir and the roads were all but deserted. This time the freshness of the day and the sweet smell of the jacaranda flowers did not produce any inspiration or new ideas.

I went to court early because I still needed to talk to Labuschagne about the likelihood of his being found guilty. I went up the thirteen steps at the main entrance on the Square. The main atrium was deserted except for the security officers at the front desk. The smell of dust and detergent hung heavily in the air and shiny particles floated in the streams of sunlight coming through the large skylights overhead. The echoes of my footsteps followed me up the staircase to the robing room. I left my luggage in the robing room. I fully intended to leave as soon as I could get away.

Court c was equally deserted and I put my papers down at the defence table. I took one last look around the room. The dock was cold and impersonal. I went to look for Labuschagne and walked past the prosecutors' table before I took the staircase to the cells below. Below the court there was no comfort. Everything was cold and grey, damp brick and mortar, cold cement on the bare floors and walls. There was no one in Cell 6 either. The door was open, so I entered through the narrow doorway bending my knees slightly. I went to look for the cell sergeant and found other equally cold cells and sparsely equipped toilets down the passage. The cell sergeant was nowhere to be found downstairs. Upstairs the security men told me the cell sergeant had left to fetch the prisoners for the day's cases. I went down again and sat down in Cell 6 and considered the best way to tell Labuschagne that he might be found guilty and that we needed to plan for that outcome. There was no easy way to tell him.

Wierda and I had already concluded that there was no further evidence available to us; we would have to argue the matter on the evidence already given. If the Court found that the evidence we had produced was insufficient to create a reasonable doubt, then we hoped to persuade the Court that the evidence in any event established extenuating circumstances sufficient to avoid the mandatory death sentence. But seven deaths were not easy to ignore. If we couldn't persuade the Court that the circumstances and events in Maximum had turned Labuschagne into an automaton at the reservoir we would have to argue that those same circumstances and events were sufficient to render his actions less blameworthy; that from a moral perspective they were, somehow, less reprehensible. But again, seven deaths were as difficult to justify as they were to explain.

I paced up and down in the cell. The graffiti provided an escape from the depressing business of the trial, and I again felt myself drawn to the scribbles in so many different hands.

> MANDELA
> SAYS NO EASY
> WALK TO FREEDOM

We certainly had not had an easy road to travel either. It was difficult to imagine freedom at its end.

> EK SIEMON IS NIE SKELAG NIE

Perhaps there was some hope, a possibility of an outright acquittal. I checked my watch. Court was due to start in a few minutes and there was still no sign of the cell sergeant. I went back up and found that the courtroom was filling up rapidly. I beckoned Wierda to follow me down to Cell 6.

'If he is convicted, I'll argue extenuating circumstances immediately, as we've planned,' I told him. 'And then I plan to leave as soon as the sentence has been passed. We can talk about appeals later. It will be your job to take care of him after he has been sentenced.'

Wierda nodded and then pointed at an inscription on the graffiti-covered wall behind me. It was an extract from the Freedom Charter:

> THE PREAMBLE OF THE CHARTER
> WE, THE PEOPLE OF SOUTH AFRICA, DECLEAR FOR OUR COUNTRY
> AND THE WORLD TO KNOW, THAT SOUTH AFRICA BELONGS TO

ALL WHO LIVE IN IT, BLACK AND WHITE, AND THAT NO
GOVERNMENT CAN JUSTLY CLAIM AUTHORITY
UNLESS IT IS BASED ON THE WILL OF ALL
THE PEOPLE O'POVU FIRST

I looked at the words and wondered. Would Nelson Mandela, if he were ever to be sworn in as our first black President, keep its fundamental promise, or would it turn out to be empty political rhetoric like that of the Voortrekkers and Verwoerd?

We waited for Labuschagne to arrive, but eventually had no choice but to return to the courtroom.

'How long will it be before they hang him, do you think?' Wierda asked me as we took our seats.

I did not have the strength to answer. Six months to a year.

Court started ten minutes late; there had been some trouble with the prisoners at the police cells, delaying their transport to court, and I never got the chance to speak to Labuschagne.

Roshnee took her seat at her usual place behind Wierda and me, with Marianne Schlebusch and Dr Shapiro on either side of her. The atmosphere in the courtroom was very solemn, almost funereal. Sanet Niemand came over to speak to Wierda to reach agreement about the fate of the exhibits after the verdict had been announced. In case of a conviction Labuschagne's gun would be forfeited to the State, but if he were by any chance to be acquitted the gun would be returned to him.

When she entered the courtroom, the registrar came directly to me where I was sitting at the defence table and made me a whispered offer.

'I've made arrangements with the security staff so that you can take him out through the back entrance when the verdict has been announced,' she said. I felt the heat of her breath in my ear.

Before I could discuss the significance of the registrar's offer with Wierda, Judge van Zyl and his Assessors were escorted into the courtroom.

'The defendant may be seated,' said Judge van Zyl when he had made himself comfortable. 'The judgment will take some time.'

He waited for Labuschagne to sit down before he continued.

'We are not united in our findings on the facts and there will be a majority verdict. I shall read the judgment of the majority first. Their verdict will be the verdict of the Court. After that, I shall read the opinion of the dissenting member of the Court. I would ask the spectators to remain calm and behave with the decorum that they have maintained until now in this very difficult case.'

Wierda swallowed hard next to me. I was about to put him out of his misery, but when I turned towards him he had his pencil between his teeth again.

Tap, tap, tap.

I didn't listen to the judgment with any degree of attention. The winner only wants to know that he has won. The loser, on the other hand, wants to know the reasons why he has lost. I busied myself with the Death Sentence Registers dating back to 1902. They were full of curious details, and as the Judge neared the end of the judgment, my finger found my friend Oupa's murderer in the register:

NO.	DATE	NAME OF PRISONER	JUDGE	PLACE	OUTCOME	DATE
1266	7.2.63	Johannes Hendrik Buchling (E.M.)	De Vos	Pretoria	Executed	24.5.63

Through the skylights I could still see banks of clouds moving slowly across the city. When I turned to watch the spectators they were straining to hear; Judge van Zyl was making no effort to ensure that they could hear him in the last rows of the gallery. There were nods of agreement when the Judge dealt with particular facts or events, when he recorded the Court's acceptance or rejection of items of evidence, and when he noted the Court's impressions of the demeanour and credibility of the most important witnesses. From time to time the spectators made their views heard. There were sighs of assent every so often, and murmurs of dissent, but otherwise the courtroom was quiet, eerily so, with the clouds outside dictating the mood below the skylights and the copper chandelier within.

The judgment ended with the words, 'Mr Labuschagne, please stand up.' Labuschagne stood up but kept his eyes on the floor. The Judge addressed him directly. 'Mr Labuschagne, we therefore find, by a majority, that the State has not proved that your actions at the reservoir were the voluntary acts of a conscious mind, and you are found not guilty and you are discharged. You are free to leave. The Court is adjourned.' When Judge van Zyl and the Assessors had left, Wierda jumped up and went over to the dock. His handshake ended in a huge hug. Labuschagne's parents and Antoinette joined him in an emotional scrum. Eventually Wierda broke loose and came back to his seat.

'You didn't tell me what we would do if he was found not guilty.'

'I'm going home. You can take care of it from here,' I said.

I stayed in my seat and pretended to fuss with my papers until the courtroom had emptied. Antoinette came back to give me a hug. My tears stained the collar of her blouse.

I found James Murray in the robing room, stuffing his robes into his bag.

'Well done,' he said, extending his hand.

I didn't know what to say. When he released my hand, he added, 'I wouldn't have thought anyone could pull that off.'

'I suspect it would have been very different if the Warrant Officer hadn't gone and killed himself,' I ventured.

'For sure,' he said.

'But you know,' he added, 'in a way I'm glad. Pretoria can't afford a case like this.'

I asked Murray to accompany me to the Judge's chambers to say goodbye. I had been a visitor to his jurisdiction and I had to pay homage to convention.

Judge van Zyl was not very talkative. The Assessors were filling in their claim forms for submission to the Chief Registrar's office. They were being paid per day for their participation and were to be reimbursed for expenses.

I saw a blank death warrant on the Judge's side table.

We shook hands and James Murray and I left.

'Who do you think was the dissenter?' I asked him when we had returned to the robing room.

'The Judge,' he said.

'Really?' I was stunned. Usually the Judge is able to persuade the Assessors to his view. 'What makes you think so?'

'I know.' He let the answer hang in the air.

Murray and I parted company with another handshake.

After a while I slipped out through the back entrance, leaving Wierda with Labuschagne to brave the gauntlet of flashbulbs and television cameras on the front steps. In the street behind the Palace of Justice I found a taxi driver who was prepared to take me to the airport. I closed my eyes when the door slammed shut behind me.

> *Kellunck*
> *Shoosh*
> *Wham*

I looked back at the Palace of Justice as we went round the Square. It stood serene in the afternoon light and gave no hint of the history that had played itself out within its walls. In the taxi I closed my eyes and tried to think of ships and shipping and of boys running on the beach.

The flight attendant on the Boeing handed me the paper. An elderly couple had been murdered on their farm. Two men had shot dead a taxi driver. There were rumours of a battle in Angola, with many casualties. A policeman had shot his wife and children and then turned the gun on himself.

On page three I found the names of the men who were in the Pot when we had our second inspection. They were the ones who must have felt the tremor in the walls when we had the Major push the lever and let the trapdoors slam against the stoppers:

MORE EXECUTIONS AT CENTRAL

The following men were executed on Wednesday in Pretoria Central Prison: Damon Willemse, Japie Samuels, Willem Lewis, Abraham Koelman, Tholi Selby Mnguni, Alpheus Banda.

Willemse, Samuels, Lewis and Koelman were sentenced to death in Cape Town on 2 February last year. Mnguni was sentenced to death in Durban on 29 January this year and Banda in Vanderbijlpark on 21 April this year.

There are more than 200 prisoners still awaiting execution at Central.

In the cycle of killing there is a beginning, but no end.

Glossary

17:   **Pak!** Pack!

18:   **Trek jou dagklere aan! Geen onderbroek of kouse en skoene nie!**
Put on your day clothes. No underpants or socks and shoes!

19:   **Maak soos ek sê en maak gou!** Do as I say and hurry up!
Dit is tyd om te gaan. It is time to go.

21:   **Staan stil en staan regop!** Stand still and stand up straight!
Ruk jou reg, man! Staan stil! Pull yourself together, man! Stand
still!

28:   **Staan vorentoe!** Stand towards the front!
Ek wil niks kak van julle hê nie! I don't want any of your shit!

36:   **Trek hom op! Maak gou! Maak gou!** Pull him up! Hurry! Hurry!
Een, twee, drie! One, two, three!

76:   **koppie** hillock

78:   **Jammer, Baas. Ek rus net hier.** Sorry, Boss. I am just resting here.

82:   **Aan die tou. Van die tou af.** On the rope. Off the rope.

94:   **Roer julle gatte daar onder! Kry hierdie fokkers van die toue af!**
Move your backsides down there! Get these fuckers off the ropes!

110:   **Moenie vir my vertel perdedrolle is vye nie!** Don't tell me horseshit is fruit! Literally: Don't tell me horseshit is figs. A colloquial
Afrikaans expression for 'bullshit'

116:   **Nou wie gaan met die meisie begin?** Now who's going to start
with the girl?

117:   **My baas, my baas!** My boss, my boss!
Ek voel fokkol vir die lewe. I feel fuck-all for life.

121:   **GULZMAR EBRAHIM WAS HIER VIR ROOF EN KAR DIEFSTAL EN
HET AGTER SY ADWORKAT GEGAAN EN SKELDEG GEPLYT SY VON-
NIS WAS 9–15 JAAR TRONKSTRAF SHALOET** GULZMAR EBRAHIM
WAS HERE FOR ROBBERY AND CAR THEFT AND WENT BEHIND HIS
ADVOCATE AND PLEADED GUILTY HIS PUNISHMENT WAS 9–15
YEARS SALUTE

125:   **Veroordeelde** Condemned

136: **Ag kak, man!** Oh bullshit, man!

174: **Dit is tyd! Trek jou dagklere aan, geen onderbroek, skoene of kouse nie.** It is time! Put on your day clothes. No underpants, shoes or socks.

Uit met jou skoene! Off with your shoes!

Sit jou hande hier, teen die muur, palms oop, vingers uit. En bly hier tot ek sê jy mag roer. Verstaan? Put your hands here, against the wall, palms open, fingers out. And stay here until I say you may move. Understand?

175: **Het jy gevoel? Presies sewe-uur?** Did you feel it? On the stroke of seven?

Vat hom terug na sy sel toe. Take him back to his cell.

Ek wil nie weer kak van jou hê nie, verstaan? I don't want any more shit from you, understand?

227: **Julle sallie vir my kry nie. Frikkie Muller is te slim vir julle, my Kroon.** You won't get me. Frikkie Muller is too clever for you, my Crown. 'My Crown' is a mocking and sarcastic mode of address by coloured people for a white person

228: **Dood is Muller.** Dead is Muller.

230: **bakkie** pickup truck

231: **Ek sal gaan soos Jesus.** I'll go like Jesus.

As ek gaan soos Jesus sal God my vergewe. If I go like Jesus, God will forgive me.

Ek sal gaan soos Jesus, vir ander se sondes. I'll go like Jesus, for the sins of others.

296 and 301: Trek hom op! Maak gou! Maak gou! Pull him up! Quickly! Quickly!

317: **Ja, my Kroon …** Yes, my Crown …

My Kroon se gat. My Crown's arse.

318: **Wat sê jy?** What did you say?

Niks nie, my Kroon. Nothing, my Crown.

353: **Fok daai liefde!** Fuck that. Literally: Fuck that love. A colloquial expression

463: **EK SIEMON IS NIE SKELAG NIE.** I SIMON AM NOT GUILTY. Pidgin Afrikaans

Author's Note

In July 1989 Nelson Mandela, a survivor of Cell 6 and Court C above it, was released from prison for the day to meet the State President P W Botha. Mandela asked Botha to release all political prisoners but Botha refused.

In August 1989 F W de Klerk became the new State President.

In October 1989 de Klerk released the first batch of political prisoners in the sweep of reforms that led to the end of apartheid. Negotiations for a handover of power to South Africa's black majority began in earnest. Years before, the names of some of those who would take up the reins of power four years later had been scratched into the walls of Cell 6.

In November 1989 de Klerk announced a moratorium on executions.

The moratorium came a week too late for Kukaleni Solomon Ngobeni, destined to be the last man to be hanged in Pretoria:

SERIAL NO	NAME	V-NO	PLACE SENTENCED	DATE	JUDGE	OUTCOME	DATE
4965	Kukaleni Solomon Ngobeni	V4906	Tzaneen	28.2.88	J. J. Strydom	Executed	14.11.89

In February 1990 Nelson Mandela was released by de Klerk. On 10 May 1994 Mandela was sworn in as President, the first African to hold that office, exactly as Dr Verwoerd had reportedly told Dimitri Tsafendas nearly thirty years earlier.

During the moratorium judges around the country continued to impose the death sentence until June 1996 when the Constitutional Court held it to be incompatible with the right to life guarantee of the Constitution negotiated between de Klerk and Mandela. Special legislation was passed and those awaiting execution were given long terms of imprisonment instead.

By then more than four thousand men and women had been hanged in Pretoria, the first on 12 August 1902 and the last on 14 November 1989.

Acknowledgements

I would like to thank the following persons for their assistance: my nephew and now my colleague Etienne Botha of the Pretoria Bar, for finding and copying the Capital Cases registers and the trial records of the thirty-two men who were hanged between 26 November and 10 December 1987; Johan Steinberg, once an escort in Maximum Security Prison, for sharing the secrets of the execution process with me; my friend and colleague Fanie Olivier, for reading the manuscript, then raw and unsophisticated, and for encouraging me to send it to Umuzi; Frederik de Jager, my editor at Umuzi, for his fearless editing, for smoothing the rough spots, and for his expert advice; my wife, Ansie, for suffering my pursuit of the subject matter of this book with such grace and tolerance, and for proof-reading it more than once.

CGM
6 March 2008